ONE-LANE BRIDGE

dan krzyzkowski

iUniverse, Inc.
New York   Bloomington

This is a work of fiction. All of the characters, names, incidents,
organizations, and dialogue in this novel are either the products
of the author's imagination or are used fictitiously.

iUniverse books may be ordered through booksellers or by contacting:

iUniverse
1663 Liberty Drive
Bloomington, IN 47403
www.iuniverse.com
1-800-Authors (1-800-288-4677)

Because of the dynamic nature of the Internet, any Web addresses or links
contained in this book may have changed since publication and may no longer be
valid. The views expressed in this work are solely those of the author and do not
necessarily reflect the views of the publisher, and the publisher hereby disclaims
any responsibility for them.

ISBN: 978-1-4401-8395-9 (sc)
ISBN: 978-1-4401-8394-2 (ebook)

Printed in the United States of America

iUniverse rev. date: 02/26/10

For my mother.
I think of you every day, Mom.
I miss you. I wish you were here.

"Diamonds aren't forever."

PROLOGUE

My father died the day I turned sixteen. We were in the dining room when it happened. Ma was cutting the ice-cream cake—a four-dollar Carvel special with *Happy Birthday, Simon* arced across it in nuclear-pink syrup—when Dad quietly got up and left the table. I watched him from the corner of my eye as he slipped out of the room and eased up the stairs. I knew precisely where he was going, and the barely suppressed smile on my face probably said as much. He was going to fetch my final gift, my *special* gift—the gift he always saved for last. This had been a pellet rifle the previous year; two years ago, a pair of high-power binoculars. Anyway, when his cake began to melt and run off the sides of his paper plate, Ma frowned and went up to look for him. She found him dead at the top of the stairs. My father had suffered a massive heart attack. He'd sat down on the top step and died with his chin touching his chest. Cradled in his limp hands was my gift—wrapped in newspaper and trussed with twine. It was the last thing he ever gave me.

*   *   *

In the years that followed, I would ask myself scores of questions: How well had I known my father? Could you truly ever know a person, even a loved one, down to his core? My father was a hard worker. He manned an assembly line at American Standard in Trenton for nearly twenty years. Two decades of lifting urinals and toilet tanks, of coming home with aches in his back and calluses on his hands, had made him a humble man. At home he was peaceably quiet, generally keeping to himself and his newspaper.

Occasionally, though, he would break his silence to offer some small snippet of wisdom. My father was the sort of man, given his blue-collar background and taciturn nature, who could shock you with his prescience. When I was thirteen, I boldly announced to my parents that I was destined to someday become a doctor. Ma clapped her hands and began enumerating the lavish items she wanted when she retired. Dad smiled gruffly, ruffling his paper. A year later, I decided instead to become an astronaut. Ma told me to bring back some moon rocks. At the age of fifteen, I came to realize the future was in entomology. "Oh, Simon, I hate bugs." I went on to make a dozen career changes before I finished high school. Zookeeper. Restaurant owner. Baseball statistician. And finally, a practicing attorney.

"The courtroom is where the money is, Dad. I'll wear the best suits and the best shoes, and I'll carry a big, shiny briefcase. And maybe, when I get to college, I'll double-major in English and Religious Studies. That way, I can quote scripture and poetry while I'm litigating. What do you think?"

My father studied me over the top of his newspaper. He lowered the paper and removed his reading glasses. "You want to know what I think, Simon? You want to know what I *really* think?"

I straightened up in my chair. "Well … sure, Dad, of course."

"I think you should become whatever your heart damn well pleases. Do open-heart surgery. Make snow angels on the moon. Chase fruit flies with butterfly nets. If it makes you happy and someone pays you to do it, then go for it. The one piece of advice I'll give you is this: take some time, either during your college years or immediately after, to work with your hands—to work hard every day like most Americans do. That way, ten years down the road when you're working in your chosen profession, you'll have a greater appreciation for what it is you have." He donned his reading glasses and disappeared behind the newspaper. Four months later, he was gone, and the storm was upon us. The rudderless months following my father's death are some of the darkest I've ever known. Ma began tipping the bottle, and Catherine … well, Catherine is another story. My sister was just a God-awful mess.

As for the wisdom Dad shared with me … well, I've had a lot of time to think matters through, and I've come to recognize it as possibly the single best piece of advice anyone's ever given me—but for far different reasons than those intended.

In any event, I'll give the old man credit where credit is due. I never forgot what he told me.

PART I

Spit Bugs

CHAPTER ONE

ALISHA

THE CONCRETE STAIRS DESCENDED into darkness. Above the header—where one was apt to crack his skull if he wasn't careful—a faded sign proclaimed Microsystems Incorporated – Independent Contractor. Beneath this: Authorized Personnel Only.

I navigated the stairs and ducked into the tunnel, pausing to adjust my shoulder pack and to allow my eyes a few moments to acclimate. Water dripped in the distance, and shadows crouched along the walls. A dervish of mist curled around my ankles and crawled up my bare legs. This place was more a cave than an office. I suffered a brief image of what the foreman might look like—a Cro-Magnon holding a club in one hand while sketching buffalo on the walls with the other.

Silly Simon.

I got moving again. The tunnel jagged to the left, then opened on a subterranean chamber illuminated by banks of overhead fluorescents. The room stank of nicotine, mildew, and personal odor. Loose papers lay everywhere. An old coffeepot, rimed brown from overuse, sat atop a metal filing cabinet to my left. I noticed there was an ashtray on every desk, and every ashtray was overflowing with cigarette butts. Taped to the cement walls were posters and calendars depicting topless women posing next to vintage Corvettes, Harleys, and construction equipment. One poster to my right showed a frizzy brunette wearing only leather work gloves, straddling a jackhammer. She pouted at me with lips the color of stoplights.

A short, stocky man sat behind a computer near the back of the room, hunting and pecking as he smoked an unfiltered Camel. He had a crew cut and wore silver studs in both ears. The black gruff covering his face suggested that he hadn't shaved in a week. His white tank top was blotted with oil stains. Tattoos rode up his biceps and shoulders like a green-black leprosy. I cleared my throat loudly. He turned, waving a hand in front of his face to clear the smoke, and saw me standing inside the room's curved archway.

"Hi, there." I indicated the lascivious ad to my right. "Do I get to work next to her?"

"What do you need, kid?" he jawed at me, his cigarette clamped between his lips. His voice was a flat mason's grind.

The first thing I needed was to set my shoulder pack down. The LSAT prep books weighed a ton.

"My name is Simon Kozlowski. I'm here for …" I pulled a swatch of paper from my front pocket. "It's Project Forty-nine Forty-four. I was given a transcript with a worker ID. It said on the transcript to report here. I just rode in from New Jersey."

He leaned back in his chair. "Forty-nine Forty-four? The Bridgepoint Extension?"

"Yes. You say it as though you've already finished it."

He laughed bitterly, tamping his cigarette in an ashtray. "You union, kid?"

"No. I was hired for the year."

"Well, I got bad news for you. You've been laid off for the year."

I stared at him, speechless.

"The Extension project was cancelled a month ago. More than a month."

"Are you kidding? Hey, there has to be some kind of mistake here." And a very big one at that. From my home in Lake Hiawatha, I'd caught a bus to the train depot in Metro Park. Amtrak had carried me north to Springfield, Mass. From there, another bus into Manchester, New Hampshire. A straight shot up I-93 in a cab, through the capital city of Concord. The cabbie took me as far as Northfield. I hitched a ride with a friendly farmer who drove an old Ford pickup, who took me as far as Ashland. I had hiked the remaining four miles west into the town of Swan Lake. My knees were sore and my shoulders were shot. It had taken seven hours and cost me a 194 dollars to get there.

"Look, pal," I said, squatting down to open one of the overstuffed pouches in my shoulder pack, "I've got a paper here that says—"

He waved me off. "Never mind the papers, kid. What happened is, last winter some pussy toad environmentalists went out to the Stratford site with video recorders and surveying equipment and clipboards and fuckin' rectal thermometers for all I know. They claim that the sixteen-mile stretch of land where we want to build the Extension encompasses vital wintering grounds for the endangered short-eared owl. So these idiots are out there for three weeks, walking around taking pictures and measuring shit. I had an inkling to go out there with my over-and-under and start shootin' at 'em."

"The environmentalists or the owls?"

"Both. These left-wing nut jobs are ruining this country. They complain how bad the economy is, and yet they're the ones killing it. Anyway, the National Wildlife Defense Coalition got involved. They filed a request for an injunction in early July, which was granted, so now the whole thing is mired up in the courts. I'm told it may be three years before we can break ground."

"Three years," I said.

"More like four, realistically. Look, we sent letters out two days after the injunction was issued. You should've gotten one."

"Do I look like I got a letter?"

He lit another cigarette. "Hey, I'm sorry you came this far for naught. But I got a third of my workforce collectin' unemployment during a peak time of the season, and I can only play so many fuckin' violins at one time."

I thought of the housing arrangements Microsystems was supposed to have made on my behalf. So, in addition to being unemployed, I was also homeless.

"Well, then perhaps you could find it in your charitable heart to point me toward a reasonable motel in the area."

Laughing. "A motel? In Swan Lake? Nobody ever comes here. There's a bed-and-breakfast off of 513, about five miles south of here. You could try that."

I rolled my eyes. *Do I look like I can afford a bed-and-breakfast, mister?* Even if I could, I didn't have a set of wheels, and there was no way I was hiking another five miles.

"Can you at least tell me where I can get a good cup of coffee?"

He had turned back to his computer. "Try Molly's, down on Main Street," he said without bothering to look at me.

I lifted my heavy pack once again and swung it across my throbbing shoulders. "Well, thanks for nothing."

"Happy trails."

*　　　　*　　　　*

I re-emerged into late afternoon sunshine. On the sidewalk, I turned right, moving west along Aldridge Street. Walking with my head bowed forward, I pondered the unfavorable circumstances in which I suddenly found myself. Fatigue muddied the waters. I was too tired to think up a solution and too poor to buy one. A quick calculation of my assets told me I had fifty-one dollars in cash left in my pocket—not nearly enough to get me home considering what I'd paid to get there. My checking account was down to 140 dollars and seventy cents. I carried one credit card with a two-thousand-dollar credit line. *All the months of planning that went into this, plus travel time—and already you're looking for a way out?* Maybe that was the crux of the matter—once in, you couldn't *get* out. I imagined Swan Lake as the world's largest pitcher plant, and me as its latest victim.

I smiled in spite of myself. I tilted my head back and filled my lungs with sweet, late-summer air. I'd never traveled this far into New England before, and I'd be damned if I wasn't going to get something out of it. If I pinched pennies, maybe I could stay a few days and absorb some of the sights and sounds.

The row of buildings to my right was predominantly brownstone and turn-of-the-century brick, with none taller than two stories. To my left, on the other side of Aldridge Street, a lush, green lawn sloped upwards away from the sidewalk. On top of the hill a hundred yards off the road, recessed in a grove of poplars and white pines, was a large three-story colonial. The house was beige with black shutters. There was a parking lot next to the building, with a brown sign that read Dolan, Packer & Spencer, Attorneys-at-Law. I considered suing Microsystems for failing to affix proper postage.

I arrived at the intersection. There, Aldridge T-boned into Main Street. I looked to the right, where a rickety wood bridge spanned Whiskey Creek. A fiftyish-looking man stood by himself halfway out across the bridge. Unmoving, wearing old dungarees and a white undershirt, he leaned forward against the wood rail smoking a cigarette. He could have been Rodin's *Thinker* standing up. I wondered if he was collecting unemployment on behalf of Microsystems Incorporated.

I crossed Main Street, turning left when I reached the sidewalk. If I didn't get this pack off my shoulders soon, I was going to wind up in traction. I surveyed some of the shops as I passed them. Most were small and quaint—a pharmacy, a bookstore, a Hallmark store. Poplars and cedars filled the spaces unoccupied by sidewalk benches or post office drop boxes. I came to a place that sold artwork. The sign in the window said Arts & Wares. I decided to stop for a gander. A dozen paintings in beveled frames were on display on the sidewalk in front of the store. Some were propped in chairs, others sat on wooden easels. One even leaned against an upside-down bucket.

Nine of the twelve canvases depicted a lake. This intrigued me, for I had yet to see an actual lake here in Swan Lake. I hadn't seen any swans, either. The first piece to catch my eye was a detailed portrayal of a beach. In it, people swam, lazed about on rafts, and ferried around in paddleboats. A square, floating dock in the middle of what I surmised was the same lake became the centerpiece of a second painting. A lone swan stood on a corner of the dock at sunset. With its head turned to the south, both the swan's body and the graceful arch of its neck appeared silhouetted against the fiery backdrop of the western sky. The piece effected a lonely, if not haunting, Impressionist quality.

I moved a few feet to the left … and my eyes seized upon a third canvas. This time I was looking at a lakeside house. I had the impression that whoever had crafted this painting had done so while sitting on the floating dock shown in the previous piece. It had that sort of perspective. The lake house was an architectural gem. Partially ensconced in the forest, the front of the house featured six-foot-high windows, a wraparound deck, and dormer windows on the second floor.

From one of the dormers emanated an eerie phosphorescence.

It was a pale light that wasn't quite a light, yet was sufficient enough to draw the eye. I took a step back to gain some perspective ... and an incredible thing happened. I noticed that the suffused light was coming from *all* the windows but in varying degrees. The glow was the strongest from that dormer in the upper right—that's where the source was. The light grew weaker the farther it got from the source.

I glanced at the lower right corner of the painting, where I saw two words: *Crawford Daze.*

"It's on sale, if you want it."

The woman's voice startled me. I looked up and saw her standing in the doorway of Arts & Wares. She was short, with black hair, probably pushing sixty.

"The price has been lowered to seven-ninety-five."

I was digging for my wallet before I knew I was doing it. In my mind, I envisioned myself peeling off a ten (dropping my cash kitty to forty-one dollars), handing it to her, telling her to keep the change—

I looked up at her. "You mean seven dollars and ninety-five cents?"

She rocked her head back and laughed.

"No, Charlie—try seven *hundred* and ninety-five. That's a twelve-hundred-dollar piece you're looking at."

"Actually, the name's Simon."

Her smile was genuine. "And I'm Millie."

"Molly?"

"No, Molly's down the street a bit. I'm *Millie.*" A little white dog appeared in the doorway behind her. "And this is Minnie."

"Did Crawford Daze paint all of these?" I asked.

Millie came forward so she could see the painting of the lake house also. She chuckled.

"No, silly. Crawford Daze is the name of the *house.*"

"Oh. What's the glow coming from the windows supposed to be?"

Millie shrugged. "Enchantment, I guess."

There is no happiness in that home. I had no idea where the thought came from. *But there used to be.*

"Enchantment?"

She smiled suggestively. "Creativity, magic, warmth. Those sorts of things—when you put them together, they shine. You believe in magic, Simon, don't you?"

"Not really." I wasn't sure what I believed in. "Does this mean there's actually a lake around here?"

"Well of course there's a lake." She stared hard at me, offering no mention of where this lake might be found. I felt myself sliding deeper into the pitcher plant.

I looked at my watch.

"Millie, I've got to be going. It was really nice to meet you."

She smiled. "Stop in again."

I slung my pack across my shoulders for the umpteenth time, then turned up the sidewalk. Six or seven stores floated past in a blur. I saw flowers through one window, then jewelry in another. Finally I looked in and saw barstools and a long counter and some tables. This had to be the café. I pulled open the glass door and went inside.

*   *   *

"Afternoon, weary traveler," said the woman standing behind the counter. I had hardly gotten through the door yet. "What can I do ya for?"

She was a portly woman of medium height, with healthy round cheeks and a double chin. Her dark hair was tied back beneath a blue and white bandana. She observed me with brown, wholesome country eyes as I moved along the vertical counter and chose a stool. I glanced around as I lowered my heavy pack to the floor. Along the opposite wall stood a row of booths. Half a dozen square tables occupied the open space between the booths and counter. The linoleum floor tiles were checker-patterned red and white. I fully expected to find a jukebox leaning against the back wall, with selections that hadn't changed in forty years. There was no jukebox, however, which for some reason came as a relief.

"You must be Molly."

"The one and only. What'll it be?"

I took a moment to consider my limited funds. "Well, I could certainly use a cup of coffee."

"I can do that." She stuck a saucer and cup in front of me. While she poured, I looked around again. There was only a handful of customers in the place. To my right, hunched over on the stool closest to the front door was an old crow with her face buried in a Martha Grimes novel. I turned to my left and saw, four stools down, a fortyish woman wearing black dress slacks, a V-neck shirt, and a satin scarf embroidered with fall patterns. Her silver-blonde hair spilled past her shoulders. The fingers of both hands were curled around a tall cappuccino. She saw me looking, and offered a smile. I returned the gesture.

I turned to survey the booths. In the last of these, in front of the Restrooms sign, was an elderly man with a mop of white hair busily sipping tea as he rummaged through a newspaper. In one of the middle booths, three township workers sat with their heads huddled together, mumbling about politics and the rising cost of haircuts.

I sipped my coffee. It was good and strong, the way I liked it. A plaque affixed to the wall behind the counter, to the right of the milk dispenser, advertised: Main Street Café – est. 1913. It was bracketed by black and white photos of various celebrities who had stopped in over the decades. There was a photo of Frank Sinatra with his signature scribbled across the middle. I saw signed photos of Roberto Clemente, Bing Crosby, and Henry Ford as well. I had read somewhere that Ford had been an ardent Nazi.

"Gonna have something with your coffee, honey?" Molly asked me.

"Can't afford to right now. I'm broke, unemployed, and a long way from home."

"We have a saying around here: when you're in Swan Lake, you're never far from home."

I smiled. "That's cute." I sipped my coffee. "Hey, speaking of the lake, I understand there is one. Is it far from here? Or does it exist only in paintings?"

"Oh, it's around," Molly ceded. "But we like to keep it a secret."

"I only ask because I grew up in Lake Hiawatha, New Jersey. There is no lake in Lake Hiawatha."

"What brings you to Swan Lake?"

"A job, supposedly. Looks like it fell through though." I sipped more coffee. "I've gotta find some way to get home."

"You know what you need?" she asked. A wisp of her raven-dark hair was riding out from beneath the bandana, just above her left ear. "You need a slice of pie. You need a slice of *Molly's* pie."

"No, really, I shouldn't—"

"Relax, honey, this one's on me."

"Simon."

"Huh?" She turned to look back at me, a pie cutter in one hand.

"The name's Simon. And I thank you kindly for the pie."

A smile brightened her face. "Well, you're welcome, honey."

She went over to the dessert tray, slid one of the glass panels aside, and pulled down one of the half-dozen pies that were on display. She removed a slice of the pie, set it onto a plate, and slid the plate into the microwave. Just for twenty seconds, to warm it. Then she put the plate in front of me with a fork.

"This is rhubarb pie, made fresh this morning. All of my pies are fresh. Have you had rhubarb pie before?"

"Can't say that I have."

"Well, I think you're gonna like it."

I slid the fork into the slice of pie and then into my mouth. Molly stood with her elbows propped on the counter, waiting for my appraisal. She could read it on my face, I'm sure. It may have been the best piece of pie I'd ever tasted. It was sweet and delicious with a soft, chewy crust.

Before I'd uttered a word, I'd cleared the plate. Perhaps Molly was looking for someone to help wait tables?

She took the plate away. "I usually interpret that as a good sign. Too bad you have to leave town so soon. I start my apple dumplings in the second week of September. Doc Benson's trees come ripe, and he brings 'em down handpicked every morning."

"Mmm," the woman to my left crooned. She seemed to favor Molly with a look of sumptuous longing. She turned to me and said, "Now, there's something to look forward to. People come far and wide for Molly's dumplings."

Molly asked me, "What job were you fixin' to start, honey, if you don't mind my asking?"

"Construction of the Bridgepoint Extension. I was hired by one of the contractors. Apparently they sent out letters announcing the project's cancellation awhile back. My name slipped through the cracks somehow."

"That was quite a fiasco, as I recall," the woman to my left added. "It was front-page news for a month."

"Are you telling me you traveled all the way up from New Jersey for nothing?" Molly asked.

"Not for nothing. The rhubarb pie sure was good." I finished off my coffee.

"Say, I may have an offer for you."

I thought it was Molly who had spoken. But I looked up and saw she was looking to my left, toward the woman sitting four stools down. I looked that way also. I found the woman gazing thoughtfully at her cappuccino and dancing her fingers against the glass, with the faintest hint of a smile playing on her lips.

Moments later, she *did* smile, and then uttered a laugh. "This is totally spontaneous, but I …" She glanced at the ceiling, then down at her hands. She quickly resembled a person who's fast come to grips with the absurdity of her inklings.

She shook her head. "I—I'm sorry, I shouldn't—"

"No," I bade her. "What were you gonna say?"

"I have a five-year-old son. His name is Corey. I'm a single mother, and I'm extremely busy. He starts kindergarten next week, and I've been searching for …"

"A babysitter."

She hesitated. "Well, I was thinking *chaperone*."

"Another word for babysitter."

"Not exactly. I need someone who can drive. My son needs to be driven to and from school, then ferried around to his various activities in the afternoons. And since Corey only rarely sees his father, I was hoping I could find someone who's … Let's just say he would do well with a little male influence."

I had to laugh myself.

"I'm Alisha, by the way. Alisha Caldwell."

"I appreciate the offer, Alisha, but I came here to work. Not to be a nanny."

"I'd match your wage, of course."

"Don't be silly. Microsystems was supposed to start me at twenty-seven dollars and forty-three cents an hour."

"I'll pay thirty."

I stared at her. "Are you out of your mind?"

She smiled. "No. Just a little desperate. I've spent most of the summer trying to find the right person."

"The right person? You're aware I just hitchhiked into town? I could be a vagrant, a dissident, a chainsaw killer. How do you entrust a person you know nothing about with taking care of your child?"

I was vaguely aware of Molly's eyes flashing east and west, absorbing this exchange. The coffee must've been awfully strong, for I felt a sense of hyperawareness.

Alisha smiled. "Actually, I'm pretty good at reading people."

"Oh, yeah? You think most road construction guys would qualify as babysit—excuse me, *chaperones*?"

"But you're not a road construction guy. You have a college degree. The construction gig was going to be temporary for you."

I have to admit, she'd caught me off guard. I watched her with my mouth partly open for a moment. If I'd remembered my father telling me that you can sometimes see the end before you see the beginning, I may have gotten off my stool and walked out of Molly's café, and out of Swan Lake altogether. But it wasn't my father's voice I heard. Instead I heard the foreman's mason's grind, speaking from behind a shifting curtain of smoke. *You've been laid off for the year.*

I said to Alisha, "How would you know that? Supposing it was true?"

"Quite frankly, young men without college degrees rarely demonstrate the sentence structure and vocabulary I've heard you use since you walked through the door. And young men who have their degrees don't normally pursue careers in road construction."

She shrugged, as if that explained everything.

"Look, Simon, here's the deal. Try it for a week. You'd be looking at free room and board, use of an automobile, and thirty dollars an hour. By the end of next week, if you don't think it's going to work out, I'll pay for your trip home."

I stared at Alisha Caldwell for a long time. I didn't like kids all that much, to tell you the truth.

I moved my eyes from Alisha's to Molly's, as if Molly would have the rational answer. *Go home, Simon. Catch the first bus out of town, then hitchhike the rest of the way. Because this pitcher plant is a lot deeper than you think.*

But Molly didn't provide the answer I was half hoping for. Her brown, country eyes instead promised better things to come. "The first dumpling's on me," she said.

CHAPTER TWO

COREY

ALISHA CALDWELL DROVE A Saab. It was black, and there was not a scratch on it. Sparkling in the late summer sun of that clear, cloudless day, it appeared as though it had just rolled off the detailing line. I walked around the front of the car and saw that the headlights had cute miniature windshield wipers on them.

"Is it a 2005?"

"It is," she said. "We'll put your stuff in the trunk, okay?"

"All right."

There was plenty of room in the trunk for my shoulder pack, but very little room in the front passenger seat for me. Both the front seat and floor well were piled high with loose papers, file folders, and individual boxes containing dozens of thick ten-by-thirteen-inch manila envelopes. "You'll have to excuse my slovenly vehicle," Alisha said. "It's organized chaos." She began gathering stuff in her arms.

"Never mind, Alisha. I'll sit in the back."

She peeked at me over her shoulder. "Really? You don't mind?"

"Not at all. Just take it easy on any back roads, or you'll be wiping rhubarb pie off your backrest."

I climbed into the backseat, right-hand side and buckled myself in. Alisha slid into the driver's seat, stuck the key into the ignition, and got us going. As we crept slowly down Main Street, she asked,

"Had you pre-arranged for lodging? Is there someone you need to call?"

"Actually, Microsystems was supposed to make arrangements for me. If that answers your question."

Her eyes flicked to the rearview mirror, where they made contact with mine. I thought they were silver, similar to some of her rogue strands of hair. Her eyes were a wet, shimmery silver, like mercury or quicksilver.

"Gosh, they really dropped the eight-ball on you, didn't they?"

"Look," I said, "I'm gonna write down a short list of names and numbers of people with whom I'm well acquainted. I want you to call them at your first opportunity."

"It's not necessary, Simon."

"It would make me more comfortable if you did. I'll make up the list tonight."

You didn't have to travel far to escape the Swan Lake town proper. Near the end of Main, Alisha turned right onto Elm Street, then passed through a blinking light. Beyond the blinking light, Elm formed a Y, splitting two ways. We took the right fork, and at this point the roads shed their namesakes and became numbers. The sign read simply: Road 30.

"I'm good at reading people. I did say that, didn't I?"

"Are you a psychologist or something?"

She smiled. "No. I'm a good judge of character, that's all."

"What do you do, then, if you don't mind my asking?"

"I'm an artist and a businesswoman. I dabble."

"Oh." Judging by the avalanche of folders and files currently riding shotgun, I'd have surmised she was a CPA. Or, quite possibly, an attorney.

Road 30 turned and twisted through thinly forested countryside. There were houses here and there on either side of the road, but their numbers dwindled the farther we got from town.

"Where did you go to school, Simon?"

"William & Mary, on a full boat."

"Athletic scholarship?"

"No. Academic."

"What did you study?"

"Pre-law."

"Good for you. Take your LSATs?"

"Studying."

"That's a half-day exam, I've heard."

"I look forward to the challenge." I surveyed the landscape flying past the windows. We were passing through an expanse of open fields now, bronzed with day lilies and goldenrod.

"Well," she said, "attorneys certainly have their place in our world. People love to give them a bad rap, until they discover they need one. I have several clients who're lawyers, actually. I'll introduce them to you sometime, if you're interested."

"That might be nice." I remembered the three-story colonial I'd seen while walking up Aldridge Street. Dolan, Packer & Spencer. It already seemed like eons ago. "Where did you go to school, Alisha?"

"I went to Smith, in Northampton, Mass."

"That's all girls, isn't it?"

"It was then, and it is now. I studied history."

"Ouch."

She smiled. "When I went for my first job interview, I was asked to take a typing test. I went home and cried."

"Did you get the job?"

"No. I did administrative work for two years, making ten thousand dollars a year. So I went and got an MBA."

Suddenly, we were turning off Road 30, and Alisha had her Saab barreling down a stone driveway. A line of oak trees flanked both sides of the driveway, which was a good half-mile long.

"Is this your house?" I asked.

"No, we have to stop to pick up Corey. This is his friend Samantha's house. They had a playdate today."

"Oh, a playdate." These days, kids had playdates. When I was a kid, every day had been a playdate. "Did you say Samantha?"

Alisha smiled. "Yes. She and Corey are best friends. Samantha starts first grade next week, Corey starts kindergarten. One can only wonder how much longer it'll last. Although they've both come out already and said they want to get married."

"Have they set a date?"

The house was a white split-level with a circular drive in front of it. Alisha put the Saab into park, left it running, and popped her door open.

"I'll be right back."

"Okee-dokee."

I watched her move briskly around the front of the Saab toward the house. As she approached the porch stairs, the front door opened and a woman's gaunt but smiling face appeared behind the storm door. Samantha's mother opened the storm door and exchanged pleasantries with Alisha. Then Alisha made a half turn with her shoulders, motioning to the Saab with one hand. Samantha's mother craned her head, peeking past Alisha's body to get a better look at me. *Look what I picked up at the unemployment office! Can you believe it?*

I turned away, feeling my cheeks flush. When I looked toward the house again, Alisha was walking carefully down the porch stairs and holding hands with her son. Corey had blond hair and blue eyes. He wore a red jacket even though it was seventy-five degrees outside. The tag stuck out from the back of the jacket's collar. In the boy's hands was a large coffee can. So, here it was coming toward me now—not a jackhammer or an asphalt shovel or even a line-painting device … but a boy of five who needed to eat, sleep, get up, get dressed, use the bathroom, and brush his teeth before bedtime. Was I going to be required to hold his hand whenever I walked him to and from the car, the way Alisha was doing now? Because I really couldn't see myself doing that.

Alisha walked him around the car and opened the back door for him. She knelt down beside him and pointed at me like I was some kind of zoo animal. I wasn't sure whether to grunt or cackle.

"Corey, this is Simon. Remember we talked about having someone live with us? Someone to help out and look after you?"

Corey didn't appear as though he remembered what he'd had for lunch that day, but he nodded anyhow. "Hi, Simon."

"Hi, sport." I offered a weak smile.

He climbed in next to me. Alisha buckled him in, then shut the door.

As we went speeding back down the driveway (Alisha had herself quite a lead foot), I looked over at the boy sitting next to me. He was holding the coffee can in his lap, with both hands pressed firmly around it.

"What's in the can, sport?"

"Why, um … why are you calling me sport?"

He spoke with deliberate innocence. The unassuming, questioning nature of his tone caused me to chuckle. I thought I heard Alisha laugh softly under her breath.

"What do you have in the can, Corey?" I revised.

"Bouncy balls."

"Bouncy balls?"

"Yeah. Wanna see?"

"Sure."

He passed the can over to me. It was a Maxwell House 34.5-ounce can, which meant that it was wide enough to require two hands in order to hold it. I took the can and looked inside. It was half filled with SuperBalls, the little rubber kind you could make bounce from floor to ceiling if you threw them hard enough.

I laughed aloud. "Where did you get all these? There must be three dozen SuperBalls in here."

"They've been collecting them," Alisha explained, "over the course of the summer. The gumball machines in the supermarkets sell them for a quarter apiece. Corey keeps the can for a week, and then Samantha keeps it the next."

I handed the can back to him. "Is there some sort of master plan in the works?"

We'd gotten off Road 30, onto Road 49, and we were now sailing through the woods at a high rate of speed. Alisha was forced to slow down, however, as we rounded a tight corner and then crossed a narrow, one-lane bridge. The bridge was arched, with fine stone sidewalls. A sign advertised that we were spanning Pine Creek. Another half mile of curvy, twisty road, and we came to a second one-lane bridge—this, an old, rick-rackety plank board bridge with wood railings. The floor planks thumped and bumped as the tires went over them. The accompanying sign said that we were crossing Birch Creek.

"I'm guessing the bridge makers of yesteryear weren't anticipating heavy traffic in these parts."

"There are a lot of these around," Alisha replied. "They're historical, for the most part, and actually quite serviceable. Eight different creeks exit out of Swan Lake. We've just crossed over two of them."

"And Whiskey Creek, back in town?"

"That's one of them, yes," she said. "Amazingly, Swan Lake has not a single visible tributary."

"It's entirely spring-fed? That's what you're saying?"

"Yes. The lake itself is a miracle of nature."

Road 49 came to its terminus when it T-boned into State Street. Alisha turned left. State Street, despite its fanciful name, was one of the ruttiest, backwoods dirt roads upon which I've traveled. Where there weren't potholes there were washboard bumps. The Saab rocked and rattled. I was glad I wasn't wearing dentures.

"Do you live in a tree house?"

"I have a Land Rover for the winter time."

Finally, we turned right into a pebble stone driveway. We descended a gradual hill, which turned into a steeply pitched hill, wherein the driveway became a series of switchbacks. We made descending S-turns in and around banks of intervening pine trees. Around each line of trees was yet another S-turn. Finally, I began to see daylight between the tree fronds. I also saw water. At the base of the driveway, the trees parted, and there was the lake.

The lake was not nearly as large as I'd envisioned it, which may have rendered it all the more beautiful. It was large enough to be a vista, yet small enough to call your own.

"You didn't say you lived on the lake."

"You didn't ask." Alisha put the Saab into park.

I climbed out of the car and found myself standing in a spacious, square-shaped driveway. A green Land Rover was parked in front of one of the closed garage bays. There was also an older Saab, a red one. A set of stairs built from old railroad ties curved upward around the right side of the house—which I now took to be the front insofar that it faced the lake. The house itself was perched partway up a ridge and yet embedded within the forest at the same time. And despite the staggering lakeside view it afforded, I couldn't escape the disquieting notion that I'd been there before. That's when I looked up and saw the front deck wrapping around the corners of the house. And above the deck, on the second floor, the dormer windows. I hadn't been there, but I'd seen it not more than an hour ago.

Alisha Caldwell lived at Crawford Daze.

THE HOUSE ON THE LAKE

ENTERING CRAWFORD DAZE FOR the first time, I felt a sudden coldness unfolding in the pit of my stomach. A shimmer of dread wormed through my viscera, then worked its way up my spine, tapping each vertebra like a piano key. I remembered the voiceless words that had filled my head as I'd studied the painting in front of Millie's store. *There is no happiness in that home. But there used to be.*

Nonsense, I decided. For the house was a spectacle of warmth and hospitality. I lowered my pack to the floor so that I could absorb the layout. Corey went flying by me and began running in circles around the spacious den in which we were standing. An open fireplace stood at my immediate right. The den consisted of solid oak flooring with thick Persian rugs, a dining room set, sofa and loveseat, chaise lounge, and television.

Alisha walked by me, her arms laden with files. "Settle down, Corey. Let's get your jacket off."

Corey had set his coffee can on the dining room table and was now doing laps around the sofa with his arms held over his head.

"He's usually not like this," Alisha confided, going after him. "He must be happy you're here."

"I do have that effect on people."

She caught him in both arms and hugged him tight to her body, more to still him than as a show of affection, I thought. He squirmed and giggled in her grasp.

A spiral staircase in the back left corner of the den ascended into a loft. The loft extended a third of the way over the den area, buttressed by a wood handrail.

Alisha saw me looking. "That's the loft. Come on, I'll show you the house."

I followed her up the spiral stairs, and Corey followed me. At the top was a sitting area furnished with a thick green carpet, a pair of chaise lounges with end tables, and an antique coffee table. This would be a perfect reading place on a cold rainy day.

A hall led past the sitting area and continued down the length of the house. I skimmed my right hand across the wood banister, looking into the den below. This place was downright beautiful.

"This hall leads to some bedrooms." Alisha motioned to the first room on the right. "This is my room." Peeking in, I saw a four-poster bed, a mahogany armoire, a triple dresser, a wood floor.

"And then these others are spare rooms."

Back in the den again, as we came off the spiral casement, Alisha pointed to an office appended to the front side of the house. The office was accessed by a single French door.

"That's my work room in there," she said. I saw two computers, a fax, a copier, and several bookshelves. The office would look out over the lake, of course. Must be nice.

"What kind of work?" It was the second time I'd asked.

"Investment strategies, market research, some other stuff."

We came around to the fireplace again. I picked up my shoulder pack and followed Alisha around the hearth, and then to the right. There, a single wood stair led up to the kitchen slanting to the left, and a separate hallway diverging to the right. We went into the kitchen first. A round table with five chairs stood in the near left corner. The kitchen itself was a long and rectangular room with an island counter. The cabinetry was all cherry. The fridge and freezer were New Age chrome, as was the oven and microwave. There was even a convection oven.

Corey, seeing the island counter, felt compelled to do a lap around it. The front door of the chrome fridge was covered with his crayon drawings, which had been hung beneath magnetized plastic letters.

"This is really something. Very nice."

"Come on, I'll show you your room."

We exited the kitchen and moved into the diverging hall. Corey came charging past us.

"You wanna see my room?" he asked. His round face was flushed red with verve. "You want to, Simon?"

"Sure."

Corey's was the first room on the right. It was the only room I'd seen thus far that had been furnished with wall-to-wall carpet. The carpet was indigo. Toys lay scattered. A bunk bed stood against the right wall—the kind in which the lower bunk lay perpendicular to the top bunk.

"See, this is mine!" He went and sat down in the middle of the floor among his toy trucks and Matchbox cars and plastic airplanes. Then he jumped off the floor and hopped onto the lower bunk. "Maybe we can have a sleepover."

"Do you sleep on the top or the bottom?" I asked him.

"The bottom mostly."

What would be my room was the next room on the right. The colors were neutral, the furniture was Pennsylvania House, and the bed was a queen with a white, down coverlet. I liked it a lot. Most of all, the Pella windows looked down over the lake. I threw my shoulder pack onto the bed and walked over to the windows. A square floating dock rocked gently over the water a hundred yards off shore. I stood there at the window, wondering if anyone had ever swum to the dock before, and how many times. Again I felt the strange coldness seeping into my stomach, an alien presence that seemed totally at odds with the firmaments of my surroundings. I thought of the painting I had seen of the floating dock, the one with the swan standing on the corner with its head turned to the south. Who had the artist been, I wondered, and how had he given the house its name?

I must have stood there for longer than I thought, for soon a hand touched my shoulder. I jumped.

It was Alisha. "You all right?"

"Yeah. Fine. It's a little hard to believe I'm standing in Crawford Daze."

"Standing where?"

I turned to face her. "Crawford Daze. The name of the house, right?"

She smiled and shook her head. "I've never heard of it. Where'd you hear that?"

I described the painting I'd seen on Main Street. Little Millie and her dog, Minnie. I left out the part in which I'd reached for my wallet without knowing it.

"How interesting. I'll have to check that out."

She turned to leave.

"How long have you lived here?" I asked.

She paused at the door. "Almost two years. This will be our second winter." She checked her watch. "It's five-thirty. Get yourself unpacked, Simon. I'll get some dinner ready."

*   *   *

Dinner was leftover turkey, mashed potatoes, green beans, and sliced pumpkin bread. Getting Corey to eat everything on his plate was like pulling teeth. I, on the other hand, ate heartily.

"I'll have you know, I eat like a Mack truck."

Alisha smiled around a forkful of green beans. When she'd cleared her throat, she said, "If only my son would eat that way."

It occurred to me that I knew nothing about raising a child. Or taking care of one, for that matter. I voiced this concern to Alisha.

She brushed it off. "He likes pizza and chicken tenders. And french fries, of course. That stuff is all in the freezer. I buy the chicken in bulk."

"When is his normal bedtime?"

"Between eight-thirty and nine. He likes to have a story read to him."

Corey's face lit up. "Story! Story! Story!"

As Alisha cleared the table and began doing the dishes, she demonstrated the basic layout of the kitchen. "Drinking glasses are up here, dishes are here, silverware's there. Help yourself to anything in the fridge."

I opened the fridge to have a look. There were two jugs of cranberry juice, two half-gallon cartons of organic milk, and lots of strange leafy vegetables. I expressed to her that whereas I did drink large quantities of milk, I could do without the organic variety.

"That's fine. But I prefer that Corey drink the organic."

"Okay."

When the dishes were done, Alisha whipped up a cappuccino for each of us. Corey drank hot cocoa. We sat on the deck overlooking the lake and ate cherry cheesecake. The cheesecake was lush and creamy.

"You made this yourself?"

She nodded. "I used to own a catering company."

"I'm impressed."

As twilight sank into evening, I sat on the bed in my new room composing a list of names and phone numbers. Once finished, I carried the list out to the kitchen. Corey sat at the table coloring in a coloring book. Alisha was removing dishes from the dishwasher and stowing them in their respective cabinets.

"This is my list of references. I want you to use it."

She glanced at me once, then returned to the task at hand. "You can just leave it there on the counter."

Later that evening, I lay propped on my bed reading an Alice Hoffman novel. I found it difficult to concentrate. I had come so far in the course of this day, and the day had taken a great many unexpected turns. I would read several lines of prose, and then my mind would start to wander. I thought of the thankless foreman in the smoky, cave-like office telling me I'd been laid off for the year. Prattling on about short-eared owls and pussy toad environmentalists and court-ordered injunctions. Somehow I'd wound up in the backseat of a car, next to a winsome if not impulsive boy with a can of bouncy balls. This was not what my father had meant when he had told me to spend some time working with my hands. This was not what I had signed on for.

From the next room, I could hear Alisha reading her son a story. At some point she must have kissed him goodnight and clicked off the light, because suddenly I heard a gentle rap on the open door to my room. I looked up and saw her standing next to the bulwark.

"Get some sleep. We'll have a pretty busy day tomorrow. I would like for us to be up by eight, if that's okay."

I nodded, indicating that eight o'clock was fine.

She noticed the book I was reading. "It's a fine choice. I'm a huge fan of P. D. James and Mario Puzo. Good night."

"Good night."

I gave up on reading and clicked off the light. I lay in a strange bed in a strange house, wondering what I was doing here and why, and too exhausted to examine those questions any further. A three-quarters moon reflected a pale, ghostly white off the surface of the lake, whereupon it shone through my windows and moved in aqueous patterns over the ceiling. My eyes fell slowly shut without my knowing it. My final thoughts as I drifted off were of the sweet tang of the rhubarb pie against my tongue and the roof of my mouth, so soft and chewy, and going down, down, down.

CHAPTER FOUR

Smashing Pumpkins

"In what ways is the ending of this novel ironic?" Ms. Spaide was lecturing us on *Ethan Frome,* the Edith Wharton novel we'd been assigned that semester. Ms. Spaide was an elfish woman who wore her raven-black hair in a tight bun. She wore loose-fitting clothes and a pair of professorial black spectacles that made her look more like a librarian than a sophomore English teacher. Word had it she lived with her parents in a small home on the outskirts of town, in which she occupied a second-floor bedroom. There were rumors that her hair was three feet long untrussed, and that she'd never traveled more than sixty miles from her home. A modern-day Rapunzel-slash-Emily Dickinson. Today she was rambling on about character dichotomies and something about a sledding accident that was supposed to mask a double suicide (myself, I sat in the back row wondering why the characters hadn't simply stepped in front of a moving train, or drunk Jim Jones' spiked Kool-Aid), and growing markedly perturbed at the enduring silence in the room.

"Now, class, I assure you this question will be on the exam. So, for those of you who haven't completed—"

There came a knock on the door. Ms. Spaide stopped in mid-sentence and went to the door to see who could be so bold as to interrupt her lesson. She cracked it open ever so slightly and began conversing with an unseen person standing in the outside hall. None of us could hear what exactly was being said, but there was an audible note of exasperation in Ms. Spaide's replies.

Finally she turned to face us once more, her chin raised as though to address someone near the back of the room.

"Mr. Kozlowski? Would you come here, please? Bring your things."

Well, either I was in trouble for having done something bad, or our cat had gotten run over in the street. Either way, I was getting out of Ms. Spaide's class, and that was a check for the plus column. As I moved past her, however, she said to me in a remonstrative tone, "Be sure to get today's notes from someone, Simon."

I looked down at her. Ms. Spaide was a string bean of a woman who stood five-two with heels. At age fifteen, I was already four inches taller than her. "I will, Ms. Spaide."

I stepped into the hall and found Mrs. Goronsky, one of the office aides, waiting for me. She offered me a kind look but didn't smile. "How are you today, Simon?"

"Pretty good, I guess. Am I in trouble?"

"Come with me, please."

I fell in step behind her as she marched up the hall in her hard-bottomed shoes. I made a concerted effort to recall any events of the past three days that might land me in detention, or worse, the principal's office. I could think of none.

Mrs. Goronsky led me upstairs, then past the gymnasium, toward the front entrance of the Parsippany Hills Regional High School. I followed her into the main office, my sack slung over my shoulder. At no time had I felt any thread of true fear—until, that was, I saw my father. He was standing at one of the windows, turned partly away from me to look out at the front lawn. It was a Tuesday in mid-October—a workday for him and a school day for me. My father was wearing his work fatigues. His arms hung still at his sides, and I saw the calluses on the edges of one of his hands, and for a moment I felt an overwhelming surge of love for him.

"Dad? What are you doing here?"

He turned to face me. "Oh, there you are, Simon. Hi-ya, howya doing?"

"I'm fine, Dad. What's going on? Is everything all right?"

One of the aides stuck a clipboard in front of him with a pen.

He signed his name on whatever form was on the clipboard, then came toward me, and put a hand on my shoulder. "Let's go for a ride, son."

*   *   *

My father drove an aged, grumbling Ford pickup, which our neighbors called the Roadgrader. A piece of shit on wheels is what it was, but my father liked it just fine. He said it had character. Last winter, he'd struck and killed a deer on State Route 46 west of Parsippany, incurring major damage to the front grille. There hadn't been enough money to have it fixed, so my father had simply ripped the old grille out and driven the truck without one. A week later, Mr. Van Ness from next door had walked over holding a round cooking grill he'd taken from an old barbecue. Affixed to the grill with thin wire were a plastic sausage and, below it, a hamburger patty. "Now, Carl," Mr. Van Ness had said seriously, "you can't be driving that old rust bucket around without a working grille." My dad had found the idea so funny, he'd strung Mr. Van Ness's "grille" onto the front of his truck himself using pieces of an old coat hanger. It was still there on this day.

I also noticed, as I moved around the back of the truck to get into the passenger side, a row of eight or nine pumpkins lined up along the bed's sidewall. The pumpkins weren't large ones—they were roughly the size of an average cantaloupe. Faces had been painted on them in hurried brushstrokes.

"What's with the pumpkins, Dad?"

"Hop in, Simon."

We drove in silence, moving out of Parsippany, onto Interstate 80. Dad drove west. He cranked his window half open. I opened mine a notch. The warm midday, mid-autumn air rushing through the cab space in a whirlwind made my hair stand up and fly around. The sun rode high in a cobalt sea of aqua blue. We drove past freshly harvested cornfields, bordered by forests blazing with red, orange, and yellow leaves. Halloween was a week away. It occurred to me in a loud kind of way that if ever there were a pinprick moment that could be dubbed the avatar of a season—the so-called "crease in the center of the book"—that moment was here and now. This was autumn in its quintessential flesh, and it was bigger than me. It was larger and rounder than any secrets, wishes, or ambitions I may have harbored at that early age.

"Hey, Dad, where we going?"

"Let me ask you something, Simon. Do you believe in opening new doors? New beginnings, fresh starts, that sort of thing?"

"Sure, I guess so."

There was an optimist's gleam in his eye, a sparkle I'd never seen before. He wasn't smiling, but he was wearing the sort of guarded expression that made you know he was smiling somewhere on the inside. Had my father just won the lottery? And then quit his job?

"Do you have dreams, Simon? I mean … well, I've heard you list a half-dozen career choices and such. Putting all that aside, though. Do you have *dreams?* Big ones, I mean—the stuff behind and beneath the career choices?"

This was heavy stuff for a high school sophomore. "Sure, I guess so. I'd like to get rich and … and live the good life, I guess."

"Yeah, get rich. Get rich." He was quiet for a while. Then, "When I was a kid, my father had a saying. He said that you can sometimes see the end before you see the beginning. You'd do well to remember that yourself." He turned to look at me. "Will you remember it, Simon?"

"Sure, Dad."

We drove into the high hills of Allamuchy. Dad got us off the interstate and onto a network of rural county roads. Off one of these county roads, we made a right onto a gravel road with a sign that read Towpath Lane. We went down this lane for several miles, cutting through forest and hayfields. There were no houses or buildings to be seen, and the gravel lane didn't appear to be going to any particular place. Finally, Dad pulled the truck aside and threw the brake. Pinecones crunched beneath the tires as we rolled to a stop.

"Okay, we're here." My father bent forward, reaching beneath his seat for something. He pulled out what looked to me like a chamois cloth wrapped around an object three or four times.

Outside, Dad drew down the Ford's tailgate, and we sat down upon it. There were tree stumps nearby where trees had been felled recently. Beyond the stumps was a grove of dark pine forest. To our right and left, open fields lay spread like the hands of God, resplendent with high whispering grasses, fall flowers, and milkweed.

"Look here, Simon, I want to show you this." On his lap was the object wrapped in the chamois cloth. He unfolded the cloth. I stared in disbelief at the gun that lay there. "This is a Colt .45 handgun. I first learned to shoot when I was about your age. I thought maybe it was time for you to learn."

"Really? You mean it? No fussing?"

"No fuss and no muss. Now look, I want to show you how to load this. It has a clip which pops right into the handle." He popped the clip. It slid out of the handle into the palm of his hand. He popped the clip back in. "Very easy."

After that he showed me where the safety was. He showed me how to hold the gun, then how to aim it. I was surprised by how heavy the gun felt in my hands. In a strange way, its heaviness was its realness. It wasn't like the plastic toy guns of my childhood, which shot rubber balls or little arrows with suction cups on their tips. This was a heavy piece of equipment with genuine working parts that fired real bullets at true speeds. It made me think of all the cop shows I'd seen on TV and in the movies, in which the good guys and bad guys just grab their pieces and start firing away one-handed.

Dad went about setting up the pumpkins on the severed tree stumps. He produced a set of earplugs for each of us. We took turns shooting. He showed me how to stand with my legs spread for balance and stability, and how to hold the gun in front of me with both arms straight. I had trouble with the recoil, and as a result most of my shots sailed high. I didn't hit any of the pumpkins dead-on. The closest I came was obliterating one of the stems off the top of the very last pumpkin.

"Whoa! Nice shot, Simon!" my father lauded. "That's like taking the apple off the guy's head!" He was smiling ear to ear, genuinely impressed at my marksmanship.

When the shooting was done and the pumpkins blown to pieces, my father showed me how to clean the gun. Then he wrapped the Colt in the chamois cloth once more and slid it under the front seat.

After that he clapped his hand on one of my shoulders and said, "Walk over here with me, Simon. I want to show you something."

I followed him past the tree stumps (now riddled with bullet holes) and through the pumpkin mush that now covered the ground, into the open grove of the pine forest. At the edge of the grove, where the ground was covered with brown pine needles, he knelt down into a squat and picked up a pinecone.

"Squat down here, Simon, so you can see this."

I did. I squatted down next to my father.

"You know what this is, right?"

"Sure, Dad. It's a pinecone."

"Do you know how it works? You know what it does?"

"It … well, it's … you know, it grows on the tree, and falls to the ground, and …"

"And what, Simon? What does it do after it's on the ground? Does it just take up space? If so, then why does it grow in the first place?"

I looked down at the pinecone in my father's hand, then back up at my father's inquisitive face. I knew, didn't I? Surely, I *knew*.

"Well … the seeds are in there, aren't they?"

"Yes, they are. Trees have some ingenious methods of spreading their seeds, Simon. This pinecone is actually a husk. The tree's seeds are inside. But as you can see behind us, there's really no room for any more trees in this forest. So, this cone will not open. In fact, it only opens under one very extreme condition—fire. Forest fires kill existing trees while at the same time causing pinecones to split open. When the cones open, the seeds spill out. New trees take root. The forest re-grows. It's an evolutionary adaptation of cone-bearing trees. It's their way of furthering their existence on the earth."

We left the darkness of the pine grove and went into the open fields, where my father showed me a dozen species of wildflowers and other plants. He broke the arms of a milkweed—we watched as the white "milk" flowed like blood from the plant's severed limbs. He identified a poisonous nightshade plant. "Its real name is *belladonna*—it means *beautiful woman* in Italian. This stuff will kill a man standing up, Simon." And later, the poison hemlock plant. "This kills by paralysis, which progresses to the point at which you can't even move your lungs to draw air. Quails will often eat the seeds. The quails are immune to the poison, but if a man eats the quail … Believe it or not, I had an uncle once who became completely paralyzed after eating a quail he'd shot."

"You're joking."

"I'm completely serious. Oh, check this out," he said, bending down once more. He pointed to a blade of grass. Halfway down the grass stalk was a small white ball of spittle. My father plucked the stalk from the ground and held it up for closer inspection. "You ever seen a spit bug, Simon?"

"A what?"

"A spit bug." Using the pads of his thumb and forefinger, my father carefully rubbed away the ball of saliva until, sitting there on his open thumb and no larger than the head of a pin, was a tiny green insect. "There he is, the little fella. That's the spit bug. We have these in our backyard, Simon; all you have to do is look. What he does is he climbs up a stalk of grass and builds himself a home simply by foaming at the mouth. Talk about a low mortgage payment."

We drove home in silence beneath a low sun that cast its last slanting light over the harvested fields. I thought of pumpkins and falling leaves and Halloween masks. I'd missed Ms. Spaide's lecture on Edith Wharton, but I'd learned a lot of other things instead. I had learned how to shoot. I had learned how a pinecone works and where the spit bug lived and how to identify a plant that could kill a man standing up.

I had learned, most of all, what it meant to have a father. In two weeks' time, I would learn what it meant to lose one.

CHAPTER FIVE

LAY OF THE LAND

ALISHA, COREY, AND I spent the next three days in the Land Rover. Alisha shuttled us from one place to the next, having me drive part of the way so that I would learn the routes. The Ace of Spades Preschool and Kindergarten was on County 513, six miles north of the Swan Lake town proper. There were five different ways of getting there from Crawford Daze. The most direct path was to stay on State Street, go halfway around the lake, then make a right onto Road 21 at the swimming beach. Stay on 21 for four and a half miles, crossing two more of those quaint one-lane bridges, then jump onto the Scarsdale Brook Road, which took you to County 513 North. Six miles up 513 was the Ace of Spades School, on your right-hand side. You can't miss it. It was a sixteen-mile trek from the house that took close to thirty minutes owing to the nature of the roads. Starting next week, Corey would need to be dropped off at 8:00 AM and picked up at one.

The teachers were preparing their classrooms when we visited. Alisha made formal introductions.

"Simon, this is Mrs. Thomas and that's Mrs. Hayes. Ladies, I'd like you to meet Simon Kozlowski." I shook hands with them. Mrs. Thomas was a sweet, old Southern belle, with sandy-brown hair and a permanent smile. Mrs. Hayes was clearly the more reticent of the two, her face creased with lines of disapproval. I was glad I was out of kindergarten.

"Hello," I said.

"Simon will be delivering Corey in the mornings and picking him up in the afternoons," Alisha instructed.

"Oh, how nice," Mrs. Thomas crooned. "And he's a cutie, too." She reached out and pinched my cheek. Mrs. Hayes watched in silence.

"Under no circumstances," Alisha said, "will Corey be permitted to get into a car with anyone other than Simon or myself."

Mrs. Thomas produced a form for Alisha and me to sign. I felt Mrs. Hayes watching me closely as I scribbled my name on the dotted line. I got out of there before she could put me in time-out.

On Mondays, Corey would be attending Kindermusik at the Barrow Hill State Park. The state park was located five miles south of the Swan Lake town proper, which translated into a twelve-mile drive from the Ace of Spades. Corey's class didn't begin until three o'clock, however, creating a two-hour gap between school pick-up and Kindermusik drop-off.

"It'll be up to you guys how you want to chew up the time," Alisha told us. "You can go home if you want. You can go into town and feed the ducks, go to the library, go to Molly's, whatever."

Corey liked the idea of feeding the ducks. "Yeah! Feed the ducks! Feed the ducks!"

Tuesdays Corey would be going to karate class. His karate master was a sharp-looking, dark-haired fellow named Dale Andruchuk who taught in a small gym appended to his home. He lived eleven miles east of the town proper. I'd be logging some serious miles on Alisha's old red Saab. I was already getting highway hypnosis going from one place to the next. Alisha charged ahead tirelessly. She had more energy than Corey and I combined. Karate classes started at four in the afternoon. A three-hour layover.

"Wednesday is an off day," Alisha told us. "The two of you can do what you want."

"Hey, you hear that? We can do what we want, kid."

Corey was fast asleep, his head lolled against the car door.

"Thursday he goes to the worry doctor. Fridays he has horseback riding lessons."

"I'll need an appointment book for a five-year-old," I said.

"I told you a chaperone was an apt description of the job."

"What's a worry doctor?" I asked.

"Child psychologist. Dr. Andrews has an office in town, just down the street from Molly's. He just left for vacation, actually. He'll be back in three weeks."

"What worries does a five-year-old boy have to discuss with a shrink?"

"Corey never sees his father, for one. I'm a single mother working practically around the clock, for two. It's more preemptive than anything else. They do a lot of play therapy."

"Play therapy? What is that?"

"Corey plays with toys in the office, and Dr. Andrews draws interpretations based on the play style."

I wondered how much money Alisha Caldwell spent dispatching her son to this barrage of weekly activities.

We drove and drove. I shook hands and smiled and nodded. It reached the point where I could no longer correlate names with faces. There was too much new information in too short a time. On the third day, Alisha drove us to her office building in town. It was located at 18 Jerricho Avenue. The Ferguson-Bryson-Caldwell Securities and Investment Firm was a turn-of-the-century building of white brick on the outside and plaster walls on the inside. It was three stories high, with twenty-one offices.

Alisha introduced me to Richard Bryson, a dark-haired fellow with a gray beard. She towed Corey and me around the building, demonstrating the who's and where's. She took us up to the third floor, where the trading room was located. Banks of computers lined the walls in a dark hall filled with cigarette smoke. Day traders sat hunched over their screens, watching stock prices blip by and occasionally executing a series of keystrokes in fast succession. Several of the traders turned and looked at us, squinting in the darkness before turning back to their business.

We went back downstairs. I asked Alisha, "Exactly what goes on here?"

"Money-making is what goes on here, Simon. Wealthy clients with large chunks of money come to us looking to park it somewhere. We park it for them. It's a parking lot industry for the super-rich. Most of our clients—90 percent of them, I'd say—were wealthy to begin with who became super-wealthy through real estate investments."

Back out on the sidewalk again, Alisha turned north and began walking. Or maybe it was south, I don't know. Corey and I had to run to catch up with her.

She went on talking, too. "Even though this is my primary workplace, I'm not here much of the time. I'm out of town on business, sometimes a week at a clip. I have people I meet in Manhattan regularly."

"Alisha, how old are you, exactly?" I called from behind.

"Forty-one. Why?"

"I'll be twenty-three in November, and I can barely keep up with you."

"Do the best you can," she said without looking back. "And be sure to bring my son with you."

A new side of Alisha Caldwell was beginning to emerge. And I wasn't sure I liked it.

CHAPTER SIX

PULP FICTION

SCHOOL STARTED. ALISHA'S PLAN to graft Corey and me into the new routine worked rather well. The first morning saw the three of us traveling together in Alisha's black Saab, with Alisha driving. On the second morning, we did the same thing, except this time we took the older, red Saab. The third morning we again took the red Saab, but it was I who drove. "You know how to pop a clutch, I hope," Alisha said to me from the front passenger seat.

"My old truck was a manual," I said. "My father's Roadgrader. You had to grind it to get it into fifth." I turned toward her. "But what if I hadn't known?"

"Then I'd be giving you a crash course in my driveway."

"Does this car have the little windshield wipers on the headlights?" I asked.

"No. Let's go, or we'll be late."

Going to school, even if for only a half day, was a new experience for Corey, and I was surprised at how well he made the transition. He had been so looking forward to it in the days leading up to it that the requisite crying spell I had anticipated never, in fact, happened. On the third morning, Alisha remained in the car while I accompanied her son into the school. I received a bit of a shock when, upon climbing out of the backseat, Corey reached up and took my hand. My first compulsion was to pull my arm away—this wasn't my son, and I felt strange holding hands with him. But a quick glance around

42

the parking lot was enough to quell my jitters—no one was watching us, and no one cared. All the kids, in fact, were holding hands with their accompanying adults.

Driving back to Crawford Daze that morning, I tried to draw Alisha out a little. Her initial niceties and mirthful mannerisms from a week ago had worn away, replaced by a distant if not dubious silence. She seemed constantly adrift in a sea of endless thought.

"I've been experiencing an odd set of emotions the past several days," I said. "The whole thing has taken me by surprise."

She had been looking out her window, watching the landscape. Now she turned her head toward me, genuine interest flitting in her eyes. "What's that, Simon?"

"It's the first time in my life September has come around and I'm *not* on my way to school in some way, shape, or form. I feel completely out of sorts … like I should be somewhere I'm not. It's a strange feeling."

"You're feeling disconnected from a set pattern?"

"Yeah, I guess so. Especially when I see other kids going to school. I feel like I should be doing the same."

"Well, you're not a kid anymore," she said. "You're growing up. We can't go to school forever. Your notions of disconnectedness will pass in a week or so."

"How do you know?"

"Because I've gone through it myself. Classroom learning is a passive endeavor. When you make the transition from school to work, you make the transition from passive to active. That's a difficult switch. Trust me, you would have encountered the same feelings had you been working on the Bridgepoint Extension."

"You think so?"

"No question." She smiled. "And you wouldn't have met Corey. I'm getting the sense he adores you."

"I haven't registered that yet."

"Well, I'm his mother; I can tell."

"I've never really been good with kids, to be honest."

"Don't forget, you could find yourself back in law school at this time next year," she said, ignoring my comment. She swept a whip of silver hair off her brow and crossed her arms over her chest, giving me a serious look. "Have you considered which area of law you'd like to enter?"

"No, I haven't."

"Just don't become a divorce or malpractice attorney."

"Why's that?"

"You'll be rich and hated."

"Looks to me like you're pretty well off," I said.

"But not hated."

In the days and weeks that followed, I began to hammer out a rudimentary schedule for myself. I'd be up at six—showered, dressed, and shaved by quarter after. Getting Corey out of bed was no small task, often requiring much prodding and jabbing of his arms and shoulders. "Let's go, kid. Time to get up." He would moan and roll over. One morning, I seized both of his ankles and dragged him out from beneath his sheets, dazed and blinking. We ate breakfast together, often Honey Nut Cheerios. Corey drank orange juice while I drank coffee. We were on the road by seven-thirty. It was around this time that Alisha was just awakening. Some mornings she'd come down in her bathrobe in time to peck Corey on the cheek on our way out.

"Don't I get a kiss?" I asked one morning.

"Get out of here, why don't you," she muttered with a smile as she turned for the kitchen, where the coffeepot was waiting.

By the time I arrived back from dropping Corey off at the Ace of Spades, the black Saab was invariably gone. I had the ensuing four-hour block to myself every day, and I began to use it. I stripped out of my clothes and got into my swim trunks. I had never been much of a swimmer, but the prospect of making it out to the floating dock was too enticing a goal. I found it difficult the first time. It was a much longer swim than the eye foretold. My arms shook with fatigue the first time I pulled myself onto the square, aluminum dock. I lay on my back with my arms splayed over my head. I may have dozed for a while. Later I sat up, dangling my legs over the side. There were three lakeshore homes other than Crawford Daze on Swan Lake, but none as beautiful. The other houses were on the north end of the lake, situated fairly close to one another, and all at or just above lake level. Crawford Daze was an architectural masterpiece of height and build.

I dove into the water anew (it seemed ten degrees colder now), and began the swim back to shore. A third of the way in, I popped my head up to try and gauge the distance remaining between me and the land. As the water ran down my face and off my eyes, I caught a glimmer of light from one of the upper windows of the house. Remembering the painting, I shook my head and wiped my hand over my face to clear my eyes. I focused on the house again, and of course there was no light coming from any of the windows. It was probably a reflection of the sun I had seen.

Following my daily swim, I remanded myself to the reading parlor in the loft, where I forced myself through two hours of LSAT prepping. This involved timing myself during practice tests, then extrapolating what my score would have been had it been the real thing. I was very focused at these times, my mental acuity honed to a sharpened point. Somehow the swim aided my faculties in this regard. After two hours, however, I turned to mush.

I called Ma at the antique shop, where she worked from eight until four, six days a week. Her initial reaction to my going to work for Alisha Caldwell had been dubious at best. Today she picked up where she'd last left off.

"Have you thought about coming home, Simon? There's plenty of work here, you know. I'm not sure babysitting is such a great idea. What if this lady's estranged husband shows up one day in a rage?"

"I'm not really babysitting, Ma. I'm more of a chaperone," I reasoned, borrowing Alisha's rationale. "And I don't think Alisha was ever married to this guy."

"How do you know that, Simon? Did she tell you?"

"No, she didn't tell me, Ma. Just a gut feeling."

"You'd do well not to get too entwined in other people's lives, dear. Their problems can become your problems. You've got your own life to worry about."

"Everything's fine, Ma, trust me. I'm swimming a lot and studying for my exam two hours every morning."

"Well … all right. But be careful, Simon. Promise me you'll use sound judgment."

I had to laugh. "I promise I will. Love you, Ma. The world over."

"The world over." She made a kissing sound into the phone. We hung up.

At noontime, I fixed myself some lunch and drank some more coffee. I was back in the red Saab and on State Street by half past. Mondays I would have Corey's Kindermusik books in the car with me. Tuesdays his karate outfit was laid out across the backseat. On Fridays it was his riding pants and boots I had to remember to take with me. At the end of the day, we'd play video games on the Super Nintendo—Mario Brothers and Donkey Kong Country. Around six, I would fix dinner for the two of us.

"Hey, kid, what do you want for dinner tonight?"

"French fries! French fries!" Most nights it was french fries and chicken strips.

Alisha returned home after seven most nights. Some nights it was closer to nine. Corey refused to go to bed until his mother was home to kiss him goodnight, forcing me to read him a second, and sometimes a third, story.

Friday mornings, Alisha would leave a paycheck for me on the kitchen counter before she left for work. It was there waiting for me when I returned from having dropped off Corey at the Ace of Spades. The first time this happened, I gasped at the amount. The check was made out to me in the amount of $1,200.00. The exorbitant sum represented one week's pay.

"It's thirty dollars an hour, eight hours a day, five days a week. I did say I'd pay you that, didn't I?" Alisha bored into me with her quicksilver eyes.

"Yes, you did, but …"

"So, what's the problem?"

"It's a lot of money for doing practically nothing."

"You aren't doing 'nothing,'" she replied, taking files out of a shoulder bag and laying them across the dining room table. It was after 9:00 PM, and Corey had fallen asleep waiting for her. "You need to get it out of your head, Simon, that you're doing something unimportant. I told you how important this was to me and how difficult it is to find someone responsible enough to do it."

Christ, where did this lady get her money? Did the investment firm she co-owned produce enough of an income for her to fork out five grand a month for childcare alone? And that didn't include all the afterschool activities Corey was enrolled in, plus whatever tuition fees she paid to the Ace of Spades. If I stayed here for a year,

I'd make a whopping $62,400 in gross pay being a chauffeur for a five-year-old.

"Put it toward your law school tuition. Trust me, you'll need it." She grabbed up some of the files she'd laid out, turned her back to me, and went into her office, ending the discussion. Ending it for now, anyway.

*   *   *

Thursday of the following week, the phone rang in Alisha's kitchen. I had just completed my morning swim and entered the house with the towel draped around my waist. Water dripped from my knees and ankles, leaving puddles across the den floor. I ran into the kitchen gingerly, so as not to slip on the tiled floor. I grabbed up the phone, expecting to hear Alisha's voice.

"Hello?"

I was greeted with silence. Then a stumbling male voice uttered, "Um ... sorry, I've got the wrong number."

"Are you looking for Alisha Caldwell?"

"Yes."

"Then you've got the right number." I was reaching over the counter for a pen and paper. "She's not here now, but I'll take a message. Your name, please?"

A hesitation. "Who am I speaking to?"

"My name is Simon. Did you want to leave a message for Ms. Caldwell?"

"No. I'll call back another time."

There came the dry click of a disconnect.

I stared at the handset for a moment before placing it back in its cradle. "Well, that was an odd one." On the top sheet of a notepad I scribbled *strange phone call, 10:15 AM*. I normally left Alisha's messages on the dining room table, where she would see them when she first walked in. Due to the mysterious nature of the call, however, I decided to leave this one in her office.

I padded across the den in my bare feet, still wearing the towel, and entered her office. The workspace was a spacious one, and by all means a scenic one. Appended to the front wall of the house, the office ran half the length of the house, affording a full view of the lake. The view from here was every bit as staggering as it was from the bedroom in which I slept. Too bad, I thought, that Alisha spent most of her hours in here after darkness had fallen. Then again, with that sort of backdrop, working during the day might present its own set of distractions.

I dropped the note on the mahogany work counter that occupied two-thirds of the front wall space. There were two computers on this counter, a fax machine, and a Xerox machine. There were two laser printers. On the blank screen of one of the monitors had been taped a three-by-five-inch index card with the following written upon it:

> specious – 1. apparently good or right but lacking real merit; not genuine. 2. pleasing to the eye but deceptive.

The card hung by a strip of Scotch tape, an island of white in a sea of black. It reminded me of some of the vocabulary flash cards I'd seen kids use back in grade school. Was Alisha preparing herself for some sort of vocab quiz?

A wire-basket waste can took up residence in the cubbyhole beneath the monitor and keyboard, where a person's legs and knees would go while working. A single leaf of paper lay at the bottom of the wastebasket, with my handwriting on it. I bent down and plucked out the paper. It had the names and phone numbers of the references I'd transcribed. Had she called any of them? Probably not. I placed the paper back into the wastebasket in precisely the position I'd found it, and turned away.

In turning, my eyes seized upon a bookshelf that stood against the side wall at the left end of the office. Remembering Alisha's comment regarding P. D. James and Mario Puzo, I wandered over to have a look. I've always believed you could get a good read on a person by examining the books on his or her bookshelves. Does he read history? Is he partial to science and technology? Or are the shelves cluttered with Danielle Steele and Jackie Collins tomes?

The books were mostly paperbacks. I didn't recognize any of the titles at first glance. When I began looking at authors' names, my heart practically seized in my chest.

Alisha J. Caldwell.

I counted fourteen titles penned by Alisha J. Caldwell. There were titles like *Red Orchid, Trial by Fire, One Hot Summer,* and *Moonlight over Water.* The cover illustrations were pretty much all the same: a man and a woman in each other's arms, the man bare-chested and rippling with abs and pectoral muscles, the woman in a white flowing dress, her black hair flying behind her in a captive wind. The dress was invariably torn in several places, allowing the woman's thigh to gleam through, or the swell of a breast. Dark, beautiful eyes and delicate skin and high cheekbones.

In addition to partnering a company, Alisha Caldwell was a published romance novelist. I tried to imagine someone hardwired for the cold, calculatory call of securities and investments coming home from a day's work and shedding that persona like a cloak, sitting down at the keyboard and pounding out lines the likes of "… *their hearts beat as one as he brought her to climax …*" and "… *she lay in his arms, bound in eternity, wondering if she could truly ever love him the way she had loved Victor …*"

I'm an artist and a businesswoman. I dabble. Dabbling was one thing. Being sharply proficient in two fields of seemingly opposite polarity was something else entirely. It helped explain her robust income. Possibly it also explained her long bouts of silence. Was she merely romanticizing about her next book? The big question was, which identity was the real one? Did Alisha the cool businesswoman masquerade as the writer of hot, juicy romances? Or did Alisha the writer of hot, juicy romances travel by day pretending to be a stock market maven? Which portrayal was real, and which was the Halloween mask?

It was 10:30 by then. I left Alisha's office. I got out of my swim trunks and into some dry clothes. In the loft parlor, I tried to study but found it difficult to focus. My mind kept wandering off.

Eventually I gave up on the studying, closed the books, and went downstairs. I poured myself a cup of coffee and sat down at the kitchen table, my fingers drumming lightly against the tabletop. I glanced repeatedly at the clock. There were still ninety minutes left to kill before I had to leave to go pick up Corey. I returned to Alisha's office and perused the titles once more. *Fire and Ice* seemed like a good one to start with. I brought it back to my room, plopped myself onto the bed, and began to read.

CHAPTER SEVEN

THE WOMAN IN THE ICE

DOCTOR ANDREWS WAS A short, portly fellow, balding on top, who wore round, thin-wire spectacles. His smile was insatiable to the point of being annoying. He nodded continuously while he spoke—quick little jerks of the head that reminded me of a rodent. Actually, he reminded me of the Weeble-Wobbles I'd played with as a child. I stifled the urge to push him over to see if he'd bound upright again.

"It's a pleasure to meet you, Simon," he said, shaking my hand. His grip was hot and sweaty. "I grab lunch down at Molly's a couple times a week. Molly told me about the day you walked in … how Ms. Caldwell happened to be there. Serendipitous, I'd say."

"On her part or mine?"

"Both, I hope." He moved his eyes from me to Corey. "Well, if you'll excuse us, I'm sure Corey and I have much to discuss."

I'm sure you do. "You'll be about how long?"

"Fifty minutes, give or take."

While Corey went in to have his worries assuaged, I returned to the sidewalk and began strolling up Main Street in the direction of the river. I crossed Elm Street, then passed Molly's café. I continued walking.

I arrived at the storefront of Millie's Arts & Wares. I went inside, reaching into one of my front pockets to feel for the billfold. Eight hundred dollars in cash resided there in the clasp of a gold clip.

Surely, Simon, there are better things to spend money on than a silly painting. It was partly the voice of reason, but I also heard my mother in it. But Ma hadn't *seen* the painting. She hadn't felt what I had felt when I'd seen it for the first time, nor was she living in the very house it portrayed. Alisha, on the other hand, might be curious to know how her house had gotten its name. And I, for one, thought the canvas would look right at home on my bedroom wall.

Millie was standing in one of the center aisles. Her head barely rose above the partitions. She saw me but said nothing.

"Hi," I said. "Millie, right?"

"Uh-huh. And Minnie."

I glanced around briefly, but the little white dog was nowhere in sight. "I'm Simon. I passed by a couple weeks ago—"

"Yes, yes, I remember. I never forget a face, dear." She smiled brightly. "Feel free to look around. There's a sale today. Anything you see is half price."

"Actually, there was one in particular—"

"The lake paintings are in the back," she said. "You'll see them if you head right down that aisle." She pointed.

"Thanks, I'll … I'll go have a look."

"Remember now, half off."

I gravitated toward the back of the store, into the right-hand corner. The aisles were narrow, the corners hard to negotiate. Wood frames jutted out and poked me in the thigh.

Paintings were piled one atop the other, some of them stacked like decks of cards. Rimes of dust lay across the tops of the frames like fluffy, gray icing. I began going through some of the canvases, one by one. I found several lake pieces, but not the one I sought. Perhaps someone had purchased it, and Millie had forgotten she'd sold it. Still, there were hundreds of paintings in this back corner alone. Some stood at crooked angles on high shelves, festooned with cobwebs.

I began filing through another stack of oils. The third piece back depicted the square floating dock with the lone swan standing on the corner. I began flipping more earnestly. The painting I was searching for wasn't there.

But a different one was. The very last canvas jumped out at me in an explosion of icy blue light. Snow flew across the piece in rippling patterns, creating a dizzying, disorienting picture that defied my expectations of art. So much snow. A moment later, I realized there was something inside the snow. A dark shape was beginning to emerge. I took a step forward, then a step back. I re-focused my eyes … and my breath caught in my throat. There was a woman in there. I was seeing a woman. Dear God, I had never seen a piece of artwork quite like this one. Who had painted it? Whose masterful strokes had created this hidden illusion? A hidden picture is exactly what it was, in fact.

The woman was visible only from the shoulders up. There was an obvious reason for this, but the reason eluded me for the moment. I was completely captivated by the pained look of alarm on the woman's face—alarm that bordered on despair, despair that leaned over the abyss of grief. I could see only one half of that grief-stricken face because the other half was turned away from me. Her arms were reaching out across the ice, fingers splayed open and hoping. The water beneath her armpits was black and merciless. The blizzard, so artfully rendered, threatened to wipe away her existence.

The woman in the painting, whoever she was, had plunged through the ice. Her life was clearly in jeopardy. Judging by the anguish stitched across her face, however, it wasn't her own life she was most concerned about. It was somebody else's, somebody not in the picture. A person she couldn't reach. The painting could have been titled *Desperation*. It was so chilling on an emotional and visceral level that I actually felt the cold. I felt the howling wind biting at my ears. Tiny flakes of snow the consistency of fine sand sliced into my bare arms at sixty miles an hour. Moments later, the ice began cracking under my feet. I looked down and was horrified to see a network of cracks spreading across the linoleum floor tiles in web-like patterns. Black water sloshed through the openings, covering my sneakers. The floor began to sink lower. I was going to fall through. I was going to—

Gasping, I turned and ran out of the store.

*   *   *

Outside on the sidewalk, I found an empty bench and plopped myself down in it. Breathing heavily, I leaned forward with my elbows propped on my knees. *What the hell was that all about, Simon? What just happened back there? Are you losing your effing mind?* Then, in a lower voice: *Perhaps you're the one who should be seeing the shrink.*

No. My imagination had gotten away from me a little, that's all. Good artwork, powerful artwork, could do that. I bent over and unlaced my sneakers. They were dry. My socks were dry, too. I wiggled my dry toes. Everything's fine, no problem here.

Re-lacing my shoes and standing up again, however, I thought about what I'd seen in the painting. What I'd seen hadn't really bothered me. I'd been deeply disturbed, though, at what I had *felt.* Her desperation, her fear, her anguish. It had sliced through me like a hot knife, leaving a searing, throbbing wound. *Her despair leaned over the abyss of grief.*

I began walking again. The sun was warm on my face, which felt good. I encountered a heavenly aroma as I passed the café, which made me feel even better. I paused to glance through the café window. Molly saw me and waved. I waved back. I spent the next thirty minutes walking around the block. After four or five loops of warm air and bright sun, I felt more or less restored.

Dr. Andrews was just opening his office door as I entered the waiting room. He had one hand on the back of Corey's neck.

Dr. Andrews looked up and saw me. "Oh, there he is. Right on time."

"All done?" I asked.

"All done. Corey did fine. I'll see you next week, lad, all right?"

"Okay," Corey answered. He looked up at me, large blue eyes sparkling in his full, round face. "What, um … what are we gonna do, Simon?"

"Follow me and I'll show you."

On the sidewalk again, I asked, "So, what'd you guys do in there?"

"Played."

"What did you play with?"

"Trains."

"Oh, yeah? I used to love trains."

Corey was looking across the street, his eyes wandering. We were moving lazily toward Molly's. I asked, "What did you do with the trains?"

"I made them go on the track," he said innocently.

"Yeah? Was it a long train or a short one?"

"A short one."

I tried to conjure a therapist's interpretation of a five-year-old playing with a toy train on a toy track. I had an insufferable image of a boy creating catastrophic collisions at crossings, in which he would run the train into a truck or school bus, then throw the boxcars across the room. There would be no crying or display of emotion on the boy's part. He would sit Indian-style and create mayhem while wearing a stone-faced expression. The therapist would be checking off boxes and scribbling notes and tabulating the bill. I tried to imagine my parents sending me to a play therapy session when I was little. The notion was utterly laughable.

Molly was waiting for us. I lifted Corey onto a stool, then sat down next to him. He clutched at the lip of the counter with both hands, his legs swinging merrily underneath him.

Molly slid a warm, steaming dumpling in front of Corey, then a second one in front of me.

"These are on me now," she said. "Like I promised."

Corey and I tore into our dumplings. It was better than the rhubarb pie, and the pie had been superb.

"My God, how do you do it, Molly?"

Her brown country eyes spoke of homespun truths and small-town wisdoms. "Like my mother used to do it, that's how. Doc Benson was by this morning. You can't get fresher apples."

Corey was still working on his dumpling, so I asked her, "Hey, what do you know about Millie? The lady with the Arts & Wares place."

"Most of her merchandise is older than the dust that covers it," Molly replied. "She's been around for as long as I can remember. She's sweet, if not a little eccentric. I can't remember the last time I saw someone coming out of her store. I sometimes wonder how she survives."

I heard Corey's fork clink against his plate. He'd cleared the plate entirely.

"What do we say to Molly, Corey?"

"Thank you, Molly," he told her.

"Thank you," I repeated.

"You're both very welcome," she said. "Hey, you know something, I've got some old bread I was gonna toss. How would you two like to go down and feed the ducks?"

Corey's face lit up like neon. "Yeah! Can we feed the ducks, Simon? Can we?"

"Of course we can feed the ducks."

"Be right back," Molly said. She slipped into the kitchen.

A piece of paper caught my attention. It was taped to the header above the door through which Molly had just passed. The paper read, in rolling Roman script:

Introducing the 23rd Annual October Ball
October the Thirtieth at the Swan Lake Firehouse Bids Are
Now on Sale: $175.00 per Couple
Come One, Come All!

Molly reappeared holding a white plastic bag bulging with yesterday's rolls. She handed the bag to me.

"It's either to the ducks or to the garbage bin." She offered me a narrow grin. "Just look out for the one with the red foot."

Corey was already off his stool and tugging at my shirt.

"Come on, Simon, come on, let's go …"

"Okay, all right, I'm coming. Thanks again, Molly," I said over my shoulder.

"Come again," she said.

We stepped onto the sidewalk and splashed into sunshine.

*   *   *

"Hey, kid, can I ask you something?"

"Sure." He was holding my right hand, swinging my arm back and forth. I held the plastic bag in my other hand. "We're going to the ducks aren't we?"

"Of course we are. But I want to ask you something along the way."

"So ask."

"When was the last time you saw your dad?"

"Um … the last time it was my birthday."

"On your last birthday, you saw him?"

"Yeah."

"When is your birthday?" I asked.

"It's … Feb-oo-ary the twenty."

"February the twentieth?"

"Uh-huh. No, it's the twenty-two, I mean."

"You mean the twenty-second."

"Yeah, the twenty-second."

"Did he bring you a present?"

"Yep. A bike."

"A *bike*? One with training wheels, I hope."

"Mom won't let me ride it."

"No? Why not?"

"She thinks I'll fall and get hurt."

"Well, maybe when you're a little bigger, she'll let you ride it, huh?"

"Yeah."

"Do you like it when your dad comes to visit you?"

He nodded.

"How 'bout your mom? Does she like it when your dad visits?"

"She mostly likes it."

"Most of the time she likes it?"

"Yeah."

"So, sometimes she doesn't like it?"

He shrugged. "I don't know. But she cries when after he leaves."

"How do you know she cries?"

"Cause I can hear her crying in her room."

"Does it make you sad when she cries?"

"A little."

"Did I ever tell you my dad died when I was only sixteen?"

"What did he die of?"

"He had a heart attack."

"What's that?"

"It's when your heart stops working all of a sudden."

"Did you cry?"

"Yes, I cried. I cried a lot, and for a long time."

We crossed the wood bridge that spanned Whiskey Creek. Corey began to get excited the moment he saw the water. A circle of mallards paddled around in the pool below us. We maneuvered around a park bench and then down a grassy hill to access the riverbank. We walked upstream about fifty feet, where we came to an exposed piece of grassy land. The ground was inundated with goose and duck feces, however. I told Corey to watch his step. Another hundred feet upriver stood an enormous weeping willow tree. A portion of its willow fronds hung over the water.

The circling mallards had spotted us and had swum toward shore. Apparently used to being fed, the first two or three were already stepping out of the river and waddling in our direction.

Corey was pointing at them, jumping up and down. "Here they come, Simon! Here they come!"

I reached into the plastic bag Molly had given me. I withdrew a good-sized hoagie roll and handed it to Corey. "All right, break off small pieces, then toss them out."

Corey began doing that, and I did the same. Within seconds, all of the mallards were on land and milling at our feet, busily plucking chunks of bread off the ground while issuing intermittent *quacks*. I stole a quick look at Corey's face as this was going on and saw a contented busyness there—wide eyes, half smile, full concentration. I heard a chorus of low honking from another direction. A gaggle of white and gray domestic geese were doing a fast waddle toward us, coming from beyond the willow tree.

"Corey, look, there's more! They must know it's feeding time. Here." I stuffed more bread into his already busy hands.

The new arrivals, maybe a dozen of them, had no patience for mallards. The smaller, less aggressive ducks were forced to the periphery as the larger geese moved in. "Whoa, these guys are hungry!" Corey wailed. A dozen became fifteen, then twenty. I began tearing off larger chunks in an effort to speed up my delivery. The hunks of crust were seized the moment they touched the ground.

"Where are they coming from?" I uttered. The scales of supply and demand were tipping out of balance. "Quick, call for reinforcements."

Canada geese were now mixed into the fray. They were suddenly behind us and all around us. I spun on my heels and saw that we were surrounded by forty or fifty rapacious, snapping bills. I began to feel oddly like a food item instead of a purveyor of one.

A large gray specimen with an immense black knob on its head began pecking at one of my sneakers. "Someone needs to teach you some manners!" I gave it a good, swift kick. A cloud of feathers puffed out. It honked rudely.

I felt them pecking at the plastic bag, actually grabbing at it and pulling. Looking down, I saw that three of them had their bills buried in the plastic, trying to tear it open. One of them had a big red paddle-foot. I felt others nipping at my knees and calves. I could see Corey from the waist up. He was overwhelmed by feathers and wings.

"Ouch!" I heard him say, "Ow … no … get away!"

"*Ruuun!*" I yelled, throwing the plastic bag and what little remained inside it. I grabbed Corey by the wrist and towed him behind me as I went charging through a knee-high army of angry geese. I kicked at them and swatted at others with my free arm. Several bills nicked at my knees as I went.

We climbed the grassy hill, got up to the park bench, then turned to look back. A mass feeding frenzy was in progress. Five or six geese had a piece of the bag, now torn and shredded. Whatever bread had remained inside had long since fallen out, yet they were still quarrelling over the plastic as though it were a prize unto itself. It was red-foot who ultimately came away the winner. He flew off with the tattered remains of plastic trailing behind him like a shredded kite. The rest of the crowd continued to pile together until not a shaving of crust was left.

"Man, that was close!" Corey exclaimed. I half expected he'd start crying after such an event, but he simply stared with wild fascination at the frenzy of geese, then at me, then back at the geese.

I started laughing. I sat down on the bench. Corey started laughing too. I laughed so hard I hung my head between my knees, both hands pressed flat against my ears. We laughed and we laughed and we laughed.

Alisha didn't come home that night.

CHAPTER EIGHT

SOMNAMBULISM

I AWOKE THE FOLLOWING morning and began going through my daily regimen of motions. I showered, dressed, and pulled Corey out of bed by the ankles. He was wearing his Superman pajamas— slippered feet, red cape, and all. His arms and the cape slid awkwardly up the mattress as I dragged him to the foot of the bed, dazed and blinking. "Come on. Up and at 'em." I left the room and went out to the den to check the dining room table for messages. Alisha had gotten into the habit of leaving me small notes and reminders there when she happened to arrive home late the night before. There was no note this morning. I walked past the window overlooking the driveway and noticed that her black Saab was not in the place she normally parked it. I padded up the spiral stairs and moved cautiously down the hall. Her bedroom door was open. I stuck my head into the doorway. The room was empty, the bed was made up.

The bed had not been slept in.

Our ride to school was quiet and uneventful. Corey looked down at his lap and rubbed sleep from his eyes most of the way.

"It's Friday," I announced. "You've got riding lessons this afternoon. We'll be heading out to the farm. Unless you wanna feed the ducks again."

His head shot up. "No! No ducks! No ducks!"

Back at Crawford Daze, I was not surprised in the least to find the red light blinking on the kitchen answering machine. I pressed the

Play button. Alisha's voice streamed from the speaker, businesslike and unapologetic: "Hi, Simon, it's me. Listen, I'm in Manhattan, something came up quickly yesterday and I didn't get a chance to call you. From here, I have to fly down to South Carolina to tend to some other business, so I'll probably be gone a few more days yet. If you need to reach me, try my cell phone. Hope everything's all right, tell Corey I said hi. See you soon, bye." *Beep.*

"You planned that one well, didn't you?" I mumbled angrily. "Wait until I'm out of the house so you can explain yourself to the machine."

I grabbed up the phone and dialed her cell number. It rang three times. I was routed into her voicemail. I slammed the phone back into its cradle.

I eschewed my morning swim, opting instead for another cup of coffee while I paced obstinately around the den. I knew I should be using the time to study for my exam, but I didn't feel like it. I felt like a hamster running on an exercise wheel—running and running and going nowhere. So I returned to my bedroom and spent most of the morning reading. I finished *Fire and Ice*, replaced it where I'd found it, and chose another, *On the Edge of the Golden Sea*. I slogged through the first chapter before falling asleep.

We drove out to the Wurtman Farm for Corey's 2:30 PM riding lesson. It was an arduous drive of sixteen miles northwest of the town proper. Some days, I was logging close to sixty miles on the old red Saab, and this was one of them. Alan Wurtman, from what I'd learned, was a retired dentist who'd purchased the farm in a sheriff's sale, and now rented it out for various purposes. He was purportedly in his mid-seventies, a widower, and a chronic grump. Most of this information was gleaned from Corey's riding instructor, Jennifer Vernick. Jennifer was a tall, slender woman with straight blonde hair down to her shoulder blades. I had gauged her as being in her mid- to late twenties. She wore a button-down shirt, tight beige riding pants, and riding boots that came up to her knees. I'd found myself gulping for air the first time I'd seen her. She wore a prominent rock on one finger, which she made no effort to hide.

Jennifer led Corey into a dome-shaped barn. Inside was a circular dirt track. I poked my head into the barn on one occasion to find Corey straddling a gelding, which was trotting at a slow speed around the track with Jennifer jogging alongside them, giving verbal instructions to both horse and boy. When the lesson ended twenty minutes later, they emerged from the barn together, Jennifer's hand on Corey's shoulder. "Hey, nice job today," she told him. "We'll work more on that next week, okay?"

Corey nodded. As he started to walk toward me, Jennifer looked at me and asked, "I'm sorry, what was your name again?"

"Uh, Simon."

"I wanted to mention something to you." She took three or four steps in my direction. I felt my heart beating its way up my throat. "You see those signs alongside the driveway?"

I turned in the general direction of the way she was pointing. "Uhh …"

"They say *speed limit five miles per hour*?"

"Yeah …?"

"It's just a reminder … last week when you left, you went up the driveway way too fast. Dr. Wurtman is a stickler about that. I mean, *a stickler*. He must not have seen you leave, 'cause if he had, he would've come out and said something to me."

I glanced at the white farmhouse, then back at Jennifer.

"A stickler, huh?"

"Yes. To the letter." She popped open the driver's door of a shiny black BMW. "I'll see you guys next week."

Tell him to stick it up his ass, then. It was just that sort of a day, I guess.

Jennifer revved up her Beamer and began creeping up the stone drive. I started the old Saab and fell in behind her. I gathered a quick look at the farmhouse as we passed it—I had this funky image of a white-haired codger with a protuberant, knobby chin standing hunched over at the window aiming a radar gun. The windows appeared dark and empty. When I faced forward again, I was startled to see that I'd practically run into Jennifer's rear bumper. "Ho!" I hollered, slamming my foot on the brake. The Saab shuddered and stalled.

I started the car again but quickly found myself bearing down on Jennifer's bumper once more. I took my foot off the gas, and we stalled a second time. "I don't think five miles an hour exists." I waited for the Beamer to gain some separation before starting the

Saab a third time. I tried rolling us gently into first gear. The Saab bucked twice, then lurched forward, kicking out stones and dust from beneath the rear tires.

Finally we reached the main road. I pulled out behind the BMW and watched it disappear before my eyes. Jennifer must have had it up to sixty in under six seconds. "She obeys a five-mile-an-hour edict on a private farm, and then it's off to the races on a thirty-five-mile-an-hour public road."

"Huh?" Corey asked.

"Talking to myself, kid. Hey, what do you say we order a pizza for supper? We can stay up late playing video games."

He pumped his fist in front of him as though it was the greatest idea in the world. "Yeah! Pizza! Video games! Yeah!"

*   *   *

We stayed up till midnight and slept until noon the following day. Saturday afternoon, I showed Corey how to make some really cool paper airplanes. "The key is to make them thin and aerodynamic, so they cut through the air. Then you have to staple them, like this," I instructed, driving three staples into the base of the plane. "It ensures that the plane stays shut in midair and also adds some weight, which makes it go farther."

We climbed the hill in the backyard with our planes in hand. Near the top, I shouted, "Now, throw!"

We threw. The planes arced skyward, then dived. There were many tree branches with which to contend, and I was sure that both planes would get snagged in them. Amazingly, though, they didn't. Our planes were white daggers of paper cutting through the air; they carved and threaded their way through seemingly impassable, interlocking tree limbs, then dipped and dived again. They didn't bump the ground right away because the ground continued to slope downward. The two planes sailed untouched the entire length of the hill, and even crossed paths halfway down. Corey ran underneath them, his arms held high over his head as if trying to catch them. I trailed slowly behind him, for the first time beginning to take some pleasure in seeing someone else having a good time.

At the base of the hill near the back of the house, the planes had come to rest twenty-five feet apart. Corey was jubilant. "Can we do it again, Simon? Can we?" I had forgotten—indeed, if I'd ever known at all—how easily entertained small children could be. "Let's go, Simon! Come on, let's go!"

"Okay, but I want to show you something first. Follow me."

I led him to the exposed, grassy portion of lawn on the west side of the house. The leaves in the canopy had scarcely begun to shift into their fall wardrobe—that was maybe a month away—and the grass was still lush and green. I knelt down and plucked a blade of grass that had a ball of white spittle partway up its stem.

"You see that glob of spit right there?" I said.

"Yeah."

"You know where it comes from?"

"Where?"

"It's the home of the spit bug." I used two fingers to rub away the saliva, revealing the tiny green insect. Resting on the pad of my thumb, it appeared no larger than the head of a pin. "Have you ever seen a spit bug before?"

"No." He stared at the green dot on my thumb.

"Well, now you have."

"Can we fly the planes again, Simon?"

"Of course we can."

Ten flights later, we grew tired of the game (I grew tired, actually, of lugging up and down the hill) and returned to the house. Corey said he wanted to play with his bouncy balls. He went into his bedroom and returned to the den with the oversized coffee can.

"I'll show you how to play with those bouncy balls." I took the can from him. "You stand right there." I went up the spiral stairs to the loft, then hung the can over the edge of the railing. "You ready?"

"Simon, wait," he said, laughing.

"*Incoming!*" I turned the can upside-down. Three dozen bouncy balls spilled out. They hit the den floor below and bounced in thirty-six different directions. Corey waited with his arms raised, then ran about the room in crazy circles trying to gather them up. He was weak with laughter. "C'mon, faster!" I yelled. "Faster!" They bounded over his head and under his arms. He giggled so hard that he finally stopped and planted both hands in his crotch.

"I peed in my pants, Simon! *I peed ... in my ... pants!*"

Sunday we played things closer to the vest. We awoke at a more reasonable hour. We embarked on a walk along the lake around noontime. Twice I tried to reach Alisha at her cell number. Twice I got her voicemail. "Good morning, Alisha," I spoke in a cheery voice. "You see the little red button in the upper corner of your cell phone? Believe it or not, that actually turns the phone on."

Later, I pretended to be her son: "Hi, Mom, it's Corey, spelled with an *e*. I'd like to make a reservation to spend some time with you. I can be reached at 1-800-home-alone."

We played video games for a while after dinner. I got Corey to bed around eight o'clock, being that it was a school night. He was reluctant to turn in, but I could tell he was tuckered out, just the same. "Aren't you gonna read me a story?"

"Of course we're gonna read a story."

We read from his favorite Richard Scary bedtime tome. With the book on my lap and reciting in drama-filled overtones, I read the tale of a mouse that wanted to go fishing. So the mouse carved a boat out of a tree trunk, went fishing in it, and caught a whale. I felt Corey leaning against me as I read to him. Finally I closed up the book, got him into bed in his Superman pajamas, and tucked him in.

"Okay," I said, "we're up early tomorrow. Back to school, and then Kindermusik in the afternoon."

"I don't want to go to Kindermusik. I wanna come back here and play."

I clicked off the light and switched on his nightlight. "Well, if you get a good night's sleep, perhaps we can play after we get home from Kindermusik. How's that sound?"

"Okay," he said, and turned over.

When I went in to check on him fifteen minutes later, he was sound asleep.

*   *   *

I channel-surfed for a while before acquiescing to a *Law & Order* rerun. Forty minutes into the program, I sensed I was no longer alone in the room. I sat up on the den sofa and looked around. Corey was standing next to the fireplace in his blue and red pajamas, the red cape dragging at his heels. He was not looking toward me, however.

His attention was focused elsewhere. He seemed to be facing the front door, in fact. His arms hung limp at his sides and his face was slack.

I stood up. "Hey, kid, what are you doing up?" I began walking toward him but stopped halfway. Something wasn't right here. He hadn't turned his head to acknowledge me. The thought that he might be asleep didn't register at first—because of his eyes, probably. His eyes were open and staring into the night. Then he raised his arms halfway up, flapping them at his sides three times as though emulating a bird in flight. He began lightly stomping his feet in place. The slippered soles of his feet sounded like sandpaper against the oak wood floor.

I knelt down to watch, amazed at what I was witnessing. I had never seen a person walk in his sleep and had always regarded sleepwalking in general as something of a wives' tale.

But that was hardly the end of it. He turned and walked in a rough circle. It would later occur to me that he'd not bumped into a single article of furniture during this odd episode. He hadn't banged his knee on the edge of the stone hearth or lost his footing descending the single stair that preceded the den. It was as if he was *seeing* while *sleeping*, if such a thing was possible.

He stopped turning and faced the front door once again. *Why is he doing that? Why is he facing the door like that? Is it his mother? Is he waiting for his mother?*

But then his face began to contort. He started hopping up and down on the balls of his feet, and he twice more flapped his arms. He appeared so distraught that I almost went to him, but something told me to hold back. Something told me to watch and listen … and maybe learn. He moaned something that was unintelligible yet bespoke great distress.

Then: "No, stop!" The words were perfectly articulated. He waved and flailed at the air in front of him. "Stop it, Daddy, stop it!" He abruptly dropped into an Indian-style sitting position. He curled his hands into tight fists and began banging them against the floor. *"Stop it, Daddy, please stop it! Stop, stop, stop—"*

Then I had him by the shoulders and I was shaking him. Not violently, but enough to rouse him. I patted his cheek several times with my palm, trying to get him to come around.

"Hey, Corey, hey, come on, wake up, snap out of it, kid, you're sleeping."

His string of exclamations halted. He glanced around the room, blinking. Then he looked up at me.

"You all right?" I asked.

He curled up on the floor, rested his head on my lap, and was newly asleep. Just like it had never happened. I gently prodded him in the ribs and shoulders, but got no response. Finally, I scooped him into my arms and carried him back to his bedroom. I lowered him into his bed, smoothed out his pillow, and pulled the sheets up to his chin.

I sat by his bedside for a while, watching and listening and waiting. With one hand, I lightly brushed his blond hair off his forehead. His breathing was so soft and quiet that it made no noise. Had I looked like this, I wondered, when I was his age? Had I appeared as small and fragile as I slept curled up in my bed? Had my father sat over me watching me sleep, and had he felt what I was now beginning to feel? Even as he poured money down the great gulping toilet (as Ma later called it), had he watched my soft, white cheek turned against the down pillow and experienced the love a parent feels toward one who is otherwise helpless and unable to fend for himself? *What gives you the right to suppose he didn't?* a voice imposed sharply. *Or the idea that you received less than the market's share of love from a set of parents who had more to worry about than just birthdays and Christmas? You know better than that, Simon.*

I watched Corey sleep for the better part of twenty minutes. I wondered what he had seen his father do, the extent to which it haunted him, and if playing with toy trains in a high-priced therapist's office had the power to extenuate life's wrongs. Ma, in a way, was right. *You'd do well not to get too entwined in other people's lives, dear. Their problems can become your problems.*

I bent forward over the bed, softly planting a kiss on Corey's temple. He rustled slightly, nestling into the sheets.

I stood quietly and tiptoed out of the bedroom.

*   *   *

Alisha was gone for five days. Corey's Tuesday afternoon karate class ended at quarter past five. It was nearing six when we crept down the switchback driveway to Crawford Daze and saw the black Saab parked nose-first in its customary corner. Corey let out a cry of delight. "Mommy's home! Mommy, Mommy, Mommy!"

He had his door cracked open before I'd slipped the car into park. "Easy, now, easy. Wait until we've stopped."

He went running across the stone driveway and up the railroad-tie stairs without shutting his door. I gathered his bag of schoolbooks as well as his dress clothes—he was still wearing his white karate outfit—and kicked his door shut before going up to the house. By the time I got there, he'd already run into his mother's arms for a tight hug and was doing victory laps around the den, waving his arms over his head.

"Mommy's home! Yippee! Mommy!"

I smelled the good smells of a home-cooked dinner—Alisha attempting to expiate her long absence by preparing a hearty meal. As I moved past the fireplace with Corey's things, I caught a glimpse past her, into the kitchen, where the table had been lavishly set for three. Alisha was standing on the top stair, leaning against the wall and watching me carefully. She wore a black pinstriped suit. She'd had her hair cut—it just barely touched the tops of her shoulders. Her quicksilver eyes, normally inscrutable, now appeared pensive and gauging. She knew I was angry.

I glanced at Corey, who was still celebrating. "It's sort of like the dog that's so happy to see its master, it forgets to be mad." I began laying out Corey's things on the dining room table. Alisha had set out some of her own stuff here, as she normally did. There were several messy stacks of papers and forms. On top of one of them was a white card with ornate silver writing on it. It looked like a prom bid. I noticed the familiar rolling script, and the words 23rd Annual October Ball near the top. At the bottom was a perforated stub that read Admit Two.

I turned and met her eyes again. She was still watching me with that searching expression.

"So, the prodigal mother returns."

She crossed her arms over her chest. A hint of a smile went flitting across her face. But it quickly went away.

"Yes, I got your sarcastic messages. I'm sorry I was gone so long. Dinner will be ready in ten minutes."

She had prepared a roast pork loin, with mashed potatoes and gravy, fresh corn, and salad. The pork loin had been marinated to perfection, and she'd used a delicate seasoning for the potatoes and corn. The salad was made from scratch and included fresh sliced mushrooms, diced artichoke hearts, and a homemade raspberry vinaigrette dressing. The utensils and glassware had been meticulously arranged. Everything this woman did, it seemed, she did top-notch. The problem was, she either flew first class, or she didn't fly at all.

I was quiet as we ate. The food was excellent, but I offered no compliments or commendations. Alisha looked up at me several times, but I refused to look back. I kept my eyes mostly on my plate.

Corey was still wearing his karate uniform. He was bubbly and talkative—so much so that he was forgetting to eat. Alisha told him on several occasions to quiet down and work on his dinner, but he was too excited to focus on the food on his plate.

Finally I cut him off in mid-banter: "Corey, you need to settle down and eat your supper before it gets cold. If you don't clear your plate, there'll be no story tonight." I hadn't raised my voice any, but my tone had been sharp.

"Okay," he said, and began eating.

I never looked up, but I could feel Alisha's gaze on me. I felt the mixture of surprise and reproof that were both a part of that gaze. The surprise part of it might have said, *How did you do that? He's listening to you,* while the reproving part was saying, *How dare you speak to my son that way—who do you think you are?*

I longed for her to say something. I was so angry that I would have welcomed a rebuke. She must have sensed this, however, for she said nothing. She coolly returned to her salad.

Corey went to bed early that night. Alisha got him into his pajamas and tucked him in and read him his story. Her voice was a droll murmur coming from the next room. I heard the light being clicked off. I heard Alisha's footsteps as she went into the kitchen. I heard her moving around out in the den, going in and out of her office, putting things away. Her feet made soft thumps going up the spiral stairs. Her bedroom was above mine. She came back down a little while later. I heard her moving around in the kitchen once more.

When she appeared at my doorway, she was holding a glass of white wine. She had changed into jeans and a white, wool sweater. I had cranked open two of the windows. A cool lake breeze whispered through the screens.

She knocked gently, twice. "May I come in?"

I was sitting on the bed, leaning back against the headboard. I was in the second-to-last chapter of *On the Edge of the Golden Sea*.

"It's your house; you can do whatever you want."

A straight back chair stood in the corner. She walked over to it and sat down with her legs crossed. She rested one arm on the edge of the bureau that stood against the wall in front of the windows, pushing aside my ceramic fish dish (the dish was hers, actually) that held all of my loose items, including the house key with the white, plastic fob attached to it. She held her wineglass in her other hand. The glass was a third full. She used her wrist to move the glass in slow circles, making the wine swish around in the bottom of it. She appeared to do this unconsciously.

"I can see that you're upset."

"You don't seem too sorry about it."

"I am sorry, Simon—"

"You disappeared without warning, Alisha." I placed the open book facedown in my lap. "And then you show up again without warning."

"It won't happen again, I promise."

"You need to spell me on weekends," I added. "I was hired as a chaperone, not a full-time parent."

It was a comment I had hoped would ruffle her feathers. Instead, she twirled her glass again and replied coolly, "Do you want me to increase your pay?"

"*No.* This isn't about money. You're paying me too much already. Christ, sixty grand to play video games and make paper airplanes?"

"I told you how important—"

"It's also important that he have a mother," I snapped, pointing at the wall beyond which Corey slept. "And not a father-for-hire."

She watched me inscrutably. My inability to get a rise out of this woman was really beginning to annoy me.

She lowered her eyes to her glass, twirling it in her hand. "You're not a father-for-hire."

"You were congenial and kind that first day in the café. But I'm beginning to feel like I've walked into a trap of some sort."

"Please don't feel that way, Simon. I need you. You're very important to me. And you're very important to Corey. He's never taken to anyone like he has to you."

"It's a specious situation in which I find myself."

A wry smile played at the corners of her mouth. "That's my word of the week. You're misusing it, however."

"Am I?"

"Yes. It applies to logic and arguments, not situations or things."

"Does your book publishing business have something to do with your being in the city?"

"Yes."

"You could have told me in advance that you were leaving. You also could have informed me of your side-job as an author. What was it you told me? *I'm an artist and a businesswoman? I dabble?* I mean, what the hell was that all about? You've published fourteen books, and you call it *dabbling*?"

"I write seedy romances," she said plainly. "They're generic, and probably even formulaic to some extent. I'm a midlist writer who's lucky to see a first print-run of fifty thousand copies in paperback."

This admission of mediocrity went a long way toward explaining why she hadn't asked what I thought of *On the Edge of the Golden Sea*, which lay in plain view on my lap. She probably hadn't asked because she probably didn't care. I couldn't make heads or tails of it. This didn't jibe with my Alisha Caldwell color scheme. This wasn't flying first class. Hell, Alisha's books didn't even fly coach. They rode in the bathroom toilet in the plane's tail section.

"I can see the confusion on your face," she said. "Unfortunately, book writing is more business than art."

"So, in the city you were meeting with …"

"My agent and I are restructuring my contract with my publisher. I have a publicist and an editor, and there's a lot of hemming and hawing. It's not a done deal yet." She paused, and even nursed a sip of her wine.

"So, what's in South Carolina?" I asked.

"An unrelated project. It may require several more trips in the coming months. In the meantime, I'm scheduled to begin work on a new novel the first of December. So, a lot of the time I've been logging at my office in town will be spent in my office here." At this point, she held up a small scratch of paper with my handwriting on it. It was the phone message I'd taken for her last week. "Did this person say who he was?"

"No," I replied, "he didn't. But how'd you know it was a he?" My message, after all, had been *strange phone call, 10:15 AM.*

She crumpled up the slip of paper. "Listen, I spoke to a friend of mine, Alan Mercer. He runs a law firm in the city. He's been an attorney for over twenty years. He keeps a summer cottage on the other side of town, and occasionally he gets out here. I've handled some investments for him in the past. He'll be out this way next week, and he's agreed to meet with us over dinner. The two of you can talk, and you can ask him anything you want about the profession, law school, what have you. He's an especially interesting man, well-cultured in the arts, with a weakness for opera."

"He'll meet us here for dinner? Here at your house?"

"No, we'll do dinner in town. Probably at Jefferey's Steakhouse or the Hampton Riverside."

"Sounds fine by me, but who'll look after Corey?"

"Not a worry. I'll call Samantha's mom and set up a playdate."

I nodded. "All right. Thank you for setting it up."

She drained what was left in her wineglass, then stood up. "Well, I'd better hit the hay. I'm beat."

"You didn't tell me Corey had a sleepwalking problem."

That one caught her by surprise. She lowered her glass, and her normally stoic expression seemed to sag a little. For several moments, she watched the floor in front of her feet.

Finally she looked up. "How many nights?"

"Just one. It was Sunday, I think."

"Where?"

"He came out into the den. I was watching television."

"Did he say anything?"

"No," I lied. "But it took me a couple minutes to realize what was happening. How long has he been doing it?"

"Over a year now." She shook her head, clearly dismayed. "I was hoping he would one day outgrow it. But then one morning last spring, he let himself outside and walked halfway up the driveway in his bare feet. That's when I started taking him to Dr. Andrews."

"He sleepwalked *up the driveway?*"

Alisha nodded. "It's the only time he's gone out of the house, but ..."

"But you're worried he might do it again."

She nodded with resignation. "Yes, it does concern me. But Dr. Andrews tells me they're making steady progress, and this is the first episode Corey's had in well over a month, so ... so, I don't know, maybe it's ... slowly getting better."

"Has he ever talked in his sleep before? Is that why you asked if he'd done so?"

She spoke with great care. "Several times he's ... yes, it's happened. But mostly it's gibberish, unintelligible." A shadow seemed to have darkened her already tired face. How deep did the pitcher plant go? "Can we ... talk about this some other time?"

I nodded silently.

"Goodnight," she said, and left the room.

"Goodnight."

I switched off the light, stripped down to a pair of shorts, and turned over in bed. I lay facing the lake. Sleep, when it came, took me headfirst and whole. But it did not come easily.

CHAPTER NINE

THE HAMPTON RIVERSIDE

THE HAMPTON RIVERSIDE WAS black-tie, by reservation only. I hadn't packed any suits when I'd left Lake Hiawatha to do roadwork in rural New Hampshire. The truth was, I didn't own any suits. "You're going to need one or two good outfits when you begin applying to law schools, Simon," Alisha told me. She sent me over to Richie's on the south corner of Merchant's Square, where she kept an account. "Go in and ask for Melvin, tell him I sent you. He'll take care of everything."

Melvin took care of everything, all right. He was also about as gay as they come. I walked out with two suits totaling in excess of eleven hundred dollars draped over my arms, a pair of ties, dress socks, and State Street shoes. Alisha was paying for all of it. I'd offered to foot the bill myself—I had more money these days than I knew what to do with—but Alisha insisted that it go on her account. "Consider it a bonus for this week."

On the afternoon of our date with Alan Mercer—it was two Thursdays after our Tuesday evening discussion in my bedroom—I discovered I had a minor problem. I padded out to the den wearing my new navy-blue suit and black dress socks. I tilted my head back and directed my voice to the empty loft above. "Alisha, there's one small issue."

She came out of her bedroom wearing a black evening gown, two hands busily fitting an earring in her left ear. She peered over the railing with an air of preoccupation.

"What is it, Simon?"

I held out my tie in one hand. "What am I supposed to do with this?"

"Wear it around your neck, silly."

"Do I tie a half hitch or an anchor's bend?"

She got the earring positioned the way she wanted it and leaned against the railing with both hands. "Simon, are you saying you don't know how to tie a tie?"

"How often do you think I wear this stuff?"

She looked down at me for a moment, marveling at my depravity. She sighed. "You're lucky I'm a multi-talented woman. Come up here."

I went up the spiral stairs and followed her down the hall to her bedroom. She pointed to the vanity. "Stand right there, in front of the mirror."

I did. She stood slightly behind me, on my right side. "Now listen. There are several ways to tie a tie. I'm going to show you the easiest." She reached around me with both arms, holding the tie in her hands. She alternately watched the mirror and then peeked over my shoulder to make sure she was getting it right. I could feel her breath on the side of my neck. She tightened the knot, then stood back.

"There. That's it. Now you try it."

"But I hardly even saw—"

"Look, take it one move at a time. Step by step." She ran through the motions once more, slower this time. I tried to replicate them. After four run-throughs, she deemed my knot satisfactory. "It'll require more practice later, but it'll pass for now."

I stood frowning at myself in the mirror. "Alisha, I feel like a clown dressed up for the circus."

"You look dashing. Now go down and get the car ready. We absolutely cannot be late. Alan's meeting us at seven."

We drove toward town beneath pastel skies, past fields of brazen browns and oranges. It was October now, and the pumpkin meadows were stippled yellow. Alisha sent us zooming through the countryside at sixty miles an hour. She'd spent an additional fifteen minutes at her vanity applying mascara and rouge and lipstick. She'd added an amethyst stone, which hung from her neck on a delicate gold chain. She spoke intermittently of her friend and colleague, Alan Mercer.

"The only thing I'll ask of you is that you address him as 'sir.' In time, he'll probably tell you to call him Mr. Mercer, or maybe even Alan. But until that time, you're to address him as 'sir.'"

"Yes, ma'am."

"He is an extremely busy man who has taken precious time out of his schedule to speak with us—with you, really. He must be treated with utmost respect."

"Yes, ma'am."

"Also be sure to wear your napkin in your lap. And to use the silverware farthest from your plate first. And whichever wine he orders is what we drink."

"Yes, ma'am."

"You can stop calling me that."

I wasn't sure what I expected to find in Mr. Alan Mercer. I had an image of Harvey Keitel in a tuxedo and red bowtie, with a Dennis Farina mustache. He would be the kind of man who quoted Shakespeare and Milton around mouthfuls of caviar and pâté. Occasionally he might tell a joke, something he heard in the Rembrandt Room down at the Met. He drank only the finest imports and drove a luxury automobile. I couldn't wait to meet him.

The Hampton Riverside stood facing Whiskey Creek, about a quarter mile downstream of the Main Street Bridge, where Corey and I had narrowly escaped being carried away by geese. The restaurant had been built in 1912 with a facade of fired brimstone and a slate roof. The interior was a pleasing composite of pine rafters, oak wood flooring, and soft lighting. Round tables hunkered in the privacy of shadows and back corners. Booths lined the side walls. There was a bar near the front of the establishment and a terrace built over the water in the back.

The host was a tall, thin man who wore a tux and spoke in a pinched voice. "Good evening, Ms. Caldwell. So lovely to see you."

"We're waiting for a third," Alisha told him. "We're probably a few minutes early."

"No problem whatsoever," the host said, running his finger down a page in the reservation book. "And will Mr. Mercer be joining you on the terrace for cocktails?"

"That would be lovely, I think."

"This way, please."

The host led us to the back of the restaurant, past ferns and other assorted greenery, to a small patio, where a pair of wide French doors opened onto the terrace. The terrace was an exceptionally large swath of decking that extended ten feet over the water, supported from below by pilings. Six or seven other couples were out there, sipping drinks and conversing in low tongues and all in all looking sophisticated. Alisha and I must have appeared a rather strange twosome, as several heads turned our way in passing.

"A server will be with you momentarily," the host said.

"Thank you," Alisha told him.

Alisha sauntered toward an empty space by the railing. I followed, hands buried deep in my suit pockets.

"And why exactly are we out here?" I asked.

"Pre-dinner cocktails. It's a tradition, Simon."

"What if you don't drink cocktails?"

"Loosen up a little, will you?" She turned and cast a sideways glance over the water, which slid across its shallow riverbed from right to left. Whiskey Creek at its widest was only a hundred feet across. Farther upstream a fly-fisherman worked a nymph in a quiet pool, white fly line arcing behind him in picturesque curly-cues. I wondered if he'd been hired by the restaurant as part of the scenery. "It's beautiful, isn't it? It's so peaceful."

"Just don't start feeding the ducks."

Another tall employee wearing a tux approached us. He spoke in a deep, gravelly baritone. "Ms. Caldwell, good evening. So nice to see you. Cocktails for both of you?"

"I'll have a Bloody Mary, thanks."

"I'll try one of those, too."

Alisha sniggered. "Simon, that's kind of a woman's drink. Unless you're an older gent, that is. Order something else."

"You know what, bring me a Coke."

"Make it a Roman Coke," Alisha said. The waiter nodded and left.

When he was far enough away, I said, "I can order for myself, you know."

"You can tie your own tie, too," she said with a smile.

"Stop making fun of me."

"Simon, I'm not making fun of you. I'm *having* fun *with* you. Admit it, this is better than shoveling asphalt."

The waiter returned with our drinks. Alisha's was a deep red, with celery sticks poking out of it. Mine looked like an ordinary Coke. I took a sip and felt the zing of the booze.

"What the hell's in this?"

"Rum. Just drink it slowly."

Several of the couples near the downstream end of the terrace had clustered together. Among them was a fiftyish-looking fellow with sandy-brown hair, wearing a cowhide belt and sailing shoes. I thought he looked lawyerly. Well, he must have told a real rib-cracker because suddenly the whole lot began laughing and carrying on. The lawyerly fellow laughed the hardest, slapping one hand against his knee three times. I wondered if that would be me thirty years from now. Strangely, I felt as though I were stuck in some sort of time warp. It was as though Alisha had brought me to a place where I could glimpse myself later in life. I wasn't sure that I liked it.

Alisha checked the silver watch that hung loosely from her wrist. "It's ten past the hour. Alan must have hit traffic."

I slapped a mosquito on my neck. It came off bloody on my palm. A minute or so later, I whacked another on the top of my wrist. "They must like the rum."

"We'd better move inside," Alisha suggested. "Alan will show up to find us covered with bug bites."

Alisha summoned our server, who led us through the French doors to the patio area and into the host's hands once more.

"We've reserved your usual table for you, Ms. Caldwell," the host announced.

Alisha smiled. "That's very kind of you."

We followed him past the ferns again, toward the bar, and then to the right, into a dimly lit alcove. We were seated at a round table that had been set for three. A low flame flickered in a red jar on the table's center. When the host pulled out Alisha's seat for her, I saw her put something in his palm. I'd like to believe it was a twenty, but I think I saw two zeros.

"Thank you, Clyde," she said.

"Thank *you*, Madam." He stuck the bill into his pocket without looking at it, then shuffled away.

I whispered across the table, "How come I didn't get my seat pulled out for me?"

Our waitress was a tall, French blonde who spoke broken English and held her chin high. "Can I bring you ze menus, or vill you vait for Mr. Meercer?"

"We'll have a look at the menus while we wait. It can't hurt, I guess."

While the waitress went to fetch our menus, Alisha reached into her purse and withdrew one of those compact mirrors that women are always carrying. She examined herself in it, applied a dab of rouge to each cheek, and snapped the case shut. I thought I knew quite a bit about this Mercer fellow, even before I'd actually met him. But I knew something else that was just as important. Alisha had her sights set squarely on him. A crush was a crush, and a spade was a spade. Think of it this way: a wealthy businesswoman and successful author didn't go tripping over her heels for Mr. Middle Class America, did she? No, it had to be a man of wit and culture, a man who wore a rose on his lapel, who sniffed his wine when freshly poured, who read the classics and drove a Mercedes. Alisha had found her Romeo, and I wondered how much time she'd spent going after him. That I was being used didn't bother me, really. I was more interested in what made her tick, what drove her. My being bait for her trap was fine by me so long as she didn't know that I knew it. Still, if I could pick this guy Mercer's brain a little, then so be it. If Alisha thought I was going to get up and wander off so the two of them could enjoy a romantic dinner, well, she'd be wrong about that. But I promised myself not to embarrass her or hurt her chances with the man.

Our waitress came with the menus. "Anuzzuh drink vile you vait?"

"Another Bloody Mary, please."

"And fo' you, sir?"

"Ginger ale is fine."

"As you vish."

Alisha had her menu open and was running her finger down the Specials insert. "Mm, the stuffed flounder looks good." She peeked at me over her menu. "The food here has an exotic edge to it. You're going to love it."

"Am I allowed to order off the pasta page?"

"You can order anything you like, Simon."

"The veal parmesan isn't too feminine, you think?"

"Stop it."

Our drinks came. Round two. The ginger ale was as good as I've ever tasted. It probably cost five dollars. The waitress removed our empty glasses and walked away.

"Alisha, there's not a single entree under thirty dollars on this menu."

"It's a four-star restaurant, Simon. Open your eyes a little. Besides, you're not paying for it, are you?"

"I suppose not. You think this Mercer's gonna show up?"

"When he does, we make no allusions to his being late."

"Do we need to stand when he arrives?"

"Of course. You don't shake hands sitting down, do you?"

"I was hoping to kiss his feet."

She rolled her eyes and returned to the menu. I flipped past the pasta page and wound up in the seafood section. The surf 'n' turf listed at $69.95. I'd never had any real predilections for crustaceans, but I thought seriously about ordering it, if for no other reason than to see Alisha's reaction.

She shut her menu and folded her hands on top of it. She reached for her Bloody Mary and drank from it. "Did you decide on something?"

"The calf's liver looks good."

"You're welcome to eat on the terrace with the mosquitoes."

"You said I could get anything I wanted."

"Do you always have to make things difficult? What happened to the pasta?"

"It wasn't expensive enough. I'm trying to loosen up a little, try some new things."

When it got to be seven-thirty, our waitress began giving us some odd looks. "We may as well order," Alisha decided, waving the blonde over.

"Maybe Mercer thought you said eight o'clock. Is that possible?"

"Look, I'm sure he'll have a reasonable explanation. Let's try and appear as though we're having a good time."

"I am having a good time," I said.

The French woman was standing over our table, her pen poised over her note tablet.

"I am going to try the flounder Creole," Alisha ordered. "I'll have the baked potato and the sautéed vegetables. Balsamic vinaigrette on the salad, but I'd like it on the side, please."

"And fo' you, sir?"

"Mussels marinara over linguine. Ranch dressing for the salad."

"No calf's liver?" Alisha asked, once the waitress had left.

I shook my head. "Hate the stuff."

She sipped her drink. "You must have given your mother fits when you were younger."

"I suppose I still do, in some ways."

"She doesn't approve of you working for me, does she?"

"What makes you say that?"

She rested her chin atop her steepled hands. "A hunch. I imagine she found it difficult to swallow—your going north to do road construction, only to wind up chaperoning."

"Truth be told, she was never fond of the road construction idea."

"I see. You and Corey are getting along well?"

"Like sea and salt."

She smiled wholesomely. "He certainly seems to like you. He talks about you an awful lot."

"That's ironic. When I'm with him, all he talks about is you. 'When's Mommy coming home? Where's Mommy?'"

She canted her head to the side a little, adopting an apologetic look. "I promise, I won't disappear like that again. It was in bad taste, I admit."

Our waitress arrived with our salads. I tucked in immediately. I was famished. Alisha poked and plucked at hers with the patience of one who knows the main dish is yet an hour away. Instead of pouring her dressing over the salad, she used her fork to dip certain items into the ceramic side dish that held the dressing, and then slid the fork coolly into her mouth. She ate slowly and with great relish.

"I take it you got everything straightened out with your publishing people?" I asked when I was finished. She wasn't halfway through hers yet.

She nodded, then drew the napkin from her lap and gently dabbed at the corners of her mouth. "Yes, I think we got most of the kinks ironed out. I'll be ready to start writing again in December."

"You can do that? Just turn the switch on and off at will?"

"As opposed to what?"

"I thought artistic people had to sort of live for the moment. You know, wait until the spirit moves them, that kinda stuff."

"I think that's something most writers eventually outgrow. Remember what I told you last week—it's more a business than art."

"I'm sorry, Alisha, but I find that awfully depressing. Especially for a writer of romances."

She watched me carefully for a moment around a mouthful of salad. Then she looked down, poking her fork into an olive. "I'm sorry. I shouldn't have told you."

I leaned forward. "Look, I'm not casting aspersions on you or your work. I simply find it hard to believe that a perfectionist like you wouldn't set the bar higher when she sat down at her word processor."

Smiling now. "A perfectionist, huh? I'm not exactly the perfect mother, according to you."

Well, that was true, but mothering wasn't exactly Alisha's business, was it? It may have been the one business she sought to avoid … and she was one of the few whose purse was deep enough to permit her to do so.

She added, "Perhaps I'm just not a very good writer."

"Oh, come on. You read prime rib and filet mignon, but you write soy burgers and tofu. You never even asked what I thought of the two books I read. What if this Mercer fellow had read them? Would you care what he thought?"

She laughed. "Oh, he wouldn't read anything of mine. He'd rather read Faulkner or Steinbeck."

"So, you're telling me that a woman of your stature and achievement has no aspirations—"

"You know what the definition of the Great American Novel is, Simon?" She waited, watching me with eyes that were, for the first time, slightly agitated. "Go on, tell me what you think it is."

"Well, it's … it's the best and the biggest piece of literary work one can produce. It's something that all of society can identify with. It transcends social ladders, racial barriers …"

"And what happens when you're done with it? What follows?"

"Hey, I'm not suggesting that everything you write has to be—"

"Have you any idea, Simon, how many accomplished writers have set out to compose the Great American Novel, then faded into obscurity?"

"You fear greatness, then? Is that it?"

"It's presumptuous on your part to suggest I have greatness in me. But to answer your question, yes, I fear *short-lived* greatness."

I raised my ginger ale. "Here's to mediocrity."

She raised what remained of her Bloody Mary. "Here's to longevity." She finished her drink.

Our waitress took our salad bowls away. Twenty minutes later, our entrees were brought out. It was more food than I knew what to do with. Steam rose in hot curtains from the bed of linguine. A dozen mussels lay with their shells open, as though having screamed in unison as they died a scalding death.

We came to round three for drinks. I asked for a tall glass of water. Alisha opted for a third Bloody Mary.

"Looks like I'm designated driver."

"I'll be fine." She ran her fingers down the gold necklace chain and drew the stone into her hand. "It was once believed by ancient Greeks that an amethyst thwarted drunkenness."

"I feel safer already." I twirled my fork full of pasta, then moved it slowly to my mouth. The marinara did have an exotic edge to it. The mussels were tender and juicy. "How's the flounder?"

"Splendid."

Between bites, I asked, "How long did you run your catering business?"

"Three years."

"What made you give it up?"

"It was too much work. I started to develop an aversion to good food. Besides, I wanted to make more money."

Halfway through my dinner, I lay my fork down, deciding I was going to need a rest if I had any intentions of finishing. My stomach was beginning to bulge. I raised my arms, crossing them behind my head to stretch.

"I want to hear about your childhood," I said.

"Why?" She was looking down, using her fork to scoop up some crabmeat.

"Because I'm curious, that's why."

"I studied history at Smith."

"You told me that already."

"When you're a freshman, they hand out rape whistles to go on your keychain. Isn't that interesting?"

"I hope you never had to use yours."

She shook her head.

"Anyway, that's not what I meant. I meant when you were a kid."

"You want to know what color Play-Doh I liked best? Or if I played with Barbie or Lincoln Logs?"

"Who's being flippant now?"

She drank some of her Bloody Mary. "I'm sorry, I must be getting it from you."

"How old were you when you started writing? Did you like to write in your elementary school years? High school?"

She shook her head. "Never gave much thought to it until, oh, I don't know, ten or twelve years ago. It came along later in life."

"Any brothers or sisters?"

She shook her head again. "I was an only."

"Did your parents spoil you, then?"

"Hardly. I lived with my mother. I never met my father."

"What did your mother do? Was she a seamstress?"

"Simon, what is it you're looking for?" Alisha asked irritably. "A secret code, a set of ancient blueprints—"

"I'm not looking for anything. Relax. I'm trying to make conversation, that's all."

She finished her drink and ordered another. I lifted my fork and resumed eating. We dined in silence for a while. Her recalcitrance flickered in the air like an electrical current. I snuck a peek at my watch. It was 8:35. The Last Renaissance Man obviously wasn't coming, and perhaps it was this that was grating her. I wondered if Mercer had ditched us or simply forgotten. Maybe something really important had arisen at the last minute, a call from a client or something. But why hadn't he phoned the restaurant? Or Alisha's cell phone?

When she was halfway through her fourth drink, she crossed her arms over her chest and met my eyes over the candlelit table. "How did you know my mother was a seamstress?"

"I didn't. It was the first thing that popped into my head. Was she?"

Nodding. "She worked in a factory basement, sewing shawls and blankets for four dollars and twenty cents an hour. We were dirt-poor. We rented a small home from an overweight lump of shit who smoked Cuban cigars. His name was Caesar. He was from Tijuana, if you can believe it. We were like prisoners in our own country. My mom drove a battered old Pinto—remember, the ones that used to explode? She'd get home around six and make dinner for us. Dinner was peanut butter and jelly sandwiches. When peanut butter got too expensive, it was just jelly sandwiches. I had to sit there and listen to my mother prattle on about the Bible and all that the Lord had given us. 'Better is a dry morsel and quietness with it than a house full of feasting with strife.' Each night when she put me to bed, I would have to kneel on the floor and say a bedtime prayer, aloud so she could hear it. She hung a crucifix on the wall above my pillow. I grew to hate that crucifix. I hated it so much, and I didn't even know what it stood for."

"So you turned atheist."

"No. But I did learn to associate religion with poverty. After Mom turned off the light and pulled the door shut each night, I would stare at the ceiling and recite my own prayer. Except this prayer was to myself. I promised myself that when the time came, I would go to college, and graduate school if I had to—whatever it took to gain control of my own destiny. I promised myself I would never be beholden to anyone again."

"Looks as though you've gotten there."

She shrugged softly.

"Is your mother still alive?"

"No, she died while I was at Smith. Junior year."

I grimaced. I'd lost my father at sixteen, and I'd felt helpless, and I'd still had one parent to hold onto. "So, you had to make it the rest of the way through college on your own, huh?"

"Everything I've done, Simon, has been on my own. I knew from an early age that no one was going to do it for me. If more people adopted that view, we'd have less of them on welfare, we'd have lower unemployment, and fewer retirees would be living out their golden years at poverty subsistence levels."

"Spoken like a true conservative."

It was past nine by then. We eschewed coffee and dessert. The waitress brought the check. Alisha paid.

"Well, thank you for dinner," I said with sincerity as we got up.

"You're welcome."

In the parking lot, as we approached the Saab, I said, "I think you should let me drive, though."

"It's manly of you, but I'm fine, Simon."

"I'm not trying to impress anyone, Alisha. You've had four drinks."

"I told you, I'm fine." She pressed a button on her keyless remote. The locks in the Saab clicked open.

She grabbed the handle and pulled open the driver's door. It had swung open only three inches when I butted my palm against it and knocked it shut again. She turned and glared at me.

"Give me the keys," I said. She opened her mouth to protest, but I cut her off. "Or I quit."

"Simon—"

"I mean it."

We stared at one another for a good ten seconds. Alisha cast her eyes about the parking lot to see if anyone was watching. She seemed to be debating with herself whether it was worth an argument.

"I guarantee you, I will not hesitate to cause a scene," I told her in a low voice.

She plopped the keys into my open hand.

"Thank you," I said.

She didn't say a word to me all the way home.

CHAPTER TEN

RUNNING THE MUNTINS

YOU MUST UNDERSTAND, THE problem has existed all along. All it needed was an excuse. This much was true, I supposed. Addictions love excuses.

I was lying in bed, staring upward. The wan glow from the streetlamps had a way of twisting through the windows and throwing shadows from the muntins onto the ceiling in intricate, sometimes horrific patterns. Those patterns shouldn't have changed from one night to the next, but sometimes they did. Sometimes they simply looked different, that's all. I would lie flat on my back running my eyes up and down, right and left along that wedge work of dark bars … and the thoughts would begin. One thought leading to the next, followed by another, and then the dominoes were falling. As they fell, my eyes would continue tracing the same path on the maze of shadows: up, down, then right, up again …

Soon enough I had a name for it. I called it *running the muntins.*

I had turned seventeen four days ago. That my birthday corresponded to the anniversary of Dad's death was not lost on anyone. Ma had gone on one whale of a bender. She'd made a chocolate layer cake, the top half of which had tilted on a downward angle. She and Catherine had begun singing "Happy Birthday." There was nothing happy about it at all, really. Halfway through the song, the top half of the cake had begun to slide. I was the only one who noticed at first, and my eyes widened. Then Catherine saw what was happening and stopped singing, then Ma stopped … and the three of us watched in mute fascination as the top layer of the cake slid three-quarters of the way off the bottom layer before collapsing in a soft *goosh* along the edge of the plate.

"Oh, dear," Ma had uttered in a thin voice, covering her mouth with one hand. Tears started to squirt from the corners of her eyes.

"Ma, it's not a big deal," I said. "We can—"

She got up from the table and ran into the kitchen. She started opening drawers and slamming them shut again. She ran into the pantry to get something. Large mixing utensils clanked against the countertop. Catherine and I stared at one another.

"I consoled her the other night," I said. "It's your turn."

"You're the birthday boy." She got up and drew her leather jacket from the coat hook by the side door. "I'm going out for a smoke." She disappeared through the door. Five minutes later, the engine of the old Chevy wagon she drove coughed and sputtered to life. I heard the car backing out of the driveway.

I reached out and stuck my fork into a piece of the cake. It tasted awful. There was too much yeast, or too little baking powder, or too much of everything.

I got up and walked into the kitchen. Ma was at the counter, hunched over a chrome mixing bowl, and stirring angrily.

"I'm making you another cake," she said. "I'll get this one right, I promise."

"Ma, you don't have to make another cake."

"The only problem," she said, pointing the wooden spoon at me (gobs of white dough fell from it, pattering the Armstrong floor), "is that I haven't any eggs."

"Then why are you making it?"

She watched me for a moment, then shook her head. "I don't know."

She exploded into tears.

I ran the muntins till midnight that night.

Right, left, up, down, all around, my eyes moved now, marking out a new path. *Right, left, up, down, all around …*

Yesterday I had been awarded my New Jersey State Driver's License. Catherine had driven me down to the Motor Vehicles

Agency in Parsippany around ten o'clock for my behind-the-wheel test. I'd passed with flying colors.

"Congratulations," she'd said on the way home. "Now you get to drive that piece of shit truck."

"What do you call this thing?" I said, alluding to the vehicle we were currently riding in.

"Piece-a-shit wagon." She lit up a Virginia Slim, rolled down her window, and rested her elbow on the doorsill while driving with her other hand. I noticed, maybe for the first time, how gaunt she appeared. Her skin was white and sallow. Dark whorls had taken up residence beneath her eyes, and blue veins were riding out of the skin of her neck.

"Hey, Cath, I wish you wouldn't smoke so much."

"Hold your breath if you don't like it."

"It isn't good for you, you know. It says right on the side of the pack—"

"I can read, asshole." She threw me an ornery look. "Besides, it's temporary. I'm trying to quit."

That's what they all say. Quitters to the grave. I had read somewhere that every cigarette you smoked took four minutes off your life.

"Ma's worried about you, you know. She says you're not eating enough, and …" I bit my tongue.

"And *what*?" Catherine threw a cutting glare at me.

And you're a year out of high school, doing nothing and going nowhere. That's what.

"Nothing," I murmured. "And I'm worried about Ma. The episode with the cake the other night … I ran upstairs to check on something, and when I came back down Ma was passed out on the pantry floor."

A sense of dark knowledge seemed to pass behind Catherine's eyes. Her lips tightened into a line. "Ma can take care of herself," she muttered quietly.

I wasn't so sure of that, however, as I lay in bed considering the events of the past four days. I was becoming less sure of it with each passing day.

Moments later, I heard a coughing, stammering muffler in the distance, the telltale indicator that Catherine was a half mile away and approaching. I'd come to think of it as her early warning device. Two minutes later, the old Chevy was backing into the driveway, the brake lights bleeding red on my ceiling. The engine cut, a car door slammed. I craned my head around to see the clock. It was 1:47 AM.

What I didn't know was that Ma had been waiting for her. Lurking in the pantry, perhaps, or sitting at the dining room table with her eyes glued to the door and her arms folded curtly on the scarred tabletop.

Catherine entered the house. I heard Ma's tightly controlled voice through the ventilation grate in the floor next to my bed. "Where have you been, young lady?"

Next came silence, and I saw perfectly well the visage of surprise captured on Catherine's face as she looked up and saw Ma watching her. "What are you still doing up?"

"Do you know what time it is, Catherine?"

"Do I give a fuck? I'm nineteen years old."

More silence, vibrating like high-tension wires.

Ma said, "What are you gonna do with your life, Cathy? Sleep until noon every day, no job, no ambitions, hang out with your friends past midnight each night?"

I closed my eyes. Softly. The muntins were still there, emblazoned across the nightscape of my eyelids. *Go upstairs to your room, Cath. Go upstairs.*

But Cathy couldn't do that, of course. Good old Smashin' Cath had to have the last word.

"What are you gonna do with *your* life, Ma? Lie there in the closet sucking the bottle all day?"

"That is none of your stinking business!"

"The hell it isn't, Ma!"

"You have no idea what I'm going through!"

"You have no idea what *I'm* going through!"

I heard Ma kick away the chair she must have been sitting in, which meant she was moving across the room, perhaps lunging.

"Stay away from me!" yelled Catherine. "You stay away—"

"You … will … not … speak to me … like I'm some … worthless … *indigent!*" I could see in my mind's eye Ma's claw-like hands burrowed into the flesh of Catherine's shoulders as she shook her, shook her like a rag doll.

Then Cath must have pushed Ma far enough away to wind up the arm and deliver a fast one. I heard a hard *thwack!* of flesh on flesh that actually made me shudder beneath my sheets. I heard Ma's body hit the floor with a dull *ca-thud.*

Next came Catherine's crying, quavering voice: "You stay away from me, you rotten, drunk bitch! You hear me? You just *stay away from me!*"

Catherine maneuvered around our mother's crumpled form. Seconds later, I heard her feet thumping up the stairs to her bedroom. Her bedroom door slammed shut.

I stared at the lines on my ceiling. They resembled the window bars in a prison. *Right, left, up, down, all around …*

I heard Ma crying. Large, hitching gasps, leading to full-blown sobs. Why didn't I go to her, you ask? Because I was angry. I was just as angry at her as she and Cath were at each other. Why? I don't know why. That part made no sense to me. I didn't know where my anger was coming from, or what was driving it. I may have known it was irrational, but knowing it was irrational didn't make it go away. *Why is Ma so weak? Why is she suddenly so frail and miserable? What in God's name has happened to her?*

She must have gotten up and stumbled into the kitchen, for I heard her bouncing off objects and kicking at others and in general crying the entire time. And I hated her. It coursed through my veins like black crude, the hate. I hated her for her weakness. I hated her for her self-perpetuating misery. I hated her for allowing her daughter to kick her around like the worthless drunk she was.

I thought of my father. Wishing he were here.

Right, left, up, down, all around.

I remembered the gifts he gave me for my birthdays, the ones he saved for last. The ones Ma never approved of.

Right left up down all around.

I remembered his final gift, the one he'd bequeathed to me the night of my sixteenth birthday. It was resting on his lap after he sat down at the top of the stairs and died with his chin touching his chest—wrapped in newspaper and trussed with twine. It was the last thing he'd ever given me.

I kept it hidden in my underwear drawer. I had stowed it there the night of my father's death. I hadn't looked at it since.

Rightleftupdownallaround …

I got out of bed, moving quietly to my dresser. In the pantry below, Ma projected her anger onto the jars of pickles standing on one of the high shelves. They smashed and shattered when they hit the floor.

I opened my underwear drawer. I pushed aside the pile of skivvies, reaching toward the back of the drawer, groping for the gift. I pulled it out. I held the Colt .45 with both hands. Its metal side gleamed a bluish-black in the pale glow of the streetlamps. The vague odor of gun oil filled the air. I remembered the first day I'd held it, how its weight had made it real. *It's real enough, all right. It's real enough to do the job.*

I pushed the underwear drawer shut. I carried the Colt back to my bed and sat down with the gun in my lap. A pall of silence had overtaken the kitchen below. Ma had opened a new bottle and lain down with the pickles, perhaps. I turned the gun around so that I could see the black eye of its muzzle.

Do you think it's possible to turn the page, Simon? Do you believe in fresh starts? Dad's words. The day we'd shot up the pumpkins. The day he'd showed me the spit bugs.

I opened my mouth and inserted the muzzle between my teeth. I bit down on the hard metal. I puckered my lips shut to form a perfect seal. What would they think then, Ma and Cath? It would serve them right, the way they'd acted. It would teach them an honest lesson.

I pulled the gun from my mouth. I opened my nightstand drawer, moved my NIV Bible and some loose papers aside, and buried the Colt underneath. I slid the drawer shut. Could I do it, if it came to that?

Bet your ass I could.

Until then, I'd run the muntins. I'd run as far as they'd take me. *Right, left, up, down, all around.*

CHAPTER ELEVEN

SHADOWS ON THE WALL

THE LEAVES TURNED EARLY. Mid-October saw the greens beginning to disappear, replaced by brilliant hues of red and yellow. The days were getting shorter. Nights were getting chillier. Josef Frustoff, who mowed the small section of lawn on the west side of the house (we had yet to be properly introduced, although we had waved to one another several times), came to the door one morning asking to see Ms. Caldwell. He said the seasonal shift was a week or two ahead of schedule this year, and it was time to start thinking about leaf and pine needle removal. It was apt to be a heavy winter, he said, and what he really wanted to know was whether Ms. Caldwell wished to renew her contract for snow plowing.

"Did you do that stuff last year?" I asked, looking down at the diminutive man from the top step of the porch.

"Aye, sir."

"Then I don't see why she wouldn't have you do it this year. And please, call me Simon."

"It's very nice ter meet ya, Simon." He wore a small top hat with a bill on it, and scuffed-up overalls. I went down the three stairs to shake hands with him.

"Where do you live?" I asked him.

"Far side'o th'lake," Josef answered, poking his thumb over his shoulder to point.

"No shit. You live in one of those three houses, then."

"The one in the middle, aye."

"I see." I couldn't tell if he was Irish or Scandinavian. "How many years have you lived here?"

"Many years, lad."

"I'm taking care of Corey, by the way, in case you were wondering. He's at school now. Alisha's at her office in town. She's practically never here."

"If you've a moment, lad, could I show ya something?"

"Certainly."

I slipped my shoes on and followed Josef down the railroad-tie stairs into the stone driveway. The stones were half covered with fallen leaves. We walked halfway up the drive, entering the S-turns that were flanked by pine trees. The small man moved slowly but with purpose.

Halfway up, he stopped, pointing down at rogue patches of earth that lined the perimeter of the S-turns. Weeds festered in these patches. Other areas were covered in brown pine needles.

"Used ter be flowerbeds," said Josef. "All these areas along edges." He turned, pointing in multiple directions. "Come spring, tulips everywhere, all different colors. But the bulbs, I must plant during fall."

"Did she have you do this last year?"

"Nar. I not tell her. But Mr. Turner, he insist every year."

"Mr. Turner? Who's that?"

"Previous owner. Mr. Turner built yer house, lad."

"No, it's not my house, I'm staying temporarily."

He nodded. "I see, yes."

"So, you're asking if you should tend to the flowerbeds or not, because it has to be done in the fall."

"Yes, lad. Much work required. The weeds, you see?"

"Yeah, I see them. Okay, go and do it. Bill Ms. Caldwell accordingly. I'll tell her we spoke when I see her next."

"Very well."

"Tell me something else, though."

His eyebrows went up.

"Come on, walk down the driveway with me," I said. When we began walking, I asked, "This Mr. Turner … How long did you work for him?"

"Thirty-one years."

"No kidding. Three decades, huh?"

Nodding, the small top hat going up and down.

"What was he like?"

"A real gentleman. Dedicated husband. His wife, Grace, was his greatest love. He nurtured her until the day she died."

"How long were they married?"

"Sixty-one years, lad."

"Wow. Any children?"

"Nar."

"Did Mr. Turner name his house sometime after he built it?"

"Not ter my knowledge."

"Have you ever heard of the name Crawford Daze?"

"Nar, never have."

As we neared the base of the driveway, I asked, "How did they meet? How did Mr. Turner meet his wife?"

"He rescued her, lad."

"Rescued her? From what?"

"The ice, yonder." He nodded toward the lake.

"She fell through the ice?" I felt my pulse quickening in my neck.

"Aye. The young lady ran onter the ice ter fetch her dog. Th'lady broke through, and Nels went and pulled her out."

This must have been the painting I'd seen in Millie's Arts & Wares. I'd seen a woman trapped in the ice, one arm extended, reaching for something or someone. It must have been the dog she was reaching for—it was the welfare of her dog that wrought such anguish and desperation on her face. *Her despair leaned over the abyss of grief.* I'd felt the wind howling in my ears and the snow biting into my arms. And then the ice had begun to crack under my own feet. The painting had been so powerful it had very nearly sucked me in. But who had painted it? And why had it exerted such a profound effect on me?

"What happened to the dog?"

Josef looked at me. "The dog?"

"Yes, the dog. Did they get the lady's dog back?"

"Nar. But an enduring love was formed." He gave me a stern

look. "Be mindful, lad. Ye must not stray onter the ice. Th'lake does not freeze properly."

I recalled Alisha telling me that there were no natural tributaries feeding into Swan Lake. Eight separate creeks emptied from it, however.

"Because of the springs, you mean."

"Th'springs, aye. Ice can be four inches thick in one place, a half inch in others. Very dangerous."

"I'll keep that in mind. Can I get you a drink? Something to eat? Anything?"

"Nar. I best be gettin' to work."

He turned and walked toward his Tacoma pickup. He dropped the tailgate, revealing the push mower, weed wacker, and assorted gas cans he'd brought with him.

I filled several mornings combing through the two-bay garage and inner basement. Both bays were filled with junk, with narrow paths winding among the piles like a misbegotten maze. Much of the stuff in here consisted of old tools and machine parts. It wasn't anything Alisha had brought with her when she'd moved in two years ago, that was for sure. This had all been left behind by Nels Turner, and it didn't appear as though Alisha had taken the time to go through it. I doubted she'd even stuck her head in here since the closing date. The cobwebs and film of mildew clotting the windows were evidence she had not.

I found shelves of paint cans and paint thinner and lacquer against one wall—cans so old they were rusted shut. There were boxes filled with old paperbacks and knick-knacks. In one corner stood an ancient toolbox, painted a mottled green and covered with sawdust. I wiped away some of the dust and saw two letters written in black magic marker on the top of the box: C.D. I opened the toolbox and its many extendable trays and found mostly electrical implements. There were old glass fuses, coils of copper wire, cutters, splicers, and three rocker panels.

Other, more basic tools hung from a vast pegboard along the back wall of the garage. There were hammers, pliers, about two dozen screwdrivers of varying types and sizes, complete wrench sets in both standard and metric, five different saws, and other things I couldn't identify. Standing in the left-hand corner was a six-foot-high lathing machine. Piled around it were three drills, two socket sets, a power sander, and a circular power saw. I withdrew a T-square that stood in a crevice between piles and ran my hand along its cool metal frame, knocking off years of dust and webs. On the backside of it, those two letters once more jumped out at me: C.D.

Who was C.D.?

Or: *what* was C.D.?

I found a chainsaw along one of the side walls. It was an Echo, and did not appear to be very old. I hit the primer button several times and gave the cord four or five good rips. Nothing. What gas was in the tank was probably old, and the plug was likely shot. Not far from where the chainsaw had sat stood a black wheelbarrow. Inside the wheelbarrow was a long-handled axe and a sledgehammer. I thought of the fireplace in the upstairs den. Probably, the Turners had used it on a regular basis to help weather the tough New England winters.

I took the chainsaw and set it into the wheelbarrow well, then pushed the wheelbarrow closer to one of the bay doors.

The inner basement was unfinished, with a painted cement floor. Hulking in shadows near the back was the burner and hot water heater. The boxes and plastic stowaway crates stacked along the walls were all Alisha's. In the darkness beneath the wood stairs that led up to the kitchen foyer stood a small bicycle. I reached for the handlebars and pulled the bike out with one arm. I examined it beneath the musty glow of the sixty-watt bulb in the ceiling fixture behind me. It was a brand-new, blue BMX 400 Racer. I slid my palm over the black vinyl seat, removing a skin of dust. It was the bicycle Corey had received for his birthday last February. From his father. Alisha had buried it down here and likely forgotten—or hoped to forget—about it. It was a gift any child Corey's age would be ecstatic to have.

Later that week, during one of the rare dinners the three of us shared together, I said to Alisha, "Where, exactly, did you get this house from?"

We hadn't spoken much since our dinner at the Hampton Riverside. I hadn't gotten it up to ask her what had become of Alan Mercer that night, and she hadn't volunteered any information.

"What do you mean, 'where'd I get it?' I bought the house." Her voice was terse.

"Yes, I know you bought the house. But from whom did you buy it? How did you obtain it, I mean."

This was information I already had. But I wanted to see if Alisha's and Josef's stories matched.

"Public auction. Why do you ask, Simon?"

"So you never met the previous owner?"

"Not personally. He was an older fellow named Nels Turner. His wife passed away some years ago. Nels lived alone here for another five or six years before his age started to catch up to him. He had to go into a nursing home three years ago."

"What nursing home did he go into?"

"I don't know."

"Was it someplace nearby? In town, perhaps?"

"I don't know."

"He could still be alive, then, couldn't he?"

"I don't know."

I asked, "Who handled the transfer of the house? One of his kids?"

"A local attorney. Far as I know, Turner didn't have any kids."

"Who got the money from the sale of the house?"

"I'm sure Turner did. It will help pay for his long-term care."

"So, you're aware that he left behind a garage full of tools and other stuff?"

"Yes. It was included in the estate."

"Have you looked at some of the stuff that's down there?"

"No. Anything interesting?"

"I found a chainsaw."

"You aren't going to hack us to pieces, are you?"

"If I can get it running, I might try and cut some firewood for the winter. Did you use your fireplace at all last year?"

"No."

"The chimney probably needs to be swept out then."

"How would you know that? Did you once do that sort of work?"

"No," I said. "My father had a wood stove in our basement. Every fall, he'd have someone come to clean out the chimney."

"Perhaps it's something Josef can do."

"I'll ask him. He was here the other day." I told Alisha what Josef had said about the snow plowing and planting the bulbs along the driveway edges. She nodded absently.

Tuesday the following week, I picked Corey up from school and brought him to Molly's for lunch. I had a club sandwich and a cup of coffee. Corey had a corndog with potato chips.

"What are we doing today?" he asked me.

"You have karate, but not until four this afternoon. We're gonna go home first, 'cause I have a surprise for you."

His face lit up. "What is it? What? What?"

"You'll see. Finish your lunch."

In the car, he couldn't keep still, nor could he keep his mouth shut. Tell a kid you've got a surprise for him, and you've made a kid's day right then and there.

"You know, Corey, Halloween is coming up. Have you thought about what you'd like to be?"

"No."

"What did you dress up as last year?"

He had to think about it for a moment. "I wore my karate outfit."

"You dressed up as a karate person?"

"Yeah."

"Well, you can't be the same thing two years in a row. Let's see … I know, how about Cinderella?"

"No!"

"Well, then how 'bout Sleeping Beauty?"

"No!"

"Snow White, then?"

"*No!*"

"If you don't like any of my ideas, you'd better come up with some of your own," I told him.

"Can I be a pirate?"

"Sure. A good pirate or a bad pirate?"

"A good pirate."

We were on our way down the driveway now. "A pirate it is, then. In the meantime, are you ready for the surprise?"

"Yeah! Yeah!"

His BMX Racer stood in the driveway in front of one of the closed garage doors, propped up on its kickstand. I had taken most of the morning getting it cleaned and ready. The vinyl seat and rubber tires sparkled beneath fresh coats of Armor All. I'd oiled the chain and added air to the tires.

He looked at the bike at first the way a child might see a potential gift through a storefront window—some wondrous fictional item he knows he'll probably never have. Then a jubilant recognition dawned on his face as he remembered it had been his to begin with. His to start with but locked away beneath darkness and dust.

"Whoa …" His large blue eyes had become opals of awe.

When I parked the Saab, he jumped out and ran over to the bike and started dancing around it. He raised his arms in triumphant celebration.

"Can I really ride it, Simon? Can I?"

"Not without the necessary safety gear." I opened the garage door to retrieve the helmet, elbow pads, and knee pads I'd purchased in town yesterday morning. "You need to put these on first."

I helped him get the knee and elbow pads on, and then demonstrated to him how to fasten the helmet clip so that the helmet remained tight on his head.

"Have you ever ridden a bike before, Corey?"

"Yeah, Samantha's," he said.

"With or without training wheels?"

"Without. I can do it, Simon, I really can."

"That's nice, but I'm still holding onto you for the first few runs. You know how to use the brakes, right?"

"Yeah, like this." He locked one of the pedals in reverse to show me.

"Okay, good. Are you ready then? We're gonna go clear across the driveway, but I'm holding onto you."

"Yeah, let's go," he said, already pedaling and moving forward. I ran along beside him, one arm wrapped tentatively around his waist.

"That's it," I said. "Good, you've got it. Now use the brakes to stop yourself."

He did so, and came skidding to a halt in the stones, putting one foot on the ground at precisely the right moment to stand up again.

"Well done. You have done this before, haven't you?"

"Can I go by myself, Simon? Can I?"

We made five more runs together, and even rode in a rough circle, before I was willing to let go of him. And when I did let go of him, I continued to run alongside him, my arms open and at the ready. But it soon became obvious that he did not need me to hold onto him. All he'd needed, really, was for me to hold open the door; he'd gone flying through pretty well at full speed, and was on his own.

*   *   *

Corey was in love.

During the next two weeks, the boy wanted nothing more than to be able to ride his bicycle. So when he wasn't in school or engaged in one of his various afternoon activities, we rode. I went into town one morning and purchased a mountain bike. It was a Ross 15-speed. I paid in cash.

We set out on brief excursions from Crawford Daze, pedaling up State Street together. Corey often rode ahead, standing on his pedals and leaning forward to build up a good head of steam. He'd go flying up the dirt road beneath a tunnel of falling leaves, trailing thin ribbons of dust behind him. When he got too far ahead, he'd circle back to meet me.

We explored some of the other numbered roads that bisected State Street, namely Roads 24, 19, and 57. Each of these roads spanned Birch Creek and Pine Creek with one-lane bridges. Every bridge was different in its own fundamental way. No two blueprints had been exactly alike. How many one-lane bridges were there? Think of it this way: State Street circumnavigated Swan Lake. Seven numbered roads in all bisected State Street. Each of the numbered roads crossed, on average, three of the outflow creeks. Right there, you're looking at twenty-one bridges, all individuals in terms of style and architecture. We couldn't pedal far enough to explore them all firsthand, but we did find two more of the outflow creeks: Spruce Creek and Yosemite Creek.

Alisha's initial reaction toward her son's newly acquired skill was anger. It was, of course, directed at me. She was upset over the fact that I'd placed her son in a position of danger, and that I'd done so without her knowing.

Her anger was short-lived, however, superseded by her son's excitement. Corey's eagerness to show his mother what he could do on two wheels made her forget she'd ever been angry to start with. He zoomed back and forth across the driveway, tumbling leaves bouncing off the sides of his black helmet. He turned the handlebars in tight, fast arcs, slamming the brakes at the same time, making the rear end of the bike spin around in a cloud of stones and white dust.

"Watch this, Mom! Watch this one!"

He'd streak across the driveway again, teeth clenched into a tight smile, his eyes beaming.

Alisha, one hand covering her mouth: "Be careful! Oh, Corey … be careful!"

Soon, though, she too was smiling.

As he darted back and forth in front of us, Alisha turned to me and asked, "Has he fallen?"

"Several times. Banged up his shoulder pretty bad the one time, had a good cry over it. But he hopped right back up."

She appeared unsure how to respond to this.

"I was eight or nine when I learned how to ride a bike," I added. "The very first time I tried, I didn't know how to use the brakes. I crashed into the curb and somersaulted over the handlebars. He's five years old and he's doing donuts on his front wheel."

"Just promise me the two of you will be careful."

"He'll never be out of my sight, and he'll never ride without his safety gear."

Assembling Corey's Halloween pirate outfit was a piecemeal effort. We picked up a pair of old black boots at a consignment shop in Merchant's Square. The plastic machete we found in a Five & Ten store. The black eye patch I picked up at the pharmacy. The black pants and torn yellow shirt we were able to gather from Corey's existing wardrobe, which was utterly voluminous.

The day before Halloween was a Friday, and Corey was trying on his outfit *in toto* for the first time. The two of us were in his bedroom. Alisha was upstairs readying herself for tonight's October Ball. Corey stood in front of his mirror admiring himself. He waved his plastic sword through the air.

"Careful," I said. "You're gonna take somebody's eye out with that."

"Hey, I forgot my pumpkin."

"What pumpkin?"

"For my candy." He went over to his closet and rummaged through some of the toys in there. Finally he came out with a small plastic jack-o-lantern with a hole cut out of the top, made for carrying all the night's candy.

On impulse, I grabbed the plastic pumpkin out of his hands and ran out of the room with it.

"Hey! Gimme that back! *Simon!*" He ran after me.

"Catch me if you can!" I yelled.

I cut into the den, made two loops around the dining room table, then headed for the sofa. He followed me step for step, giggling and yelling at the same time.

"Simon! That's mine!"

"If you want it, then come and get it!"

"I'm gonna pee in my pants again!"

I jumped onto the sofa, cradling the pumpkin like a running back trying to protect the football. He jumped on top of me and began wrestling for the pumpkin. I let him get his hands on it, and then I began tickling him. He let go of the pumpkin and thrashed around in my grip, weakened by his own laughter. He laughed until his face was red.

"Don't tear the house apart, you two."

We quit the horseplay and turned to look over the sofa's backrest. Alisha was carefully descending the spiral stairs. She wore a white dress with frills down around the knees. The dress was sleeveless. A single white spaghetti strap curled over each of Alisha's cream-colored shoulders. She wore tan nylons, but it wasn't until she'd stepped onto the den floor that she placed her feet into what looked like a pair of glass slippers.

I said to Corey, "She looks a bit like Cinderella, doesn't she?"

"Yeah, Mom, you look like Cinderella."

"Dinner is in the fridge, you guys. There are Popsicles in the freezer for dessert." She went over to the dining room table, where she grabbed up a small silver purse. She popped the purse open, withdrew a set of keys, then snapped it shut again. The scent of daffodils filled the air, some sort of perfume she was wearing.

We had gotten off the sofa by then, and Corey ran up to her in his pirate outfit. "Hug, Mommy, hug."

She knelt down and embraced him. "You be good now." She kissed him on his ear.

She stood tall once again, looking at me. She had applied eye shadow, blush, and a purplish glossy lipstick. Her silverish hair hung mostly straight, but some of it had been wound into braids and trusses. That alone must have taken hours.

"I may or may not be home tonight," she said in a lower voice. "The ball ends around midnight. Do I need to call?"

"That won't be necessary. I'll be fast asleep. Is your date picking you up here?" I was hoping he was.

"No, I'm meeting him at the firehouse."

"Have a good time," I said.

"Try to have Corey in bed around eight, okay? Tomorrow being Halloween and all."

"Have a good time," I repeated.

*   *   *

We had our dinner and then each of us had a Popsicle. Afterward, we did some Hidden Picture puzzles on the kitchen table. Corey loved these. He'd sit quietly with his pencil, his head bent over the open book, searching diligently for the icons pictured in the legend. He adroitly circled the lost items—a rabbit, hidden upside-down in a bush; a candle lurking discreetly in a tree trunk. I sat next to him, watching. A good many of the objects he located before I did.

A bit later he wanted to ride bikes.

"No, we're not riding bikes anymore today. It's dark outside. And it's getting cold."

"But—"

"Hey, tomorrow's Halloween, remember? You need to get a good night's sleep. You've got a lot of work to do tomorrow night. You have to collect enough candy for both of us."

"Simon!"

I got him into his pajamas. We played hide-and-seek for twenty minutes and then settled down for a bedtime story. Corey went to his bookshelf next to the window to choose a book. I have to say, he looked as cute as an ace standing there in his yellow bunny outfit—slippered feet, a fluffy, white cottontail poking out, and even a hood that wrapped over his head with a pair of rabbit ears sticking out on top. One of the ears stood erect, the other was bent limply to one side. I almost had to laugh at just how adorable he was in all his innocence. It made me want to scoop him up and cradle him to sleep in my arms.

The story he chose was predictable enough: *Go Dog Go*.

"We read that last night," I told him.

"I know, but it's my favorite."

"Well, how 'bout tonight, we read *my* favorite?"

"Yeah!" He ran back to the shelf, returned *Go Dog Go* to the slot from which it had come, and withdrew *Wacky Wednesday*. This had been a favorite of mine when I'd been Corey's age. I read him the tale of a boy who wakes up one Wednesday morning to find his shoes on the ceiling; who later goes outside to find adults sitting in strollers being pushed by infants; who sees a world that is basically upside-down and inside-out.

Later, I tucked him in and clicked out the light. When I checked on him ten minutes later, he was lying on his side, asleep in his bunny suit. I bent over him and planted a light kiss on his forehead.

I went through the den and admitted myself into Alisha's office. I moved over to her bookshelf to select a new title. A row of hardbacks on the bottom shelf caught my attention. I hadn't seen them before, but then again I probably hadn't been looking so low to the floor. Down there were eight novels by Jonathan Dent. The name rang familiar because it had been in the news five or six years ago. Tragically, Dent had killed his wife and then himself in their Georgia home in the aftermath of a violent killing spree in a nearby South Carolina town. His final book, *The Real Deal*, had been published posthumously. Panned by critics, the book had sold millions of copies due in part to the horrific events surrounding it. I withdrew Alisha's copy of *The Real Deal*, opened it, and skimmed the synopsis on the dust jacket. It seemed a bit violent for my tastes.

I chose instead a paperback rendition of Alisha Caldwell's *Gods of Komodo*. I took it back to my bedroom. I flopped onto the bed and read for close to an hour. It was a story of a suburbanite schoolteacher named Sally Hayes. Shy and single, Sally is a typical

American wallflower—oversized black glasses, hair trussed up in a bun, the whole bit. She's dated several men, been jilted more than once, and shudders with revulsion at the thought of portly beer bellies covered with "a mat of black fur." Frustrated with the inequities of life, she opts to go on a cruise, where she hopes to meet some interesting men. The cruise ship is capsized by a huge freak wave, and all hands are lost. Sally, the lone survivor, wakes up on a beach. She has managed to cling to a hunk of flotsam, and, well, here she is, all alone on some strange island. Except she isn't alone at all. The island is home to a populace of men. Maybe thirty or forty of them, all between the ages of twenty and thirty-five. All are soap-style hunks. And none have seen a woman in years' time. Their tan chests are sculpted in muscle and sinew, and their libidos are in full strut. The once sexually repressed Sally Hayes can now pick and choose from this lost culture of exotic male specimens. Pick and choose she does, sometimes two or three at a time. Sally lets her hair down, and we discover that she really is quite gorgeous. She renames herself Shalla and anoints herself queen of the island.

I didn't have to read on to figure out what happens. Some sort of curse is handed down, and overnight all the men are transformed into the belly-dragging, fork-tongued, venomous lizards known to inhabit the island of Komodo this very day. If the story itself wasn't bad enough, some of the sordid metaphors were enough to make me wince: "… *she climbed his taut body as if it were a trellis of muscle …*" or "*… she moaned with delight as their sandwiched bodies gyrated to the staccato of ocean waves …*"

I had reached page 109 when I heard the front door bang open. I slid the book underneath a pillow (so embarrassed was I by its content), then turned to check the clock. It was 9:45.

I got out to the hallway in time to see Alisha stumbling across the den floor. One of her ankles buckled and turned beneath her.

"Ow! Shit!" She paused long enough to pull off both slippers, and then threw them across the room.

"What's going on? Was the ball cancelled?"

She didn't look good. Her hair was askew. Some of it hung in stringy, damp dewlaps in front of her face. She used one hand to toss some of it back, and I noticed right away that her eye shadow had streaked. The eyes themselves were red and inflamed.

"Oh, it was cancelled all right. It might as well have been."

She went to the dining room table, where she opened the small silver purse she'd taken with her and began dumping its contents. Out came her keys, followed by a tube of lipstick, several credit cards, and other feminine items. She shook the purse until she was convinced it was empty and then tossed that aside, too. Some rogue strands of hair had fallen over her eyes once more. She used one quick hand to whisk them away.

"And there I am, standing by the entrance, all dressed up and smiling and feeling like a fucking idiot."

The bottom fell out of my stomach as I realized what had happened. I genuinely felt bad for her.

I went down the lone stair and walked over to her. I tried to stand next to her, and I even put a hand on her shoulder. "Jeez Louise, I'm really sorry—"

She whacked my hand away, though. "No, Simon, it's quite all right. I'm a grown woman, I don't need to be placated. Just go back to your room and leave me alone."

Instead, I pulled out one of the dining room table chairs and sat down. "Was it Mercer again?"

She was trying to stuff her credit cards back into her wallet, but was having a rough go of it because her hands were shaking.

"I told you, I don't want to talk about it." She fiddled with the wallet a moment longer before putting it down. "You know what I'm gonna do? I've got a big bottle of brandy in the cupboard. I'm gonna take it out on the deck and get drunk. Wanna get drunk with me, Simon? Drown some sorrows? Misery loves company, you know."

"I'm not getting drunk, and neither are you."

"Oh no? Says who?"

"The Gods of Komodo."

"Oh, very funny, Simon. Is that supposed to make me feel better?"

"Look, if it makes you feel better to vent your anger on me, go for it. I can stand it."

Instead, she put both hands on the edge of the table and sighed deeply. Looking down between her arms, she said, "You know, all a woman wants is to be able to dance. I mean, nine-hundred-dollar dress, two-hundred-dollar shoes … Is one dance too much to ask?"

"I'll dance with you, Alisha."

She chuckled. "That's quite all right."

"I'm serious," I announced, getting up from my chair. "I haven't danced with anyone since my high school prom."

I reached for the remote control that operated Alisha's state-of-the-art Sony stereo system. I pointed the remote toward the TV set, beneath which the stereo unit had been assembled, and pressed the power button.

"Simon, honestly, you don't have to—"

"Look," I said, "just one dance before you open the brandy. If you still want the bottle afterwards, I promise I won't stop you. Is that a deal?" I was already holding my hands out, waiting for hers.

Her smile bore a hint of resignation. "Yes, all right." She gave me her hands.

The CD table spun around several times, choosing at random. It fell onto a Moody Blues track.

> *"When the fantasy we live in*
> *Lies in pieces on the ground*
> *And there is no false illusion*
> *That can turn your heart around ..."*

My right hand was the high hand, clasping her left hand up around her left shoulder. Her hands were considerably smaller and very soft. I stood maybe four inches taller than she did. I watched her eyes for any signs of the sadness that, despite all her commercial successes, seemed to encircle her body like a nimbus most days of the week. I didn't see any just now, and that was fine. Now, there was only the music. It was the music, and the two of us inside it, rocking slowly back and forth on the edges of our feet to its sure and gentle rhythm.

> *"Only the silence that I feel*
> *Only the lonely road is real*
> *If only I didn't lose you*
> *If only we could be*
> *If only we could be ..."*

I risked a quick look down and saw the dark cleft between her breasts. There was a flash of warmth in my loins, a sensation that had no business being where it was. But it was late, and the music was good, and now we were turning in a slow circle, and I promised myself I wouldn't look again.

The tired smile on Alisha's face had faded into a kind of dreamy vagueness. She met my eyes several times, and each time the vagueness seemed less and the appreciation more. She moved closer to me. I felt the soft swell of her breasts against my sternum. Until finally she laid her head on my shoulder, relaxed and perfectly at ease, and letting the music do its thing. I had the sense that her eyes were closed. I closed my own. For a moment I had come home. I had come back to my beginnings and forgotten about the ends.

> *"Chasing shadows on the wall*
> *Chasing shadows as they dance the floor*
> *Chasing dreams that were forever young*
> *Now I'm on my own*
> *Chasing shadows on the wall ..."*

I held Alisha in my arms, and she held onto me in return. We danced the tune through. When it was over, she looked up at me with a slightly bashful smile. "Thank you." She stood on her tiptoes and kissed me lightly on the cheek.

"You're welcome."

She turned toward the spiral turret and began slowly climbing the stairs in her white dress, her head down. I flicked off the lights and the stereo, and returned to my room. I turned on my side and stared through the windows for over an hour until a thick, black sleep finally pulled me down.

CHAPTER TWELVE

DRIVING WEST

"YOU'RE AWFULLY QUIET, SIMON." Ma was sitting on the passenger side of the Roadgrader, her pocketbook in her lap, her hands folded neatly on top of it.

"When I think of something to say, I'll let you know," I muttered.

"Oh. Well. All right."

She turned her head to gaze out her window. We were moving west on Interstate 80. It was mid-November. Dark clouds clotted the sky. Today she had begged for me to cut school so that I could drive her into Hackettstown for her eye appointment. Ma had lost her driver's license. She'd been pulled over by a municipal cop who'd caught her driving down the wrong side of the road south of Lake Parsippany. Ma had agreed to take a breathalyzer test. Her blood-alcohol level had been twice the legal limit for the state of New Jersey. A local judge had seen it fit that Ma not drive for six months.

"Get Cath to drive you," I'd protested initially. "It isn't as if she's got a busy schedule ... although she *would* have to drag herself out of bed before noontime."

Ma had looked down at the floor. "Your sister isn't speaking to me at the moment, Simon."

"Have you asked her?"

"Yes. Would you like to know what she told me to do? In her own words?"

"No."

I had the Roadgrader up to sixty—pretty much her upper limit these days. Traffic sailed past as though we were standing in place. Ma flinched as an eighteen-wheeler went hurtling past her window, perilously close to sideswiping us.

"Heavens be! Did you see that truck? Someone's gonna get killed on this road someday."

"People do get killed, Ma. Every day. Don't you watch the news?"

I saw her looking at me from the corner of my eye. I could feel the hurt expression on her face. She turned away again.

We cruised in silence for several miles. Finally, Ma turned and said, "I promise you, Simon, things are going to get better for us. Just as soon as I get my license back, I'm going to get a job and—"

"You need to quit drinking, Ma."

"What?"

"I said you need to quit drinking."

I still hadn't turned to look at her directly, but I could see her face turned fully toward me, a white pall spread across it.

"Are you insinuating that I have a p—"

"No, I'm stating the obvious." I hesitated, finally turning to look her squarely in the eye. "You get caught driving drunk again, Ma, they're gonna take your license away for two years. A third time, and it's a decade … and they send you to jail for six months."

She stared open-mouthed at me. Tears must've begun to cloud her vision, because the next moment she was rooting through her pocketbook, pulling out tissues.

"You're as bad as your sister." Her voice quavered.

"How much trouble are we in, Ma?"

Dabbing at her eyes with the tissue now. "I'm not quite sure what it is you're talking about. You and Catherine both, saying hurtful things and—"

"Financially, Ma. That's what I mean. How much trouble are we in?"

"There's no trouble, Simon, who gave you the id—"

"A man called the other day," I injected. "From the phone company. He said we haven't paid our phone bill for the last three months. He said we owe them four hundred dollars."

"Oh. Well …" She fell quiet for a while, fiddling with her fingers, wrapping the damp tissue around one of her pinkies.

That's not to mention the pile of unopened bills on the dining room table. Last month, I counted perhaps half a dozen. Yesterday I counted sixteen.

"All right, so maybe we're … a little behind in some areas. It happens, you know. But I've got a handle on it. Trust me."

"Can I ask you something, Ma?"

"Of course."

"Didn't Dad have a life insurance policy with his job? So that, when he died—"

Ma rocked her head back and guffawed. When she'd finished laughing, she rolled right on: "Barely paid for his funeral, Simon. *Barely.*" She turned to glance out her window, quieting down and becoming serious once more. A patchwork quilt of yellows and reds flew past her solemn face. "It costs a lot of money to bury a person, Simon. It's almost an insult, him dying, considering what he left behind him."

"Ma … if the problem gets to the point … Look, if you need the money, I'm not averse to you tapping into my college fund. I just want you to know—"

"There isn't any college fund, Simon."

I stopped, looking straight at her. We looked at each other. I searched her expression for hints of bemusement or guile. She appeared to be searching mine for hints of sobriety, and never mind the irony. That she was doing so scared the living stuff out of me, I'll say that much.

"But …"

"Whatever gave you the idea there was a college fund, Simon?" A wretched smile cracked her icy veneer. She laughed bitterly. "Don't you think that if there *had* been, your father would have tapped it out long—"

"No, we had this discussion, him and I. I know we've talked about it more than once because … well … he told me …"

He told me to take some time, either during my college years or immediately after, to work with my hands—to work hard every day like most Americans do. So that someday, I'll have a greater appreciation for what I have. Surely he would have never mentioned college if he didn't have the money to send *me to col—*

"—get one thing straight," Ma was saying. "Your father said a lot of things that weren't true. Oh, and sometimes he said things that *used* to be true ... and he even uttered things he hoped *might someday be true.* Certainly, he had his moments, Simon, moments when his hopes and optimisms ran high—but hope alone doesn't have a dollar sign in front of it. Believe me, if it had had a dollar sign before it, it rode away long ago on a last-place blueback at fifty-to-one odds."

Had Catherine heard any of this? I was beginning to wonder if she knew more about our parents than she was letting on. If so, did it have something to do with her aimless purgatory today? I was in my junior year of high school. I was slated to take my SATs next spring. I had begun ruminating on where I'd like to attend college. That had all changed, suddenly. Where was I going to go on an empty tank? What school was I going to attend on a fund that didn't exist? Why had my father told me something that wasn't true? Why had he lied to me?

CHAPTER THIRTEEN

JOSEF

OCTOBER BOWED OUT WITH a curtsy. November swept into place, steeling the sky with gray woolen mats of sagging clouds. A chilly breeze shook the handfuls of dead leaves still clinging to their respective branches, rattling through them like castanets. Some of the leaves tore free and clicked off the windows of the house. Drifts had formed on the roof and clogged the downspouts. Josef and I spent two days up there working. We spent the first day sweeping the rooftop and cleaning out the gutters. A brisk wind blew in off the water, making the air feel a lot colder than it was.

The second day was devoted to sweeping the chimney. We hung a heavy drop cloth over the fireplace down in the den and then climbed the ladder onto the roof once more.

"Aye, she's a clogged up good!" Josef grimaced through tight rows of teeth. He was able to lower his black chimney sweep about four feet before striking an unseen obstruction. He used both arms to piston the long pole up and down, trying to drive it through whatever had jammed up the chimney.

"This isn't normal, is it?" I asked.

He laughed, and added, "Say, lad, 'tis a good thing you didn't try ter use the fireplace! All yer smoke woulda gone right in ter yer—"

He was interrupted by a progeny of squeals. He relinquished his grip on the pole as the first squirrel shot out of the chimney. Five gray, furry forms came bouncing out behind it, dancing on the rim of the chimney and leaping in all directions.

Josef threw his hands in the air. "Blimey! Make a run fer it!"

He turned and ran one way, I went the other. I'd gone four or five steps before I stopped. *Why are we running from squirrels?* I turned and looked for Josef, located him on the opposite corner of the roof. He started laughing, and then I started laughing too.

We got the chimney cleaned out. We were both black with soot when the job was done.

Later that week, I got the chainsaw running. I'd changed the plug, cleaned the filter, and poured the old fuel out of the tank. I mixed up a new oil/gas mixture and added an ounce of fuel stabilizer. The saw sputtered to life on the sixteenth pull, coughing out purplish-gray clots of smoke that made my eyes water. I went into town and bought replacement blades. I also bought some heavy-duty work gloves, steel toe work boots, and a sharpening stone. I used the stone to hone the axe to a fine cutting edge.

I began making daily forays into the woods along the west side of the house, searching for felled trees—wood that would already be dry and ready for use this winter. I found three likely candidates. The first was so hard that my chainsaw literally bounced off the bark. An ash, maybe? I'd never been much of a tree person. The second candidate was a pine or evergreen, and I began cutting away. The tree was either too fresh or still alive, however: I was covered with sap after the first fifteen minutes, and my new blades became so gummed up with the stuff that they'd no longer cut. My four-letter expletives flew unabridged through the forest.

I decided to call it a day.

It was an uneventful month for the most part, comprised of days that seemed to flap by like a deck of cards. I logged frequent flyer miles ferrying Corey to and from his endless string of daily activities. Alisha began making more frequent appearances around the house as her December 1st starting line drew nearer. She spoke little and smiled less. I was outside working most of these times, cutting up the third tree (a far more serviceable maple, thank God), and then using the wheelbarrow to cart the pieces of wood into the yard, where I separated them into piles according to size. Several times I ducked into the house for a cup of joe or a snack, where I found Alisha walking in and out of her office, moving things and frowning and muttering small intangibles to herself—what I began to think of as "Alisha-speak." Her preparations were more mental than physical, I thought—getting her office workspace cleaned and ready was a method of getting her mind cleaned and ready.

Part of it was getting *me* ready, as well. I asked her one day, "So, how's it going?"

"Fine." Looking down, her lips moving.

"Do you know what you'll be writing about?" I asked, sipping my coffee. "Do you have an outline? Do you know what page one will look like, or what your first sentence will be?"

"Simon," she said, giving me one of her trademark cynical smiles meant to convey that I was intruding on her delicate train of thought, "let's get something straight, shall we?"

"Yeah, sure. Anything."

"It's of utmost importance that once I begin writing, I not be disturbed. I'll be sequestering myself in my office four days a week, beginning December 1st. I cannot have Corey running in to interrupt with every fanciful whim that befalls him, and I can't have you knocking on the door with unimportant phone messages or dinner queries. Is that understood?"

I stood up straight and gave her a military salute.

She rolled her eyes. "I have a separate phone line in my office, which only a few people are privy to. My agent, my publicist, Mr. Bryson down at the office, to name a few."

"How 'bout Alan Mercer?"

"I'll probably start around nine each morning, and work until two, depending on how the juices are flowing that day. The good news is that I'll be here most nights to prepare dinner for the three of us."

I called Ma two nights later. We spoke for twenty minutes.

"I'm probably gonna stay here for Thanksgiving, Ma. Is that okay with you?"

"That's fine, Simon. There are plenty of places I can go. Don and Betty have already invited me to their place."

We talked about Catherine for a while. Ma didn't want to talk about Catherine. She never did. I changed the subject by asking her how work was going. Work was work, she said. "Plenty busy, always things to do, always people in and out of the store. How about you, Simon? Are you getting along with that woman?"

"Like peaches and cream," I said.

"I read one of her books last week. It was pretty awful."

I laughed. "There's more where it came from, Ma."

"Have you been studying for your exams, Simon?"

"Every day," I lied.

"Good. I think about you a lot, you know."

"Likewise, Ma. I gotta run. I love you. The world over."

"The world over," she replied, blowing a kiss through the receiver.

I began splitting wood with the axe. The first two or three days of this were difficult. My upper arm and shoulder muscles weren't prepared for the repeated motions of swinging a long-handled axe. Gradually I grew stronger. I would raise the axe high over my head and drive it downward in a tight, whistling arc. When the axe wedged and got stuck, I used the sledgehammer to drive it the rest of the way through. But I used the sledgehammer less and less. More often than not, the axe blade struck true, sending wedges of split wood flying in three directions. Several times, I turned toward the house and saw Alisha watching me through a kitchen window, a cup of coffee in one hand. I began stacking the wood along the front of the house to the right of the front door.

Josef was on the property practically every day. When he wasn't using a high-power blower to drive the leaves and pine needles into neatly arranged piles, he was working diligently along the driveway fringes with his spade and hoe, carving out shallow holes in which to plant his bulbs. He demonstrated to me how this was done, and I even helped him some mornings.

Corey experienced two more sleepwalking episodes later that month. The first was three days before Thanksgiving. It happened in the wee hours of the morning. He came into my room, actually. My alarm was fifteen minutes away from sounding, which is probably why I was awake when the episode occurred. I heard Corey's slippered feet making sandpaper rubs against the wood floor, and I opened my eyes to see him moving across the room. I sat up in bed, blinking and rubbing sleep out of my eyes as he headed straight for the bureau in his cottontail bunny pajamas, as if he had some kind of business there. He stopped in front of the bureau without running into it or banging a knee or foot on it, and started running his hands across the top of it. His hands found the ceramic fish dish and closed on the keychain with the white fob on it. He made a half turn with the keys in hand before dropping them on the floor. Then he turned back to the bureau once more and began opening drawers. He pulled three drawers open, leaving all three in that position before lowering himself to the floor, curling up into a fetal shape, and resuming normal sleep.

I carried him back to his bedroom.

As I lowered him into his bed and pulled the covers up to his chin, his eyelids flickered. Open, then shut … then open again. He was staring straight at me. I couldn't tell if he was asleep or not. For a moment, I thought he'd truly awakened.

His lips parted, gummy with sleep. "I saw … him."

"You saw who?" I asked.

"… saw him … saw … the man … in black …"

"Corey, are you awake?"

For those several moments, he may have been. His eyelids flickered again. They fluttered briefly, then fell shut. He was sound asleep.

Two nights after Thanksgiving (a quiet affair, mostly; Alisha made one of her lavish dinners and was surprisingly in a pleasant mood), Corey walked into my room again, got into my bed next to me, and curled up against my back. I have no idea how long we inadvertently slept together; I stirred around 3:45 and felt his knee poking into my shoulder blade. I clicked on the light and found him sleeping like a baby, thumb in his mouth, head on the pillow as though he belonged there. I again carried him into his room and lowered him into his own bed. I watched his face to see if his eyes would open again, but they didn't.

I told Alisha the following day. She was sitting at the dining room table transcribing notes onto a steno pad.

She leaned back in her chair and sighed as I described both occurrences.

"The episodes tend to increase in number around the major holidays," she parlayed. "Be sure to tell Dr. Andrews on Thursday, okay? He'll want to know."

"Has Corey ever mentioned this 'man in black' before?"

She afforded herself a moment to think about it, then shook her head. "No."

I thought she was lying.

"But he has crawled into my bed with me, as he did with you," she added.

"He crept up the spiral stairs in his sleep?"

"Yes."

"That's a little scary, don't you think?"

"It's very scary, Simon," she agreed. "And I'm very concerned about it. That's why Dr. Andrews is working with him."

"I don't think Dr. Andrews is helping him."

She eyed me skeptically, twirling her pen with her fingers. "And what makes you say that?"

"He sits and watches while Corey plays with trains and race cars and toy boats. I think he's taking advantage of you."

She crossed her arms over her chest, tilting her head to one side. "And you got your Ph.D. from where?"

"Does Dr. Andrews ever debrief you on his and Corey's sessions?"

"Of course. We speak on the phone periodically."

"What does he tell you?"

She paused. "That's private. It's between me and him."

"Oh, I see. I guess I'm just background furniture."

"You're not Corey's father, if that's what you mean."

The words stung, despite the fact that I'd uttered them myself two months ago. The truth was, I spent more time with the boy than Alisha did. I had grown close to him in ways that words couldn't measure.

"So, it's not my business to get involved, that's what you're saying?"

"I hired you as a chaperone, not a social worker, is what I'm saying."

"What did Corey see his father do that was so traumatic? Did he witness the two of you having a bad fight?"

She said nothing, but I saw the surprise flash through her eyes. Her lips formed a tight purse.

"Did this man hurt you, physically? In front of your son?"

"That is none of your business, Simon. I told you to drop it."

"He hit you, didn't he? I'm willing to bet on it."

I was pushing the envelope now, for sure. But I didn't back down. For I had found a way through Alisha Caldwell's outer defenses. Earlier reproofs on her character had been parried like ping-pong balls bouncing playfully off of an armored tank. Now I had discovered her weakness, her kryptonite. I was partially amazed to see her lower lip trembling as she glowered up at me. I was even more amazed to see a tear squirt free from one eye. For a moment, she was too furious to even speak.

Then she rose slowly to her feet and leaned toward me, her arms propped on the table. I thought she was going to slap me.

Instead, she leaned closer and said in a thin voice, "What gives you the right to make such heavy-handed assumptions on my past, you arrogant ass?"

"Am I right?"

"Why don't you start minding your own business from now on?"

"Has it occurred to you I might be trying to help?"

"It's occurred to me that you're being nosy." She began gathering her materials into her arms.

"Look, all I'm saying—"

"It's occurred to me, Simon, that you ask too many damn questions."

She turned and strode away from me toward her office. I called out behind her, "I'm an aspiring lawyer; it's my job to ask questions."

She slammed the door shut, locking it behind her.

*   *   *

Alisha didn't speak to me for a week. The woman could hold a grudge, I'll give her that. What little we saw of one another was punctuated by imperceptible nods and awkward silences. I made several concerted efforts at making eye contact with her—if for no other reason than to break the ice a little—but she had a crafty, cunning way of brushing her silver hair over one shoulder and looking away at just the right moment. Her sullenness leeched into her interactions with her son, and this angered me.

One morning after having dropped Corey off at school, I walked into the house to find her sitting at the kitchen table with a mess of papers spread out in front of her. She was drinking coffee. She was still in her robe.

"Can I say something?" I hadn't taken my coat off yet.

She glanced at me momentarily before turning back to whatever she was working on. "You can say anything you like, Simon, but I can't guarantee I'll be listening."

"It would be unwise for you to allow your displeasure toward me to rub off on Corey. You didn't even give him a kiss this morning."

"I'll give him two this afternoon." She seemed to think about these words and began laughing. It was the first smile I'd seen on her face in some time, even if it was wry and humorless. "That sounds like something you would say, doesn't it?"

I ignored her bitterness. I shed my coat and hung it over the back of a chair. As I poured myself a cup of coffee, I asked, "How come you're not in your office, writing?"

"I'm on my way there, trust me. In the meantime, why don't you make like an insect and buzz off?" Apparently she found this funny also, because she began chuckling again.

Sipping my coffee, I asked, "Where am I supposed to go?"

"Don't you usually go off into the woods with your axe? Like Paul Bunyan?"

I was almost finished splitting the wood from the maple. What remained was a handful of thick pieces from the lower trunk section.

"I didn't hear you complaining about the fire I made the other night."

"The only thing missing was the marshmallows."

She got up and went into her office. I went outside and swung the axe.

Wednesday of that week, I was fifteen minutes late picking up Corey from school. No big deal, really. Children of tardy parents are ushered out to the playground behind the school, where they're allowed to cavort happily on the swings and jungle gym under supervision until their rides show up. Corey loved playing on the footbridge. I'd arrived late several times before to find him hanging onto the side ropes with both hands, lined up with other children on the quaking bridge, a smile spread across his face from ear to ear. I found him this time sitting on one of the steps leading down from the school's rear entrance. Both shoelaces were untied. He was trying unsuccessfully to tie them.

I knelt down in front of him. "You get sand in your shoes again?" I quickly tied them and stood up.

"Uh-huh."

"Let's go, come on. Sorry I'm late."

In the Saab, I helped him get his seatbelt clicked into place. I started the car. I looked at his face and noticed for the first time that his cheeks were flushed. His eyes were slightly red.

"Hey, what's wrong with your eyes?" I asked. "Have you been crying?"

He nodded. His lower lip was puckered out.

"Why? It's not because I was late, was it?"

He shook his head. "Tommy pushed me."

"Tommy … Another kid pushed you?"

Nodding again, the lower lip puckered out.

"Why did Tommy push you?"

He shrugged his shoulders. "He just pushed me down and told me to get out of his way."

"Is that how you got sand in your shoes?"

He nodded.

I didn't know who this Tommy was or what he looked like. So I pointed to the five or six children who still remained in the playground area and asked Corey, "Is Tommy still here?"

He shook his head. "His nanny came and got him."

"Did you tell the teacher that Tommy pushed you?"

Nodding. "She saw me crying and came over."

"Did she reprimand Tommy?"

He turned and looked at me. "What—what does that mean?"

"It means 'punish.' Did she punish Tommy?"

"She told, um, him not to do it anymore."

I got the car going. I turned onto County 513 heading south.

"Has Tommy ever pushed you before?" I asked.

"No. But he says mean things a lot."

"Like what?"

"He calls me 'dirtboy' sometimes."

I put my hand over my mouth to stifle a laugh. "Why does he call you that? You're not dirty at all."

"I don't know."

"Does Tommy pick on other kids, too? Or just you?"

"Mostly me."

"Why does he pick on you?"

He stuck his hands out. "I don't know."

The answer was obvious, though. The bullies always pick on the gentle ones because they know they can. It's almost a natural law. Corey was a quiet, meticulous, gentle child. He may as well have worn a bull's-eye on his back. I remember being in third grade, the first week of school. It was lunchtime, and we were all in the cafeteria when Carl Kevin decided to reach over my tray and overturn my milk onto my grilled cheese sandwich. He cawed in his oddly ass-like banter. Before the caw was three-fourths complete, I had turned and planted my fist into the side of his nose. His nose caved in, and a parachute of blood pattered the linoleum floor. Some of the blood landed on my arm. Carl Kevin wasn't cawing after that. He was bawling and covering his face. I had gotten in a lot of trouble for that. But Carl never laid a hand on me again.

I had pulled into the driveway and begun the switchback descent when Corey asked me, "Hey, are you … um, are you coming to the father-son breakfast?"

"The father-say-who?"

He giggled. "The father-son *breakfast.*"

"What's that again? The mother-daughter dinner?"

"The *father-son breakfast!*"

I tapped the side of my head as if trying to clear out my ear. "The cousin's in-laws literary lunch?"

"*Simon!*"

"Of course I'll be there," I said. "When is the father-son breakfast?"

"After New Year's."

"Sounds like fun. Can we go in our pajamas?"

"No!"

"Can I go standing on my head?"

"No!"

"Can we go dressed as—oh, shit."

We were halfway down the driveway when I saw Josef lying on his side. I dropped my foot on the brake pedal a little harder than I should have. Corey bounced forward in his seat. I forgot to step on the clutch. The Saab bucked and stalled.

Josef was lying in the barren flower patch off the left side of the driveway as the driveway jagged to the right. The metal spade was loosely clutched in one hand. One leg lay straight out beneath him, the other was bent slightly at the knee.

I opened my door. "Stay here, stay in the car," I told Corey. I got out and ran over to Josef's still body. I grabbed him by the shoulder and rolled him onto his back.

"Josef," I barked, "hey, can you—"

He looked up at me through half-slitted eyes. The pupils were large and unmoving. I grasped his hand and began squeezing; the meat of his palm was cold in the flesh of my own. I moved my finger to the top of his neck, feeling around underneath his chin for the barest inkling of a pulse. The skin there was cooling and beginning to stiffen.

"Shit." I knelt there in front of him for several minutes. Then I reached forward and lay a hand on his forehead. "I'm sorry, Josef. Shit, man, I'm sorry." I moved my hand slowly down his face, closing his eyes.

*   *   *

The United Methodist Church of Swan Lake was a boxlike structure with a steeple crudely affixed to the top of it. It had, in the 1800s, doubled as a schoolhouse. As the congregation had expanded proportional to the town's growing population, periodic renovations had rendered the church more of a rectangle than its original square—additions that became obvious with one glance at the siding.

The season's first snow flurries drifted lazily down from the soft gray pillow of sky as Josef Frustoff was laid to rest in the nearby cemetery. A green canvas tent had been erected above the gravesite to provide some semblance of shelter. A line of five folding chairs sat facing the casket. I had wondered earlier how many immediate family members might occupy those chairs when the time came. I was dismayed and saddened to recognize the answer was one: the lone widow sat slightly bent over in the middle chair. She was dressed in a black fur coat, black scarf, and top hat, with a black veil drawn over her face. She clutched a white rose in one hand.

I glanced around at the makeshift crowd. Perhaps two dozen people were in attendance. Molly from the Main Street Café was there. Richard Bryson, of Ferguson-Bryson-Caldwell Securities and Investments, was there with a woman of similar age, who I surmised was his wife. Bryson was a stoic figure who stood tall and still, the fingers of one hand nestled in the gray strands of his beard. I could almost see minute-by-minute stock prices blipping through his head. I didn't recognize any of the other attendees. Probably, they were people for whom Josef had worked over the years. I saw an older gentleman in a seersucker suit, impervious to the cold. He stood perfectly still in the falling snow, his hands planted deep in his pockets.

"When we reflect on the life lived by Mr. Frustoff," the white-haired priest recited, "we are reminded of the overall hardness of life. We are reminded of the many fruits to be reaped by hard labor and dedication. We are asked to consider the difficulties embraced by those hopefuls who leave everything behind and arrive with nothing more than determination and personal will. The Lord is my shepherd; I shall not want. He maketh me to lie down …"

I cast my eyes down the gently sloping cemetery, past some of the older tombstones. The hard ground was beginning to whiten. I glanced at the property just east of the church, trying to imagine wood swing sets and picnic tables and children playing.

Corey took hold of my right hand. He stood between his mother and me. Alisha had bundled him in so much clothing that his face was barely left exposed. I looked down at him and smiled. He swung my arm back and forth a little, growing restless. This was Corey's first funeral, of course. I would spend most of the ride home answering a barrage of questions. "What happens when we die?" "Why do they put the basket (meaning to say 'casket') underground?" "Does the stone grow where they bury the basket?"

The priest finished his psalm and took a moment to gaze at the small gathering. "I will now read from Romans."

I glanced over at Alisha. She wore a pinstriped suit and a heavy coat with a mink collar. Flakes of snow clung to her silver hair like garland, and her black eyelashes flickered up and down. Alisha had seemed more perturbed by the interruption caused by Josef's death than saddened by the relevant loss of a neighbor and dutiful employee. But it's hard to say, exactly. She was taciturn by nature, not given to discussing her emotions openly. Her writing was going badly, that much was certain. I had passed by her office door on several occasions during the week to find her sitting cross-legged in her chair, absently holding a cup of coffee while gazing through the windows at the lake beyond. Her computer screen was entirely blank on all of these occasions, save for the cursor blinking tirelessly in the upper left corner. It was hard to know what she was thinking in those moments, but her body language did not shed a positive light on the matter. She prepared dinners in an ornery silence. Her participation in mealtime conversation was limited to contrite, one-word responses and a burgeoning new phylum of shoulder shrugs. The only one of the three of us in a perpetually good mood was Corey, who was simply thrilled to have his mother home on a more regular basis.

I'd spoken with Dr. Andrews briefly on Thursday, per Alisha's request. The human Weeble-Wobble had been less than forthcoming in regards to his understanding of Corey's "issues." Though he did acquiesce as to his knowledge of Corey's "man in black," he made little effort to elaborate on his progress in dealing with it.

I heard muffled voices. I looked up and saw that people were moving. The graveside service was over, and the small crowd was starting to disperse.

I said to Alisha and Corey, "You two head on down. I'll catch up to you in a few minutes."

I made my way through the smattering of people, cutting toward the canvas tent. The snow was still falling, and the hard ground was becoming slippery in places. Josef's wife was being led away from the gravesite by the priest, who had one arm around her shoulders and was speaking to her in a low voice.

The priest let go of her to exchange some words with one of the funeral directors, and it was just the widow shuffling along by herself, clutching her purse with both hands, and tipping her head forward as if watching the ground.

I approached her pensively.

"Mrs. Frustoff?"

She raised her head to look at me through her veil. "Yes, dear?"

"I just wanted to say that … that your husband was a fine man."

"Thank you, dear. That's very sweet."

The voice was oddly familiar, with a rustic, antique quality one does not quickly forget.

The veil parted with one gloved hand, and Millie looked out at me with sore, solemn eyes. She regarded me closely for several moments, looking me up and down. "Thank you for coming, dear. I do appreciate it."

Then she was shuffling past me, moving slowly down the sloping cemetery toward the church. I stood and watched for several minutes as her diminishing form moved away from me in the falling snow.

CHAPTER FOURTEEN

SMOOT

I ANSWERED THE DOOR wearing an old pair of sweatpants and a thinning, tie-dye T-shirt. The man standing on the porch stoop wore a crisp white suit and a white Stetson. The half loop of a gold chain hung from a breast pocket. His brown mustache was neatly trimmed to fine perfect points at both ends. He was clean-cut and redolent of aftershave. I thought he looked like a banker out of some fifties' Western movie.

It was a dreary though mild day for this time of year, which explained why he wasn't wearing an overcoat. I cracked open the storm door and asked him, "Are you looking for the O. K. Corral? It's the next street over."

"My name is Norman Smoot." His voice had a dry Nebraskan timbre. "I'm a processor with First Equity Savings. I'd appreciate if I could speak with your mother."

"She's not home today," I told Smoot. "In fact, she'll be out of town until tomorrow."

His brown eyes sized me up for several moments. The clarity and directness of those eyes told me that he knew I was lying. "How about an older sibling, then?"

"Nope, they're outta town together." It was partly true, figuratively speaking. Ma was passed out in the back sewing room, and Catherine was upstairs getting thinner. Either way, neither would be making an appearance. "Is there something I can help you with?"

Smoot tipped his head forward briefly, as if glancing down at his shoes. I saw the top of his Stetson for a moment. He looked up again, made a half turn as if to leave, then hesitated. He turned back to me and said, "Perhaps you and I could have a talk. You mind if I come in?"

My first instinct was to shut the door in his face. Talking to strangers was a bad thing, and letting them in your house was worse. But the sagacity in Smoot's eyes suggested that closing the door on him would be imprudent.

"I can't let you in, no. But I'll come out, if that's all right."

He nodded, signifying that this was fine. I grabbed a jacket hanging from one of the gold coat hooks to the right of the door and stepped out onto the side stoop.

"Have a seat, young fellow," Smoot said. We sat down next to each other, him on the left, me on the right. For a minute or so, neither of us spoke. The resulting silence should have been awkward, but somehow it wasn't. Somehow, the silence more closely resembled the day: *dreary*. It was gray, uncharacteristically warm, and damp. The yard, unkempt in places, was blotted with wet leaves of yellow and brown. I glanced over at the Roadgrader, a hulking pile of metal in the stone driveway. The chrome barbecue grill with the plastic hotdog and hamburger patty, the one Mr. Van Ness had brought over a few years ago, had come loose and fallen off a few weeks back. There was a crack in the windshield. The tailpipe was strung fast to the chasse with a strand of wire.

Smoot asked me, "What's your name?"

"Simon."

"How come you're not in school today, Simon?"

"Had a headache." In truth, I'd stayed home because I hadn't felt like getting out of bed. Running the muntins had become a burdensome task, and sleep was getting hard to come by. Staying in bed because you felt like there were anchors strapped to your feet was starting to seem like a passable excuse for cutting school on a Monday morning. Who was gonna make me go, anyway? Who was going to kick my ass into gear in this house? *Hate to say it, pal, but you're straying down Catherine's path. Aren't you?*

I was shocked to discover that this sudden awareness, this self-realization, utterly terrified me. It scared me to such intimate depths that for a moment I physically shuddered. Both Ma and Cath had set down their swords, opting instead for the bottle and the ease of darkness. What might happen were I to toss aside *my* sword? Was my life an every-man-for-himself contest, or was it still a team sport? If it was still a team sport, at what point did you jump ship to avoid going down with the crew?

I should have closed the door on Smoot and gone back to bed. The Path of Cath was easier. *So much* easier.

"Mind if I smoke?" Smoot asked.

"I'd prefer you didn't."

He produced a pack of Winston Lights and shook one out, lighting up anyway. "I was sorry to hear about your father."

I said nothing. I watched him puff smoke for a while.

"We've been trying to call, you know. Can't get through. A recording comes on and says the line's been disconnected."

"That's what happens when you don't pay your phone bill, I guess."

Smoot stuck his hand inside his suit and withdrew a batch of letters bound by a thin rubber band. He held them out to me.

I took them. "What're these?"

"Certified letters. Half a dozen of them, sent by our office."

I noticed the green sticker with the black bar code on it curling over the top of each letter. The address was the same on each one: Ms. Carol Ann Kozlowski, 16 Williams Way, Lake Hiawatha, NJ 07843.

I said, "How come these weren't deliv—"

"Your mail carrier *tried* to deliver them. Five of the letters were scanned as 'attempted.' The other was scanned as 'refused.'" Smoot paused, tapping the ash off the end of his cigarette. "We sent some letters by regular mail, to circumvent the need for a signature. But we've received no return contact."

"My mother … hasn't been opening the mail lately," I said. The drift of unopened letters on the dining room table had begun spilling onto the floor, actually.

Smoot nodded, as if this was a fact he'd already known.

He remained quiet for a while, which unnerved me. I asked, "What company did you say you were from?"

"First Equity Savings. Your mortgage company. Your mother

hasn't made a payment in five months, Simon. We've begun foreclosure proceedings."

I shook my head. I was looking directly at the side of Smoot's face. Smoot was gazing straight ahead.

"I don't know what that ... What does that mean, exactly?"

He tamped out his cigarette on the porch step and flicked away the butt. "It means the bank is repossessing your house."

I was shaking my head again. "No, we—we *own* the house, Mr. Smoot. We've lived here for over twenty years. My parents, see, they bought the house before Catherine was born, and—"

"They've never owned it free and clear," Smoot cut in. "In the past twelve years, your parents have taken out second and third mortgages against the house."

"What's that mean?"

"It means they've borrowed a lot of money. Now, taking into account the equity your folks have garnered over the years along with appreciation, factored against second and third mortgages and the remaining balance on the original loan ... we figure we're looking at a fifty-fifty."

"A what?"

"Fifty-fifty mortgage-to-equity ratio. Those are good numbers—favorable numbers—from a bank's standpoint. We'll be able to flip the house rather easily."

"Flip?"

"Sell. Probably in a public auction."

"You're gonna auction off our house?"

"That's correct."

My mouth had gone dry. A nauseous, empty sensation had furrowed into the pit of my stomach—like the feeling you get when the roller coaster you're riding is about to enter a series of upside-down loops.

"Wh—where are we gonna live?"

"You're gonna be homeless, son." He spoke with the easy candor of a TV newsperson forecasting the weather. The gravity of his words didn't seem to bother him at all, maybe because he'd uttered them many times before, or because it just came with the territory, or because it's the way of the world, son—the zebra eats grass, lion eats zebra, death, taxes, Darwinism, and magnetic north … maybe because *it was just his job.*

I fought for balance, struggled for the mental clarity necessary to see my way out of this.

"If … it's … How can …" *Focus, Simon. You must focus now.* I squeezed my eyes shut and bit down. It was hard. It may have been the hardest thing.

"How much … do we owe, Mr. Smoot?"

"A lot."

"How *much?*"

"With interest and late fees … I'd say about fifty-four hundred."

It hit me like a medicine ball in the chest. "You're saying … over five *thousand.*"

"Yes."

I sat in shock, numbed by what seemed an astronomical sum of cash. Fifty-four hundred. Five thousand, four hundred. A thousand dollars multiplied by five, with another four hundred on top of it. It seemed fictional to me, that any one person could possess that amount of money all at one time.

"I have two hundred and fifty dollars in a savings account," I said. "I could give that to you. There's probably another fifteen or twenty bucks rolling around my bedroom. And I work part-time at the hotdog place out on Forty-Six, so …"

Smoot chuckled wholesomely. "You're about fifty-one hundred short, son."

"My name is Simon. Look, Mr. Smoot, how much time do we have? If I came up with the money—"

"You have to understand, Simon, that this isn't like going downtown to pay for a parking ticket. A foreclosure is an involved process, with a lot of weight behind it. Once the ball gets rolling on this sort of thing, it usually stays rolling."

"How much time?"

He fell silent for a moment, looking down and shaking his head. "It's awfully late, Simon. We began lis pendens—the first step in the New Jersey foreclosure process—about six weeks ago. By law, we're required to make you, the homeowner, aware of that … and certainly, we did everything in our power to do so. Because we never heard back from you, your case is now considered what's known as an 'uncontested foreclosure,' a status that tends to speed up the overall process. At this point, I'd say you have about two weeks, certainly no more than three, before the process moves into 'final judgment,' at which point the court system takes over."

"I'll have the money, Mr. Smoot."

Smoot favored me with an indulgent look. The wan caricature of a smile played at the corners of his lips, below the points of his mustache. His brown eyes said to me, *You're noble, kid, and maybe even a little brave. But let's get real, shall we?*

"I'll talk to Ma, I'm sure she has money tucked away somewhere. We'll get this straightened out, I promise. If you could just talk to the bank people a little, maybe stall for some time, let them know we're working on it ..."

"Look, son ..." Smoot carefully removed his hat and set it upside-down on his lap. "I'm afraid you aren't grasping the complete and true picture here."

"What do you mean?"

"What I mean is that you have other debts to consider. Your quarterly property taxes are more than a month overdue. That's another nine hundred dollars, not including late fees. And we've downloaded your mother's credit report. She has fourteen active credit cards. They account for fifty-one thousand dollars of credit debt. It's my guess that your mother has been taking cash advances against those cards, probably to buy food and other essentials. Some of the interest rates on those cash advances are upwards of 24 percent." He paused, watching me carefully. Probably watching the color draining out of my face. He delivered the fatal blow. "In addition to losing the house, your mother will most likely have to declare bankruptcy. I'm sorry to have to say all this, but ... well, these are just the facts of life."

My mouth fell open. Nothing came out. I didn't know you had to pay taxes for your property. I didn't know what a cash advance against a credit card really was. I didn't know what 24 percent interest really meant, either. But I knew it wasn't good. I knew we were in a lot of trouble. I knew we were in the storm now, into the full-blown smack-dab wind-in-your-face lights-out Category 5 whistling fray of the storm. I was turned around in it; we'd all somehow gotten turned around in it. I remembered the hatred pulsing through my veins like black crude: enmity toward Ma and Cath—toward each of them as individuals but also toward their relationship with one another. Their weaknesses had helped put us here. I thought, too, of my father, wishing desperately he were here … and remembering the spit bugs and thinking there was some lesson lost of that special day, something I'd overlooked or forgotten.

"My Ma … lost her license."

Smoot, nodding. "I know."

"My Ma has a drinking problem."

"I've seen it happen." He put the Stetson back on his head. "America is a great place to live, son. Don't lose sight of that. It's the greatest country God ever gave man … if you pay your bills."

He rose to his feet. "Well, it was nice to speak to a live voice. I'll leave you my card." He produced a business card and laid it on the porch next to me. "You'll be hearing from us. Good day."

He started toward the road, where his Infiniti was parked.

"I'm going to hold you to your word, Mr. Smoot."

He turned toward me. "Beg pardon?"

"Your two-week deadline. I'm holding you to it." A pause. "I'll have the money."

He tipped his cap and left.

And where, may I ask, are you going to come up with fifty-four hundred dollars? Sixty-four, actually, if you include the property tax?

The truth was, I didn't know.

I had no idea.

CHAPTER FIFTEEN

CHRISTMAS

I WOKE FROM A sound sleep. The room seemed to spin in dark circles around me. At first, I wasn't sure where I was. Imposed on the ceiling was the wedge work of dark bars swimming in a sickly pale light ... surely, this was my bedroom in Lake Hiawatha, where I could run the muntins until hell froze over if I wanted. Slowly, the room's features came into focus, and I realized it was the light of the half moon reflecting off the frozen lake that I was seeing.

I had been having a dream, however, in which I *was* in the Lake Hiawatha house. Norman Smoot had been moving idly through the rooms on the first floor, calmly knocking things over. I trailed behind, telling him to stop that, it was impolite to go walking through someone's house upending the furniture. He'd ignored me. He'd adjusted his white Stetson and then lit up a cigarette. I told him not to smoke in here, that it was rude to smoke in another person's house without consent. He pushed over a pole lamp and replied, *Bank's house now, son. We're gonna flip the place. Flipping is what we do.* He'd gone on flipping things over. The television (the screen exploded), an end table, a reclining chair. I'd pleaded with him to stop. To which Smoot had replied, *Greatest country God ever gave man, son ... if you pay your bills.*

I sat up in bed, turning to check the clock on the nightstand. It was 1:55 in the morning. Something had awakened me. I tried telling myself it was the dream that had done it, but I knew this wasn't the case.

I had heard movement elsewhere in the house.

Go back to sleep, Simon. What you heard was Smoot knocking things over, and those noises were in your head.

I almost believed it, too. I lay halfway down again when another voice queried, *What if it's Corey? What if he's sleepwalking again?*

I tossed aside the sheets. Tiptoeing across the room was something I'd gotten quite good at. The wood floor of the hall was cold against my feet. I paused, listening to the air ducts clicking in the walls and ceiling, and hearing the hum of the kitchen fridge. Then I ducked into Corey's room, expecting to find the sheets cast aside and a little boy's impression carved into the mattress, minus the boy. But he was there, all right. He slept on his side, his mouth partly open, his thumb on the pillow. I leaned in close, listening for his breath. His breathing was so shallow that there was nothing to hear. I leaned closer yet, gently caressing his temple and planting a delicate kiss there. I adjusted the sheets, pulling them over his small shoulders so—

A floorboard creaked above me. A drawer slid open, then banged shut with a dull *thud*. This was followed by footfalls above the ceiling. I *had* heard a noise, and here was its source.

In the hall again, instead of turning right to re-enter my room, I made a left. I passed the kitchen and descended the single stair into the dining room and den area. *You shouldn't be moving in this direction*, a voice admonished. *There's no business for you in this direction.* I supposed that was true. In fact, I *knew* it was true, even as I placed my bare foot onto the lowermost riser of the spiral stairs. I started up, my right hand gliding smoothly over the wood railing. The air temperature climbed about five degrees, owing to the rising nature of warm air.

My bare feet found carpeting at the top. This made for softer walking. I passed the reading parlor to my left and started up the hall path. Two steps into the hall, I stopped.

Go back, Simon. You shouldn't be up here.

I turned around to retrace my steps, and that's when I heard her voice. I froze once more, my head cocked to one side, listening. Alisha was speaking—to whom I had no idea, and at this hour I couldn't wager a guess. Was she on the phone, then? Or was someone else in the room with her? Inexorably, I moved forward, advancing in such small degrees that I hardly knew I was moving. I couldn't decipher what Alisha was saying. Her words were somehow unintelligible, as though she was conversing in a different language.

Turn back, Simon. Please heed this warning and turn back, for you don't want to know what it is she's saying, you have no business knowing, you have no recourse but to—

But to listen. Because suddenly I was outside the door of the master bedroom, and I was gently pressing my ear against it, and now I heard. The language in which she spoke was universal. The words were warbled and unintelligible because there were no words. There were no words because she was crying. Alisha was crying. Sobbing, actually, and doing her best to keep it to herself. I experienced one of those astute mental images to which I'm occasionally prone, one in which she sat on the edge of her bed, her head tipped forward, her hands in her lap. What on God's good earth could cause a grown woman, who, upon first glance, had everything you could ever want out of life, to sob so miserably at two o'clock in the morning in a house the likes of which most would never have, overlooking a lake the likes of which most would never see? Did it have something to do with her writing? Possibly, but I was slowly coming to believe that her sadness was more subversive and pervasive than just that.

And you weren't brought here to fix it. Ma's voice. *Don't allow her problems to become your problems. Remember, Simon, why it is you're here.*

And maybe that was just it. Maybe I had forgotten why I was there.

I reached out and grasped the doorknob. The inner workings of the lock mechanism belched out a metallic *clack* that was far louder than it should have been. The noise startled me, and I fell still. From the other side of the door, the crying abruptly stopped. I waited, my pulse thumping in my ears like kettledrums. She'd heard. Or, she at least *thought* she'd heard. I saw her once more in my mind's eye: still on the edge of the bed, but no longer looking down; head turned to one side now, staring at the door and concentrating upon it … wondering if perhaps she'd heard something after all.

I let go of the knob, then tiptoed the rest of the way down the hall. It was a distance of only ten or twelve feet, but it felt a lot longer. Here the hall jagged to the left, forming a corner, before jagging straight ahead once more en route to the laundry room. No sooner had I reached the corner, standing behind it with my back against the wall, did I hear the bedroom door click softly open behind me. I stood perfectly still. I even held my breath. *What are you gonna say if she finds you here? That you were coming up to fold some linens?*

Moments later, the door clicked shut again. Still I waited. I slid slowly down the wall, dropping into a squat … and ultimately a sitting position with my back still against the wall. The back of my head barely touched the chair rail.

Ten minutes went by. Fifteen. Twenty. I felt my eyes beginning to fall shut. Only then did I push myself up. I crept down the spiral stairs and climbed back into bed.

*   *   *

The days leading up to Christmas were tumultuous ones for me, and exciting ones for Corey. His winsome blue eyes constantly glimmered in anticipation of Santa's coming. I fielded fifty questions a day concerning sleighs, reindeer, and route maps originating from the North Pole. To each question, I provided a creative answer. I was careful to ensure that none of my responses completely absolved the mystery, for it is the mystery that gives life to the magic. It was the enduring facet of the unknown that kept Corey's round, curious face steeped in wonder—that kept his large eyes shining with the deep complexity of possibilities. It reminded me in a true sense of the day my Ma had told me the truth about Santa Claus, and how saddened I'd been. When I looked into the mirror of my sadness that long ago day, it was Corey's fervor I saw reflected there.

Shopping proved to be a tricky matter. Naturally, I had to do my shopping for Corey and Alisha during times in which I was alone— primarily in the mornings while Corey was in school. Main Street had become a decorous avenue of evergreen boughs and red ribbons and oversized wreaths. The shops were busy, the sidewalks were crowded, and buoyant spirits prevailed. There was much talk about the season's first significant snowfall, which was slated to arrive late Christmas Day or the morning after. "It's gonna be a whopper," Molly

Kerrigan told me one morning when I was in the café having a cup of coffee and a muffin. "That is, if it hits us the way they're saying it's gonna hit us. But we might have a white Christmas, after all."

I wasn't sure who I trusted more—Molly or the National Weather Service. But to be safe, I made a run over to Walt's Hardware on Elm Street, where I picked up two kerosene heaters. I purchased a can of kerosene at a local gas station.

Corey and I spent much of that afternoon—and several afternoons thereafter—prancing around Merchant's Square, passing in and out of shops and stores. This was Corey's first true experience shopping for another person, and one that proved intriguing for both of us.

"Doesn't Santa bring all the presents?" he asked me one afternoon. We were sidling slowly up the sidewalk, weaving in and out of oncoming shoppers.

"Well, yes," I answered, "he does bring a lot of the presents. But not all of them. We also give presents to each other. That's what Christmas is partly about: giving."

"So, what should I get for my mom?"

"Well, that's the fun part. You have to pick some things out that you think she'll like."

I allowed Corey to select which shops he wanted to browse through. I was making a concerted effort not to steer him too much in any one direction. "Can we go in this one, Simon? And then, over there, in that one?"

"Sure."

I did have to exert some guidance, though, when it came down to choosing certain items. Corey had a propensity to gravitate toward the candy racks in the stores in which candy could be bought. He would run his eyes, and sometimes his hands, up and down and back and forth past all of the offerings. I did my best to suppress a smile.

"Do you think your mom is going to want a Milky Way for Christmas?"

He seemed not to hear. I reiterated the point, "Corey, who are you shopping for? Are you shopping for yourself or for your mom?"

"Okay, *okay.*"

We wandered into the Five & Ten on East Street, where all sorts of items could be bought at low prices. Again, I had to divert Corey from the candy aisle. "Let's go this way," I said.

The aisles were narrow. The shelves were packed with so many items that it would take hours to peruse them all. Another factor that came into play: Corey tended not to see things above eye level. For someone who was three and a half feet tall at best, this amounted to half of the store's merchandise passing beyond notice.

"Hey, don't forget to look up. There are a lot of things above your head in this place."

In the back corner of the store were some hardware and practical odds and ends. Corey was standing in front of the mousetraps. He reached forward with one hand and removed from a wall hook a double pack of Victor kill traps. He made a half turn, holding the traps up to me, awaiting my appraisal. His round white face was a landscape of pure innocence, and I had to try hard not to laugh.

"Mousetraps? What makes you think your mom is gonna want mousetraps?"

I saw his face working. Licking his lips as he attempted to crystallize his thoughts into words. "Um, it's, she can …"

"Yes?"

"She … my mom doesn't like mouses, Simon. Really, she doesn't."

"Mice," I corrected. "If it's more than one mouse, we call them *mice.*"

I advised him to at least check out the rest of the store first. Reluctantly, he put the traps back on the hook.

We made our way slowly up the center aisle, approaching the front of the store. I let Corey walk in front of me. We wandered into the pet supply section. He reached out again, taking hold of a thick rawhide bone shrink-wrapped in plastic. He turned it in both hands to better see all sides of it. I suffered one of my absurd mental images: Alisha down on all fours, forearms and elbows touching the floor, hair hanging in front of her face as she held the bone in her teeth, shaking her head back and forth so that her hair flew in a squalor. This time I *did* start laughing. I had to cup my palm over my mouth to stifle the noise.

"Wh—what's so funny, Simon?"

Those perfectly innocent blue eyes made me laugh harder, however. "Oh, God, you're killing me, kid, you know that?"

We got out of the Five & Ten.

The Town Pharmacy netted a bit more success. First Corey chose a set of colored, plastic barrettes that he thought his mother might like. They may have been the most gauche things I'd ever seen, designed more for girls ages five through nine. Alisha wouldn't be caught dead wearing them on her worst day, but I relented on this one. It was a start—and an indicator, in the very least, that Corey was at last beginning to see the world through the eyes of another. Elsewhere in the same store, we encountered a turnstile of paperback novels. Corey marveled at the way in which the stile turned from the mere weight of his hand.

"Can I … can I get my mom a book?"

"Absolutely. Books make wonderful gifts."

He couldn't read any of the titles, of course. He plucked a Linda Fairstein novel from its cradle and began leafing through it.

"How come there are no pictures?" he asked.

"Because big people don't need pictures. Words make the pictures appear in your head."

"How?"

"You'll understand in a year or so, when you begin to learn how to read."

He picked out four books.

At the counter, the young lady working the register rang up the total sale for the books and the barrettes. It came to $34.79. I gave Corey a twenty, a ten, and a five out of my wallet. "Now give that to the lady."

He did. The lady gave him twenty-one cents.

"That's your change," I told him. "Put that in your pocket."

I noticed he was pointing at something down by his knees. I took a step back from the counter to see what it was, and there were the candy bars. Corey started hopping up and down.

"Who are you shopping for? Your mom or yourself? Tell me the truth."

"Me," he said, still hopping. "Me, me, me."

I smiled. "All right. Because you've been pretty good today, you can pick one out."

"Yippee!" he cried, and clapped his hands.

He chose a pack of Rolos. I paid for them, and we left the store.

⋆   ⋆   ⋆

"Where do you normally stand your Christmas tree?"

"Last year, we had it right in that area." Alisha pointed into the corner between the spiral stairs and the dining room table. "We'll have to slide the table about four feet to the right."

"Let's do it," I said.

She was holding a cup of coffee in one hand. She wore a pencil tucked behind one ear. She had been passing in and out of her office most of the morning. It was Christmas Eve, and she seemed determined to get some solid work done before the holiday commenced. Personally, I was wishing she'd hang it up for a few days and start acting merry. Yesterday, I'd gotten under her skin a little bit. She'd gone into the kitchen to refill her coffee mug, and I began chattering away. She appeared not to listen. She stirred her coffee, then tossed the spoon in the sink and walked away. Well, I don't like to be ignored, so I followed her through the den, talking as I went.

"How's the new project coming? You seem to be spending more time out here than in there. Hey, listen, if the new book's not working out, I've got a great idea for a sequel to *Gods of Komodo*. It's called *Babes of Tasmania*. What happens is—"

She closed her office door in my face.

Now, she reluctantly set her mug onto the coffee table, then came around the sofa to help me. We carefully slid the dining room table toward the kitchen, creating an ample-sized area in which a tree could stand, surrounded by a hemisphere of gifts.

"That'll work," I said. "What I'll do is lay a suitcase on its side, then throw a white sheet on top of it. We can stand the tree on the suitcase."

"Where do you plan on getting a tree?" Alisha asked.

"I've already got one."

"From where?"

"Your backyard. You've only got about twelve acres of trees to choose from."

By mid-afternoon, I had the tree erected, firmly ensconced in its metal stand and held up with several strands of fishing line. Corey was visibly excited, and I could see that he wanted to run laps around it.

"No, you can't go behind it," I told him. "There isn't enough room. Go do laps around the sofa."

Alisha, who had finally given up writing for the day, was carefully making her way down the spiral steps, her arms laden with boxes. She simultaneously had dinner going in the kitchen.

"Okay … in this box are the lights. And most of the ornaments are in these two boxes. I'm gonna have to make one more trip up to the attic. Corey, you have to settle down, or you'll never get to sleep tonight."

I settled him down by soliciting his help in decorating the tree. We got the lights wrapped around the tree first, and plugged them in to test them. They worked fine. We spent the remainder of the afternoon carefully hanging ornaments and candy canes. Then we strung the tinsel. Lastly, I stood on a chair, making myself as tall as possible, and placed the Christmas star at the very top of the tree.

"How's it look from down there?"

"Good!" Corey exclaimed.

We sat down for an early five o'clock dinner, which began with a delicate cream of mushroom soup. Corey said he didn't like mushrooms. He raised a spoonful of the soup to his nose to sniff it. "Yuck," he said, dropping the spoon back into the bowl. "Yucky. Yucky, Mommy."

I passed my napkin over my mouth to conceal my smile. Alisha told her son curtly, "If you don't like it, Corey, you'll sit with your hands in your lap until the rest of us have finished."

He did as told, at least for the first several minutes. Then he began to grow restless. "Mom, can I have a hotdog?"

"No, you may not."

His shoulders slumped.

I said, "You know, I've heard it mentioned that Santa always brings a few extra presents for kids who eat all of their dinner."

His eyes lit up and he reached for his spoon once more. He took half a spoonful of soup into his mouth, then quickly leaned forward and spat it back into the bowl.

"Oh, Corey, that's gross," Alisha bemoaned.

"Yucky. Yucky, yucky."

Dinner was a roast duck, fresh broccoli, and seasoned mashed potatoes. All of it was exquisite, and succulently prepared. Corey, though, wouldn't touch the broccoli, and didn't much care for the duck, either.

"Mom, can I have some french fries?"

"No."

I chuckled. "Looks like you're gonna be a hungry boy tonight."

Alisha and I indulged in a Cognac after the meal was finished, and Corey had a chocolate milk. Then we got ready for church. I dressed in a pair of white pressed pants and a wool sweater. Alisha insisted that Corey wear his jacket and tie. It may have been the smallest jacket and tie I had ever seen, and Corey looked absolutely adorable wearing it.

We attended the seven o'clock service at the Methodist church, where services for Josef Frustoff had been held only a few weeks ago. The church was packed to the gills. Many ended up standing in the back, and some along the aisles. It was warm and stuffy in there, and the service seemed to go on forever. Getting Corey to keep still, let alone quiet, was a hardship. He sat between his mother and me, and a part of him was constantly moving. Four or five times, he looked over at me and whispered, "Is it almost over, Simon?"

"Almost," I whispered back. I craned my head around several times, hoping to locate Millie Frustoff. Josef's Tacoma pickup was still parked at the bottom of our driveway, and I'd been considering making an offer for it. I couldn't find Millie anywhere in the congregation. Perhaps it was the nine o'clock service she planned to attend. After the service had ended and the people were filing out the doors into the cold night, I made repeated attempts to find her. I had Corey latched onto me with one hand at all times while Alisha made small talk with a handful of townsfolk. A lot of people were conversing about the coming storm, which had been pushed back to the day after Christmas, but had been upgraded to blizzard potential. There were a great many faces to look at, and I spoke to a lot of people myself, but Millie Frustoff was not among them.

*   *   *

Naturally, Corey did not want to go to bed that night. But he eventually recognized that the sooner he got to sleep, the sooner Christmas would arrive. So we hung our stockings around the fireplace and then set out a plate of cookies and a glass of milk for Santa. Corey got into his Superman pajamas and jumped into bed. Alisha read him his story, kissed him, and tucked him in. But before she clicked his light off, he insisted on telling me something first. Alisha summoned me, and I waltzed into his room, taking a seat on the edge of his bed.

"What is it, sport?"

He licked his lips like he normally did when he was working to articulate a particular thought. "Um … you … um … Make sure that … that you don't, um … put a fire in tonight, okay?"

"In the fireplace, you mean."

"Yeah."

"Oh, I see. So Santa can get down the chimney, right?"

He nodded. "Mm-mmm."

"No problem. I'll make sure Santa has a nice clear path to work with. All right?"

He nodded.

I pinched his cheek. "Now get some sleep, kiddo." I gave him a light kiss on the forehead.

He rolled onto his side and squeezed his eyes so forcibly shut that his cheeks wrinkled. Alisha and I shared a smile before clicking off the light and leaving the room.

An hour later, I went into his room to check on him. He was sound asleep. Alisha and I started bringing out the gifts and putting them under the tree. It was good fun, actually. She switched on the radio, keeping the volume low enough that it wouldn't wake Corey but loud enough for us to enjoy. She poured us each a glass of port, and we went to work, transforming the den into a Christmas wonderland and a Santa Claus crime scene. I ate half of the cookies and drank all of the milk. Alisha stuffed the stockings with so many chocolates and miniature gifts that the red and white fabric bulged at the seams. She lugged load after load of wrapped boxes up from the basement, placing them strategically around the tree. Several of these were so large and unwieldy that I had to help her.

"What in the name of Solomon is in these?" I asked. I heard moving parts rolling around every time we turned a corner.

"Four of the boxes actually go together," she replied. "You'll have lots of fun assembling it."

"I can't wait."

It took us until 11:45 to get the den set up for Christmas morning. Alisha was on her third glass of wine and was starting to get giggly. I was exhausted, utterly wiped out. We stood admiring the tree and the drift of gifts piled around and underneath, holding our wineglasses, and surveying the room at large.

I asked her, "What were Christmases like for you as a child?"

She gave it a moment's thought. "Spartan. And you?"

"My sister and I never got cheated."

"I'm happy that you're with us, Simon. I mean it. You've brought Corey so much joy, and it does mean a lot to me. I recognize that I can be tough to get along with at times, but you seem to handle it with grace."

"Well … I'm happy to be here."

"Merry Christmas, Simon," Alisha said, leaning over and planting a kiss on my right cheek. She passed in front of me and started up the spiral stairs.

I called behind her, "We get to sleep late tomorrow, don't we?"

She laughed. "I wouldn't count on it."

I turned off all the lights and then went to my room. I gently closed the door and switched off the lamp. At the window, I peered through bare-limbed trees across the blotchy ice of the lake below. The moonlight was little, and the starlight was less. In the middle of the three houses along the far shore of the lake, there burned what appeared to be a lantern or some form of low-wattage lamp. I had the distinct, somehow ineluctable sense that Millie was awake over there. Alert, and perhaps watching from a porch window. I wondered what she might be doing at this late hour, and what she might be thinking.

*   *   *

Corey was on top of me. He had me by the shoulders and was shaking me awake.

"Simon, get up!" he spoke in a fierce whisper. "Get up, Simon, come on, get up!"

And I had only just fallen asleep moments ago. But daylight streamed through the windows as I cracked open my eyes. Not the harsh brightness of high noon, but the stillness of dawn. I reached for the clock and saw that it was almost 7:30.

"Oh, Corey," I moaned. "It's too early."

He began shaking me again, pushing and pulling on my one shoulder the way a shipman would work an oar. "Get up, Simon, it's Christmas."

I listened for general household noises and heard none.

"Is your mom awake?" I asked.

"No, but Santa was here, Simon! He was here last night! He brought lots of presents!"

I told him I wasn't getting out of bed unless his mother did so first. He climbed off the bed and ran out of the room. I heard his small feet thumping up the spiral stairs. Moments later, the footfalls were above my head. I rolled onto my side, sliding gently into sleep's warm embrace once more. It didn't last long. Minutes later, Corey was rowing my shoulder again.

"Simon … hey, Simon …"

I moaned.

"Mom says that … She said she'll come down if you get up and make coffee."

"*What?*"

"She wants you to make coffee … Come on, Simon, get up already."

I mumbled through heavy lips, "You tell that mom of yours that I'm not getting up until I smell bacon and eggs cooking."

"*Ohhh.*" I heard his feet go thumping up the stairs once more.

Moments later, he was on my bed again. "Hey, Simon … Mom says she wants you to bring coffee up to her now."

"Tell her I want eggs Benedict."

He trotted out of the room … and back into the room. He was starting to breathe heavily from all the running. "Mom … says that you're full of shit. Isn't that a bad word?"

"Tell her she's a female dog."

"What's that mean?"

"She'll understand."

He came back, huffing and puffing. "She says … that you're … an il-legit-imant child."

This went on for several more rounds, and because it was starting to get ugly and since I was wide awake anyway, I decided to finally get up. Corey and I went up the spiral stairs together and into the master bedroom, where I picked him up and tossed him onto his mother's bed, on top of her. She issued a startled, "Oh!" and then began giggling.

Corey was shaking her. "Come on, Mom! Come downstairs!"

"All right, I'm up … I'm up." She looked at her son and smiled. "Did Santa come?"

"Yeah! He was here, Mom! He left lots and lots of presents!"

We ate a rich, hearty breakfast, the three of us. We switched on the kitchen radio. A local station played nonstop Christmas carols. Alisha and I drank strong coffee while Corey drank orange juice. Finally, we sauntered into the den, a jovial Corey Caldwell leading the way. He jumped and pointed and exclaimed and smiled all at once.

Alisha gestured to the empty milk glass and the plate of mostly-eaten cookies. "Corey, look. Santa must be a real pig."

We spent the rest of the morning exchanging and opening gifts. There were many smiles and much laughter. It was by all means a joyous and celebratory occasion. Corey ripped wrapping paper right and left, beaming with excitement. "Whoa!" he would say, in awe of a new gift. Or: "Oh, yeah!" I gave him a lot of small things, but my big gift to him was a brand-new Flying Horseman runner sled. His eyes lit up like neon. "Oh, man! Look, Mom! A sled! *Simon got me a sled!*"

"Wow. Another way for the two of you to get killed together."

I told Corey, "After the snowstorm, we're gonna go sledding down the driveway."

"Yeah! Down the driveway! *Yeah!*"

I had also gotten him a small, handheld compass. It had been an impulse gift, actually. I'd seen it a week or so ago while shopping for his mother.

"What is it?" he wanted to know.

"Oh, Corey, it's a compass," Alisha realized. She came over and tried to explain to him how it worked. "See, you can hold it in your hand, and it will tell you which direction you're moving. It tells you which way is north, south, east, and west. See, watch the needle ..."

My gifts to Alisha were small and mostly basic. It wasn't easy shopping for a woman who already had everything she needed and wanted, not to mention a woman who also happened to be your employer. I gave her a French press for her downtown office, along with some flavored coffees. These had been exorbitantly priced, which, I hoped, would later be reflected in the flavor. I had found several vintage wines that I knew she liked. A thick thesaurus, laden with synonyms that she could use in her writing. An ancient, leather-bound dictionary of poetical quotations, featuring selections from British and American poets, published in 1849. And a signed copy of Benchley's *The Girl of the Sea of Cortez*, which I had found in a used bookstore down in Smithfield.

Alisha gave me a pair of suits, each with a matching set of shoes. She gave me four ties, along with a small pamphlet on how to tie them. "Very funny," I ceded, to which she smiled brightly. She also gave me a leather briefcase, replete with a combo-dial lock mechanism.

I said, "It's all very nice. All I need to do now is get into law school."

"That part is up to you."

She also gave me a full-body Carhartt snowsuit. Along with a wool hat, neck warmer, and fleece gloves. "So, you'll be ready for your sledding expedition."

"Thank you," I said upon opening each item.

Alisha smiled when she opened the barrettes Corey had given her. "Oh, how sweet ... Thank you, Corey." She gave him a hug. She ripped open the bag, removed two red barrettes, and used them to tie her hair back. "How do I look?"

"Really good, Mom!"

"Like Dorothy running to catch the tornado," I mumbled.

She threw a ball of rumpled-up wrapping paper at me.

"Here, Mom, open this one!" Corey thrust a gift at her. "Open it, Mom! Open it!"

"Okay, okay, I'm opening it, I'm doing it right now ... Oh, mousetraps! I was hoping to get these ... How did you know I wanted them?"

Corey's big gift to his mother was a white ceramic house that lit up from the inside when you plugged it in. He'd found it in a specialty shop in Merchant's Square, and even I had been drawn to it. It looked a lot like Crawford Daze. It reminded me, when lit, of the painting I'd seen on the sidewalk in front of Millie's that first night.

"How cute," Alisha said, admiring the ceramic house from all sides. "We'll plug it in tonight after it's dark out so we can see it better."

She set the house safely to one side and flashed her son a wink. "Okay, Corey, you want to give Simon his big gift from you?"

"Yeah! My gift, my gift!"

Alisha reached behind the tree and withdrew several wrapped items. She began handing them to Corey, who walked over and presented them to me. "These are from me, Simon."

"Wow, thank you," I said.

The thin, elongated items turned out to be a pair of fishing poles. "Oh, my ... look at these." Both poles were six-and-a-half-foot medium-action Ugly Stiks. There was more to follow. Corey produced two small, square-shaped boxes, which turned out to be matching reels. The reels were Shimano Stradic 2500s.

"You must have broken the piggy bank for these," I told Corey.

There was also a Plano tackle box, already stocked and outfitted with hooks, sinkers, bobbers, and an assortment of artificial lures. The final addendum turned out to be a spool of six-pound test monofilament line.

"I don't even know how to fish."

"Well, now the two of you can learn," Alisha said. "Just stay away from the deep water."

"Thank you, Corey," I told him. "That was a very thoughtful gift."

"You're welcome, Simon." He jumped into my arms for a quick hug. "When can we go fishing?"

"As soon as the ice melts."

Finally, the moment arrived for Corey to unwrap his big gift from Santa. The four large boxes Alisha and I had lugged up from the basement the previous night were the only gifts yet unopened. Corey at first cast a scrutinizing gaze at the four packages piled before him, then quickly turned to examine the open fireplace.

He looked at me quizzically. "How did Santa get these down the chimney?"

"Magic."

"Santa can do magic?"

"Of course. Should we see if we can send them back up?"

"No!" he cried and began unwrapping. He tore off large sheaves of paper, his eyes wide with joy and delight, his mouth set in a consummate smile. *"Whoa! Holy smokes, man!"* He removed more of the paper, turning the box so that both his mother and I could see it. "Look, Mom! Look what Santa brought me! Look, Simon! Look!"

"Wow," Alisha replied, "look at that."

"It's Playworld! Santa brought me Playworld!"

I was scratching my head fretfully. "That Santa's just full of surprises, isn't he?"

Corey started tearing open the other boxes. Playworld was an immense indoor jungle gym of plastic crawl-through tubes, wood ladders, secret rooms, and a slide that emptied into a pool of plastic balls. Judging from the color photos on the outsides of the boxes that illustrated what Playworld would look like when fully assembled, it appeared to me to be a cross between a hamster cage and a McDonald's Funland. And judging from the scale provided by the kids shown playing next to and inside it, it looked as though it might stand seven feet high and span eight feet wide. Holy smokes was right.

"I'd say Santa spent a lot of time on this," Alisha offered.

"Word has it he'll be by next year to assemble it," I said.

Corey was jumping up and down. "When can we play in it, Simon? When can we play in it?"

"As soon as the ice melts."

"I'm sure that Simon will be thrilled to help you put it together," Alisha offered.

I scratched my head again. "One can only wonder what Santa was thinking as to where we're gonna put this thing."

Corey appeared to consider this. "Yeah, Mom, where we gonna put it? Can it go in my room?"

"Not unless you want to sleep in it," I told him.

We spent an hour or more getting the room cleaned up. I started a fire and began burning the wrapping paper while Corey helped his mother organize the gifts under the tree. When the place looked respectable, Alisha went upstairs for a nap. I took a shower, then went outside to do some last-minute splitting before the snow moved in. I wore my new Carhartt, gloves, hat, and neck warmer. Come mid-afternoon, low-slung clouds began scudding in from the north. Eventually the sky became a swollen gray dome. The wind died, and the air developed that humid chill that lets you know snow is coming. I piled up as much wood as the front of the house would allow before I decided to call it a day.

When I went inside, Alisha was in the kitchen working on dinner. Corey was busily roaming the house, holding his compass on one open palm and watching the needle bounce around. He saw me and asked when I'd be starting work on Playworld.

"Bright and early tomorrow morning, how's that?"

"Oh, okay." He zoomed off down the hall.

I took the cordless phone into my room, plopped myself onto my bed, and called Ma. When she answered, I heard immediately the cacophony of noises in the background. There was music playing, along with laughter and people talking.

"What in carnation is going on there?" I asked.

"Oh, Simon! Merry Christmas! I was wondering when you'd call."

"Are you having a party?"

"Well, sort of. I invited some friends over. We're drinking apple cider and eating pecan pie and singing carols. We're having a wonderful time. Can't you tell?"

"Well … yes."

"How was your Christmas, Simon?"

"Really good, Ma. Quite fabulous, actually."

We didn't talk for too long because I wanted her to get back to her party and her friends. I told her how proud of her I was. I told her how much I loved her.

"Oh, Simon, that's so sweet. I couldn't have come this far without you, you know."

"Yes, you could have."

"I'll talk to you later, dear. Love you."

"Love you, Ma. The world over."

"The world over." She blew her customary kiss through the receiver and hung up.

I laid the phone on my chest and gazed up at the ceiling for a while. It had been as enjoyable a day as I could remember having in some time … perhaps since the day Dad had pulled me out of school to go shoot at the pumpkins. My four years in college had not produced the happiness I was feeling now. I felt my eyes drifting shut, and I was content to let them. There may have been a smile on my face as I listed off. I dozed for close to an hour before Corey came launching onto my bed to wake me for dinner.

*   *   *

I got up at seven the following morning to begin work on Playworld. I put the coffee on and jumped in the shower. When I emerged from the first-floor bathroom and stepped into my bedroom to get dressed, I stole a glance out the window and saw that the sky was spitting snow. The storm's first flakes swam past the window in disorganized gusts and cartwheels. The flakes themselves were small, and weren't yet falling in any kind of high density, but the wind sure was picking up. It blew in from the west, meaning that it moved from left to right across the lake, being that Crawford Daze was on the lake's southern shore.

By the time Alisha descended the spiral stairs around 8:30, the northern shore was obscured from view by a moving curtain of white froth.

"Wow," she remarked, looking out the front windows.

"The leading edge," I said. "Coffee's on."

"Great, thanks." She turned and walked over to check my progress on Playworld. I could see she had just showered, as her hair was still wet. She had dressed in loose jeans and an open flannel shirt beneath which she wore a tight-fitting white blouse. "How's it coming?"

"Swell."

She chuckled. Her eyes found the assembly diagram, which I'd opened and lain flat on the wood floor. It looked like a scaled-down architectural blueprint.

"Oh, geez. That's pretty intense."

"Yes, it is." I was holding a flat screwdriver between my teeth while holding a Philips with my left hand. "Oh, shit, now I need an Allen wrench."

"Corey's still asleep, huh?"

"Probably worn out from all the excitement," I said.

"True. Let him sleep." She wandered into the kitchen.

I went down into the basement, then into the garage to search for an Allen wrench. I found a complete set hanging on the pegboard along the back wall.

When I got back upstairs, Alisha was sitting at the dining room table close to the tree, taking her coffee and a bowl of cereal, and leafing through a magazine.

I said, "You know, we're gonna have to permanently move some of the furniture in here to make room for this thing."

"I had considered that, yes," she answered, without looking up from the magazine.

"You're not writing today, are you?"

"I wasn't planning on it. Why?"

"Just wondering." The truth was, she'd been in such a good mood the last couple of days, and I wanted the trend to continue. With any luck, she'd wait until Corey went back to school to begin work again.

"Well, shit, now I need a hammer," I muttered. "I just made a trip down there."

"What could you possibly need a hammer for?"

"There are wooden pegs that have to be driven through the side posts into the platform edges."

"Well, that'll get him up, I'm sure." She pushed herself up from the table and carried her cereal bowl and empty mug into the kitchen while I made another trip down the stairs to fetch a hammer. I returned a minute later, holding a claw hammer in my right hand.

I felt a raw chill wrap itself around me. "My God, it's cold in here," I said. "Did you turn the heat—"

I had taken three steps into the open den when I realized what was wrong. Snow was billowing through the room. It was actually snowing on me right where I was standing.

The front door stood wide open.

"Jeezus Jiminy!" I ran up to the door and kicked it shut with one sneaker. I turned and saw Alisha coming out of the kitchen, drying her hands in a dishtowel, a disconcerted look on her face. "Did you open this door?"

She shook her head. I saw the first frown lines beginning to crease her eyebrows and forehead, and it took me a moment to catch on.

I dropped the hammer onto the hearth and went jogging past her, into the hallway. She remained rooted in place, and the frown lines I had seen were now worry lines.

I made a sharp right turn into Corey's room. There was a tangle of bed sheets rolled into a ball near the center of the bed, a pillow nearby … but no Corey.

No.

I jumped on the bed and peered over the rail onto the top bunk, hoping he'd be up there, and knowing in my sinking stomach that he wouldn't be. The top bunk was empty.

Alisha started to scream. It was a curdling shriek that made my blood run cold.

"Corey! Oh, God, Corey, no! Nooo!"

Instinctively I went to the window. I pressed my face close to the glass. It was just in time to glimpse the small, red and blue form streaking across the ice below, the red cape billowing and fluttering in the blustering wind.

I heard the front door pop open.

"Alisha, no! Alisha, no, wait!" I pushed away from the window, tripped over one of Corey's Tonka trucks, and fell flat on my face. I scrambled to my feet, banged my left knee on the edge of Corey's bed frame—"Ow, shit!"—and banged into the right-hand bulwark of the doorframe.

Finally, I got into the hall, around the corner, and down the single stair into the den. There was the front door yawning open once more, a maelstrom of snow churning and turning in a clockwise pattern through the room, like a white merry-go-round.

I went shooting through the open door, making sure to pull it shut behind me. I wasn't wearing much, I knew: jeans, a gray sweatshirt, socks, and sneakers.

The icy wind carved around me, driving a million tiny bullets into the side of my face. The storm was really picking up steam now.

I squinted into the wind, throwing a hand up to shield my eyes, and was just in time to see Alisha as she reached the bottom of the hill and bolted onto the ice after her son. I could hear her muted screams, shrill and terrified, but the wind was growing stronger.

Don't lose sight of her, Simon.

I went running down the hill after her. "Alisha!" I yelled. "Alisha, come back! *It's too dangerous!*"

I went hurtling past trees whose branches whipped against my face and neck. I had to dodge a large boulder in the last instant, and then I sprinted onto the ice. The wind slammed into me with such force that I actually slid ten or twelve feet to the right while in a standing position. The bottoms of my sneakers slid uselessly across the snowy ice. I had to pitch myself forward and fall flat on my stomach to stop the slide. I got up and began running again.

Thirty yards ahead of me, Alisha's darkened form turned and twisted in the murk. I saw her arms wheeling as she slid and fell. She got up and began running again. I could barely detect her voice, even though she was no doubt screaming at full lung capacity. Never mind Corey. Corey was gone, swallowed in the blizzard. I thought, *How will we ever find him in this?* But more so, it was Josef's admonition I was thinking about, how the ice could be four inches thick in one place, half an inch in others. This truth was made clear and bold when my right foot suddenly broke through on one of my down steps. Cold water leeched through my sneaker. Had I been moving slowly, I might have fallen through *in toto*. Because I was running, however, the hole succeeded only in tripping me. I went in up to my ankle, then flew forward in a face-first spill, bumping my chin hard on the ice.

Don't lose sight of her, Simon. Get up, get up, get up.

I was already climbing to my feet, listening to the banshee howl of wind in my ears. At the same time, I felt an irregular sensation against my lower back, as if something was pricking my skin. I wondered if I'd been hurt, somehow. I ignored whatever it was and kept going.

I saw the shadow of Alisha's body banking to the left. I wondered vaguely if she could still see Corey the way I saw her. I tried screaming again: "*Alisha! Please stop, Alisha! Please stop—*"

She began to falter and stumble. It took me several moments to

realize what was happening. I saw her go down to one knee. Dark
blotches of water went flying through the air. She tried to pull herself
out. For a moment, she looked like a baby crawling on all fours. My
thumping heart was a drumbeat of horror in my throat as the ice
beneath her finally gave. Alisha plunged into the water.

God and sweet Jesus this can't be happening. This can't possibly
be—

I saw the back of her head sticking out of the hole. As I got
closer, I could see her wet hair clinging to the nape of her white neck.
Beneath my feet, a medley of cracks could be heard webbing out
in multiple directions. I cautiously slowed down. Torrents of snow
bulled past my shoulders, screaming in my ears, all the dark things of
the north let loose and shrieking in devil tongues. Instead of coming
up behind her, where the ice was apparently weak, I made a wide
circle to her left, went around the front of her, and lay flat on my
stomach near her right shoulder. She appeared completely oblivious
of my presence. Her arms were working to try and pull herself onto
the ice, but her clawed fingers slid uselessly against the slippery
surface. Her mouth was working to produce the exclamations in
the shape of her son's name, but very little was coming out. She was
disoriented and growing weak.

I screamed at her: "Alisha! Alisha, look at me!"

Finally, she did. Her white, desperate eyes turned and found me.
In them I saw the fear of one who knows she's in mortal peril.

"You need to grab my hand! Grab onto me!"

She simply stared. Water was streaming off the point of her chin.
The lake water beneath her armpits was black and pitiless. The hole
she'd created was ten feet across by now, and was filled with shards
of floating ice.

"Give me your hand, Alisha! Reach for me!"

I slid forward on my belly as far as I could go. I heard the ice
cracking beneath me, and I felt the ice actually lowering as it started
to give away.

She stuck her arm out just enough for me to reach it. I swiped
up her hand and started crawling backwards. The ice beneath me
broke and fell away. I pulled Alisha through the new channel. But
when I got back to solid ice, I realized I could pull her no more …
not without pulling myself in. There was nothing for me to grasp

with my free hand, nothing to hold onto. I turned and looked back at her. Her eyes were starting to roll in their sockets. If I was going to somehow locate Corey in this wintry hell, then I was going to have to let Alisha go. As I stared into her eyes, I could see a final moment of lucidity … and then she mouthed the words, *"Let go …"*

I remembered the pricking sensation I'd felt earlier. I reached around with my free hand, and there was the Philips screwdriver. I'd inadvertently stuck it in my back pocket when I'd gone downstairs to fetch the hammer. I pulled it free, turned it around so that its handle lay firmly in my palm, and drove the pointed end as hard as I could into the ice. Now with a firm handhold, I pulled with one arm against the screwdriver while holding Alisha with the other. I got her partway out, then had to drive the screwdriver quickly into the ice again. I felt every muscle and tendon in my right arm popping and stretching. I gritted my teeth and screamed, *willing* myself to muster the strength.

She slid up and onto the ice like a wet seal. Amazingly, she was trying to clamber to her feet. She was between me and the hole, and she actually tried to bound over me in a renewed pursuit of her son, but I reached up and grabbed the toe of one of her slippers, which was enough to upend her. She went flying stomach-first onto the ice.

What about the dog? I remembered asking Josef. *Did they get the dog back?*

Nar.

The will of a mother must know near-limitless resilience, for Alisha was astonishingly trying to regain her feet. But she didn't get far. The cold was now taking its hold on her. I got up to find her crawling on hands and knees in a continued trajectory of the path she thought Corey had taken. She went about five feet before she collapsed and rolled onto her side. A sudden, nasty gust of wind blinded me, forcing me to shut my eyes. When I finally got to her, I saw that her face was a ghostly white. There were bluish-black circles around her eyes. Within seconds, her clothing, having been fully immersed in water, was frozen completely solid from the sub-zero wind. I saw with amazement that the outsides of her jeans were clear-coated with a perfectly translucent rime of ice. Her flannel shirt was as stiff as plywood. Her clothing had been transformed into a suit of armor. She couldn't have moved if she'd possessed the strength to do so.

I got my arms beneath her and lifted her up. I stood on wobbly, trembling legs. Alisha watched me the entire time. I don't think she had the strength to move her mouth. Braids of ice now clotted her hair. Her cheeks were lined with frost. She was dying in my arms. I cradled her body close to mine. I started moving. I looked for the hole in the ice, but couldn't find it. It was out there somewhere, dangerously close. The wind wailed in my ears. I stopped and looked around, attempting to pinpoint my position … and I made a horrifying discovery.

I couldn't see the shore. I made a full circle with Alisha in my arms, and I couldn't see land in any direction. Visibility had decreased to perhaps twenty feet, and we were caught in a whiteout. I'd gotten turned around, somehow. I'd gotten turned around in the storm, and I'd lost my bearings.

In the blizzard's twisting, circular ferocity, I tried using logic to deduce where Crawford Daze might be located judging by which direction the wind was blowing. If the wind was moving out of the west, I would want it blowing directly into my right ear as I moved perpendicular to it, going south. Okay, then. I made a three-quarters turn until I felt the wind biting into my right ear. Then I began moving perpendicular to it. But it changed, the wind did. It gusted into my face several times, and even slammed into me from the left side on one occasion. I never re-located the gaping hole in the ice. I was quickly coming to grips with the likelihood that all three of us were going to perish out here.

And then I saw a light over my shoulder.

I turned in that direction, squinting against the blinding gales. The strange light pulsed twice more, like a slow-action camera flash hidden in the storm. I moved faithfully toward it. Renewed strength filtered into my legs. I had read and heard of lightning and thunder being observed during snowstorms, but this hadn't been lightning. This had been …

It had been something else.

I increased my pace to a slow jog until, finally, I grew aware of a darkened wooded hillside rising in front of me. I drew closer and saw the first trees. Looking up, I saw the dark crag of the house towering above us.

I started to run.

Minutes later, I burst through the front door into the den. Alisha lay motionless in my arms. I kicked the door shut and carried her around the corner and up the hall to the bathroom. Her body was coruscating with shivers. I lay her face-up in the bathtub, her feet underneath the faucet. I cranked on the water, adjusted the valve so the water was warm but not overly hot, took one glance at her white face, and said, "You'll be okay. Stay here."

I ran out of the bathroom.

In my bedroom now. Working efficiently, I stripped out of my wet clothes and climbed into dry ones. Thinking, *He's already been out there at least fifteen minutes. You probably have another fifteen minutes to find him, Simon.* I pulled on dry socks, grabbed my boots. I ran out to the Christmas tree and pulled out the Carhartt snowsuit. I climbed into the suit, and began lacing up my boots. By this time, I heard Alisha splashing around in the bathtub. I stood up. I pulled on the neck warmer and hat, then the fleece gloves. I turned around and there she stood, dripping wet, water pooling on the wood floor at her feet, arms wrapped around her torso, chin rattling ... but coherent.

She could barely speak. "He's ..."

I pointed at her. "You need to stay here!"

She came up and grabbed the front of the Carhartt. She was shaking her head, her face a landscape of misery. *Her despair leaned over the abyss of grief.* "He's ... all I have. He's all I have." Tears ran from her eyes.

"Promise me you'll stay here!" I repeated. "Stay here and call for help."

I went over to the dining room table to retrieve one final item: the handheld compass I'd given Corey only yesterday.

Alisha was trying to scream behind me, but could only manage a strangled hiss: "Please, Simon ... Please, I'm begging you ... he's all I have, he's all—"

"I won't come back without him!" I thundered, heading for the door. I was on my own now.

As I closed my gloved hand on the brass door handle, I turned and looked back. Alisha was kneeling on the floor, her stringy, matted hair hanging in front of her face. She cried in great, gulping sobs. I was suddenly seized by what may have been the most selfish thought I've ever known: *I'm not doing this for you, Alisha. I'm doing it for me.*

I opened the door and went back into the storm.

CHAPTER SIXTEEN

THE SURPRISE PARTY

I FOUND A DIARY of Catherine's.

It was an accidental discovery. I hadn't known she'd kept a diary. I'd been searching for a laundry basket, actually. Because Cath had an irksome bent for carrying loads of clothes up to her bedroom, then tossing the basket aside and leaving it there, her room was one of the first places I looked. There was the basket, all right, crowned atop a pile of laundry in the center of the room.

I made a quick survey of the room's disheveled contents. The bed was unmade. Ashtrays overflowing with cigarette butts cluttered the end tables and vanity. A foul odor clung to the walls and ceiling: staleness, decay, nicotine. One of Cath's Bob Marley posters had come partially detached from the wall, the top half now hanging over the lower half. The lampshades were covered with dust and had yellowed from ceaseless smoking.

I grabbed the basket and made ready to dump the clean clothes it contained onto the bed. The diary was lying underneath it, on top of the dirty clothes. It was a brown hardcover book with one of those cute gold locks that held the book shut. In the center of the latch was a small keyhole. Had the lock mechanism not been present, I probably wouldn't have given the book a second glance. But a locked book is bound to pique my interest on most days, and this day was no different. It was a bright sunny morning in late November, three days after Norman Smoot's visit, and the house was quiet. Ma was still in bed. She slept through half the day these days, it seemed. That Cath wasn't in her own bed at the moment meant she hadn't come home last night. In fact, I couldn't remember having seen my sister for the last two days.

I dropped the laundry basket and picked up the book. I set my thumbs against the insides of the covers directly above the keyhole and pried the book open rather easily. The lock's lone protest was a feeble pop-clack. *Not exactly maximum security, is it?*

I began riffling through the pages, expecting to find juvenile entries from a years-ago era. What I found were drawings and poems, mostly. The drawings were benign, and the poems were meaningless. Halfway through, the pages became blank. I stopped riffling forward and began riffling backward slowly in an attempt to find the most recent entry. I found a lengthy note, written in blue ink. At the beginning of the note was a date: Nov. 19th. That was just last week, assuming it hadn't been written a year or more ago. Cath had written a letter, actually. A letter to our father.

> *Dear Daddy,*
>
>   *I hope you can hear this and yet I know you can't. You have left us to be on our own and we have lost the way. I wish you were here, Daddy, I miss you so very much. I don't know what to do anymore, and I don't know how to fix it. Everything is wrong. I have lost sight of the person I am someday to become. That person, Daddy, that woman—the adult me—had dreams and ambitions and hopes. But you are gone now, and you will never be here again. The adult version of me will never have you in her life, do you see? The me without the you. You'll never get to know that woman, the woman I was someday to become. I can't seem to get it through my head that you'll never know me, Daddy. You'll never know me.*
>
>   *Ma does not talk to me, but takes to the drink. I fear that she hates me, and yet and I can't go on protecting her much longer. She is so angry, Daddy, and I think she resents your leaving us, and she*

does not know what to do. She does not know how much danger she is in. The men who come, they say awful, dreadful things. The woman I was someday to become—I think of her as Caroline, *and she is dying—cannot let these things come to bear, even though I suspect* Caroline *detests Ma to some degree for allowing you to get us into such trouble in the first place. She has no fight in her, Ma. Why is she so weak? How is it that she permitted you to bring this scourge upon us? The men who come are filthy creatures. Their eyes are filled with alternatives. They send their friends. And they send their friends' friends. There is no end to this madness. Ma drinks through it, Simon stays away. And I am the glue holding the sinking ship together. There is not much time. There is not much of me left. You can't squeeze blood from a stone, but I guess you can squeeze the life out of a whore.*

I love you so much, Daddy, and I miss the dickens out of you, but I can't pay your debts much longer. You'll never know Caroline, *but I may never know her either. I don't know what to do anymore, Daddy. I am so scared, and I don't know what to do. Please, please help us.*

Catherine

I closed the diary. I had read enough. And so there were the answers, pulsing in stark boldface three inches in front of my nose. That, precisely, had been the problem: the answers had been too close, too close for me to see correctly. I'd been looking past them all this time, blinded by what should have been obvious.

You'll never know me, Daddy. You'll never know me.

There were several answers, of course, but they all had a common denominator: *pain.* Ever since Dad had died the night of my sixteenth birthday a little more than a year ago, we'd all been wrapped up in our own pain. We'd been nothing more than a bunch of spit bugs, foaming at the mouth and trying to make ourselves as small as possible. That's really what it came to. I was reminded of a saying: *A person wrapped up in self-pity is the smallest package in the world.* I guess we were one small, fucking package.

I was sitting in Catherine's pile of dirty clothes. Shafts of dust-filled sunlight penetrated the grimy windows. I had cut school again. Cath was out. Ma was asleep. We were losing the house. The question was: was there enough time left? Enough time to fix it?

Ma's birthday was coming up next week. It was going to be a real whopper, I thought. As a shaft of sunlight edged up my face, bathing my right cheek with its morning fire, an idea began to coalesce. It wasn't much, but …

Stand up with what you have … to thine own self be true.

*   *   *

"Simon, I insist on knowing where we're going. Do you hear me? I *insist.*"

It was the third time she'd put forth the question. We were bumping along Route 80 in the Roadgrader. I exited the interstate near Succasunna and got on 46. Darkness flew past the windows, tempered with icy raindrops that fell in occasional spats. I tried not to look at Ma. Sooner or later, though, I knew I would have to.

"If I told you, it would ruin it," I said, repeating my mantra. "You trust me, Ma, don't you?"

"Well, of course I *trust* you, Simon, but …" She stole herself for a moment, then leaned closer and asked in a conspiratorial whisper, "Did Don and Betty arrange a surprise party for me? Oh, Simon, just tell me, *the suspense is killing me!*"

I took a moment to glance at my mother, and couldn't help but feel a stitch of guilt at the look of excitement in her eyes. She'd gone a little heavy on the lipstick; there was a faint red smear in the shape of a comma at the upper right corner of her mouth. Her hair was okay, but her clothes didn't match. She was wearing pink cotton pants and a gray Villa Nova sweatshirt. But far and away the crème de la crème: white athletic socks and bedroom slippers.

"Ma, you can't go out like that," I'd told her back at the house.

"Why not?" She'd looked down at herself, apparently found nothing wrong, and looked up at me again. "Why can't I, Simon?"

"At least put some shoes on, Ma. It's forty degrees outside, it's almost December."

"Why don't we stay home, then. I'd prefer not to go out at all."

"No, Ma, we have to. This event has been planned, it's—"

"Then this is what I'm wearing. I don't dress to impress, Simon. I wear what I like."

Now she hovered in again. "Okay, look, I know it's a surprise party, just tell me whose doing it was. It's Don and Betty, isn't it? I'm right, aren't I?"

"Well … yes."

She punched the air with a fist. "Oh, I knew it, I just *knew* it. Those crafty little devils! But I can smell a plot cooking, Simon, I always could. I was always good that way."

"Look, Ma … You have to at least pretend—"

"Oh, I won't give it away! I'll act totally surprised, you'll see." She jiggled her loose fists in front of her. "Ooh, this is so neat, I haven't had a surprise party since my sixteenth. Tell me, how long have you known?"

"Oh … awhile, I guess."

We passed the town of Netcong to our right. I stayed on 46 heading toward Budd Lake and Hackettstown.

Ma said, "Oh, but we passed … Don and Betty live over that way …" She was turning her upper body in an attempt to peer out the foggy windows, trying to gauge where we were.

Don and Betty Reinhardt lived on the Stanhope side of Lake Musconetcong, which we were now leaving behind us.

"The party's not at their house, Ma."

"Will Catherine be there?" she asked in a low voice.

"I'm afraid not."

"Just as well. She treats me like dog poop, you know. She never would have spoken to her father the way she speaks to me." Ma fell silent a moment, and I could tell by the tone of the silence that she was beaming at me across the dark cab space. "But you're different, Simon. You're a *good* son."

Unlike the town of Lake Hiawatha, the town of Budd Lake does have a lake. It's a 376-acre dishpan bordered by Route 46 along one shore and a cedar swamp along the opposite shore.

I made a right onto Sand Shore Road just prior to the point at which Route 46 parallels the lakeside. The lake was now swaddled in darkness to our left as I steered the Roadgrader down the bumpy, potholed avenue.

"Well, this is different," Ma mumbled. "I can't imagine where we're going. I don't recall there being any restaurants or civic centers down this way …"

The homes on her side of the street were mostly one- and two-bedroom clapboard bungalows that hunkered square-backed in the night. Sand Shore Road was bisected here and there by narrow lanes that ran in east-west grids through old tracts consisting of these tenements. Tree limbs listed and swayed in a rain-driven breeze.

A wide, sand-gravel parking lot appeared on Ma's side of the road. The church lot was full this Monday evening. Floodlights mounted in the peak of the church eaves and also on several utility poles overlooking the parking area accentuated the slanting rain.

"This is Budd Lake Chapel," Ma said, reading from the wooden sign. "Of course, a church, I should have known …"

"Make sure you put your coat on," I said. I parked the truck as close to the church as I could get and killed the engine.

"Are they all to yell 'surprise' at once? Do you think they know we're here? Simon, maybe you should run in first—to tip them off, you know. I'll pretend I'm brushing my hair or something, and I'll come in like a minute or two later, so everybody'll be ready."

"Let's just go, Ma. Everything's going to be fine." I opened my door, aware of the sinking, somehow sickening feeling in my stomach.

I went around and helped her out. I had to steer her around the small puddles that were beginning to form in the sandy parking area. "I told you you should have worn real shoes."

Three Harleys leaned against their kickstands just outside the church entrance. Ma noticed these as we passed.

"My oh my, look at those motorcycles … Simon, who do we know who drives—"

I had already pulled the door open for her. "Never mind the bikes, Ma. Let's go."

We entered into a rectangular foyer. Off to the right were chrome coat racks with hangers on them. In front of us stood a pair of wooden doors. Both doors were propped open. We passed through the opening and paused. We were standing in a short hall space. In front of us, and on the right, a half-dozen stairs climbed upward, to what I knew would be the sanctuary. Also in front of us, but on the left, another half-dozen stairs descended to the basement.

I took Ma's hand. "Come on. We have to go downstairs."

"Oh … Well, all right."

Her eyes had lost their excitement and had acquired a new wariness. She cast disparate glances up and around as we went down the stairs. I held onto her hand very tightly.

We went through the double-swing doors at the base of the stairs and into a wide room with old wood flooring. Roughly three dozen people—maybe more—sat in metal folding chairs in the center of the room. The chairs were arranged in concentric circles. I had heard a man's voice speaking as Ma and I had entered, but now the voice fell silent. Several heads turned to look at us … and then several more … and then all of them at once. I felt the weight of all those stares, and Ma felt it too. *Be strong now, you have to be strong. The forest is burning around you, all is afire, and you are the pinecone.*

I held fast to Ma's hand. She was trying to pull back. I felt the muscles tightening in her wrist and forearm.

"Simon, I think we came to the wrong place," she half whispered.

"No, Ma." My voice was trembling. My pulse was hammering in my neck. "This is the right place. Come on …"

We advanced two or three steps, Ma's slippers going *snick-snick* against the wood floor, before she stopped again, trying to pull back.

"Simon, this is … I don't know any of these people. We can't—"

"I know, Ma. But they know you. They all know *you*, Ma."

Her eyes flitted right and left. A frown line had formed a crease going straight down the middle of her forehead. Her mouth opened. Her lower lip quivered. Resentment crept into her voice. "Simon, you … you tricked me. You tricked me into coming here." The first tears were welling in her eyes and rolling down her cheeks. Her voice was trembling and angry and hurt. "How could you do this, Simon? How could you do this to me?"

I felt her starting to pull her arm back, and I knew I was going to lose her, that she was going to rip her hand out of mine and that I wouldn't be able to hold it, and coming here had been a grisly error, a big fat joke, and Ma would never trust me again—

"I was hoping," said a deep male voice, "that you might join us tonight."

A man had stood up from one of the chairs on the inside ring of the circle—close to us and toward the left a little. He was tall, maybe six-two. He wore black biker gear to a tee. Leather pants, leather jacket, dark stubble on his face, a goatee, and one earring. His hair was black and squirrely. He wore black, fingerless gloves. Had I seen this fellow coming toward me on the sidewalk on a bright afternoon, I may have turned and gone the other way, or ducked into a store to avoid any trouble.

"This here," he went on, pointing down to his chair, "is your seat. I've been saving it for you."

A second biker next to the first stood also. That, of course, would be my seat. Several of the other members were looking up at the two bikers, nodding in agreement, before turning their attention back to us.

"We would be honored, ma'am, if you would join us," said a man wearing a gray suit on the back ring of the circle. A ripple of horror undulated through me when I recognized him as Mr. Brunvald, my school principal.

A young lady surely no older than nineteen or twenty with Pollyanna pigtails and wearing jeans and a sweater added, "All you need to do is listen. You aren't here to speak."

My mother stared at these people as though she were in some sort of trance. The clash of dissonance in Ma's eyes was perfectly legible: she couldn't possibly back out now ... not when the people before her were being so *nice.*

The first biker guy motioned us with one hand, again gesturing to his chair. "Please ..."

I began edging forward once more, pulling Ma with me. She came reluctantly, but she came. Her slippers dragging across the floor like sandpaper was easily the loudest noise in the room. I didn't need to look at her eyes to know she was terrified, because I was right scared myself.

We sat down in the vacated seats, on the innermost ring of the circle. Ma sat primly with her knees touching, her arms wrapped protectively around her large black purse. Her wide fearful eyes wandered around the room.

Before the meeting could resume, I quickly rose to my feet. I began rooting around in one of my pockets. I said, "Ma, I brought you here because tomorrow is your birthday, and I wanted to give you your birthday present."

I removed my hand from my pocket, then uncurled my fist to reveal the gold coin that lay flat on my palm. I held it out for Ma to take.

Slowly, hesitantly, she did. She held it in front of her face for close examination, turning it. On the topside of the coin was a triangle with a raised dot of black plastic in its center. Along each of the triangle's three sides was a word. They were: *unity, service, recovery*. And wrapping around the entire triangle, along the outer edge of the coin, was the maxim: *To thine own self be true.*

I took my seat again, but I never looked away from Ma's eyes. "You've lost the way, Ma. You haven't been true to yourself, nor to me, nor to Cath. Nor to Dad."

Normally this would have drawn a protest, but it didn't tonight. Her mouth hung open as she watched me.

"It isn't your fault, Ma. It's no one's fault. I didn't bring you here to ascribe blame. I brought you here to save you. To save *us*. We're in a lot of trouble, Ma." *We're in the storm. We're turned around in the storm.* "There isn't much time."

Her lips moved feebly. "Trouble? Simon … there isn't any—"

"Oh, yes, we're in a heap of trouble. We're losing our house, Ma. A man from the mortgage company stopped by last week. His name was Norman Smoot. You haven't made a payment in over five months. They've started foreclosure."

I saw a narrowing in Ma's eyes … the first glint of truth poking through perhaps. It wouldn't be pleasant, that feeling. But that's what I wanted. It's why I had brought her here. There was an old proverb, *Better to be stung by the truth than comforted by lies.*

"You haven't paid the property taxes either. We owe about sixty-four hundred dollars combined, Ma, and we have maybe a week left to pay it. Or we're gonna be homeless."

"Well, surely …" She looked at the coin, then looked at me

and shook her head, trying to be shut of it. "There has to be an explana—"

"*How's this for an explanation?*" I had removed several papers from my other pocket, which I now unfolded and waved in front of her face. At the top of each, in bold block letters, was: Notice of Foreclosure. "They've been taping these to the side and front doors every day for the past few days, *so what more explanation do you need?*"

My mother shrank back in horror. Her lower jaw was shaking badly, and her eyes were glistening again. "Oh … oh, I …" She opened her purse and began rooting through it. My first thought was that she was searching for a small mirror, or a clutch of tissues. Her hand reemerged holding a small bottle of scotch. Her quivering hand went to the cap, trying to loosen it.

"No, Ma, you can't … you can't drink that here." All emotion, all conviction, had been stripped from my voice. "That's … it's …" *It's blasphemy, to take a drink in the middle of an AA meeting. Dear God and Jesus.*

She had loosened the cap and was now unscrewing it.

I looked wildly around the room. "Somebody help her. Make her stop. Please make her stop—don't let her do it …"

For a moment, though, no one in the room said a word. All eyes were on Ma and me, on the drama unfolding. Ma was staring at the open fifth in her hand, though she appeared to be staring *through* it—looking, instead, at something else.

"We can't make *anyone* stop drinking," a voice calmly spoke. It was the girl with the Pollyanna pigtails.

"It's not what we're here for," another woman added.

A man in jeans and blue chambray shirt sitting across from us said, "You give us too much credit. We simply don't have that power."

I stared at them, uncomprehending. "Then … what are you here for?" My voice was barely a squeak in the basement. "What power *do* you have?"

The girl with the pigtails replied, "We have the power to help someone who wants to stop."

I turned from her, and from the group at large, toward Ma again, who was still clutching the small bottle and staring decidedly through it as though it were a looking glass into another place. The bottle was moving up and down in her quavering hand. I took her in as a whole for a moment. I saw the red comma of lipstick at the corner of her mouth; it suddenly meant nothing. The mismatched outfit, white athletic socks, and bedroom slippers all ceased to exist. What I saw beneath those things in the dim but eerily penetrating basement lights was in fact my mother, and it was the only mother I would ever have. This was the woman who had given birth to me, nursed me, changed my diapers, and cared for me at a time when I could do none of those things for myself. This was the woman who had scolded me when I'd filched a pocketful of Tootsie Rolls from the supermarket at the age of five, then marched me right back into the store to return them and make me apologize to the store manager. It was she who'd flushed my mouth clean with Ivory dish soap when I'd muttered the F-word in front of her at age seven. It was she who'd grounded me for a week my freshman year of high school for talking back to my math teacher and being put in after-school detention. She'd been the one to kiss my right cheek before I left for school every morning; the one to stuff wads of lunch money into my knapsack every day; the one who had dinner ready at a timely moment each night; the one who kept the house neat, kept the laundry done, made sure my homework was completed, made sure I learned how to swim, and that my teeth were seen by a dentist every six months, and the list went on and on.

This was my mother, with the smear of lipstick riding up one cheek, with the pink circus pants and brown bedroom slippers. This was my mother, holding the little bottle in front of her and staring through it like a prism. This person sitting in the chair next to me was my mother, and I loved her.

I loved her.

The words were free from my mouth before I knew I had uttered them. Can words heal? I don't know. But love can.

Love *can*.

She put the plastic cap back onto its threads and started screwing it back on. She dropped the bottle into her purse. She clutched the top of her purse with claw-like hands, her eyes moving from me, over to the next person, and so on around the room. She gave a small, imperceptible nod that was felt in the room's silence more than seen.

The meeting resumed. The man who'd been speaking when Ma and I had entered picked right up where he'd left off, as if no interruption had occurred. Others spoke after him. Ma listened, and I listened too.

*   *   *

I took the side roads home. The rain had stopped, leaving behind it a cold mist that rose in tall shrouds along the edges of the woods. It made the night appear darker and deeper than it really was.

Ma hadn't uttered a word since leaving the church, and I couldn't help but wonder whether this was good or bad. She would recognize and embrace the new door I'd helped open for her, or she'd backtrack, running for cover in the comfort of her old paradigm. Choosing the latter would rekindle the resentment she'd undoubtedly felt for my bringing her to the church in the first place. All would be lost, if it wasn't already.

"Ma? Ma, are you mad?"

Silence unrolled like the damp road beneath us. I was relieved, in a way, for the darkness that cloaked Ma's face. I wasn't sure I could shoulder whatever hurt and betrayed expression now lived there. Would my mother ever trust me again? That depended, I suppose, on which door she chose: the old door behind her, or the new one in front.

"I'm … a little wounded, I guess. A little surprised. But mostly, I'm ashamed … and embarrassed. About my behavior, you know. I haven't really acted like an adult lately. At least not a responsible one." She turned to me. "But how did you come to learn of that meeting back there? Where did you get the gold coin?"

"It doesn't matter where I got it right now," I said. Behind us was a car with its high beams on. I reached up to flip the rearview mirror to the night position. "What matters, Ma, is that you keep going back. To meetings, I mean. You have to attend ninety meetings in ninety days. If you miss a day, you've gotta go to two the next day."

"That's quite a commitment, isn't it? How am I meant to accomplish that without a driver's license?"

"I'll drive you," I answered. "Every day, there and back."

"Oh, Simon, you don't have—"

"Yes, I do, Ma. I haven't got a choice. You were supposed to begin attending meetings when you got your DUI, and you never did. Now look, they don't let you speak until the ninety-first day. All you do until then is listen."

"Well, I … I don't think I'd have much to talk about, anyway."

"So, you'll go back then? Starting tomorrow?"

"Oh … well, I don't know … I guess we could give it a try. The people there certainly were nice."

Ma and I had listened intently, and with ease, as the meeting had continued around us. People had spoken as if the little scene Ma and I had raised had never happened. I even began to feel a small sense of homecoming, as if we actually belonged in those two metal chairs among that small throng of anonymous persons. I felt as though we were being spoken to.

When it was over, though, a sense of awkwardness had come creeping back. What did we do now? Did we stay and talk? Or did we run to the door as fast as our feet could get us there? I had tried to allay this fear by giving Ma a quick hug and then holding one of her hands again. Before we had taken a step toward the double-swing doors, though, people had begun lining up next to us. They all wanted to shake Ma's hand.

"My name is Mary. Thank you for coming."

"My name's George. Nice to meet you."

"I'm Stan."

"I'm John."

"My name's Stella. Keep comin' back."

After the initial shock had worn off, Ma had begun responding to these fast introductions. "And I'm Carol, it's nice to meet you, too …"

The driver behind us flashed his headlights on and off twice in succession. High beams, then off … High beams, then off … High beams again. I was starting to get annoyed. *Switch on your low beams, asshole, or get off the road.* Actually, it reminded me of that old urban legend, The Killer in the Backseat. Remember that one? Every time the killer raises himself up, with the steak knife held high, an alert driver behind flashes his high beams to scare the killer into hunkering down again.

My thoughts diverted to the small bottle of scotch still taking up residence in Ma's pocketbook.

"Ma, you'll need to quit drinking. The Program won't work otherwise."

"Yes, Simon, I'm well aware of that."

"You will, then? Quit?"

"I don't know, Simon. It isn't that easy."

"But you'll try?"

"I'll … yes. I'll try."

"Promise me."

"What?"

I said, "Promise me you'll try to stop. Promise me that you'll make a concerted effort."

Silence for a while. Then, "Okay, I promise."

"Throwing that scotch out the window might be a good start."

"What? Oh … Well, I suppose it wouldn't hurt, yes. I mean, what's a bottle of scotch, right?"

She spoke like a woman partially unsure of herself, like a person trying to weigh an object she's holding in her right hand against an object she's holding in her left. But she began going through her purse again, and, once more coming up with the small bottle, rolled her window partway down and tossed it out.

"Anything else in there?" I asked.

"No. Shall I turn it upside-down?"

"What are we gonna do about the money, Ma?"

"I think I can only handle one crisis at a time, Simon." Her voice was quivery again. *Better to be stung by the truth than comforted by lies*, I reminded myself.

"You'd better adapt in a hurry," I told her.

We drove in silence for some time. The high beams flicked off again, then on. This meant little in the rearview mirror. However, it was blinding in my two side-view panels.

"Ma, do we have any money?"

"No."

"There are no side funds, no rainy-day accounts, no nest eggs you can borrow fr—"

"Which part of 'no' do you not understand, Simon? The N or the O? Either way, it comes to the same."

"Can you borrow it from somebody? Your Aunt Dorothy in Cleveland?"

"Aunt Dorothy's more of a drunk than I am, Simon. And part senile, to boot."

I felt despair steeling its way into my innards again, the way it had the morning Smoot had paid his visit.

"Perhaps I could apply for a home equity loan," Ma thought out loud.

"There isn't enough time," I told her. "And you'd never be approved anyway. You have fifty grand worth of credit debt."

She rounded on me. "How do you know about that? What business of that is yours?"

"Smoot told me. He knows. His people know a lot of things about us, Ma."

"They do, do they?" She faced forward again, her jaw rigid, her features set against the night. "Well, they don't know everything, Simon. They don't know quite everything."

PART II

Man in Black

CHAPTER SEVENTEEN

THE STORM

I'm not doing this for you, Alisha. I'm doing it for me. But now I have returned, and I fear I may have failed. So what happens next? Where do we go from here? These thoughts, lost in the storm. My thoughts, lost in the moment. Our thoughts, one and the same. *I stood with what I had. I stood as tall as I could. It wasn't enough. This time, it wasn't enough.*

So disjointed were these bits and fragments swirling round the cyclone in my mind that I didn't know where one ended and the next began. At times I wasn't sure where exactly I was. White may as well be black. I felt the pressure of wind sucking at my ears and the wantonness of cold leeching at my soul. But the end was coming near. It was all winding down, and things wouldn't be the same anymore. Catherine was gone, the man in black was beyond reach, and Crawford Daze had changed forever. It was a different house when I came back to it, that's what I know.

But I *did* come back to it, and our thoughts may have yet been one and the same, because the woman kneeling before the stone fireplace suddenly looked up, and I saw myself through her eyes. I saw a young man coming home empty-handed out of a snowstorm, his arms wrapped around himself, the brown Carhartt encrusted with snow and ice. He may have been the Yeti, as white as the suit was. His cheeks were a pale gray, and blue rings encircled his eyes. As he staggered across the threshold, with snow blowing torrents around him, he turned to press the door shut … and it was as he fashioned himself into a side profile that the lump in his suit became visible. His arms wrapped tightly around his torso were actually holding that lump fast against his body. The small head was barely visible where the chest zipper came up to meet it, and partly covered with the red cape.

Then she got up off her knees (had she been praying?), and I wasn't seeing through her eyes anymore. I was seeing through my own again, and I was aware of different things on different levels. I saw her hair hanging in damp tresses across her shoulders. It was also chilly in the house—far chillier than it should have been. And it was dark. Not a single light was on. This could only mean that the blizzard had knocked out the power. She had been down on her knees trying to light the fireplace with hands that quivered and shook, as evident by the half-dozen spent matches that lay on the stone hearth.

Alisha wore blue jeans and a denim jacket. When she saw Corey's head tucked beneath my chin enwrapped in the red cape, she literally flew at me.

Her hands were on the Carhartt and the lump beneath it.

"Oh, you brought him back, God and Jesus in heaven you brought my son back—"

"—hypothermia from prolonged exposure …"

"—thought you were both gone, I waited forever, none of the phones are working—"

"—you have to calm down, Alisha."

Finally she got the zipper down, and she grabbed her son away from me, and she was rocking him in her arms, hugging him, and kissing the top of his head. Her voice was a crying, hysterical mess. "Oh, God bless you! You're a saint, you're an angel! How did you find him? How did you find him in that horrible, awful mess?"

He was dead when I found him. That is the truth. For some time after, I had carried the boy's body close to my own, pressed up against my beating heart. I held him so tightly to my chest I must have crushed him. I willed him to be alive. I carved my way through a twisting headwind, pushing snow aside that drifted to my knees. I talked to him and told him to come back. I was on the beach, and then a road. At some point, I was in the forest, walking backwards at times to avoid having to face the pernicious wind. As I was climbing a steep hillside, my thighs beginning to cramp with exertion, I felt him move against me. A bit farther on, I felt his head turning against the underside of my chin. I continued to talk to him. I told him to stay with me because there was someone close by who loved him.

*   *   *

The most prudent course of action would have been getting him into a bathtub partially filled with warm water. But lack of electricity meant lack of water pressure.

"Get him out of his pajamas!" I yelled. "Fast as you can now. Take him into the kitchen."

I kicked off my boots and shed myself of the cumbersome suit, and went up the hall in a half run. My legs were so weak and wobbly that I lost my balance at one point and had to place both hands on the wall to steady myself. Then I limped into the bathroom and started grabbing up as many towels as I could.

I ran back to the kitchen.

Alisha had laid Corey on his back on the kitchen table. She was just peeling off the Superman pajamas. His white naked body lay face-up on the table. His eyes were closed. His extremities had gone blue. The farther down the arm or leg you looked, the bluer the skin appeared.

He was beginning to shake as he warmed. His arms were bent in at the elbows, his forearms held in the air an inch or two above his belly, his hands closed into tiny fists. Those fists and forearms were shaking and shivering uncontrollably.

"He's hypothermic, and possibly frostbitten," I said. "Okay, now lift him up, and I'll lay a towel down."

She did as told, and I spread a towel flat onto the table. She lay him down once more. We wrapped the towel around his pale shivering body. "Now another one," I said. We wrapped him in a second towel. We now had his small body completely swaddled so that only his head showed. "Now bring him into the den. You have to hold him against your body while I get a fire started."

Alisha followed me, holding her son tightly against her, as I had done out in the storm. She sat down in the loveseat facing the fireplace.

"I tried to start a fire after the power went out, but I couldn't get it to work."

She had tried lighting the big logs directly, instead of getting it going with kindling and newspaper first. I pulled out the four logs she'd thrown in and set them aside. I tore up some newspaper and set kindling atop of it. In minutes I had a real blaze going. I added the larger logs in two-to-three minute increments, allowing the fire to catch. I blew on it, nursing it along. Finally I had all four pieces in the flames. The fire hissed and crackled and spat.

I stood up, noticing for the first time how wet and cold I was. So beyond my own physical limits had I pushed myself out there that I'd begun to perspire. Sweating is a dangerous matter in the winter. I had worked up such a sweat that within twenty minutes my inner layer of clothing was soaked. In cold, windy climes, what becomes wet quickly becomes frozen. My constant movement, in turn creating more heat, had kept me alive.

"I'm going to change," I said. "Stay here with him."

She nodded wordlessly, never taking her eyes off Corey's face. She spoke to him in a low tongue while she rocked him slowly back and forth in her arms.

As I turned away, my eyes captured the partially constructed frame of Playworld in the background. It had a grounding effect, reminding me where I was and what I'd been doing before this madness had started. It made me think of the screwdriver I had unknowingly carried in my back pocket when I'd run out the door after Alisha. It made me think of the way her eyes had rolled in their sockets as she'd floundered in the icy water.

"Simon? Do you know what time it is?"

I was ascending the single stair, en route to my bedroom. I paused to peer into the kitchen, toward the battery-powered clock mounted on the wall high above the kitchen sink. It was 11:45 AM. Corey and I had been out in the storm for more than two hours.

*   *   *

I peeled off my wet clothing. I used a fresh towel to better dry myself before climbing into dry clothes. It was noticeably colder in here than it was in the center of the house, and the temperature had nowhere to go but down. Beyond the windows was a frothy white curtain moving left to right. I could barely make out the shadowy forms of trunks and tree limbs. The lake itself had been completely erased from view. The wind screamed along the eaves; it whistled and hooted through the gutters. The house swayed and shifted on its foundation. I had never seen or dreamed of anything like this.

I was rubbing the towel against my thighs and pelvis in hard, angry motions when suddenly I began to cry. It hit me without warning. I allowed myself to collapse into a sitting position in the corner created by the bed and the nightstand, naked save for the towel wrapped clumsily around my waist. I sobbed uncontrollably for two to three minutes. Shudders wracked my bare shoulders. My stomach muscles throbbed and quivered until they hurt. My eyes burned hot and wet. The banshee cry of the wind obscured my hitching, gasping sobs.

It ended as quickly as it had come. I used the towel to dry my face and the corners of my eyes.

There is more work to be done, Simon. Be mindful of that.

Sound logic got me going again. I climbed into fresh dungarees, T-shirt and sweater, socks and moccasins. Dry, warm feet have never felt so good.

Out in the den, Alisha was still rocking Corey gently in her arms. "His eyes are open now."

I sat down on the loveseat next to Alisha, looking closely into Corey's face. His large blue eyes flicked toward me, registering my presence. His cheeks were flushed red. His lips were slowly returning to their normal shade of pink.

"How you doin', kid? You with me?"

He nodded. The movement was slow and somewhat labored, but he was definitely improving. I couldn't help but smile.

"You listen to your mom, okay? She's gonna help you get warm. I've got some things I have to do."

"Like what?" Alisha asked.

"Little things," I said.

I added more wood to the fire. Using the cast iron poker, I jabbed and prodded at the already burning logs to keep the flames spitting and hissing. Then I went outside to fetch more wood. The pile stacked along the front of the house was buried in snow. These new logs I lay at both ends of the stone hearth so they could dry in preparation for later burning.

My next task was setting up the kerosene heaters I'd purchased in town last week. The first of these I put in Corey's bedroom. I struck a match and the heater hissed to life, producing a steady blue flame. I stood and watched as the coils going up the center of the unit began to glow red. The outlay of heat wouldn't be exorbitant; it would, however, be sufficient to keep the room modestly warm.

I set up the second of the two heaters in the kitchen, for the time being. When that was done, I went around the house opening the water taps on all the sinks and bathtub faucets. Not full tilt, but partway—enough to create an aperture through which water could move if the standing water in the pipes began to freeze.

I explained this to Alisha, adding, "We'll find out how well Nels Turner insulated his house."

"You really think the pipes might freeze, Simon?"

"With this wind, there's a high possibility, yes. Next order of business: I need you to tell me where you keep any flashlights, candles, and matches you may have."

"Oh, geez … You can try under the kitchen sink."

I found a pair of tall, thin candles burned two-thirds of the way down their stems. There was one flashlight containing a pair of dead batteries.

Dammit. I lowered my chin to my chest and closed my eyes, forcing myself to rein in my mounting frustration. I had done more in the last month to prepare for emergency than Alisha had done in a year and a half.

I went down to the garage. I had more luck rooting through Nels Turner's junk pile than anywhere else. I came up with an old propane lantern—its small tank still had some gas in it, as evident by the hissing sound when I opened the vent—as well as four thick candles, yet unused, and a box of wood matches.

I set my finds onto the dining room table, saying as I went, "There's an old generator down there, but it's so badly rusted it's not worth slaving over. There's only so much gas anyhow. I'd be lucky to get twenty minutes out of it if it did run."

By 6:00 PM, the combination of darkness and the storm's wrath had encircled the house like the tightening coils of a python. You could hear Crawford's ribcage popping and cracking as it worked overtime to hold Mother Nature's fury at bay. A loose window or two rattled in its frame. The upper rafters groaned with discord. Every now and again, something would bang against the roof. I had all four candles lit: one apiece in the den, kitchen, my bedroom, and Alisha's bedroom. The kerosene heater in Corey's room provided minimal, albeit sufficient illumination. I moved the second kerosene heater to Alisha's bedroom and lit the old propane lantern in the kitchen. The propane lantern threw enough light to disclose two-thirds of the kitchen, enough for us to enjoy a modest dinner by.

"This is quaint," Alisha said.

Had he been his normal self, Corey would have found these conditions exciting and worthy of considerable chatter. Tonight, though, he was unnaturally quiet. I wondered several times if he wasn't experiencing some form of semi-shock. He poked his spoon disconsolately at a bowl of Honey Nut Cheerios. "I'm not hungry, Mom."

"Try to eat a little bit, honey, okay?"

For Alisha and I, it was peanut butter and jelly sandwiches and warm ginger ale. I discovered that I wasn't all that hungry, either. Actually, what I craved was a warm beverage. I was cold on the inside.

Corey was already wearing his bunny rabbit pajamas, the cute little hood pulled over his head, one ear lopped in front of his face. After dinner, Alisha helped him climb out of the PJs so we could look at his extremities. He sat on a kitchen chair in his underwear and began to shiver.

"Cold, Mom."

"I know, love, it's only for a minute. Simon needs to look at your toes."

Alisha held the lantern while I held Corey's left foot, then his right, in my open palm. The dark coloration had gone mostly away. Some of his smaller toes were still inflamed, though, and I knew he'd come awfully close to losing them.

I rubbed the pad of my finger lightly against the underside of one of his toes. "Can you feel this, sport?"

He nodded.

"Can you feel this?"

Nodded again.

"How 'bout that?"

Nodded still.

I began tickling the sole of his right foot. "And how 'bout this?"

He smiled dimly, yanking his foot away.

"Now I think it's time for you to go to bed," I said.

He was too drowsy to protest. He asked, "Can you both read me a story?"

"A story?" Alisha said. "Of course we can."

"In the dark?" I asked.

Fortunately, the lantern had a metal hook on its top, which I slung over one of the crossbars of Corey's upper bunk. I turned down the intensity so that the light wouldn't overwhelm us, and the three of us crowded ourselves into the space beneath the upper bunk, with Corey sandwiched in the middle and enough light to read by.

He scrunched into his bunny suit once more, and he was as cute as pie. He asked, "Simon …? Why did …?"

"Yes?"

"Why, um … why were we out in the snow before?"

"We went out to build a snowman."

"We did?"

Alisha broke in, "No, honey, he's being silly. You walked in your sleep again. The dark man in your dreams chased you. You ran out of the house and into the snow, and Simon went out to get you. Simon brought you back."

I rubbed one hand against my left leg, trying to warm myself. "Corey, do you remember running out of the house?"

"No."

"Do you remember the dream you were having this morning?"

"No."

I marveled at the depth and complexity of sleep one would have to attain to not be immediately jarred awake by bitter cold and piercing winds. I wondered at what point the storm *had* awakened him. Had he cried out there, before I'd stumbled across him? Had he known on a conscious level that he was lost? Had he tasted terror?

Smelled the closeness of death? Had he felt the pain, and later the numbness, of exposure?

Alisha began reading from Corey's favorite tome of Richard Scary's assorted tales. He was sound asleep in minutes. His small head rested on my right shoulder. I could scarcely hear the smooth rise and fall of his breathing through Alisha's voice and the hiss of the lantern.

She stopped reading in mid-sentence. "Simon, what's wrong?"

"Nothing. Why?"

She reached over her son's slumping form to lay a hand on my shoulder. "You're shaking."

"I'm fine." I wasn't, though. I was cold on the inside, and getting colder. "I'll check the fire."

I went out to the den to kneel in front of the dancing flames. I added another log, then held my hands as close to the fire as the heat would allow. Alisha was doing something in the kitchen. She came out moments later holding two glasses and a bottle of dark liquid.

"Christ, Simon, you're *shivering*. I can see your arms moving."

"I told you, I'm all right. I'm just a little … a little shaken up."

I heard liquid decanting into a glass. "Sit down and drink this. It'll help."

I backed into the loveseat and accepted the glass from her. She poured some for herself and set the bottle on the wood floor. She sat against the armrest with both legs curled beneath her, watching me closely. "Go on."

I raised the glass. It burned my lips and felt like acid going down. But I felt a slow warmth beginning to spread through my belly. I nursed the liquid, taking several more sips. Gradually, the shaking in my hands and arms subsided.

"What is this stuff?"

"Something to warm you up after a heroic day."

I shook my head. "No, not a …"

"Simon … Simon, I told you to let go of me. I told you to let go … and you didn't. You *didn't*."

But I was about to. That's the part you don't understand.

"You saved two lives today," she added in her dusky voice. "We both could have been lost. Mother and son. You brought us both back. First one, then the other."

"You don't … understand—"

"Yes, I do," she said, nodding. "I understand perfectly well what you did …"

"… was lucky to cross paths with him. I was lucky to stumble … it wasn't …"

"Tell me what happened out there," Alisha beckoned. "Tell me what happened that has you shaking so badly."

I had already resolved myself never to speak of what had happened out in the storm. But that didn't mean that I wasn't somehow going to have to find a way to live with it. Or reconcile some of the strange events that had happened along the way. What was I to make of the light I had seen over my shoulder? That light had come from the house. From *this* house. With Alisha freezing solid in my arms, as frost hardened her cheeks and the life went out of her eyes … I'd been turned around, I'd lost the way. Extricating her from the icy water had been one thing, but my luck had run out now for sure.

Except it hadn't. One small stroke remained, and I had gone toward it. Gone toward it remembering, *There is no happiness in that home. But there used to be.*

And what was I to make of what had happened later? How could I explain to Alisha that I had given up? If I had saved two lives, if I was the hero she claimed me to be, then how could it be that I felt so bad? So guilty? So dishonored? How was it that a man could stand tall with all he had, and come up so dreadfully short? How was it that he could come up so dreadfully short in what had been a mismatch from the very beginning … *and still win?* How were these things so?

How was it that I had found the boy dead, yet brought him back alive?

He probably wasn't dead, Simon. Probably he was so cold that you misread his vital—

But I didn't think so. Corey hadn't had a pulse when I'd found him. His heart had not been beating. Peeling back his eyelids had revealed dilated pupils.

So, how was it that I had gone from giving up and coming back with nothing … to coming back with a dead body … to coming back with a living, ultimately healthy young boy?

"Simon, you're starting to shake again."

My glass was empty. Alisha raised the bottle and refilled it. She put the bottle down again.

"Simon, I want you to look at me."

She moved closer. Her hand was touching my shoulder, then sliding down my arm. I could feel the warmth of her breath. I could feel the warmth of her body.

"Simon … you're cold." Whispering now.

"I'll … be okay."

"Then why won't you look at me? I can help you."

"I … don't—"

"Just once, Simon. Look me in the eye one time …"

I looked her in the eye. Orange flames dancing off quicksilver glass. Her lower lip curling outward. She came toward me, and I didn't turn away. Her face was inches away from mine, and she stayed there for a moment, as if she could see something not visible from farther away. One of her hands came up to caress my cheek. The pads of her fingers moved over my chin and danced across my lips, as if testing what was there, what I was made of. My tongue moved out just enough to wet the last of her fingers. She slowly lowered her hand. Her eyes watched me, moving up and down as she fell closer, angling her head slightly and pressing her lips to mine.

She kissed me slowly, softly, gently. Her lips were moist and supple. I felt the tip of her tongue brush the inside of my upper lip. She broke away momentarily, looking down at me questioningly with black eyelashes at half-mast. I looked up at her, and decided I wanted more of her. I reached up with one hand, holding her face and caressing her cheek with the pad of my thumb. I moved my hand around the nape of her neck and pulled her toward me.

We kissed a second time. My tongue was inside her mouth now. Hers was inside mine. Light came to darkness, darkness came to light. Snow clicked and whickered off the windows. The walls popped and groaned against the wind. Alisha's breathing was deepening. She lifted herself partway off the loveseat, pivoting around on one knee and planting her other knee on the other side of me, straddling me with her thighs. Again I was looking up at her. She held my face with both of her hands, and came down to meet my lips again. We kissed with a predatory lust this time, one feeding off the other.

She pulled away again, both hands resting on the tops of my shoulders. Her silvery hair spilled over her own shoulders, backlit by the flames. She tilted her head forward, never looking away from me, speaking to me with her eyes.

I moved my hands slowly up her thighs, which were firm and taut beneath the jeans she wore. Worked them around both sides of her hips. I felt the warmth of her underneath the clothing. She was so warm. She was so *warm*.

She unzipped her denim jacket. Shook it off. Underneath was a white, long-sleeve cotton turtleneck. She lifted this off with slow, unhurried precision, letting it fall to the floor. I placed my hands on the front of her bare belly, moved them around to the small of her back, then brought them to the front once more. She reached behind herself with both arms, her elbows pointed upwards, and seconds later her bra fell away. I cupped her breasts with gentle hands, kneading them into hardness. I leaned forward and put my mouth on them. I tasted her and relished her. The more of her I got, the more I wanted.

She moaned wantonly. "Oh, Simon … take me … up … stairs …"

Her bedroom had been sufficiently warmed by the kerosene heater. The coils glowed and hissed. The lit candle on the nightstand stood unwavering, casting a soft yellow light on Alisha's body as I undressed her. I knelt before her, sliding my hands up the fronts of her thighs, watching and feeling at the same time. There seemed a dissonance between sight and texture of the feminine perfection that stood before me. But gradually my hands verified what my eyes saw. I leaned closer and kissed her, moving my lips along her inner thigh, and then skipping up to her navel, and then both sides of her hips, until finally I took her true womanhood into my mouth. She crooned and grew weak and trembled before me. I stood up and pushed her gently backwards, onto the bed. She lay down and waited there for me as I undressed. "Oh, come to me, Simon. Come to me now."

I went to her.

She lay on her back watching me, legs bent up at the knees, her chest rising and falling rapidly. I moved between her thighs, preparing to meet her, hovering over her with my hands pinning her wrists against the mattress, and we spoke to one another with our eyes once more. Her chest rose and fell to a faster cadence, faster and faster, her cream-colored breasts swimming below me. Alisha watched me tirelessly, saying nothing, then lifted her head once, her chin touching her chest, as if to examine her own body. Then her eyes were looking into mine once more, telling me she was ready.

And still I waited, holding her down and hovering over her as her breathing quickened, rising to a crescendo, and I felt her warm thighs, so soft and warm, as they closed and rubbed against the sides of my torso, preparing to accept me and at the same time rein me in, and I was aware of her head beginning to rock back as her chin lifted toward me and—

Our bodies met. Darkness came to light, light came to darkness. The wind shook the house, windows rattled in metal frames, tree limbs batted and swished and cracked at each other. I thrust myself into Alisha and she rose up to meet me. Her climax was immediate, and mine was close behind. She pressed herself so forcefully into me, and me into her, that I temporarily lost sense of my singular being, and embraced our union as oneness. There was a flash of light accompanied by a fleeting of thought, and I no longer knew where I was or how I'd gotten there, but I knew I'd come home, knew I was home at last, I was where I belonged, there was happiness in this home again, as we paused and waited and rested and then rose up again, our bodies melding together, Alisha pressing her hot flesh into mine as the python tightened its coils around us, around all that there is, as light comes to darkness, darkness comes to light.

*   *   *

I slept in her arms. She slept in mine.

Twice I awakened and began to shiver. She moved closer to me, held me tighter. "It's okay, Simon. Don't be cold. Don't be cold." She rubbed her hands across my back and shoulders, scissored her bare legs against mine. It worked both times. I fell asleep against her.

Later, I woke a third time. It was hard to know when without working clocks, but I'd surmise it was around three. The storm hadn't abated. That freight train roar of wind oppressed all things great and small.

I started to climb out of bed. Alisha stirred. "Simon, what is it?"

"I thought I would check on Corey."

"I'll check on him. You stay here."

When she returned minutes later, she nuzzled up against me, and her body was as warm as ever. She laid her cheek on my shoulder, inches from my neck. "Mmm, he's fine. He's sleeping like an angel. Thanks to you."

"I got lucky, Alisha."

"My hero …"

"I got lucky," I reiterated.

*   *   *

An hour later, I woke again and this time managed to slip free of her grasp and out of bed without rousing her. I crept down the stairs in my bare feet to check the guttering fire. I added three more logs and got it going again. Then I went into Corey's bedroom. He was indeed sleeping peacefully. I sat next to him, watching him closely and stroking his forehead. I stayed with him for close to twenty minutes, listening to his gentle breathing and watching him sleep. I checked the kerosene level in the heater to ensure it would burn through the night. It would.

Back in the hall, I turned right to glance into my own room. It was strange seeing the bed made up and unslept in.

I ascended the spiral stairs and returned to the master bedroom. Carefully, I turned the sheets aside and slid back into bed. The mattress was warm, the sheets were warm, Alisha was warm. She turned and rolled her body into mine. We lay on our sides facing one another, front-to-front, my loins against hers, hers against mine, our arms wrapped around one another.

Sleep rose up and took me down again. I didn't wake up this time.

*   *   *

The blizzard raged right on through the following day. Around 6:00 PM the winds began to taper off. Snow continued to fall, but it was slackening.

I was jolted awake in the middle of the second night by coughing, sputtering spigots, followed by the sounds of running water. Alisha raised her head off the pillow, squinting as lights flickered on. "What's happening?"

"Power's back on," I said.

I rolled out of bed and moved through the house turning off lights and faucets alike. The thought of utility crews working in the dead of night to restore power while others slept, literally trapped in their homes, both warmed me and gave me goose pimples. The real victory would come when the burner returned to duty down in the basement. Nothing happened at first, though. Then I remembered something my father had showed me ten or twelve years ago. I went down the basement stairs, went around to the back of the burner, and slid off the metal safe-plate. The plate revealed some wires and fuses, and a black panel with a single red button in the middle of it. A reset button. I pressed it. The furnace roared to life.

*   *   *

The storm cleared out, the python relinquished its grip. The sun swam through a sky of aqua blue so pure and clean that no brush could have painted it. The return of electricity brought TV and radio reports of just how bad the blizzard had been. It had dumped thirty-four inches of snow and claimed eleven lives throughout the New England states. Two dozen people were still unaccounted for. In western Vermont, a family of three had been traveling a county road when the serpentine belt in their old Ford had snapped. They'd waited for help alongside the road, the engine running and the heaters on. They'd run out of gas in the middle of the first night. They'd frozen to death. At least four elderly folks had died inside their homes from extreme cold due to the no-heat conditions.

We took showers and gave Corey a bath. It felt downright rejuvenating to be clean again.

It took three more days for a municipal spreader to get far enough out, and ultimately plow out our long, switchback driveway. Those may have been the best three days of my life. We spent them together, reading stories and making up stories, and playing board games in front of the fireplace. We played board games for eight hours straight one day. Corey loved Candyland, but he cried any time he drew a card depicting a piece of candy that sent him backward on the game board. So we gave him a mulligan. He loved Chutes and Ladders even more, but he cried anytime he landed on one of the chutes. We gave him a mulligan for that, too. As a result, Corey almost always won.

It was Alisha's idea to try Monopoly. Corey had no idea how to play, but he loved rolling the dice and marching around the game board. He loved collecting money, even if he couldn't count it. He bought properties and built houses. When he landed on the Boardwalk, finding himself in a position to put a stranglehold on the upper half of the game board, Alisha told him that buying it would be a bad investment.

"Why?" he asked. "I thought you were supposed to buy places."

"Yes, honey, but you'll never be able to afford the taxes on it."

"What are those?"

I leaned over. "I think your mom's giving you bad advice, kid."

Alisha won, eventually, by talking Corey into allowing her to stay in his hotels rent-free.

We went outside and built snowmen. When that was done, we had a snowball fight. We came inside afterward, hot and sweaty and thirsty, and we sat around the kitchen table drinking hot cocoa, telling jokes and laughing.

Corey, still recovering from his trauma in the blizzard, took occasional naps during the three-day period. They were much needed naps, too, judging by the swiftness with which he fell asleep. While he slept, Alisha and I made love. She wore jewels on one occasion. Diamond earrings, gold necklace, pearl bracelets, a diamond-studded ankle bracelet. I looked down at her, brushed her hair away from her eyes. Kissed her forehead. We napped in each other's arms.

Later, we showered together in Alisha's master bath. Afterward, while sitting in front of her vanity and combing her wet hair, a towel wrapped about her midsection, she said she wanted to ask me something.

"It's silly. Trivial, really. But I've always wanted to ask it to a man."

She was watching me through the mirror. "So ask," I said. "I'll give you an answer, if I can."

"When a woman walks down the sidewalk, what part of her does a man notice first? If she's attractive, what attracts him? What part of the woman's body does he find the sexiest?"

"That's three questions, but the answer's the same to all three. The answer is her heart."

Alisha studied me through the mirror. "That's not really what I meant, Simon."

"No. But it's what I meant."

"So, how does the man know what the woman's heart looks like, then? How is a woman to know what a man's heart is like? The heart is invisible, Simon."

"It's one of life's great challenges, I suppose."

She turned and glanced at me over her shoulder. "You're different, Simon, you realize. Most men would never give such an answer."

"I'm not trying to be different," I said quietly.

"I know you're not," she answered, resuming her brushing once more. "I know you're not."

*   *   *

On the third day, the plow came, an enormous beast of a truck with a giant V-shaped blade that stood six feet high and parted the snow as though it were dust. The Public Works man at the wheel appeared as though he hadn't slept in a fortnight, but he kindly cleared out the base of the driveway for us, the diesel engine grinding and cutting and coughing clouds of grayish smoke. When he was finished, what he'd left behind was a flat, solid snowpack—perfect for sledding. We spent the remainder of the day making runs down the driveway on Corey's new runner sled. I'd sit with my feet on the steering bar, Corey sitting between my legs, and down we'd go, fast as lightning. We'd go crashing into the snowdrifts the plow truck had left, laughing until our faces turned rosy red. Then Corey and Alisha would run together. Then Alisha and I. Corey couldn't get enough of it. "One more time!" he'd yell, jumping up and down in his blue snowsuit. *"Let's go one more time!"*

The sledding wore him out. After a huge, delicious home-cooked meal, one could tell just by looking that he was ready for the pillow. He was fast asleep by quarter to eight.

Alisha and I stayed up until ten or so. We had a brandy and sat by the fireplace and talked. We touched on a variety of topics, from politics to art to history. Eventually we retired to the master bedroom, where we talked some more before making love. I brought her slowly to climax, building steadily toward it, until neither of us could hold out any longer, and we peaked together, as one.

We slept.

*   *   *

Around midnight, I nudged her awake. "Alisha. Alisha."

"Mmm …"

"There's something I've been meaning to tell you."

She rolled over to face me. She brushed her hair away from her face. "What is it, Simon?" Her voice was thick.

"The day of the blizzard," I started. "The morning … that it happened."

"What? Tell me."

"All these dreams Corey's been having … The sleepwalking … Dr. Andrews is wrong, we've all been wrong. Corey's not running *away* from the man in black." A pause. "He's running after him."

She thought it over awhile before turning onto her other side again. "Try to get some sleep, Simon."

CHAPTER EIGHTEEN

INSIDE THE VAULT

THEY DON'T KNOW EVERYTHING, Simon. They don't know quite everything ... We were in the Roadgrader again, Ma and I. We were always driving these days, it seemed, running from one thing while chasing something else. My foot hard on the gas, trying to outrun the past and stay ahead of the rain. Ma clutched her purse to her chest with both arms. She held an item in her right fist. I couldn't see the item now, but I saw that the fist was shaking. Ma was shaking, too.

"Are you sure you're all right, Ma?"

"I am definitely not all right, Simon. You've no idea what I'm about to do."

I switched on my left turn signal. The Midland County Savings & Trust was a one-story building of white brick. It was one of the few remaining small-town banks not yet swallowed by the larger conglomerates. I had never been inside it. To the best of my knowledge, neither of my parents had ever carried an account there.

"No, not yet, Simon. Keep driving."

"But I thought—"

"Just keep driving, will you? Christ, I'm not ready yet."

I disengaged the turn signal and stepped on the gas again. I was honked at twice for driving like a lost tourist.

"Where are we going, Ma?"

"Just drive, dammit. Drive while I get my nerve." She turned and looked out her side window. In a lower voice, as if speaking to the glass, "God and Thomas, could I use a drink."

Four days had passed since the night I'd taken Ma to her first AA meeting in Budd Lake. She'd held mostly true to her promise—we'd attended a meeting every day. We'd gone to one in Lake Parsippany one day, another in Lake Hiawatha the next, then another in Randolph. There were meetings all over the place, we were learning—held in churches in every town and city in the country every day and evening of the week. Those who peopled them hailed from all walks of life: gardeners and florists, doctors and dentists, executives and CEOs, teachers and grocery store clerks and trash collectors. There were husbands and wives, there were brothers and sisters, there were parents and children.

Ma had suffered a setback. She'd had three drinks on the second day. She'd stopped after the third, ashamed and angry at herself. When told in Randolph last night that the ninety days would start over, a black man in the second row had comforted Ma, telling her not to feel too badly. "I relapsed on my eighty-sixth day," he told her. "Don't know why, really. The urge to have a drink that day was strong, and I was weak."

"What constitutes a relapse, exactly?" Ma had asked him.

"One drink. One sip."

Ma was just beginning to grasp the long-term nature of her recovery. "Oh, dear. That means never again. Never ever."

"Never again," the black man told her. His smile was full of reassurance, his eyes full of hope.

"Where am I driving to, then?" I asked Ma.

"I don't know. Drive in circles. Go around town for a while."

"The last time I pulled into the Sunoco, they didn't give me the gas for free."

"Courage isn't for free either, Simon. You have to work at it."

I turned onto Lake Drive West—pretty funny, I thought, considering there was no longer a lake in Lake Hiawatha. Lake Parsippany had a lake. Budd Lake had a lake. What did Lake Hiawatha have?

"Besides," she went on, "there's something I wanted to tell you. About your father. He won once."

One-Lane Bridge 199

I risked a glance at Ma. She was staring straight ahead, her lips firm, her cheeks hardened and set, her face unreadable.

"I'm not advocating what he did," she said. "His addiction was every bit as bad as mine, Simon. Probably in some ways it was worse. But for the record … let's just say it would be unfair not to give him his due. He won once. One time."

She held up her index finger to accentuate her point. *One time.*

"What did he win, Ma?"

A whole lotta nuthin, was what I thought she'd say. *A big fat headache, an enema, a four-valve blockage leading to myocardial infarction and an early retirement. How's that for winner-take-all?*

"Your father began placing bets online. It was three years ago, I'd say. Maybe not even that long. That's not to say he lost interest in his ponies—nothing would pry your father away from the racetrack. But Internet betting was virgin territory for him, and he wasn't one to allow new waters to go untested for very long."

"I wasn't aware Dad knew how to use a computer."

"Neither was I, Simon, until our credit card statements began showing large balances."

I gawped at her. "You're saying Dad gambled on his credit cards? I didn't know you could do that."

"He gambled on *our* credit cards, Simon. And yes, you can do it, and it's highly illegal."

"Did Dad know it was ill—"

"Oh, Simon, I doubt he cared one way or the other. Most online casinos operate outside the Continental U.S., and they're easily accessed via the World Wide Web."

I waited, staring ahead with my hands fisted around the wheel. Ma's silence was loud. It was so loud it was almost scary. She held her purse against her bosom as though it were her last earthly possession. Her eyebrows were bunched together in tight scrutiny. For the first time, I saw her as someone dealing with her own issues instead of merely representing a symptom of my own. This was a woman who had her own pain, her own anger, and her own losses.

"Several years ago, your father placed a bet on the college basketball tournament. NCAA—is that what they call it?"

"More or less."

"It had gotten down to where there were only sixteen teams remaining."

"Sweet Sixteen," I told her.

"Your father rightly predicted which teams would be the final four, and then the final two, and ultimately the winner. One of his final four teams was a Cinderella pick, with extremely long odds to win, which of course upped the ante. Your father placed a bet of five hundred dollars. He won."

"How much did—"

"It was a six-figure sum, Simon. It was a lot of money. The only problem: the company that operated the site was a scam. They took the five-hundred-dollar wager, but never doled out the winnings."

"But didn't you go after them? You could've filed a lawsuit."

"We tried, Simon, we tried." Ma sounded tired as she said it. "We contacted the Better Business Bureau. And then the New Jersey Division of Gaming Enforcement. The Division placed us on a list with hundreds of others who'd been scammed and were trying to collect their winnings. They told us online betting was illegal because it's unsanctioned and unregulated. We even contacted the Nevada Gaming Commission and State Gaming Control Board, and they told us the same thing. For heaven's sake, it's not even legal in *Nevada*."

"So you gave up, then?"

"Not that easily, no. We hired a private investigation company— the Carl Landis Firm. We paid them a five-thousand-dollar retainer, then three thousand a month thereafter, for four months."

"Oh, Christ, Ma." I was beginning to feel sick to my stomach. Seventeen large out the window. Where was that money now? We could sure as hell use it.

"Carl Landis was able to track down the company that ran the online gaming site we were looking for—to a small town somewhere in South America. And from there to Bermuda. From Bermuda to southern Denmark. There, the trail went cold. These companies are like ghosts, Simon. They exist as a series of electronic routing offices in the basements of private homes, the back rooms of Laundromats, and hotel broom closets. They never stay in one location for very long."

"So Dad went from losing the five hundred, to winning a six-figure sum he couldn't collect, to spending seventeen thousand trying to recoup the six-figure sum that he couldn't collect."

I was beginning to feel downright nauseous.

I recalled the day Dad had pulled me out of school and taken me for a ride: the day of the pumpkins. That had been the day I'd learned the difference between a spit bug and a pinecone. It had also been the day Dad had spoken of fresh starts and new beginnings and turning the page and all that other bullshit. My father had been on such a high that day that his feet hadn't touched the ground.

I realized now that he'd probably won his bet—or *thought* he'd won, that is—the previous March, when the NCAA tournament took place. He would've spent that spring and summer paying the Carl Landis Firm large sums of money in hopes of collecting his winnings. It would have been a night during that summer when, upon my wandering ruminations of what I someday wanted to be, my father had lowered his newspaper and delivered what I would later recognize as the best piece of advice I ever got. *Take some time, during college or immediately after, to work with your hands …*

There was, in truth, no money for college … but he genuinely believed there *would* be because he was still nurturing hopes of collecting his winnings. Come October, he'd finally come to grips with the grim fact that there would be no winnings. He'd made the decision to quit betting altogether. That's what he'd meant by "turning the page." That's what his "fresh start" was meant to symbolize.

"Ma?"

"Yes, Simon?"

I was remembering something Mr. Smoot had told me the day he'd visited. About all the debts Ma and Dad had incurred in the past years. Second and third mortgages.

"Where did you and Dad come up with seventeen thousand dollars to pay to the Landis Firm?"

Ma fell silent. I turned and saw her biting her lower lip, and knew at once that I'd stepped on the land mine.

"He … borrowed it."

"Borrowed it from who?"

"I'm not sure. It was someone in Trenton, near the factory. One of your father's co-workers knew somebody, who knew someone else, who knew this guy. A guy by the name of Blackstone."

And he never paid Blackstone back. I knew this without having to ask. Knew it by the way my heart sank in my chest, by the way my stomach churned and tumbled. *He probably thought he was justified, too, in reneging on this Blackstone. After all, he'd been cheated out of* his *winnings. So, why shouldn't the cheat-ee become the cheat-er?* It was one long, sick line of dominoes. Each one cheating the next.

The only problem: Dad had died, but Blackstone hadn't. And Blackstone hadn't forgotten. Blackstone sent messengers. Or clients of his own. Possibly even creditors to whom he himself was beholden.

They came for Catherine. They came for an easy lay. Catherine was using her body to protect Ma, to protect *us.* All this time … all the fights and feuds Ma and Cath had had … and it had been Cath doing dirty deeds behind the scenes, trying desperately to preserve the estate.

Cath was five-foot-nine and under a hundred pounds. She was starving herself to death.

Did Ma know? Did Ma know what Cath was doing?

Maybe. But I couldn't bring myself to ask. I didn't want to know the answer to that question.

*   *   *

Moving up the sidewalk that led to the bank entrance, I caught Ma by the elbow, stopping her.

"What is it now, Simon?"

I'd been struck by a thought, sparked by a scene from the movie *Thelma & Louise.* "Ma, we're not robbing the place, are we?"

She read my face closely. "Yes, Simon, we are. It's good of you to finally catch on. Be sure to lay down a covering fire while the teller empties the vault into my pocket book. And have the getaway truck ready when I come bounding out the front entrance—we might make it down to the ShopRite before they catch us."

She turned her back on me as she pulled open the front door and went in. I went in after her.

The bank interior was small and cozy, with green carpeting. Instead of approaching the front desk where two tellers stood waiting, Ma walked into one of the office cubicles. The desktop nameplate read: Elizabeth Roas, Astnt. Mngr. Ms. Roas was an attractive lady in her mid-thirties, with long sandy hair and blue eyes. She wore a blue wool sweater and a French dress.

"Yes, ma'am, how can I help you today?" she asked.

"I need to access a safety deposit box," Ma told her.

"Okay. I just need to see ID. A driver's license will suffice."

"How 'bout a birth certificate?"

Ms. Roas paused. "We really prefer a photo ID."

"Passport?"

"That'd be great."

When Ms. Roas was satisfied that Ma was who she said she was, she smiled and said, "All right, follow me. You have your key, right?"

"Yes, I do." Ma held up the small key she'd been holding since we'd left the house.

We followed Ms. Roas past the tellers' counter into a narrow corridor. The assistant manager stopped in front of a thick, formidable-looking door halfway along the hallway, pausing long enough to tap a nine-digit access code into a keypad inset below the doorknob. There was a triple-clack as multiple security devices temporarily disengaged. She pulled the door open and held it long enough for us to pass through. We proceeded another six feet down the corridor before making a left turn. We went another ten feet before encountering a second door on the right. Ms. Roas entered another series of numbers into an identical keypad, and this time slid a white access card into a card slot. A red light above the card slot blinked over to green, indicating the magnetic lock mechanisms had disengaged.

We entered the safety deposit vault. The vault was a rectangular chamber with an island counter. Three of the four walls were composed entirely of gold lock boxes. The face of each box displayed a number and a pair of keyholes.

At the island counter, Ms. Roas withdrew a black ledger. She opened the ledger and began writing on a blank line on what looked like an oversized index card.

"And your box number?"

"Fifty-two," Ma answered.

"Okay … and I'll need you to sign here, please."

Ma scribbled *Carol Ann Kozlowski* into the blank space indicated by Ms. Roas's index finger.

"And the date, please."

Ma dated it.

Ms. Roas closed the ledger and pushed it aside. She turned to the wall of lock boxes behind her. Box fifty-two was located about chest-high in the right-hand corner. I was aware of my heart starting to thump in my throat as Ms. Roas inserted her key into the right-hand keyhole, and Ma inserted her own into the left.

"And turn …"

They both turned their keys. Ms. Roas grabbed the gold handle and pulled. The lock box slid partway out of the wall. Ma reached up to help her. The box looked about a foot wide and two feet long. Together they pulled the entire box out of the wall, and Ma was able to cradle it in her arms.

"Got it?"

"Yes, thank you," Ma said.

Ms. Roas led us to a private viewing room off one corner of the vault. "You can lock the door if you like. And you can slide the curtain over the window for privacy."

"Thank you," Ma said.

"There's a buzzer with an intercom out by the vault door. Just buzz me when you're ready to come out."

"Okay. Thanks."

Ms. Roas departed. Ma locked the viewing room door and drew the curtain over the window. It was just the two of us sitting in a locked room in a locked vault in a locked wing of a secure building. Ma set the lock box on the scarred tabletop. Before she slid aside the ceiling door, I asked her, "Does that manager lady know what's in this box?"

"Of course not, Simon. None of them know what resides in any of the boxes. Nor do they want to know."

I found this intriguing, if not outright fascinating. "But … aren't they curious?"

"Most people who lease safety deposit boxes use them to house precious documents, Simon. Things like house deeds, insurance papers, wills, and trusts. The vault is fireproof and blast proof. If World War Three were to break out just now, we might be among the few to survive it." She turned her face toward mine. "Wouldn't that be ironic?"

I somehow couldn't find the humor in it. "What's in the box, Ma?"

She slid aside the ceiling plate. I'm not sure what I expected to see … the Star of Africa, maybe … or a lost Fabergé egg. I expected something wonderful, something magnificent … something that would solve all of our problems.

An object wrapped in white oilcloth lay in the center of the box. Ma's forearms were visibly shaking as she reached in to remove it. She set it gently onto the tabletop between us, and slowly began peeling away the layers of cloth. Pulling back the final layer revealed a rectangular object that I first thought resembled some kind of designer belt buckle. It was three inches long, this object, and two inches tall. I saw a white, glittering stone set dead center into it … and heard, simultaneously, Ma's breath catch in her throat. One hand went up to her mouth to stifle a muted whistle.

"It's … more beautiful than I remember it."

I saw lots of gold. None of this gold appeared solid, however. It was thin and lacy, woven in intricate filigrees in ever-largening rectangles around that glittering centerpiece. Mounted in and among those gold filigrees were rows of what appeared to be small white pearls. The pearls had a waxy-shiny gloss to them.

"Simon … do you know what it is?"

"It …" *It looks like a belt buckle*, I wanted to say. "It's a piece of jewelry, I suppose."

"It's a Victorian brooch, Simon. The gold is 18-karat. It has forty-one seed pearls built into it. And that thing in the middle … you know what that is, don't you?"

"Judging by the tremor in your voice, I'm guessing it's a diamond."

"It's a *flawless* diamond, Simon. It has no physical defects. It's a two-and-a-half-carat stone."

"What does that mean?"

"It means that it's heavy. One carat equals two hundred milligrams."

That still didn't mean much to me. I'd always thought of a carrot as something orange that you could eat.

"The brooch itself was made in Scotland. The diamond was probably unearthed in South Africa."

"Is it true," I asked, "that a diamond is the hardest substance in the world?"

"The hardest naturally-occurring substance, yes. It's believed that diamonds were formed millions of years ago, when carbon was subjected to intense heat and pressure. Most of the world's most valuable diamonds were found in vertical rock formations deep in the ground, thought to be the throats of extinct volcanoes.

"This brooch was given to one of my great ancestors, Lady Rowena Versailes, by a French prince in proposal to marriage. Lady Rowena wore the brooch on her wedding dress the day she was married. It has subsequently been bequeathed to the first-born daughter of each successive generation, and worn on that daughter's wedding day. It made its way across the Atlantic when my great-great-grandmother, Agnes Darnelia, emigrated from Amsterdam with her husband, James. The brooch is roughly a hundred and fifty years old, Simon. It is a genuine family heirloom."

"You're saying … that this thing makes an appearance but once in a generation?"

"That's correct."

I asked, astonished, "You wore this, then? The day you and Dad got married?"

"Yes. I have pictures."

"And how long has it been locked up here?"

"Twenty-four years."

"So, this was meant to be passed on to …"

"Catherine. That's right."

I paused, realizing now why Ma's hand had been shaking out in the truck when she'd uttered the words, *You have no idea what I'm about to do.* What she was about to do was break six or seven generations of family legacy.

"Ma, wait. Maybe you shouldn't—"

"I've already made my decision, Simon. There's no other way to get us out of the mess we're in."

I swept my eyes across the floor, trying to suppress a tide of guilt, as if I were somehow to blame for this.

"Does Cath know this brooch exists?"

"Yes. I first showed her the day she turned thirteen. And again, the day she turned sixteen."

"Ma, she'll be devastated."

"Devastation is relative, Simon. Would you rather be homeless?"

I had no answer to that. I had somehow turned the tables on Ma in the past week, forcing her to look reality true in the face. Now she was turning those same tables on me. Looking reality true in the face requires one to make arduous decisions. That Ma was finally beginning to undertake those decisions on her own was laudable.

I recalled with sobriety the dollar figure Smoot had thrown at me. "How much is this thing worth?"

She took a moment to think it over. "In today's market, the diamond alone is worth between fifty and fifty-five thousand dollars."

"Fifty *thousand*?"

"That's right."

"Holy shit with pudding and whipped cream." This changed things. This changed *everything*. There was a way out now, and I could see it. I could see it, and Ma could feel it. There was a way to wipe the slate clean and start fresh. "You're sure you want to do this, Ma?"

"I'm sure, Simon. It's the only choice I have, really, given the circumstances." She picked up my hand in her own, squeezed it. "To thine own self be true. Right?"

I smiled. I even laughed a little.

"Now let's get out of here," she said. "The getaway truck is waiting."

CHAPTER NINETEEN

NIGHT WRITER

LIGHT COMES TO DARKNESS, darkness comes to light …

Corey went back to school on Tuesday, the tenth of January. It was one of those bitterly cold, bright, clear days. A sky of piercing blue stretched from one horizon to the next. The northwest wind drove dry snow into powdery windmills along the crests of drifts and dunes. The air temperature alone was twenty-six degrees. But the wind made it feel more like ten.

I began using Josef's Tacoma because it had four-wheel drive. The keys had been left on the console.

Corey was silent on the way to school. He sat looking sleepily out his window at the white landscape.

"Are you happy to be going back?" I asked.

He shrugged both shoulders.

"Well, we're back to the normal schedule again. Today's Tuesday. That means karate at four o'clock."

He sighed. "I don't want to go to karate anymore."

"Why not?"

"Can't we stay home and go sledding instead? That's more fun."

Something in his voice made me smile. It may have been the excitement reverberating around his words … or his eyes lighting up like neon. It brought to mind the sight of him in his blue snowsuit, jumping up and down and hollering, "One more time! Let's go one more time!" It made me think of the way he'd hunched down on the sled in front of me, my legs spread around him with my feet on the steering bar, one arm wrapped around his upper body to keep him close. Or going down with Alisha sitting behind me, her legs tight against my sides, her chin resting over my shoulder so that our cheeks touched, screaming in my ear all the way down. Sometimes whispering in my ear. Her silverish hair blowing helter-skelter, sometimes draping over my nose and mouth, redolent of her shampoo.

I dropped Corey off at the Ace of Spades and drove home. Crawford Daze had indeed changed. It looked different from the outside and felt different on the inside. I went inside and sensed that budding newness the way I had when I'd come out of the storm with Corey's body stuffed into my Carhartt. The angles of the rafters had changed. The shadows in the high corners had shifted positions. Some of the shadows had receded. I stood still in front of the fireplace, trying to gauge what else appeared different. The spiral staircase looked wider, but shorter … yet the balcony above looked to have retained its normal height.

The changes aren't physical, Simon. They're in your mind.

I shook my coat off and went into the kitchen for a cup of coffee. The pot was half empty, meaning Alisha was awake and in her office. Out in the den, I stoked the fire and sat in front of it for a while. I got up and maneuvered around the abandoned Playworld (unchanged from the day of the storm), moving up close to the closed door of Alisha's office. I peered furtively through the glass. She sat statuesque in her swivel chair, legs crossed, holding her coffee mug with both hands. She stared past her blank computer screen—the cursor blinking unfailingly in the upper left corner—at the snow-swept lake beyond the windows. Did she get ideas from out there? I wondered. She'd been staring through those windows for a month and a half now. It occurred to me I might be witnessing a rather severe case of writer's block.

Knowing better than to interrupt, I sat down on one of the sofas with my coffee and waited for her to emerge. Twenty minutes later, she did, holding her empty mug in one hand.

She saw me sitting on the sofa with my legs propped up on the coffee table and halted. "Oh, hi, Simon. What's up?"

"Nothing much."

She started toward the kitchen once more, then seemed to catch a better glimpse of my face, and stopped again.

"Is everything okay? What are you thinking about?"

"Everything's fine."

She came forward and sat down on the neighboring sofa, watching me intently and rubbing her hands over the tops of her thighs. She crossed her legs, laying one arm on the sofa's backrest. "Talk to me."

I couldn't help but laugh a little.

She smiled. "Why are you laughing? What's funny?"

A month ago, you would've come out of your office ready to bite someone's head off—that's what's funny.

Instead of answering her question, I said, "It's a beautiful day, isn't it?"

"Yes, it is. It's cold, though. It's one of those days that makes a great photograph for a New England postcard … yet if you're living in that postcard, the day finds you longing for summer."

"I want you to stop paying me."

"Ah, I knew we were thinking about something."

"I mean it," I said. "I don't want to be paid anymore. Not another dollar."

"That's not an option," she replied. "I won't hear of it."

"I won't deposit any more of your checks."

"I'll direct-deposit them, then. I know your account number."

"I'll change my account number."

"Simon, you still have a job to do here, and you *will* be paid for—"

"Well, it doesn't feel like a job anymore," I said. "I don't feel like I'm working. I can't say it any other way."

"Work doesn't always have to be unpleasant. Besides, you're going to need every dime you can possibly get for law school. Have you any idea what tuition costs these days?"

I paused, staring down into my coffee. I lifted my gaze slowly but couldn't meet her eyes. "I'm not sure I want to go to law school."

This was met with silence. She tilted her head to one side and said softly, "Simon, don't say that."

I lowered my eyes to my coffee cup again, shaking my head a

little. "I don't know, things are ... changing, I guess." *Like the house. They're changing like the house around us.*

"Well, look, don't make all your important decisions in one day. Time will bear them out." She stood up and came toward me. She bent over and kissed me on one cheek. "And if you bring up this matter again, I'll have to force you into accepting a raise."

*   *   *

Thursday around one, I pulled into the Ace of Spades to find Corey sitting glumly on the long wooden bench inside the enclosed corridor that connected the preschool with the kindergarten. His coat was on and his small knapsack was on his lap. His oversized hat and mittens made him appear smaller than he actually was.

"Ready?" I asked.

He nodded wordlessly. His lower lip was puckered out, and one of his cheeks was slightly red. It was a face I'd seen before.

"What's wrong, kid?"

"Tommy threw snow over me."

"When? Just now?"

"A little while ago. There was a fire drill, and we all had to go out—outside in, um, the parking lot. And he got some snow and threw it over my head."

Again I felt the urge to laugh at the trivial strife of child warfare. Again I controlled it. Because the corridor was crowded with kids and parents alike, I had to sit down on the bench beside Corey in order to be heard, and to avoid being overheard.

"Did you cry?"

Nodding.

"Well, did you tell the teacher?"

Still nodding.

"And what did the teacher do?"

"She put Tommy in time-out. And then he called me a dirtbag."

"Tommy called you a dirtbag?"

Nodding again.

I put one arm around him. "Okay, look. Tommy is preying on you because you're gentle. You need to learn how to fight back."

Corey lowered his head and stuck his lower lip out again.

Fighting back wasn't his nature. I wondered where all those karate lessons had gone to.

I asked him, "Is Tommy still here? Can you point him out?"

He nodded, pushing himself off the bench. He moved to the left, toward the kindergarten classroom, pausing at the doorway, his eyes scanning the room. His arm came up in a point. I saw at once why Corey didn't feel compelled to retaliate. The boy at whom he pointed stood six inches taller and probably weighed thirty pounds more. He was washing the chalkboard along the back wall of the room. I cast a cursory glance around the rest of the room. Mrs. Thomas—the friendlier of the two teachers—was involved with four or five kids up close to the front of the classroom. They were preparing the room for the upcoming father-son breakfast by stapling nametags to the bulletin board.

I turned to Corey. "Go sit down on the front step and wait for me. I'll be right out."

He did as told. I discreetly made my way toward the far end of the classroom, where Tommy was just completing his task of washing the chalkboard. Upon closer inspection, he was a chunky meatball of a child with dark hair and pudgy cheeks and a face full of freckles.

I came up beside him. "Hi, there."

He looked up at me silently.

"Are you Tommy?"

He didn't answer. His brown, vacant eyes and protuberant nose reminded me of the finger holes in a bowling ball.

I knelt down in front of him, so we were eye-to-eye. "Answer me, son. I asked you a question. Is your name Tommy?"

He nodded.

"Well, look, I understand you've been giving Corey a hard time. Is it true you dumped snow on his head earlier? During the fire drill?"

He only stared at me.

"Is it true that you called him a dirtbag?"

The same stare. His meaty lips came together above a double chin. His eyelids blinked up and down.

"Corey tells me you did. He also says that you've picked on him in the past. Well, guess what? I'm Corey's big brother. And I'm going to keep an eye on you, Tommy. If I find out that you've been mean to Corey in any way, I'm gonna come and get you. You got that, you overweight pig-faced lump of shit? Answer me, Tommy. You got it?"

Tommy nodded. His vacuous expression didn't change.

"Atta boy." I clapped him once on the shoulder and then left.

*　　　*　　　*

The phone rang at ten-thirty that night. It was past my normal bedtime, but I was still awake. I was lying on my bed with one knee drawn up, reading an Ed McBain novel. Who would call at this hour? I wondered. I waited for Alisha to pick up—there was a phone in her bedroom, of course—but the kitchen line continued to ring. And ring. And ring.

"For the love of Pete," I uttered finally, tossing aside the paperback. I jogged out to the kitchen and lifted the portable handset from its cradle. "Hello?"

I was met with silence. When I took a moment to quickly peek at the Caller ID screen, I saw Private Caller. "Hello? Going once, going twice …"

"I'm, uh, calling for Alisha Caldwell," a man's voice stumbled.

"If she didn't answer herself, she must be dead asleep. Who's calling?"

Another moment of silence. "Well … who are you?"

"I think I asked you first."

More hesitation. "I'm a friend. Kind of an old friend. Think you could wake her?"

"No." By this time, I had wandered out of the kitchen and into the den area. The only light came from the flames whickering in the fireplace. "But I could take a message. Say, haven't you called several times before? Your voice sounds familiar."

The man hung up.

"All right, then. Be that way." I clicked the off button on the portable phone as I approached the spiral stairs. I had put one foot on the bottom riser when I caught a dim glimmer of light from the corner of my left eye. The light was coming from Alisha's office— from underneath the door, to be precise. The blinds had been lowered to cover the glass, something she rarely did in the daytime. The thin line of light escaping beneath the bottom edge of the door and skating several inches across the wood floor before diffusing entirely was too dim to be coming from a desk lamp or overhead light.

It looked like the soft gray light that might be thrown from a computer screen.

Still holding the phone in one hand, I stepped softly to the closed door, holding my ear close to it. From the other side came the busy clack of computer keys. I stood for several minutes listening to the nonstop march of keystrokes. It was a noise the likes of which I'd never heard emanating from this room.

I stood listening for several more minutes. There came a brief pause in the gush of keystrokes, and then they started up again.

I backed away from the door as softly as possible. Tiptoeing across the den, I made my way into the kitchen to replace the phone. At the fridge, I poured myself half a glass of milk, drank it down, and set the cup in the sink. I slunk back to my bedroom and climbed into bed, where I slipped into an easy sleep.

*   *   *

Later, she came to me.

It was half past midnight when I heard movement in the hall. My eyes flicked open, searching. She was a spectral form standing in the doorway. Her white negligee came to mid-thigh. The negligee was open in the front, and Alisha was naked underneath. Bathed in partial moonlight, she came forward. I saw her white sliver of belly between the open folds of her gown, and the dark patch beneath her sloping navel. I captured the sickle-shaped shine of her sternum between the swell of her breasts.

When I started to sit up, she whispered, "No, Simon, don't get up. Don't get up." She pressed a finger to my lips. "Shh, don't speak. Don't speak …"

She slid onto the bed next to me and folded back the sheets. She worked her hands slowly down my bare chest, over my tightened stomach, and then her fingers were plying at the waistband of my underwear.

Slowly and delicately, she pulled the shorts off of me with warm, careful fingers. She tossed the briefs aside. Now she splayed the pads of her fingers across the tops of my thighs, slowly working her hands upward along the sides of my groin. Her dancing fingertips sent titillating bolts of electricity through my entire lower torso. I began to quiver uncontrollably.

"God, Alisha, what are you—"

"Shh, Simon, quiet now …" she whispered, and began to lower her head toward my waist. "Let me do the talking. Let me do *all* the talking." My penis was rock-hard, and I saw the curvaceous form of her lips inches from its engorged tip. She brushed it with the side of her nose, and then her cheek. Her tongue touched me next, and then I was inside of her mouth.

"Oh, God, Alisha," I moaned, "oh, *Jesus Christ Almighty.*"

"Stay right there," she said when she was finished. She sat up and brushed her silvery hair away from her eyes. "I'm not done with you yet."

She sat up straight and straddled herself on top of me. She positioned herself slowly and methodically, holding my erection with one hand to guide it. Moments later, my penis was sliding past her clitoris and I was inside of her.

She seemed to sense that I was on the verge of peaking, for she said, "No, Simon, not yet, not yet … Wait for me, wait for me … That's it … slowly, yes … slowly …"

She allowed the negligee to slip off the points of her shoulders. Looking up, I saw her cream-colored breasts dancing above me, basking in a slash of moonlight. Her head rocked slowly back, showing me the underside of her chin and the white flesh of her throat.

"That's it, Simon, yes …" She was crooning now, getting close. "Yes, Simon, that's it, now take me with you … yes, oh, yes, take me with you … oh … take me … with …"

I erupted into her in a series of explosive, galvanic thrusts that pitched her body up and down. She rode me out tirelessly, her body pulling as mine pushed, hers pushing as mine pulled, our bodies in perfect harmony, pushing and pulling, pushing and pulling, as we went over the edge together, into that blissful white zenith lovers know as rapture.

*   *   *

"I heard you writing earlier."

"Mmm …" She lay against me with her cheek on my right shoulder, one open hand caressing my chest. I felt her breasts pressing the side of my ribcage, her pubic hair brushing the side of my hip. Our legs were entangled. Her silvery hair spilling over her top shoulder looked like a waterfall forever frozen. She smelled of lotion, and Dove body soap, and that exotic shampoo she used. She smelled like a woman in the velvet dusk of night. Knives of partial moonlight stabbed into the room, slicing the darkness into black and white piano key daggers.

"The spirit moved you, then," I said.

"It happens. What were you doing up?"

"The phone rang. Didn't you hear it?"

"No. I have a private line in my office, but not the home line. Who was it?"

"Jack the Ripper."

"That's not funny. Who was it?"

"The IRS."

"Simon, I'm not kidding. Who was it, really?"

"I don't know. He wouldn't identify himself. When I told him I thought his voice sounded familiar, he hung up."

"Hmm …" She turned her head so that her chin was squarely resting on my shoulder. She nuzzled me that way several times before stretching her neck in such a way that she could land a quick kiss on my lips. A quick kiss turned into a long kiss. We kissed for several minutes … slowly and passionately, our tongues entwined, our lips moist with each other.

Finally, she broke away and laid her cheek on my shoulder once more. "It may have been Corey's father," she said.

That caught me by surprise. Alisha had never spoken of Corey's father.

"Why would he call so late?" I asked.

"How late is late?"

"It was after ten."

"I don't know."

I asked, "Were you ever married to him?"

"No."

"Engaged?"

"No."

"Feel free to elaborate," I said.

She chuckled, muffling the laugh into my shoulder.

"What was his name?"

She said nothing.

"What was his name?" I repeated.

Silence.

"Alisha?"

Her voice was a half whisper when she spoke. "His name was David."

David. His name was David.

I allowed the name to hang in space before me, rotating as though suspended from a string. *David. His name was David.* I tried to form a mental image of what this man might look like judging solely by that name. *David.* The little movie projector in my head showed me a man who stood six-foot-six, who wore a beige suit, who drank martinis at lunch and always ate the olives, a man who conducted six-figure transactions over his blackberry, whose hard chiseled face garnered the attention of voluptuous women wherever he went; he was the sort of man who had a woman (maybe two or three) in every city. The movie projector clicked and flickered, showing me another image of *David*: James Brolin with long hair and an overgrown beard in *The Amityville Horror*, holding an axe. Getting to know the axe. Sharpening the axe. And later, actually *throwing* the axe, practicing with it.

"He hurt me once."

"What?"

"He … hurt me once," she repeated. "It was somewhat accidental, but … well, Corey saw it."

"How did David hurt you 'accidentally?'"

"It wasn't entirely his fault," Alisha remarked. "He's bipolar, see. When he stops taking his medication, he's unpredictable."

"Why would he stop taking his medication?"

"It's actually pretty common for bipolar patients to intentionally stop taking their meds now and then. You know why?"

"The manic phase?" I remembered reading it somewhere.

"Yes, the manic phase. It's like being on a super-high for several days in a row. People like it. But sometimes they go too high and can't control themselves."

"What happened?"

"David … he … well, he chased me around the house with a knife."

"*This* house?"

"No, another house. North of Philadelphia. Where Corey and I were living before we came here."

"Jesus Christ, a *knife?* What made him so angry?"

"I don't know, some silly argument we were having, and it got out of hand, he started screaming, and … and suddenly he drew a carving knife from the knife block in the kitchen."

"Was he living with you at the time?"

"David? No, he has a house in Bergen County, New Jersey. He was staying with us for a few days, that's all."

"What did you do when he came after you with the knife?"

"I turned and ran."

"Corey was how old?"

"Three."

"He remembers it," I said.

"I bet he does. I'm surprised he told you, Simon. He's never talked about it."

"He didn't tell me. He re-enacted it." I described the sleepwalking episode I had witnessed, how Corey had sat on the floor out by the fireplace, pounding the hardwood with his little fists, yelling, *Stop it, Daddy! Stop it!*"

Alisha was stunned. She lifted her head once more, so that her chin was propped on my shoulder again. "When did this happen?"

"Early in the fall, I think. Remember when you disappeared for a week? You went to New York City, and then South Carolina? It happened one of those nights, I think."

"How come you didn't tell me?"

A sardonic laugh escaped me. "Come on … We weren't exactly seeing eye-to-eye back then."

"You're right, we weren't. And it's my fault, I apologize, but … but Simon, I would've liked to have known. Really."

I thought about it for a while. "Okay. I apologize for not bringing it up. But now you know."

We were silent for several minutes. The moon slid behind a shimmer of cloud, passing the room into transient darkness. *Light comes to darkness, darkness comes to light. Daytime runs a'falsehood high, tho' truth distills the night.*

"At what point did David hurt you?"

"What?"

"You said that he hurt you. When did that happen?"

"By the front door. I was undoing the locks so that I could open the door and throw him out. He caught me from behind. He grabbed one of my arms and spun me around. I saw the knife in one hand, but I never saw the other hand. The other hand was coming up to hit me in the face. At the last second, he seemed to realize what he was doing, and he tried to restrain himself. He ended up striking a glancing blow to my temple. I staggered back against the side of the piano, stunned."

"What did you do then?"

"At first, nothing. All I could do was stare up at him in disbelief. He immediately recognized he'd crossed the line. He dropped the knife and made a feeble attempt to apologize. I told him to get out, just to go."

"Did he?"

"Yes."

"Any repercussions?"

"Well, I didn't speak to him for six months. But he's apologized a hundred times over since, so gradually I forgave him. He is Corey's father, after all."

I asked, "Do you ever worry about him stopping his meds again?"

"No, not really."

"When was the last time you and Corey saw him?"

"Last February. He drove up for Corey's birthday. He gave Corey the bicycle."

"So he knows where you live, then."

"Yes."

"Do you suppose he intends to visit again? For Corey's next birthday?"

"Possibly," Alisha allowed. "Would you disapprove of that?"

"Not necessarily," I answered. The coil of jealousy in my gut, however, spoke of a different truth. "I wonder how Corey feels."

"Corey is always excited to see his daddy."

"He's never talked about him very much to me," I said. "Little snippets here and there, but …" An idea occurred to me. "Hey, maybe David should come up next week for the father-son breakfast. Corey would love that."

"Sounds to me like you're trying to get out of it."

"Nonsense. I'm looking forward to meeting men who are older, wealthier, and more accomplished than I am."

"Good," she said, giggling girlishly. Then she put her lips to my ear and whispered something so unbelievable—so *unexpected*—that it rendered me speechless. "You're the best father that boy has ever had, Simon, and both you and I know it."

She pressed her finger to my lips before I could utter a response. "Shh, Simon, no more talk. Now we sleep." She laid her head in the crook of my neck, her body nestling closer to mine beneath the sheets. "Now we sleep."

CHAPTER TWENTY

THE FATHER-SON
BREAKFAST

BLANKETS OF RAIN STOLE the morning. The wipers on Josef's
Tacoma, even on maximum speed, had trouble keeping pace with
the deluge. Visibility was horrendous, and driving conditions were
worse. Because of the unseasonably warm air temperature—mid- to
upper forties—the combination of steady rain and melting snow
resulted in a fog so thick that the road seemed to disappear twenty
feet in front of us. Water rushed along roadsides in crashing gray
rivers, overriding gutters and pushing storm drains to their limits.
At one point, a low peal of thunder rumbled beyond the massing
clouds.

"Did you hear that?" I asked Corey. "Thunder in January, eh?"

He was quiet, as he had been the last week or so whenever we
were traveling.

"There's more water than road," I said. "We should've taken the
Bat Boat."

"The what?"

"The Bat Boat. Whenever Batman leaves the Bat Cave, he has
the option of taking the Batmobile, the Bat Plane, or the Bat Boat."

"But we don't live in the Bat Cave."

"Oh, you're wrong about that, Chunkycheeks."

221

He laughed. "What, um … what happened to my compass, Simon?"

"What compass would that be?"

"The one I got for Christmas."

"It got eaten by the Bat Computer."

"Simon!"

"I haven't seen your compass," I told him. "I'm sure it's lying around the house somewhere. Why, you planning on going someplace?"

Instead of answering, he asked, "Are you, um, ever gonna finish building Playworld?"

"You want me to?"

"Yeah."

"It takes up a lot of space. I've been thinking about moving it to the basement, but the ceiling down there may not be high enough."

I turned onto County 513 north. There wasn't a great deal of traffic, but what traffic there was plodded along through lanes inundated with water and slush. I saw red hazard lights flashing and great waves of water being thrown to the sides.

"You've got a birthday coming up next month," I said plaintively. "Anything special on your wish list?"

He shook his head. "I have everything I want."

This was a surprising response for a five-year-old going on six. "You do, do you? I'll have to return the Bat Copter, then."

"Simon!" he cried with a laugh. "There is no Bat Copter."

I pulled into the Ace of Spades. Half of the parking lot was underwater. "Oh, good. Watch this." I gunned the engine. We surged into the submerged back section of the parking area, parting huge waves on both sides. Corey giggled.

I killed the engine. "Well, we're here. Better put on your Bat Boots."

"I don't have Bat Boots!"

"Hope you can swim."

"Simon!"

I carried him over the flooded section, setting him onto his feet once we reached exposed pavement. As we walked toward the school entrance, passing the back bumpers of other vehicles, I inquired,

"Are the girls in your class gonna be here, too? Or is it just fathers and sons?"

"It's just fathers and sons. Next week is girls and mothers."

I noticed a gold Jaguar parked in front of the playground. It was parked between a gray Volvo and a red Ford Escort. On the lower left corner of the Jaguar's bumper was a red, square-shaped sticker. When I saw what it said, I had to look again to ensure I'd read it correctly. *Fuck the money, show me the pussy.*

"Now there's someone who should've parked in the puddle."

"What?" Corey asked.

"Nothing." We went inside.

*   *   *

Mrs. Thomas stood inside the classroom doorway, greeting people and shaking hands and smiling. Mrs. Hayes stood on the opposite side of the doorway, silently handing out programs. The latter gave me the look of death as I accepted the leaflet. "What's this?"

"It has the songs in it, Simon," Corey answered.

"What songs?"

"The ones we'll be singing," Mrs. Thomas replied, beaming.

"We're going to *sing?*"

"Well, of course, dear. The kids have been practicing for weeks."

"I thought it was coffee and bagels, then off to work."

"There's coffee, Simon, look," Corey said. He pointed to an area by the windows overlooking the playground where a pair of coffee urns and condiments had been set up. A half-dozen men wearing expensive suits had formed a loose semi-circle in front of the urns. They stood with hands in their pockets, suit jackets flayed out, glancing awkwardly around the room.

I was wearing a pair of pressed pants and a white wool sweater. As I removed my coat and followed Corey to the coat closet, I quickly scanned the room, hoping to seize upon a father dressed in janitor's fatigues or a Public Works outfit. I saw none. At the classroom entrance, fathers and sons were continuing to file in.

Corey grabbed one of my arms and began towing me across the room. "Come on, Simon. Come on, let's have some orange juice and bagels."

We parted the half circle of suits en route to the coffee and food table. Corey took special pains pointing out what was where. "What do you want on your bagel, Simon? Cream cheese or butter?"

"I'll take marmalade."

"What's that?"

"Never mind. Cream cheese is fine."

I fixed myself a cup of coffee while Corey prepared my bagel. I raised the Styrofoam cup to my lips and took a sip. The coffee was awful.

"Here's your bagel, Simon."

"Well, thank you," I said, accepting the paper plate from him. He'd managed to smatter a layer of cream cheese so thin it was hardly visible. "It gives new definition to the meaning of a plain bagel."

"What?"

"Nothing," I said. Several of the suits chuckled.

Corey spent the next fifteen minutes dragging me around the classroom, explaining the various workstations, pointing out bulletin boards, and showing me his desk. He was too excited to take so much as a bite of the half bagel he'd fixed for himself, and he'd only drunk half of his orange juice. I glanced repeatedly at my watch.

"It isn't that bad, is it?" a voice asked.

I turned to my left and found a short, smiling man standing next to me. He wore gray slacks, a white shirt, and a tie, minus the jacket. "I've been checking my watch, too, so don't feel bad. My name's Joe. Joe Graves."

He offered me his free hand. I shook it. "A pleasure. I'm Simon."

"You must be Corey's dad."

"Well, no. I just look after him."

Joe smiled. He was a pleasant-enough looking fellow who was balding on top. He had reddish-brown patches of hair along the sides of his head and wire-rimmed specs that gave him the appearance of either an engineer or a geology professor.

"I see," he said. "You're sort of like a live-in babysitter, or a nanny, right?"

"More like a chaperone, Joe."

"Oh. Right."

"What do you do?"

"I'm a math teacher. I teach advanced calculus. Mostly to high school senior honor students."

"Sounds kind of heavy."

He laughed. "Well, it's not for everyone, that's for sure."

"Which one's yours?" I asked him, gesturing to the kids spread among the classroom.

"Oh, Jerry's mine. The short one over there, wearing the bright red overalls."

"If you'll excuse me," I said.

"Sure."

Corey had wandered to the far side of the classroom. He was playing tic-tac-toe on the chalkboard with another boy. It was the chalkboard I'd found Tommy washing when I'd confronted him last week.

I'd gotten three-fourths of the way across the room when a hand grabbed my arm. The contact startled me, and I jumped a little. I turned to my right and saw a woman standing there.

"I'm sorry. I didn't mean to spook you."

"You didn't," I uttered quickly. "You just … well, maybe you did a little."

"My name's Vivian. I'm sort of new to the area, so I don't really know anybody here. You're Corey's dad, right?"

"Well, no. I'm his designated driver."

"Oh." She smiled. Heavyset though not entirely unattractive, Vivian wore her metallic blonde hair in a messy bun, so that rogue strands of hair frizzed out at crazy angles. She wore her blouse about as far open as the buttons would allow. One more button and her left bosom was going to fall into my lap. She struck me as the type of woman who spent large chunks of time snacking on Double Stuf Oreos while watching the QVC channel.

"Hey, I thought this was the father-son breakfast. How'd you get past security?" I nodded toward Mrs. Hayes.

"My Derek doesn't have a father. His father left us for a younger woman when Derek was four months."

"I'm sorry to hear that."

"It was for the better, actually. He was a real drip."

I asked, "So, what do you think of the party?"

She spared a dismissive glance around the room. "Well, I can't remember the last time I saw men in twelve-hundred-dollar suits drinking coffee out of Styrofoam cups." She turned her focus back on me. She gave me a salacious look-down and bobbed her shoulders. "Say, I've been looking for a handyman to help me with some odd jobs around the house. Preferably someone with strong hands. You look like the sort of guy who's got strong hands."

I looked down at my hands, flexing my fingers slowly. "Actually, my hands are in pretty rough shape."

"Oh? Why's that?"

"I'm recovering from carpal tunnel surgery."

"No kidding. At such a young age?"

"Yes, well—"

"I don't see scars."

"What?"

"Your wrists," she said, pointing. "I don't see any scars. You must have a great surgeon. Who did you use?"

"Uh, Stevens."

"No shit? Phil Stevens?"

"Actually, it was Wolfgang."

She cupped her chin with one hand, thinking. "I haven't heard of that one. Did you have it done at Mercy Medical?"

"I thought you were new to the area."

"Eight months is kind of new, isn't it?" She sipped her coffee.

Peering past Vivian's shoulder, I caught a glimpse of Corey's nemesis, Tommy. He was standing beside an Italian-looking man wearing a pinstriped suit and a rawhide belt. The man's black hair had the wet and shiny gloss of hair gel. They were standing in the half circle of suits—what I'd begun to think of as the Power Circle. I saw with a small measure of dismay that Tommy was pointing at me while whispering into his father's ear. His father was slightly hunched over to be at ear level with his son.

"Vivian, you'll have to excuse me," I said.

I turned away before she could respond, continuing toward the chalkboard. I'd taken a half step when I noticed that Corey was no longer there. Three scribbled-out tic-tac-toe games on the chalkboard were all that remained. He'd somehow snuck past me while I'd been involved with Vivian.

"I think he's over there," she said, pointing toward the classroom entrance. I spotted him huddled among four or five other boys in front of the teachers' desk.

I started in that direction. I didn't make it. As I was passing in front of the open coat closet, I was accosted by a tall fellow wearing jeans, a gray suede vest, and a wide-brimmed hat. He looked like a cowboy. The only thing missing were the boots and spurs. At least he wasn't wearing a suit.

"Hey there, partner," he said, pointing at me and grinning.

"Hey." I didn't feel like talking anymore, and I was tired of bullshitting. "I was just on my way—"

"You must be Corey's dad. Are you Corey's dad? You are, aren't you?"

"I'm … yes. Yes, I am. And I was just on my way—"

"Name's Pete. Pete Skillman. It's a damn thrill to meet you."

He stuck his hand out. We shook. His grip was so tight I thought my eyes were going to pop out of my skull. What is it with some men? You go and shake their hands, and it's like they have to try and break your fingers or something.

When my hand was safely in my pocket and I was sure nothing was dislocated, I nodded politely. "The thrill's all mine, Pete. Now if you'll excuse—"

"I've been meaning to ask you … What's it like?"

"What's what like?" I asked.

"Being married to a smut writer. What's that like, man?"

Well, I hadn't seen this coming. "It's swell," I said.

"Swell," he repeated, nodding and staring at me with a fascinated half smile stuck to his face. "Swell, huh?"

"So, you actually read my wife's books, then?"

"Hell, no. But my wife, Marge, she's into 'em somethin' fierce." He lowered his voice. He inclined his head toward me, as though divulging a secret. "She's always telling me all the sex and stuff she's readin' in 'em. And I says to myself, 'Where does that woman get her ideas?' Meaning your wife—not mine. Where *does* she come up with her ideas?"

I lowered my own voice to a confiding whisper. "Well, Pete, in the bedroom, of course. Some of those ideas were mine originally. But don't tell that to Marge, okay? It's our secret."

At that point, Mrs. Thomas stood in the front of the room and called for everyone's attention. It was time to sing. I was actually relieved. It would at least put an end to my bullshitting, which was getting out of control in a hurry. All of the fathers were to form three rows in the middle of the room. There was an awkward scuffle amid some low groans and reluctant mutterings. Mrs. Thomas orchestrated this. "That's right. Shoulder-to-shoulder. Yes, one row behind the other. Come now, men, look alive and smile; this sort of a day doesn't come around too often."

"Thank heavens for that," a man to my immediate left uttered. It was Joe Graves. He was a good five to six inches shorter than me. To my right, towering above me, stood Pete Skillman. Pete continued to stare down at me with a perfect blend of awe and adulation. *You've got to be kidding me. How could I wind up between the two of them?* Just then, someone pinched me on the ass. I jumped. Vivian giggled in my ear.

I turned halfway around. "Knock it off, will you?"

She whispered over my right shoulder, "Carpal tunnel, my ass."

Pete Skillman said, "You had carpal tunnel? No kidding. That must've made things difficult for you. You know, generating ideas."

"It did," I said, "but I'm getting over it."

Joe Graves whispered, "My wife had that done a year ago. She plays piano."

"Ask him to show you his scars," Vivian said to Joe.

Ignoring her, Joe asked me, "Who did your surgery?"

"Some Chinese dude," I muttered. "Can't remember his name."

"Sure he does," Vivian said. "It was Wolfgang. You know Wolfgang, don't you?"

"Stop it, will you?" I barked through clenched teeth.

"Are you talking about Wolfgang Hewitt?" Pete Skillman asked. "He's a client of mine. Last I heard, though, he was doing root canal work."

"Talented, isn't he?" Vivian offered.

"If you'll refer to your programs," Mrs. Thomas addressed, "we'll begin on page three, starting with 'Joy to the World.'"

Mrs. Hayes pressed the play button on a small Sony cassette player. A crackling, static rendition of "Joy to the World" stumbled out of the speakers, bereft of lyrics. Only the little boys' voices could be heard through the first several lines, because they were the only ones singing (save for Mrs. Thomas). Most of the fathers were grunting or lip-syncing.

"Sing, fathers, *sing!*" Mrs. Thomas bellowed over the music. "Let's hear those lovely baritones!"

And so the fathers began to sing. It was easily the worst thirty minutes of caroling I've ever heard. Mrs. Hayes, who didn't appear to be singing (she seemed content, in fact, to press the stop and play buttons on the cassette player), seemed to recognize the desultory performance taking place in her classroom, for she grimaced and frowned most of the way through it. Mrs. Thomas went on singing and smiling without a care in the world, swinging her arms in front of her as though conducting an orchestra. The only marvel to be had, I suppose, was that the children had been forced to memorize these tunes verbatim. Most kindergartners, after all, cannot yet read.

We went from "Silent Night," to "Rudolph," to "Jingle Bells," ultimately ending with "The Twelve Days of Christmas." Vivian chose certain stanzas to exercise—at my expense, mind you—her full range of vocal abilities. She would belt out a particular line, dwarfing all other voices at once, and my left ear would bear the brunt of the punishment. The next time it would be my right ear being dealt the blow. This truly came to light during "The Twelve Days of Christmas," for Vivian felt compelled to air out her soprano skills with each passage of *"f-i-i-i-v-e g-o-o-lden r-i-i-i-ngs!"* Anyone familiar with the song knows that you must pass through that stanza eight times in order to bring the song to completion. It got worse with each passage, so much so that I grew to dread its coming. I would bow my head forward and clench my teeth as Vivian let it rip. When I turned to scowl at her, she responded by singing louder.

When the final partridge in a pear tree had been sung, the fathers clapped and hoorayed as their sons whooped and hollered. Vivian pinched me on the ass again. I chose that moment, amid the confusion and chaos, to head for the door. My coat hung aloft in the coat closet, and there it would stay. Luckily, I had dropped my keys into my pants pocket, and those were all I needed. The next moment, I was ducking out of the room, into the enclosed corridor that bridged the kindergarten with the preschool, and then I slipped out the front entrance, into a full-fledged rain that slanted into my face and soddened my clothes in seconds. Mrs. Hayes had turned her watchful eyes on me as I'd fled, but I didn't care. Mrs. Hayes would get over it.

By the time I'd fished the keys out of my pocket, extracted the correct one, then managed to insert it into the keyhole of Josef's truck door, I was every bit as soaked as the day was wet. I launched myself into the cab space, pulled the door shut, and hit the auto-lock button. I started the engine. Flipped on the heaters, the windshield defoggers. Not the wipers, though, or the headlights. I slouched lower into the seat, waiting.

*   *   *

Five minutes later, fathers began streaming out of the building. Some had umbrellas. Others threw their arms over their heads in mock protection as they sprinted for their vehicles. One by one, and then in twos and threes, engines roared to life; mufflers coughed smoke and spat rainwater; brake lights bled in the dismal January gloom. Vehicles backed out of parking spaces and departed.

Tommy's father was one of the last to leave. Maybe Vivian was putting the moves on him, I thought. He exited the school wearing a long, tan trench coat, without an umbrella. He approached the gold Jaguar, pulled the driver's door open, and got in. The small, square-shaped bumper sticker was little more than a red speck in the rain-slashed morning. What sort of a man, I wondered, doused his hair with Vitalis, wore an expensive suit, and drove a gold, super-charged Jaguar bearing that sort of a slogan?

Fuck the money, show me the pussy.

I felt an urge to find out.

*   *   *

Surveillance can be fun—actually, I found it quite exhilarating. As bad as the weather was, it provided terrific cover for me as I tailed the Jaguar south on County 513. I was able to hang back fifty or sixty feet, keeping the red taillights centered in my windshield. I would appear as nothing more than a pair of white headlights in his rearview mirror. The Tacoma's overall body shape would be obscured by the rain and fog.

The Jaguar exited 513 onto Nutley. We dog-eared onto an underpass, proceeding toward the Swan Lake town proper. We made a left onto Pear Street, followed by a right into Main Street. We crossed the Main Street Bridge. Whiskey Creek, now an angry, foaming river carrying with it entire tree limbs and garbage can lids, went roaring beneath the overpass going left to right. Ahead, the Jaguar turned left onto Aldridge Street.

I turned left also, hanging far enough back to avoid detection. The Jag began slowing down. To my right, I saw the sloping, snow-covered yard studded with tall leafless poplars. When last I'd seen this gorgeous estate, the lawn had been a lush summer green beneath a full canopy of leaves. The transformed three-story colonial building was still there, however—beige with black shutters. I passed the wood sign that advertised: Dolan, Packer & Spencer, Attorneys-at-Law. The Jaguar continued past the main parking lot, then slowed considerably. A second, smaller driveway appeared on the right. This one was marked Employees Only. The Jag turned here, disappearing from sight behind a stone wall and a row of hedges. I drove past the mouth of the drive in time enough to capture the rear half of the Jaguar disappearing behind the back corner of the colonial. I continued along Aldridge Street.

So, Tommy's father happened to be one of the three senior partners in the law firm of Dolan, Packer & Spencer. Either he was Dolan, or he was Packer, or he was Spencer. Judging by his demeanor back at the school, and by his expensive attire, and not to mention the car he drove, it was reasonable to conclude that he wasn't merely a clerk or a process server or even a junior partner. No, he was one of the three honchos. Interesting.

As the road curved to the right, banking away from the creek, a row of stone buildings cropped up along the left side of the road. At the bottom of one of them was a curved arch that served as the entrance to the basement offices of Microsystems Incorporated. A chain had been strung at waist level in front of this opening. From the midpoint of the chain hung a white sign: Out of Business.

I continued on Aldridge, making my way to the north quadrant of Merchant's Square. I hung another right, onto Elm Street, which took me back down to Main Street once more. I turned right again, passing by all of the shops with which I was now familiar. Molly's café was bulging with business on this wet and sloppy day. Customers sat inside drinking coffee and tea, and savoring cups of hot minestrone. Farther up the street, I passed Millie's Arts & Wares. A sign hung in the doorway: Closed Due to Illness. I knew as I passed the darkened storefront that I couldn't postpone my meeting with Josef's widow very much longer. Not only was I driving Josef's vehicle, but I felt intuitively that Millie held the answers to a handful of questions that needed asking.

I came to the bridge that spanned the raging Whiskey Creek. When I got halfway across, I stopped and slipped the Tacoma into park. I opened the door, stepping into the drenching downpour once again. As I headed toward the handrail overlooking the downstream side of the river, I dug into my pants pocket. I came up with the small, handheld compass I'd given Corey for Christmas. I wasn't sure it could be trusted. I wasn't sure I wanted to allow *Corey* to trust it. I tossed it over the handrail. It disappeared into the foaming, frothy river with nary a splash. Corey would eventually forget it was missing, and he would never know that it had once saved his life.

CHAPTER TWENTY-ONE

TALL OAKS

LET'S GET OUT OF this place. The getaway truck is waiting ...
Right now, the getaway truck was sitting in an empty parking lot
outside of an Applebee's restaurant on Route 46 westbound. Ma and
I were the only customers in the place, save for two bar patrons who
sat on stools sucking on Coors Lights while watching a daytime
hockey game on the large color television. Ma and I sat in one of
the booths that lined the front edge of the establishment. We spent
lengthy interludes staring through the tinted glass window to my
right (Ma's left), watching the traffic. The autumn day had grown
dark. A thick mat of gray clouds streaked across the sky. A sharp
wind blew out of the northwest, pushing drifts of dead leaves across
the front parking lot.

A waitress came to take our order. Her nametag read Bev. She
was an older woman, possibly in her early fifties. She had black,
shoulder-length hair, and enough rouge to stop traffic.

Ma ordered a Caesar salad, and I had a bacon-cheddar burger.
Our lunch was mainly reflective and mostly quiet. I remember it as
being one of the saner, more relaxing moments of that tumultuous
time. We were coming out of the storm. We had found an exit. There
was a way to be free again. There was a way to start fresh.

"Can I ask you one thing, Ma?"

"If you like."

"This heirloom, this brooch ..."

"Yes?"

"It sat in a safety deposit box for more than twenty years …"

"I believe we've covered that territory, but for the slower people in our audience, yes, it sat there for more than two decades." Ma getting her sense of humor back meant that I was getting my Ma back. I laughed heartily, not because I found the quip funny. I laughed because I was *happy*.

"Didn't Dad know you had it? If you wore it on your wedding day … well, wouldn't he have seen it?"

"Yes and no," Ma answered.

"'Yes and no?' What's that mean?"

"What it means is that your father was a man, Simon. Jewelry tends to be a woman thing. He probably saw it and had no idea what he was looking at, and just as quickly forgot about it."

"But did he know how valuable it was? Did he know where you kept it stored? Did he have a key to the safety deposit box?"

"I have the only key, Simon. Only Catherine and I knew where the key was kept. Your father couldn't have gotten at the brooch if he'd wanted to."

"But if he'd *known*," I persisted, "if he'd consciously *known* its net worth, had *known* how to get to it—"

"Would he have stolen it, is what you're asking. And I can't answer the question—partly because I don't know, and partly because it's a moot point. Try not to think of this as a secret that I kept from him. That's what's bogging you down. An old, ugly brooch handed down through the years isn't really a husband-wife type of thing. It's a mother-daughter type of thing. Your father probably wouldn't have cared way back when. Not caring lends itself to not knowing, over time. You understand?"

"I guess." I drank some of my Cherry Coke. I asked, "Would you have ever told me?"

Ma shrugged. "Sure, probably on Catherine's wedding day. Would you have felt angry and resentful for my never having told you until then?"

I sighed. "No. I probably wouldn't have cared."

Ma smiled. "My point exactly."

*   *   *

Thinking about secrets.

I was thinking about the secrets a family keeps. You know, the ones that build up over time—like dust on a mantelpiece or webs in a corner. So many secrets. They aren't always maintained out of spite, meanness, or duplicity. It's what families do, that's all. It's part of their nature.

My father had been a reserved, practical man. A man who'd known his limitations, who had abided by life's natural boundaries. At least, that's what I had always thought, for he'd also been a compulsive gambler. Ma had kept it hidden. She'd kept it hidden for as long as she could. There'd been a side of my father I had never seen, a part of him I'd never known—a darker element I'd have sworn time and again didn't exist, if asked. Husband-wife secrets.

Mother-daughter secrets. What had Catherine's reaction been the very first time Ma had allowed her to see the brooch? To touch it? To hold it? On Cath's thirteenth birthday, and again on her sixteenth? Had they laughed together? Smiled together? Had they hugged one another? What words had Ma used, exactly? *It will one day be yours, Catherine. To be worn on your day of marriage. And later, bequeathed to your first daughter …*

Father-son secrets, too.

Ma and I were sitting in the truck in the parking lot of Tall Oaks Jewelers, which was located four miles west of the Applebee's. I asked her, "Ma, did Dad ever tell you about the day he pulled me out of school last year? The day we shot up the pumpkins?"

Ma's hard, inquisitive stare was enough of an answer. She shook her head.

And so I told her. I told her about being pulled from Ms. Spaide's sophomore English class, about being led to the main office where Dad had been waiting. Ma listened with attentive fascination as I described Dad's newfound optimism and listed some of his hallmark quotes during the truck ride. Quotes like "fresh starts" and "turning the page" and "new beginnings." And then showing me the gun and teaching me how to shoot it.

"It was a good day," I told her. "It was a special day. If nothing else, I can guarantee I'll never forget the evolutionary advantage of a pinecone."

Ma reached over to touch my hand. Tears had moistened the

corners of her eyes. "Simon, that's so sweet. Your father did have a special place for you in his heart, even if he never told you outright. I'm glad he took you out of school that day, even though I wouldn't have approved of it at the time. But hearing it now makes me happy. I'm glad you told me."

And now a mother-son secret, a new truth about to be forged. Ma was about to sell off the most precious artifact she'd ever owned. In a way, she was selling off an item that no longer belonged to her. I suppose Ma was about to become the world's most notorious Indian-giver. Her relationship with Cath already in tatters, the question became: how much further would this new betrayal push the envelope? Could there ever be a reckoning after this?

Let's get out of the storm first. Let's save the house and appease the creditors. Broken fences can usually be mended. And when they can't be mended, they can be razed and rebuilt.

Tall Oaks Jewelers was part of a strip mall, sandwiched between Farino's Pizzeria and a Radio Shack. It was owned by a pair of Lebanese brothers. Only one of the brothers was manning the shop today. His name was Karem (pronounced *Ka-reem*), and he was assisting a stately blonde woman when Ma and I entered. Karem was changing the woman's watch battery, actually. When he saw us, he called out, "Yes, I be right with you."

"Take your time," Ma told him. She began browsing some of the diamond earrings on display in the glass showcase. I stood several feet away from her, perusing the watches.

"Ma, why would someone want to pay five thousand dollars for a wristwatch?"

"So, he can tell time richly."

"Yes, let me help you now," Karem said. He had come around behind the showcase counter. "How are you today?"

"Very well," Ma answered. "I'd like to have an item appraised."

"Yes, of course, no problem. You have item with?"

Ma withdrew the cloth-wrapped item from her purse. She reached over the show counter to hand it to Karem, her arm quivering. "It's a Victorian brooch, very old, been in my family for generations ..."

"Let me see," Karem said, accepting the cloth from Ma. He moved to our left behind the counter, toward the register, where he kept some simple tools and devices stored. "Come, come, walk this way."

Ma tittered somewhat as she walked. I laid a hand on her shoulder. "It's okay, Ma. It's all right."

Karem had parted the oilcloth. He was now looking at the brooch through a monocle. He uttered a series of grimaces and grunts. Washboard lines formed on his forehead. His lips seemed to pucker like those of a fish as he scrutinized the piece.

Without looking up, he asked, "Were you looking to unload this today?"

"Well ... I'm not sure yet."

"Have you gotten other appraisals?"

"Not recently," Ma said.

Still peering through the monocle, he said, "Well, the pearls are small and not worth much, but they're in good shape. The gold is badly in need of a polish, but it's eighteen-karat and its quality is fine." He stood tall again, allowing the monocle to fall into his hand. Looking at Ma, he said, "I give you twelve hundred dollar."

"Twel ... What ..." But her mouth fell open and hung there for a moment. Mine fell open, too. At first, Ma looked stunned. Then she looked stupid. Then she looked angry. "What ... Did you ... did you say *twelve hundred*? Did my ears hear you correctly? Please tell me you didn't just say—"

"Ma'am, yes, the gold, you see, it is filigreed, and therefore not very heavy, maybe you get another fifty or sixty dollar from a different jeweler, but I cannot—"

"Another fifty or sixty?" Ma bellowed. Her face was brightening. "Are you out of your mind? Do I look like I fell off the turnip truck? Do you think I'm stupid or something?"

"Ma, calm down," I implored, tugging on her sleeve. "Try to—"

"No, Simon, I will *not* calm down! I will *not* be silent! This man is trying to take advantage of us, and I will not stand for it."

Karem moved his eyes onto mine before looking back at Ma once more. "Madam, it is my mistake. You will excuse me, I hope. But I assumed you knew the diamond was a fake."

"*It most certainly ... is ... NOT!* Do you have any idea where this brooch came from? Do you know how *old* this is? A *fake*? What do you take me for? What do I look like to you? Some kind of prairie pig? Some kind of dumb-ass, dim-witted—"

"Ma, stop!" I was holding onto her shoulder, shaking her. "Stop it! Get a hold of yourself."

She looked at me for a moment, her cheeks beet-red, nostrils flaring. She seemed to recognize where we were and looked past her shoulder to survey the rest of the store. It was still empty, luckily.

I looked at Karem. In a reasonable voice, I asked, "How can you tell the diamond is fake just by looking at it?"

"This is a cubic zirconia," he said. "Any seasoned jeweler can judge the difference immediately. I can also tell by the weight. The weight is different."

I said, "When you were looking through the monocle …"

"I was examining the gold."

"You knew the diamond …"

"As soon as I looked at it, yes, of course."

"There has to be some kind of a mistake," Ma said. "I've had this appraised in the past. Your appraisal is about fifty grand off the mark, mister."

"I show you something. You will see." Karem ducked below the register and came up with a small black instrument resembling a fat-bodied pencil. One of its ends tapered down to a gold, metallic point. "This is a diamond tester. It tests for carbon content. Watch now," he said, bringing the metallic point into contact with the brooch's glittering centerpiece. Nothing happened. "These lights should all light up." He indicated a series of dark panels, all unlit, progressing along a continuum scale that ended with the word Diamond. "Now I show you." He slid open a display panel behind the glass showcase and brought out a pair of diamond earrings. The diamonds were a canary yellow. I had never seen yellow diamonds before. Karem placed the point of the diamond tester against one of the yellow stones. All of the lights on the continuum scale lit up—not in unison, but in ascending order, and progressing in different colors. The final two panels lit up red underneath Diamond. Karem said, "These earrings sell for sixty-three thousand dollars."

"Cubic zirconia," Ma breathed.

"It happens a lot," Karem said.

"You're saying … that someone—"

"Does the stone feel loose to you?" I asked. I'd picked up Karem's diamond tester and tried poking it into the fake diamond. "I think the zirconia just moved a little."

Karem produced a pair of forceps. He pulled the brooch toward him once more. We all leaned in, trying to get as close a look as we could.

"It is loose," Karem said. "It's rocking back and forth." Finally, he got the forceps firmly planted on the edges of the stone and then began to pull it free. It popped out of the brooch rather easily. The zirconia stone popped out of the forceps' tongs as well, landing upside-down on the oilcloth. Poking at the gluey white substance that adhered to it, Karem said, "It looks like gum. Does that look like gum to you?"

I looked at Ma. Her lips were moving, but no words were forming. Her cheeks had flushed to a new red. Temblors of rage shook her body. Under her breath, I heard her say, "How could she do this? That two-timing, conniving … *bitch*." Ma lifted her face to meet my eyes. Her lips were white. Her temples were pulsing. "Take me home, Simon."

CHAPTER TWENTY-TWO

DINKMAN'S

THE SNOW WAS GONE by February. What had once been white was now wet and dripping. When it wasn't raining, low shrouds of fog hovered over the earth in patchy, knee-high grave blankets. Roadside ditches overran their banks with gray, dirty runoff. Dirt roads were transformed into treacherous, gluey quagmires. Despite a holiday blizzard that had dumped over two feet of snow and killed a handful of people, none of the locals could recall ever having experienced such a topsy-turvy, turnabout winter.

"It wasn't like this last year," Alisha told me. "This place was a winter wonderland." We were taking a walk along State Street, an enterprise that now required a sturdy pair of boots. "Simon, it was beautiful. Pristine and white, and somehow clean. And quiet. It was so *quiet*." She waved an arm toward the pine forests on our left. "All the evergreen boughs were laden with white fluff. This road that we're walking on now—it was solid snowpack. Your tires would glide over it without a sound. It was as if the world was on mute. The silence had a cottony softness that I can't compare with anything else."

"And now?" I asked.

"And now the whole place is melting," she replied with a laugh. "You still need your four-wheel drive just to navigate this mud hole."

"Must be global warming."

"Global warming is a crock, Simon."

"You think so?"

"Absolutely. Global temperatures have been trending upwards for the last century or more, long before the Industrial Revolution began spewing greenhouse gases into the stratosphere. History, in fact, is filled with periodic warming trends and cooling trends."

"So you think we're in a trend, then?"

She turned to look me in the eye. Her L.L.Bean boots, which came halfway up her calves, squelched along in the mud. Her jeans enclosed her legs snugly. I watched her long, firm thighs going through their walking motions. She wore a long-sleeve flannel shirt underneath a sleeveless down vest. The top three buttons of the flannel shirt were undone, revealing the white stretch blouse she wore beneath. I took in her silverish hair and quicksilver eyes and wholesome lips embossed with lip balm. "Yes, I do," she replied. "And what are you looking at?"

"Nothing. Are all Smithies as opinionated as you?"

"Yes. And they're always right."

We walked in silence for a while. She reached down and took my hand in hers. I felt her thumb moving back and forth, caressing the inside of my palm.

"I've been meaning to ask you something," I told her. "About your writing."

"Yes?"

"It's … well … slowly becoming nocturnal."

"I've always been more prolific after dark, Simon. You of all people should know that by now." She elbowed me in the ribs.

"You know what I mean," I said. "I can't recall seeing you enter a keystroke during your normal, mid-morning hours. And yet, after dark …"

"So, you're keeping tabs on me? Should I start calling you the Writing Police?"

"I'm not keeping tabs. It's a casual observation."

"You won't report me to my agent, will you?"

"Enough said, I get the point. I won't ask about it anymore."

She jabbed me in the ribs again and laughed a little. "You're adorable when you're angry, Simon. I love it when your eyebrows bunch up the way they do."

I shook my head. "You can be a real pain in the ass sometimes, you know that?"

"I'll bet you were dying to say that to me last autumn."

"My tongue is still recovering."

We walked as far as the intersection of State Street and Road 35 before turning and heading back. We walked hand in hand, and the silence was good.

"Simon?"

"Yeah?"

"I've been meaning to ask you something as well."

"Sure," I told her. "What is it?"

For a minute or so, the only noises punctuating the silence were those of our boots belching in and out of the mud. "It concerns the nightmares Corey's been having. In relation to his sleepwalking."

"He hasn't had an episode since—"

"I know," she cut in. "I know. But you mentioned something awhile back about this 'man in black' he claims to dream about. You said you thought it was Corey chasing this man instead of the other way around. Do you still believe that?"

"Yes, I do."

"Then I'd like to know why. And I'd like to hear any other thoughts you might have pertaining to the subject."

Obviously, she had remembered what I'd said, and had put some considerable thought into it, as I had known she would. Alisha was far too intelligent to eschew the advice of others in hopes of clinging to her own stubborn beliefs. And the truth was, I did have some thoughts concerning the dark-robed figure eluding Corey in his preternatural dream world. I had a theory, as well, as to why Alisha was burning the midnight oil in her writing room instead of making hay while the sun shined. But I wasn't sure Alisha was ready to hear either one of them.

"Corey isn't having nightmares," I said.

"How do you know?"

"He isn't bursting out of sleep in a cold sweat. He doesn't wake up crying or screaming. It's the other way around. You see that, don't you?" I looked into her eyes, and the soul of the mother within her looked back. She neither agreed nor disagreed. She neither nodded nor shook her head.

"He's almost impossible to wake up," I continued. "While in the throes of one of these dreams, you practically have to shake him out of sleep. He sleepwalks up the spiral stairs, he sleepwalks up the driveway, he sleep*runs* across the lake in the middle of a snowstorm. Those aren't attributes of a person having a nightmare. He doesn't *want* to wake up, Alisha. The reason he doesn't want to wake up is that he's pursuing a mystery. He's chasing something that he very much wants to catch."

"What is it, then? What could a six-year-old boy possibly be chasing in his sleep?"

I was hoping you could tell me. For if the answer resides in his subconscious mind, then that same answer must also reside in your conscious mind.

"I have no idea," I lied. "But let me ask you something else. Do any of Corey's sleepwalking episodes predate your living here?"

She had to think about it for a moment. "Well … no. It started after we moved in. You're saying the house has something to do with it, then?"

"I'm not sure. But Crawford Daze is a unique place, that much I do know."

"Who is Crawford Daze, Simon?" She'd apparently forgotten my mentioning of the name.

"I don't know. I thought at first it was a person. Then I was told it's the name of the house we're living in. But lately I've begun to wonder if it really wasn't a person after all."

"Oh, Simon, you're not making sense."

How could I tell her? How could I describe the light I had glimpsed in the storm? I'd gotten turned around in the storm somehow, and I couldn't see the shore … and then a light had flashed—once … twice … three times. Like a beacon at the top of a lighthouse, and at the same time a heartbeat in someone else's chest. The only problem is that there was no lighthouse standing alongside Swan Lake. There never had been.

But there *was* a heartbeat. There was a heartbeat in someone else's house, and it had saved all of our lives. I didn't know how, and I didn't know why. More than anything, it reminded me of one famous author's quote: *History rarely repeats itself—but it often rhymes.*

*   *   *

I moved Playworld into the basement. Corey wasn't thrilled with the relocation, but once he saw construction picking up again, his enthusiasm grew. It took me a little more than a week to have the whole thing up and done. Height restrictions did play a role. The ceiling ductwork coming off the burner forced me to abbreviate Playworld's upper level. That is, I had to leave off the top-level side rails. "You're going to have to avoid visiting the top floor," I advised Corey. "Unless, of course, you're willing to lie flat on your belly. Try and sit up, though, and you'll smack your head into the ductwork."

Playworld was so wide that it covered practically the entire floor of the basement. Spatially, I arranged it so that a person coming down the basement steps, upon reaching the lowermost stair, could readily access Playworld through a side portal. Once inside, you were free to move around. Corey especially loved climbing up to the chute, then sliding into the pool of multi-colored plastic balls.

One night after dinner, I announced to Alisha that I was going to run into town to do some shopping. Corey expressed his desire to come with me.

"Actually," I told him, "you're gonna stay with your mom tonight. Think of her as your babysitter this time."

He looked at his mother with wide, excited eyes. "Hey, Mom, can we play in Playworld? Can we?"

"Of course we can."

I left to the sounds of their shrieking voices clamoring up from the basement.

I drove into town through a wet, standing fog. Curtains of dewdrop mist slanted out of the night sky. The wipers thumped back and forth on an intermittent cycle. By the time I reached Elm Street, however, I had the wipers running constantly. Living in Swan Lake these days was like living in a cloud.

I crossed Main Street, making my way into Merchant's Square, where I parked the truck and fed the meter. The square was sparsely populated this evening. Several shoppers moved along the sidewalks holding umbrellas, pausing to gaze wistfully through storefront windows before slowly moving on. Others advanced at a brisk pace, carrying briefcases or shoulder satchels, hurrying toward their cars or ducking into a restaurant or watering hole. I spent the first half hour browsing through a high-end toy store called Gatsby's Toys 'n Stuff. The notion of discovering the perfect birthday gift in a toy store had begun to wane in previous days, though. It may have been Corey telling me in plaintive terms that he already had everything he wanted. Or maybe it was the monstrosity of Playworld blocking out the light of the sun. How could Playworld be bested? *It can't be. And that shouldn't be your objective, either. Try and find something neat and cool that he'll like. Something small and creative.*

I found a section of shelves filled with remote-controlled cars. Above these, I found remote-controlled boats. Here was a possibility. A battery-powered boat zooming over the waves scaring up geese in response to a joystick in Corey's hands had its merits. I decided to put it on the back burner for now.

Craft and hobby shops began to accrue more of my interest. I thought of the fishing poles Alisha had given us for Christmas. It had been a stellar idea. I'd heard and read of people spending hours, if not days, alongside their favorite streams and lakes. But Corey was young, and only time would tell whether or not he'd develop the patience required for fishing. But how about astronomy? Might the stars and distant planets tickle his fancy? I started looking at high-powered telescopes. Prices ranged dramatically. I perused manuals on isolating the constellations, when to look for Mars, and the best nights to watch for meteors. This eventually fed into another idea—and perhaps the best one of all.

Corey was in kindergarten now. Kindergarten was where you learned the individual letters and the phonetic sounds they represented. Next fall he would enter the first grade. In first grade, you were taught how to put the letters together. You were taught how to make the letters form words. You were taught how to read.

So, how about books? How about *books?* The idea lit up my head like neon. Corey *loved* books. Corey loved *stories.* He was always asking me or Alisha to read him stories. So why not get him some elementary-level stories … those that relied a little less on pictures and a little more on words? By this time next year, he'd be starting to read on his own. Why not set him on his way? Why not put him on the path of becoming an independent, self-motivated reader?

I exited the hobby shop through a back door, which accessed a dark alleyway leading toward a set of stairs. The stairs were made of slate slabs, and they would be treacherous in the dark. But the bookstore I wanted to visit was down on Main Street, and this was the quickest way of getting there.

I was so excited at the prospect of snatching up an armful of some of my favorite childhood tales that I never heard the man who must have slipped out the back door behind me. As I moved over a round slab of wet stone toward the stairs, I heard the door being pulled shut behind me, followed by rapidly approaching footsteps. The vague outline of a dumpster cringed in the shadows to my right. Lazy cords of fog drifted through the dark alleyway. Old gutters dripped water.

A voice muttered, "Hey, buddy, you forgot this."

I spun around on my heels. The fist slammed into my face before I knew a fist was coming. I saw a white flash of light in my left eye. My head rocked back like … well, like a punching sack, I guess. I tottered backward, finally falling on my ass on the wet stone. Through my right eye, the tall figure loomed, coming toward me again. I went into a backward crabwalk, kicking out with my feet. A low thudding pain was starting to bloom in the left side of my head.

"Little bastard." The man's voice was gravelly.

I tried to get up by flinging my body to the left and getting my feet under me all in one motion. He was ready for it. He grabbed me by the shoulders and flung me backward into the side of the dumpster. I hit the dumpster hard and went down again. I was on my ass a second time. "Shit," I stammered under my breath.

"That's right, Commando. That's what you get for picking on little kids. You get this, too." He lunged forward again. I raised my right leg at the last second, planting my foot into his gut. He cried out, "Ahhhrrrgg!" as he doubled over at the waist. Before he could right himself, I planted my left foot onto his left shoulder and kicked out with all my strength. He went flying backward, spinning in a kind of human whirligig, before landing on his can.

I rose weakly to my feet, trying to ignore the throbbing pain on the left side of my face. I passed a hand gently over my left cheek. The skin there felt raw and swollen.

The attacker pushed himself onto his knees and snarled up at me. His teeth flashed white in the darkness.

He stood up and brushed himself off. "Okay. Now we'll see what you've got. You can push little kids around, but now we'll see if you can dance with the big dogs, huh?"

"I don't know what you're talking about, mister."

He raised his fists and came at me. This time I was ready. As he swung, I stepped inside the blow and grabbed his right arm in one motion. Furthering his own momentum, I quickly spun him around and sent him crashing back-first into the dumpster. He hit hard. "Ahhh! You sonofa … bitch!"

He ran at me again. This time he ducked low and bull-rushed me, driving his shoulder into my midsection and propelling me backward into a brick wall. My shoulder blades and left elbow absorbed the brunt of the impact. My knees buckled, but I managed to stay on my feet.

He pulled away from me, retreating into the center of the dark circle. He danced around in a boxer's pose, gesturing me toward him with his fisted forearms.

"Come on. Come on, you little pussy. My boy pointed you out at the father-son breakfast. I knew you were a pussy the moment I laid eyes on you. I was right, wasn't I? Huh?"

I was shocked by this man's overwhelming arrogance. But even more, I was angered by his overconfidence. I went at him.

He stepped toward me and swung. I ducked beneath his heavy swing and dealt two quick blows to his stomach. He groaned twice, then kicked me in the shin.

"What the fuck?" I shouted at him. I swung high and connected with the underside of his chin.

"Aaahhh!" He reeled two or three steps backward and fell in a pile. There he stayed, massaging his left jawbone. "Damn you, I had dental work done last year. I could sue you, you know."

"For what? Defending myself against a ruthless attacker?" I lowered my arms. My left cheek felt like a balloon ready to pop. "What's this bullshit about kicking below the knees? Your sister teach you that?"

Still rubbing his chin, he said, "All right, ace, you've got a pretty good swing. You've earned yourself a draw in this one. Now help me up, and I'll buy you a beer."

Actually, I rather thought I'd earned a win, but I saw no harm in letting him see it his way. I grabbed his hand and pulled him up. "I don't want a beer."

"Don't be a pussy." He stood brushing himself off for a second time. "I just had this fucking coat dry-cleaned."

"Look—"

"'Look,' my ass," he said. "We're going to Dinkman's for a beer. Come on." He opened the rear door of the crafts and hobby shop and pushed me through it. Suddenly I was passing through the astronomy section once more, only this time I was moving in the opposite direction, and my face felt as though it had a tennis ball growing out of it. From behind me, Tommy's father added, "It's the least you can do for putting an old guy down on his can."

"What, so this is my fault now?" I became vaguely aware of people watching us as we passed. One store employee, a young woman, must've noticed the welt blooming on the side of my face, for she stopped what she was doing and covered her mouth with one hand. "It's nothing, I'm fine," I said.

Dinkman's was one of those places with a lengthy L-shaped mahogany bar, a billiards table, a pay phone, and two pinball machines. We found a pair of empty stools in the middle of the bar, so that's where we sat. The bartender's name was Owen. He was built like an oak tree. Short brown hair and a brown mustache. Tommy's father asked for two Amstel Lights.

"Don't I get to choose what I'm drinking?"

"No. I'm buying, so I choose." He pointed at the color TV mounted to a wall bracket at the far end of the bar. It was showing an episode of *The Best Damn Sports Show, Period.* "You ever watch that shit? They bring these hot chicks on sometimes, right? Pure fucking eye candy. And these guys, they sit in a circle and talk absolute bum-fuck nothing. And they call it a sports show. By the way, I'm Karl. Karl Spencer."

The next moment, I was shaking hands with Karl Spencer while massaging my left cheek.

"Simon."

"My kid tells me you been pickin' on him after school."

"Your kid is lying through his big fat teeth."

"He says you gave him a cheap shot in the shoulder."

"*What?*"

Karl toped on his beer. "Sure, yeah. He said that after you told him you were gonna beat him to a pulp, you gave him a quick punch in the shoulder."

"I gave him a *clap* on the shoulder after I politely asked him to stop picking on Corey." Well, the *politely asking* part was a stretch, but if Tommy and Karl could molest the truth, then so could I.

"So, this Corey then, what's his problem? Can't take care of himself?"

"His problem is *your son*. Tommy's a bully, and you need to speak to him. You need to have a little father-son chat on how to respect one's peers instead of dumping snow on their heads and calling them dirty names."

Karl laughed. "Look, I kinda think this playground-pushing is a healthy thing. Kinda gets 'em ready for the real world, you know? It's a dog-eat-dog world."

"No, Karl, it isn't. These are children we're talking about, not dogs."

"Look, all I'm saying is that I was brought up to fight my own battles."

"Corey's not looking to fight anybody. He's quiet and gentle. He also weighs about thirty pounds less than Tommy."

He nodded thoughtfully over his beer. "Okay. I'll talk to Tommy, tell him to leave your boy alone. No more playground crap. But I still think you should try and instill a little more toughness in your kid. Corey'll grow up the better man for it, trust me."

"He's not my kid," I said. "I'm just looking after him."

"Yeah? Where's his real father at?"

"I don't know. His father's not married to his mother. It's a long story, Karl." I drank some of my beer.

"What's his mother do? Does she work here in town?"

"Sometimes she does, yes. She's a romance novelist, so she splits her time—"

"Oh, Caldwell. Alisha Caldwell, yeah, sure. Corey's her kid, huh? Christ, I never knew that."

"So, you know her?"

"Ah, just through business." Karl finished his beer. He waved to Owen for another. "I sold her the house. House on the lake, right?"

I paused a moment. "*You* sold her the house? I thought she got it through auction."

"She did. I handled the transfer. 'Bout two years ago."

"No shit? That was you, huh?" Quite suddenly, Karl Spencer had my attention. Karl Spencer of Dolan, Packer & Spencer, Attorneys-at-Law, who happened to be father of the schoolyard bully giving Corey so many problems, had also been the man to oversee the legal transfer of Crawford Daze from the Turner family into the ownership of Alisha Caldwell. I asked, "Did you handle the closing?"

"Well, yes, I represented the seller during closing. Ms. Caldwell hired her own attorney as buyer. Boy, what a prime piece of ass, that woman. I tried to get into her pants a couple times, but she wouldn't budge. Couldn't even get her to go out for a drink."

"So, you represented the seller—Nels Turner."

"Turner. Yup, that's right."

"I understand he was forced to enter a nursing home. Do you know if the facility was nearby?"

"He went to Stonegate over in Franklinville. I know because I had to work with them to help set up his finances. I heard he died eight, maybe nine months ago."

"What can you tell me about him?"

"Well, he died eight, maybe nine months ago." He laughed. "Hey, Owen, bring this kid another beer, will you?"

"I don't want another beer."

"Bring him something for his face, too. It's blowin' up like a fuckin' balloon."

Owen said, "Hate to say it, Karl, but your face ain't much prettier."

"Yeah, well, who asked you?"

An attractive blonde sitting several stools to my right was following the exchange. She asked me, "Did the two of you get into a fight, or something? What's with your faces?"

I shook my head. "Don't ask."

Owen slid another beer in front of me. He tossed two blue ice packs onto the bar. "Do both yourselves a favor. This'll reduce the swelling."

Karl scowled. "The hell with that shit."

I lifted the ice pack and held it against my bruised left cheek. "Karl, what else can you tell me about Nels Turner?"

"Not much. What sort of information are you looking for?"

"Anything. What kind of a man was he?"

"Old and sick."

"How 'bout his wife?"

"Never met her. She died before Nels got out of the house."

"So, as an attorney, you never did any work for them? Before the auction, I mean?"

"How old do I look to you? Nels was probably retired before I ever passed the bar."

"What sort of work did Nels Turner do?"

"He owned a variety of businesses. Some delis, a restaurant, a gas station. He eventually started his own real estate holding company."

"He was pretty successful, then?"

Karl shrugged. He had snatched up the ice pack and was now pressing it firmly to his left jaw line. "Yeah, I guess, sure. His family was always regarded as being somewhat reclusive, though. You know, living in that house out by the lake. Especially after their kid died."

I laid down the ice pack and reached for the second beer. *So, they did have a child, after all.* I remembered going through the junk down in the basement and finding the letters C.D. scrawled in permanent ink on some of the tools and tool boxes.

"What happened, Karl? How did their child die?"

"Beats me, pirate. Hey, far as I know, most people never even *saw* their kid. That's how private they were. How the kid died is beyond me. Some kind of accident, I s'pose." He tipped his beer. And then, almost as an afterthought: "People did say the kid was special, though. I remember that."

"Special in what ways?"

Karl shook his head. "Sorry, kid, I just don't know. Like I said, they were a reclusive lot."

"Can you think harder?" I implored. "It's important."

He was starting to become annoyed. "No, I *can't* think harder because I don't *know.* Why's it so important? That house haunted or something?" He chuckled and tipped his beer.

I clearly recalled asking Josef last fall if Nels Turner had ever fathered a child. Josef Frustoff, having worked for Turner most of his adult life, would have had an inside track on the who's and what's within the Turner household. But then why had Josef lied to me? What had he been trying to protect? None of it made sense to me.

Karl chose this moment to redirect the conversation. "Let me get this straight. Corey's not your kid, but you bring him to school every day, and you pick him up, and you show up for the father-son breakfast. Judging by all the questions you're asking about the Turners and the lake house and shit, I'm guessing you must be living there with Corey and his hottie Ma. So, you're … what? Like, his fuckin' nanny or something?"

Owen laughed. "No shit? Are you a nanny? Really?"

I rolled my eyes. "Chaperone, fellows, chaperone."

The attractive blonde to my right added, "Oh, that is so cute. A male nanny standing in as a father figure."

"No, it's not really—"

"Do you have to help him get dressed in the morning?" Karl jived. "Tie his shoes for him?"

"Actually, he can dress him—"

"What about when he takes a bath?" Owen said. "You don't have to scrub him down, do you?"

"Does he wet the bed?" Karl asked.

I took a moment to remind myself what it felt like to read Corey a story before tucking him in and administering a gentle kiss to his forehead. I thought about how dashingly cute he looked in his Peter Cottontail pajamas. And I remembered the night of the storm, how Corey had sat sandwiched between Alisha and me, the lantern hissing above our heads—how we had taken turns reading and Corey had fallen sound asleep between us. I remembered the warmth and tenderness of Alisha's body later that night. I had been cold and shivery from the nearness of tragedy, and she had driven those demons out of me. She had taken my hand and helped guide me the rest of the way out of the storm, back onto solid ground once more. Corey was so special to us both, perhaps in ways similar to the specialness endeared by a young Crawford Turner to his parents.

Recalling these things, I said to Owen and Karl, "You know what? Fuck the both of you. It may not look like it, but I have a college degree, and I came here looking for temporary work before applying to law schools."

Karl slammed down his beer. "Law school? *Law* school? I shoulda known a young whippersnapper with that kind of an uppercut had law school in his blood. What schools are you applying to?"

"I haven't even taken the LSATs yet, Karl."

Karl spent the next twenty minutes extolling the rewards and incentives of becoming a practicing attorney. He drank a third beer and started a fourth.

"Law is all about attitude, kid. It's about *nerve*. It's about knowing when to pull the string and kick the caboose. It's about knowing when—"

"How about knowing the law?" I asked.

"Listen, have you thought about what type of law you'd like to enter?"

"Not really."

"Let me ask it in a different way. Do you want to litigate? Most attorneys don't litigate in front of crowded courtrooms, you know."

"You're getting a bit ahead of yourself, Karl."

"Let me give you some advice, pirate. Malpractice and divorce. Remember those two words."

"You know, I seem to recall a close friend advising against those two arenas."

He jabbed a finger at my chest. "No, fuck that, man. *Fuck* that. You take it from me. Malpractice and divorce. That's where the money is, that's where the pussy is. Look, these highly paid doctors and the hospitals they work in, they're always fucking up. All the time, man. You gotta understand the system. They screw up, you sue their ass, their insurance company settles out of court to keep things quiet. Bango, you take 40 percent, clean fucking sweep.

"And then there's divorce. People will *always* be getting divorced, from now until the end of time. One study concluded that today's divorce rate in the United States is roughly six out of ten. Can you believe that? Six outta fuckin' ten, man. That's what I call an investment. If you live in an affluent area where people are rolling in dough, that's even better. And here's a little secret. Always represent the woman. Talk to her, let her cry on your shoulder. You'd be surprised how much free pussy is out there. It's a win-win, man. And, hey, if you ever get married yourself and your wife screws you over, you'll have the edge in court. I fucked my ex-wife over for everything she had. Even got full custody of my kid, and look how he turned out."

He jabbed a finger at my chest again. "Invest in other people's divorces, man. It's like investin' in fuckin' *rain*—you know it's coming eventually."

"That's some pretty compelling advice, Karl."

"Tell you what I'm gonna do," he said, digging into his pants pocket. He fished out his wallet, from which he plucked a business card. He slid the card across the counter in my direction. "You get yourself into a reputable school and get your law degree. When you pass your bar, you give me a call."

I picked up the card. "Well, thanks, Karl, that's awful nice of you." I got up to leave. "You'll remember to have that little chat with Tommy, won't you?"

"Oh, yeah, sure, consider it done, man."

"Thanks for the beers, then. Thanks for the shiner."

"Yeah, you, too."

"Thanks for the ice pack, Owen."

"Anytime, guy."

I dropped Karl's card into the trash on my way out.

CHAPTER TWENTY-THREE

MILLIE'S SECRET

THE FRUSTOFFS' HOUSE WAS a one-story ranch with wood shakes siding and a roof that was more moss than shingles. It was a long, rectangular structure that began at the base of the driveway and ended at the edge of the lake. I pulled into the crumbled shale driveway and parked Josef's Tacoma behind Millie's Pathfinder. For a moment, I sat hunkered over the wheel with my foot on the brake, listening to the idling engine. Finally, I cut the ignition and got out.

A wet snow was falling. Mingled within were fat dollops of rain that had an unseemly penchant for locating the open places behind my ears or across the nape of my neck. The bruised, swollen sky hung low. Clouds sagged and dripped.

I searched for a doorbell and didn't find one. When I pulled open the Plexiglas storm door, I found the inside, front door ajar. I knocked gently on the glass insets, causing the door to swing most of the way open.

I stuck my head inside. "Hello? Millie?" I was looking down a center hallway that transected the entire length of the house. At the hallway's extreme far end, I saw porch windows overlooking the water. "Hello?"

Stomping my boots on the outside welcome mat, I stepped into the house, then gingerly restored the door to its ajar status. I was standing in a compact living room or maybe even a parlor. The house was mostly dark save for a low-wattage light emanating from farther down the hall—the kitchen, probably. I took several more steps.

"Millie? It's Simon, from across the lake." *Far side o' the lake*, Josef would have said. "Are you here?"

I advanced slowly down the hall, passing two closed doors on the right and two open ones on the left. Three-fourths of the way down the hall, I came into the kitchen, which opened along both sides of that central walkway. A pair of overhead lights accounted for the wan illumination I'd seen back in the front parlor. I glanced to the right, where I saw a sink overfilled with dishes. To the left was the kitchen table. It was cluttered with newspapers, outdated *TV Guides*, and unopened mail. The sight of unattended bills piling up lifted a sour taste in my throat.

I stepped into the enclosed back porch. For the very first time, I found myself looking across the lake at Crawford Daze instead of the other way around.

"Do you know they say it takes five years to mourn the loss of a loved one?" She was sitting in an old pine rocker to my right. Her legs were crossed, and her hands were folded around a cup of tea—I smelled the lemon and honey. I don't think she ever turned to look at me.

"It's true," I told her. "My father died seven years ago."

"Did he? You know, I didn't know that. And to think that he's your reason for being here."

I stared down at her. I suppose I shouldn't have been surprised, but just the same I was.

"How do you know that, Millie?"

Chuckling dryly. "Main Street is anything but a vacuum, dear. Come, sit."

She patted the empty chair to her left. I walked around the front of the chair and sat down in it.

"I'll pour you some tea, if you like."

"I'm okay," I said. But moments later she was pouring hot, steaming tea from an insulated decanter into an empty mug.

She slid the mug toward me over the small island table. "Mind yourself, it's hot."

"Thank you."

"Josef and I used to sit out here together in the mornings. He especially enjoyed watching the migrating birds in the spring and fall. In the summertime, we used to watch the sky for falling stars."

I tilted my head back to look up. The ceiling of this enclosed back porch was also composed of glass panels. I could readily imagine two people lying flat on retractable chairs, holding hands while searching the sky.

"That must have been special, Millie."

"Twas," she said softly. "It's funny, you know … some of the twists and turns life takes. Things don't often go the way you want them to, or even expect them to. I never would have imagined myself coming to live in a place like this. But somehow I did. And I've never regretted it.

"You know what I find even more amazing, Simon? The people. The people who pass in and out of your life. They just kind of wander in and wander out. Some stay longer than others. Some stay forever. It's the people, I believe, who represent life's single greatest variable. You know why? You know why, Simon? Because they change you. Whether you know it or not, they change you. And you change them."

This was not the sort of conversation I'd imagined myself getting into with Millie Frustoff. I sipped my tea heartily. It was very good, and it was hot, and it warmed me. The snow-sleet-rain struck the windows and ran down the glass with wintry abandon. This was one of those dreary February days that causes one to think about unresolved issues and unfulfilled goals. If I had them at age twenty-three, and Millie had them at age sixty-three, then maybe they were things that never really went away. I found that a hard thought to swallow.

"What happened to your face, dear?"

"Oh, I got into a fight a few nights ago." I'd had a devil of a time explaining that one to Alisha, who had wanted to know every minute detail, including the guy's name, address, eye color, and place of employment. I told her it had been a simple misunderstanding. I told her I'd kicked the guy's ass, too.

"I'd have thought someone your age would have outgrown that sort of thing," Millie said.

That was sort of funny, I thought, considering the guy who'd actually picked the fight was twice my age.

"Millie, I came to talk to you about the Turners. Namely, their son, Crawford."

"Of course you did, dear."

"What, you knew I would?"

"How could you not?" She turned her head to look me in the eye, but only for a moment. "How could you live in that special place, and not ask? And not wonder?"

I leaned forward in my rocker. "It *is* special, Millie. I know it, yet I can't explain it. I feel it, but I can't touch it. And ..." *And, yes, one time I even saw it. I saw it with my own eyes.*

"It's special, dear, because of the people who lived there before you. Love is an extremely powerful emotion, Simon. Its bonds are stronger than any cement, its properties more dynamic than those of any atom or molecule. And at exactly the right doses ..."

"Yes? What?"

In a lower voice: "Well, there are those who say it can produce a kind of magic."

"I'm not sure I believe in magic."

"But you're a little more sure than when you first arrived last August."

"Millie, why did you and Josef hide the fact that the Turners had a son?"

Millie opened her mouth but then closed it. She took some tea and allowed her eyes to wander across the lake. She was quiet for what seemed a very long time. Three minutes became five minutes. Five minutes became ten. Icy rain ticked the windows. The gray sky hung so low it seemed conjoined with the gray surface of the lake.

"Crawford wasn't like other children his age," Millie said finally. "He was ... he was different. He was just *different*. But he was special. He was oh, so *special*."

"How was he different?" I asked.

"He didn't communicate well in school. He was withdrawn, shy, quiet. Teachers had a difficult time getting through to him. They said he would pull himself into a shell or a bubble, and at times be unresponsive. Sometimes, the other kids picked on him.

"Keep in mind, this was during the mid-sixties. Education has come a long way since then. In today's world, Crawford might well be labeled as borderline autistic."

"Do you think that's what he was, then? Autistic?"

"I don't know, dear, I'm not a psychologist. But I know that Crawford didn't fare well in a public forum. He didn't fare well at all."

"What made him special, then?"

Millie smiled. It was the sort of smile you saw on a person who's thumbing through an old album and has come across a photo she especially likes, one that raises nostalgic memories.

"He *himself* was special. He radiated a warmth, a kindness, a general overall *benevolence* that I can't compare with any other child I've met. There was an aura around him, and everything about it positively glowed. That's why I found him special. I found him special because he was easy to love and eager to *be* loved. And I loved him, despite the fact that he was someone else's child. I loved him very much. Josef did, too."

I guess you kind of had to be there, then, huh? Because the words Millie was using to describe the late Crawford Daze Turner were the same words most parents would likely use to portray their own kids. Most kids radiated warmth, didn't they? Most kids were easy to love and eager to be loved. Most kids were inherently benevolent—except Tommy Spencer. Most kids were so cute and loveable, it made you want to hug them ten or twelve times a day.

"Is that all?" I asked.

"No," Millie answered. "That's only the beginning."

*   *   *

She got up to make more tea. When she returned five minutes later with the newly filled decanter, the mixed precipitation had changed over to pure rain.

She refilled my mug. "Our weather doesn't quite know what to be, does it?"

"What did you make of the blizzard?" I asked her.

"'Twas the worst storm I've witnessed in the forty-plus years I've lived here. I've never seen anything like it, Simon. And to be without Josef … I was very worried."

"Were you here? In this house, I mean?"

"Yes, of course. Where else would I be?"

"Did you happen to see anything unusual through these windows? Out over the lake, specifically?"

She retook her seat. "I don't believe I was able to see twenty feet in any direction. It was like a wall of white moving horizontally. And it got so *bad* so *fast*. People actually perished, Simon."

We were almost among them—Corey, Alisha, and me.

"Were you able to remain warm?" I asked. "With the power outage and all?"

"Oh, yes. I kept the woodstove going around the clock. Several years ago, Josef purchased a pair of kerosene heaters. Both of those came in very handy. I kept one in my bedroom and the other in the kitchen."

"Good for you. I'm sure Josef would have been proud."

She smiled meekly. "Now, where were we? You wanted to hear more about the young prodigy across the lake."

"Crawford was a prodigy?"

"Oh, yes, dear, he was that and more. Despite Crawford's social ineptitudes, he had two extraordinary gifts. Both involved his hands. The boy could paint, and he could build things."

The painting I had known about. The ability to build things I hadn't. But it did explain the garage full of tools, machines, implements, and tool chests with the letters C.D. writ upon them.

"Millie, I'm not sure I fully understand."

"What's not to understand, dear?"

"Well …"

Crawford Turner may have been borderline autistic. It was even possible that a learning or behavioral disability had hindered his performance in a public school setting. However, it wouldn't have been the first time (far from it, actually) that a learning-disabled child exhibited extraordinary artistic talent or adroit craftsmanship skills. There were dozens of stories—*hundreds*, really—of kids who—

"These are amazing abilities, Simon, for a child born without the gift of sight."

My train of thought ended as abruptly as it had begun. Millie never turned to look at me. Her gaze remained focused out over the lake. Snow was once more mixing with the rain.

"Millie, you're not … You're not saying Crawford was *blind?*"

"Yes, dear, that is what I'm saying. Crawford came into the world with congenital blindness."

I was shaking my head in disbelief. "Millie, no. That's not possible. That can't *possibly*—"

"And yet it is. It's not only possible, Simon. It's true."

"But, Millie, think of all the paintings he did. I mean, he painted the house to a T." I pointed across the lake as I said it. "He—he knew exactly what the house looked like from the outside. He knew what the lake looked like, with the floating dock in the middle."

Millie, nodding. "Yes. He did."

If you thought about it, you could carry this argument several steps further. "How does a person who's never seen the world know how to paint a tree? How—how does he know what a tree looks like if he's never seen one? How does he know that the trunk is brown and the leaves are green?"

"Funny, I asked him that once. He sort of shrugged and said he was only painting what he saw in his head."

"Still … how could he raise a brush to a canvas and know exactly where to put the brush? How could he know where he'd last left off on the canvas without being able to see it?"

"I asked him that, as well. He said he had a good memory. Simon, I used to sit here on this very porch and watch Crawford paint." She pointed to the left. "He would stand right over there in front of his easel with his brush in hand. That brush would go from the canvas down to his palette and back to the canvas without pause or worry. And he would talk to me while he worked. We had long, detailed discussions as he stood there painting away, working the brush blithely and merrily."

"At the very least, he must've asked you to describe what the house looked like. The lake, too. And the floating dock."

"He never asked me those things."

"How could he swing a hammer without being able to see the nail? How could he run a power saw without cutting his finger off? How could he build something—*anything*—without being able to *see* it? Hell, it took me a week to assemble Playworld."

"The eyes can deceive, Simon. The trained mind has a much sharper focus, a more astute eye. Blind people will often compensate for their lack of sight by heightening their other senses. Crawford had an uncanny sense of smell. And I've never seen a person with a more acute sense of hearing. He could identify who was walking through the house by the pattern of the footsteps. When a car pulled into the driveway, he knew instantly whose it was by the sound of the engine. He could hear a bird chirrup three miles away. He knew when a plane was flying over the house at an altitude of forty thousand feet."

I fell quiet for a while. I drank some more tea while I digested this new information. Certainly, there were no reasons to doubt Millie's words. And if what she was saying was true, then I suppose Crawford had indeed been special. Maybe even remarkable.

"Was Crawford able to finish school, Millie?"

"No. The school system asked his parents to pull him out. He was home-schooled by his mother."

"What was the school's reason? The autism? The blindness? Both?" An idea occurred to me. "It's possible that Crawford's presence among other, non-blind students was what contributed to his social withdrawal. I don't think Crawford was autistic at all. Especially given that the two of you shared detailed discussions while he stood here painting."

Millie smiled in a rueful sort of way. "It was his paintings that got him kicked out."

"What?"

"That's my belief, anyway. The school cited a litany of reasons. An inability to learn. A disruptive presence to a classroom environment. One school official even described Crawford as 'a menace and possible source of danger to other children.' Hogwash. It was his paintings they didn't like."

"What's not to like about his paintings, Millie? They're products of a gifted talent. You said so yourself."

"I did, didn't I? And I stand by it. But there were some people who experienced strong emotional reactions to some of his paintings— reactions they later found disturbing, and to some degree even frightening."

I know the feeling. It's happened to me twice. The question is … There were a lot of questions, actually. *A lot* of them. On my first day in Swan Lake, I'd seen the painting of the Turner house on the sidewalk in front of Millie's store—the one with the light in the window. I'd reacted fairly strongly to that one, hadn't I? In a strange town with no job, no housing, and practically no money, I'd been reaching for my wallet without so much as a second thought. And later, there'd been the painting of the woman trapped in the ice, up to her armpits in water that was black and pitiless, but reaching still … reaching for something beyond view, something that was out of the picture. I'd been swept off my feet by the haunting detail, by the indescribable and yet ineluctable anguish on the woman's face—so much so that I'd literally felt the harsh, wind-driven snow clipping my ears and raising my hair.

Both events had later come to fruition, albeit in an inverse order. Alisha had wound up trapped in the ice—and yet reaching, reaching for her son, who was getting farther and farther away. Minutes later, as I'd held her freezing body in my arms and realized with horror that I'd lost my bearings, that the storm had turned me around— that's when the light had come. And to think that I'd first glimpsed that light from over my shoulder … I'd been moving in the wrong direction, and the house had *signaled itself*—had shown me the way.

Consider this, then: had Crawford forecasted these events in painting them? Or had the events themselves happened as a result of my seeing the paintings? Which came first—the chicken or the egg?

Another question: was the woman-in-the-ice painting meant to be a rendition of Crawford's as-yet unwed mother reaching for her dog? Or an eerie prelude of Alisha reaching for her son? Had Crawford been illustrating the past in commemorating the event that had brought his parents together? Or had he been illustrating the future by coloring the near-tragic episode that would one day bring Alisha and me together? Was art imitating life, or was art *predicting* life?

I squeezed my eyes shut and rubbed my face with my hands. All this cosmic thinking was giving me a headache. Insane thinking is what it was, and it was probably all nonsense.

But I couldn't dispel that strange and pervasive gut-level feeling of history trying to rhyme. I remembered that first afternoon in town, feeling transfixed and maybe even hypnotized by the painting of the house with the light in the window. Riding on the heels of that hypnosis had been this insight: *There is no happiness in that home. But there used to be.* It hadn't made any sense to me then, but it was starting to make a lot of sense now. Nels Turner had pulled a woman out of the ice. I had pulled Alisha out of the ice. Originally, there had been a man, a woman, and a boy living happily in the Turner house. Today there was a man, a woman, and a boy living happily in the Turner house. So startling were the similarities that I actually began to shiver.

What exactly was happening here? What was happening to *me*? Was I in control of my own destiny anymore? My own life? Or was I conforming to some external master plan, caught in some great existential tractor beam?

That's silly thinking, Simon. Rid yourself of those thoughts. Don't deny your emotions, your feelings, your love for Corey and Alisha. Are those things not real?

They *were* real. They *were*.

And their realness redirected my galloping thoughts back to Crawford Daze Turner. The boy who'd been special. The blind boy who'd painted what he saw in his head.

Crawford had been special, all right. He may have been more special than anyone ever knew.

*   *   *

When I emerged from my reverie, I saw that Millie's chair was empty. I was alone on the enclosed back porch.

I set down my teacup and got up. I went into the kitchen, but Millie wasn't there. I stood stock-still, listening for sounds of movement elsewhere in the house. Hearing none, I began walking up the central hallway toward the parlor. The front door was standing wide open.

Millie was standing out in the driveway. Wet, heavy snowflakes fell past her arms and shoulders. She stood facing the other way with her arms at her sides. My first thought was that she'd gone out to look at her husband's truck, but it became quickly evident that Josef's Tacoma had nothing to do with her being there. She seemed to be staring across the road actually, into the woods.

I pushed through the Plexiglas storm door and walked up beside her. "Are you all right, Millie? I never heard you get up."

"This is where I was on that day. This is the exact spot where I was standing."

"What day was that, Millie?"

"The day I learned that Crawford was dead. This is where I was when I found out."

"What happened?"

"He and his mother had been in an auto accident the night before. Their vehicle had turned over up on the Blue Marsh Road. It had been cold and dark and rainy. Grace had swerved violently to avoid hitting a group of deer that had suddenly appeared out of nowhere. The car smashed into a ditch and rolled over. Both had been wearing seatbelts, but Crawford had suffered a severe, side-impact head trauma. He was unconscious. Grace herself was bleeding from her forehead and both hands. It took her ten minutes, she later said, to climb out from the upside-down car. There were no cell phones back then, of course, so she had to wait for the next passing motorist. That motorist happened to be Lester Humes, who was seventy-five at the time, and whose grandson now owns the fly and tackle shop in town by the river. Lester drove to the nearest house to find a telephone. Grace ran back to her overturned car to tend to her son. She managed to get his safety harness unbuckled, and then drag him out of his upside-down position, so that he was lying face-up on the inside of the roof of the car. And then … well, a strange thing happened then."

"What happened, Millie?"

"Crawford woke up. He regained consciousness, though barely. He opened his eyes. And he looked up at his mother. He smiled weakly. And he told her she was beautiful. 'You're beautiful, Mama. You're so beautiful.' Those were his words. In the dim glow of the dashboard lights, Grace said she was sure his pupils were sharply focused and fixed on hers. She said she felt a tingling sensation in her spine and a lightness in her gut that she'd never felt before. She said that he blinked, and that his eyes remained focused on hers, knowing right where she was. And she knew that her son was seeing her for the first time. She *knew*.

"Those were the last words he ever spoke to his mother. Crawford died in the ambulance on the way to the hospital. I learned of his death the following morning. I was walking from the front door to the mailbox with a handful of outgoing letters when Lois Church from Road 37 came skidding to a stop in front of my driveway and blurted out the news. I didn't believe her at first. I didn't believe her at all, not one little itty bit. But then she threw her car door open and came tottering toward me at a half run, and I saw the stricken look on her face, and I saw the car door standing open with the car in the middle of the road behind her, and … and I knew. Then I knew. I dropped all of the letters. They landed in the wet driveway by my feet. This is where I was standing when I dropped the letters. This is where I was standing. It was right here."

Snow was piling up on our shoulders now. It had formed a white wreath around the top of Millie's hair. A lone tear slid down her near cheek in silent tribute to the lost Crawford Daze Turner—the son she'd loved as her own.

"He died on February 9th, 1976. He was eighteen years old."

"Millie, do you really think Crawford saw his mother's face that night? That he acquired eyesight after the crash? We're talking about rods, cones, and retinas that have never functioned. An optic nerve that's never transmitted an image."

"I don't know, Simon, whether he did or not. But Grace remained steadfastly convinced of it through all the remaining years of her life. She never once wavered. And I never tried to convince her otherwise." Millie turned to look me in the eye. "What do you think, Simon? Based on everything else you've learned today?"

"I think you were right when you said that Crawford was special." Millie turned away, looking toward the road again as if she could still see Lois Church's car idling there with the front door hanging open. "What happened later on? In the aftermath?"

"Grace lapsed into a severe depression. I ministered to her every day for three years to help her cope. To help her get by. To help her get back on her feet."

"Did she? Get back on her feet, I mean?"

"I suppose she did, in time. But a mother never fully recovers from losing a child. Grace was never the same again. She never fully regained her bright, bubbly self. There were new lines in her face. A strain hid behind every smile."

"That's a sad story."

"And yet a happy one, as well. In the eighteen years of Crawford's life, the Turners may well have been the happiest, healthiest family I've come to know. The love among the three of them was unconditional and pure."

I laid a hand on her snowy shoulder. "We should go back inside, Millie. You're starting to shiver."

"Not yet," she said. "There's something I have to show you."

*   *   *

She turned, then led me out of the driveway and into the narrow strip of yard to the left of her house. We passed through a row of small dogwoods that separated her property from that of her neighbor's. We were heading directly for her neighbor's house, in fact. I had always wondered about the two houses sitting on either side of the Frustoffs'.

"Who lives in these other houses?" I asked.

"No one. They've been empty for over thirty years."

"Who owns them?"

"I do. Josef built them. He built all three of them." We climbed a series of four wooden stairs that led to a small wood porch that accessed a side entrance. Millie reached into her pocket and withdrew a key. She stuck the key into the keyhole and turned it. As she pushed the door open and led me inside, she said, "Long ago, we used to rent these two units out as summer cottages. We had a couple good years doing so, but after that it always ended up costing us more than we made."

We were standing in the kitchen. The interior layout of this unit was much different from that of Millie's house. In fact, I liked this one a lot better—it had a more modern appeal. Facing the kitchen was a deluxe dining area replete with table, chairs, and a wraparound sofa. To the right of this kitchen/dining room combo was a plushly furnished den that overlooked the lake. The den had an open fireplace and a bearskin rug. To the left of the kitchen/dining room would of course be the bedrooms.

"Gees, Millie, this is really nice." The place was more or less clean, save for some layaway dust here and there. It was moderately warm. The thermostat must've been set around sixty.

Millie went around turning up blinds and clicking on a few

lamps. "You see, Simon, Swan Lake never really found its way onto the tourist map. It's really too far away from any major cities or towns for people to take notice. And of course, the lake isn't all that big. When Josef and I first began renting these in the summertime, most of our tenants couldn't even find their way out here."

"How come there aren't more houses on the lake?"

"Because Nels, while serving as town mayor, passed an ordinance that prohibited further construction within a 2.3-mile radius of the lake's geographical midpoint."

"Nels was mayor?"

"For a time, yes."

"It seems pretty selfish of him, like he wanted all the lake to himself. How did he get the rest of the town to go along with it?"

"Mr. Turner pretty well *built* the town, Simon. He carried most of its merchants and businessmen in his pocket." She must've read the sour look on my face, for she added, "He was also wealthy, and a philanthropist who donated thousands to local interests."

"If he was that powerful, then how did the school system manage to oust his son from their classrooms?"

"No man's power is greater than that of the board of education or the local teachers' union. And besides, Grace simply *adored* home-schooling their son. She poured every ounce of her spirit into it."

I went to the kitchen sink and lifted the tap. Nothing came out.

"Water's turned off," she said.

"And yet the heat …"

"The thermostat is set to fifty-seven."

"But why? It's as if you're saving this house for something. Like you're planning to use it, or …"

"Well, I am using it. I'm using it right now."

"For what? Show and tell?"

"No, silly. For storage." She went into the hall and opened the first door on the right. I walked up behind her and peered over her shoulder. The room was filled with paintings. Crawford Daze original prints ran the gamut from wall to wall. A narrow walkway zigged and zagged like a sharp-edged maze through the labyrinth of piled artwork. Some of the canvases were stacked flat, one atop the other, all the way up to chest-height. Others stood vertically, leaning against one another like books on a bookshelf. Some were individually wrapped either in plastic or in brown wrapping paper. Many weren't wrapped at all. It reminded me of the back of Millie's store on Main Street.

Stunned, I said, "Millie, there must be four hundred or more canvases in this room alone."

"There are two more rooms exactly like it," she said. "That's in *this* house."

I turned to face her. "And the other house?"

"Three additional rooms, all stacked to the gills."

I shook my head slowly. "I can't believe it. That's more than twenty-four hundred pieces of artwork."

"Not to mention what's in my store. And the pieces I've sold."

"How does a blind person who never reaches his nineteenth birthday become so *prolific?* What's in this room alone probably accounts for more work than most artists produce in a lifetime."

"I told you he was a prodigy."

She went up the hall, opening the doors of the remaining two rooms. The proof is in the pudding, I guess. More paintings, piled high and wide.

"It's why I keep the temperature in the upper fifties. Artwork can become brittle, and later crack, from exposure to the cold. Wide temperature fluctuations can ruin the integrity of the pigments, as well as accelerate aging. And the place has to remain dry, of course. Unchecked humidity is lethal to artwork."

I entered the cutback maze in the third "storage" room. "How did all of these get here? Were they always here?"

"Some of the rooms in the Turner house were filled by Crawford's thirteenth birthday. There simply wasn't any more room. So I told him he could begin keeping his newer pieces in here. Gradually the rooms began to fill up."

"You're not kidding."

"After the accident, Grace told me she couldn't bear having all those earlier paintings taking up space in her house. She didn't have the fortitude to go through them, and yet she didn't want to throw them away. I offered to house all of Crawford's canvases over here until she figured out what she wanted to do with them. It took Josef, Nels, and I two full days to transport them all. Nels paid us a monthly stipend of three hundred dollars for twenty-seven years."

"You're saying that you made …" I tried crunching the numbers in my head.

"It's almost a hundred thousand dollars, yes."

"Holy smokes," I breathed.

"Yes, I know," Millie said, dropping her eyes to the floor. "It's an awful lot of money for something I would have gladly done for free. And yet Nels insisted, time and again, that he pay us for storing his son's treasures. He paid the first of every month, up until the time he was forced to enter the nursing home."

"What you're saying, then, is that Grace never came up with a plan on how to get rid of them."

"She did, actually. She came up with a rather wonderful plan. About four years after Crawford's death, she took me to lunch one day and told me what she wanted me to do. She wanted me to bring some of her son's best pieces into my store, where I was to begin selling them off, one by one. She instructed me to allow the market to dictate the price, and that I was to retain 10 percent of each sale. The remaining 90 percent was to be donated to the Carroll Center for the Blind, in Newton, Massachusetts."

"What's the Carroll Center?" I asked.

"A private, non-profit organization that provides training programs and services to the visually impaired and legally blind. It was founded in 1936 and named after Father Thomas Carroll. One of their rudder projects in the mid-seventies was a program to help blind children take part in mainstream education with sighted students.

"I was so enamored by Grace's plan that I agreed to donate 100 percent of every sale of a Crawford Daze original. And that's what I've done, from 1980 up to today."

I turned on my heels, surveying the stacks of canvases on all sides of me—some of them rose to shoulder height.

"I don't get it. If there are this many pieces remaining … well, how many have you sold?"

"I sell seven or eight a year, give or take."

"Seven or eight? That's it?"

"I'm afraid so, yes."

"Sounds like you need to lower your prices."

"Price is irrelevant. I've offered them for twenty-five dollars apiece, all the way up to fifteen hundred. I still sell seven or eight a year. People love to look at Crawford Daze canvases. But they rarely buy them. In fact, when it comes to buying, most people afford them a wide berth."

"Do you find that odd?"

Millie bit her lower lip, dropping her eyes to the floor. She pushed a rogue dust bunny around with the toe of one shoe. "It is what it is, I suppose." She looked up again. "I'm going to run downstairs to check the burner. You'll excuse me for a moment?"

"Yeah, sure, go ahead."

She disappeared from the doorway. I heard another door being opened farther up the hall, followed by footsteps clomping down thick, wood stairs.

I rotated on the balls of my feet, again surveying the hundreds of paintings that filled this room. Even the closet was filled. The closet doors had been removed long ago to facilitate storage. It wasn't as if these one-time bedrooms had *beds* in them, either. There were no beds, desks, chairs, end tables, or pole lamps. Only paintings. So many paintings. Paintings that stole people's breaths away, but paintings that no one wanted to buy. How could this happen? How could a talent of such magnitude simply go to waste? How could the products of that talent be permitted to ride a receding wave into time's vast, forgetful ocean? It seemed not only wrong to me, but unfair. Time, like quicksand, has a way of killing dreams, I suppose—it quietly sucks them down.

I ran my fingers along the gilded edges of a wood frame belonging to a painting that sat atop a stack of canvases directly in front of me. The stack was waist-high. The one on top was not wrapped, and I found it an absorbing piece to look at. It consisted of geometric shapes that were all somehow interlocked with one another. Some of the shapes were partially superimposed over others. Say, a part of a circle overlapping one corner of a triangle, while a different corner of that triangle would overlap part of a trapezoid. And the trapezoid … well, you get the point. Inside each of these shapes was a primary color. Where the shapes overlapped, the colors would mix, but in perfect gradations relative to the distance from the main shape. A white square overlapping a corner of a red rectangle produced a mini-square of pink intersection. But true pink was only achieved in the very center of that mini-square. The closer to the main white square you looked, the whiter the pink became. The closer to the red rectangle you looked, the redder the pink became. It looked like an artist's exercise in the proportional mixing of colors. This sort of piece had probably been done hundreds of times, but by those able to see what they were doing.

I lifted the canvas from the top of the stack and set it aside. The canvas beneath it depicted a bird perched on a tree branch. The branch, probably that of a locust tree, had what looked like two- and three-inch thorns growing out of it. Impaled on one of these thorns was the body of a mouse. Blood leaked from the mouse's body and dribbled off the end of the thorn. Standing on the ground below was a gnome with a hooked nose and a green hat. The gnome's head was tilted back and its mouth was open, greedily accepting the dripping gore. In one of the gnome's bunched fists was a rolled-up piece of parchment. Interesting.

I lifted the mouse-on-a-thorn piece and set it on top of the shapes-and-colors piece. The next piece in the stack may have been one of the more random renditions I'd ever set eyes upon. In fact, it took me a few moments to register what exactly I was looking at. I saw the color blue, and lots of it. The blue was actually part of a tent or a pavilion. But the tent was not shown in its entirety. I was seeing one half or even a third of it. The blue tarp was clearly wet. It seemed to flutter ... or *ready* to flutter, perhaps. I felt a warm breeze grazing the back of my neck; moisture formed behind my ears. Along the bottom edge of the blue tarp were the tops of several aluminum poles—is that what they were? Yes, indeed, the poles were the things holding the tent up. My eyes followed the upward curving arch of the blue tarp to its acme. Perched there was a silver, metallic bird standing tall with its wings spread. The bird wasn't quite a hawk, and yet it was; wasn't quite an owl, yet it was; wasn't quite a gargoyle, yet it was. The bird was somehow all three of those. If I hadn't known any better, I might have deemed it a lightning rod. But there was no point at the top of the bird's head. And besides, who would ever be so dumb as to put a lightning rod on the top of a party tent, beneath which revelers and celebrants were eating hotdogs and drinking birch beer?

Is that what it is? A party tent?

I lowered my focus from that strange metal bird, following a corner crease line of the blue, glistening, rippling tarp … and my eyes seized upon something they hadn't noticed before. How I possibly could have overlooked such a thing both befuddled and scared me. But I was seeing it now, and it took the air out of me. It was a hanging bulge in the tent. Rainwater meant to dribble down the tarp and drip harmlessly off the edge had formed a sizeable pool three-fourths of the way down the tarp's diagonal slope. The weight of the water in this abscess had caused the sac to deepen, allowing it to collect more water. The bulge that resulted was large and wide enough to be considered dangerous. Soon, the weight of the water would overwhelm the integrity of the blue material. The tarp was going to tear. All that water was going to spill downward. The entire tent would react; the poles might move, perhaps even lose their earthen footings.

And what about that bird? What was going to become of the bird? What might that bird *become?* Might it become the hawk? The owl? Possibly the gargoyle?

And then—amazingly—the bulge appeared to grow in front of me. It wasn't growing, of course, but my *anticipation* of its growth was almost too much to bear.

Turn away, Simon. Don't look at it.

I felt a low-level nausea churning in my belly. That swelling crater of rainwater was going to rupture, and when it did, all would be lost. Would I be able to stand here and watch it? Would I be able to stomach it? How was I going to react to seeing the world go plundering through that rip in the tent in one wet, silvery flash?

The thought alone was too much. I felt everything being pulled out of me, as though long stiletto fingers had been thrust into my navel and then raked up to my throat. I'd been rent open. My blood was leaving my body, all of my organs and entrails going right along with it. I felt my physical self growing *lighter* as it all drained out of me, forming a spreading pool around my ankles. I was dying, I was dying while standing up, and no one could see it, no one could *feel* it, they couldn't *feel* me dying, they couldn't *know* what it—

"—okay?"

"What?" I looked up, blinking. Millie was standing in the open doorway.

"I asked if you were okay. Simon, you look awfully pale."

"I—I'm fine. Just a bit of a headache, I guess."

"Let's go," she said. "I'll give you some tea and two Advil."

"That … that sounds good." I tottered on my feet a little as I wove through the cutback maze.

Out in the hall, Millie pulled the door shut. "Are you sure you're all right, dear?"

"I'll be okay. Some fresh air might help."

Outside, rain was falling again.

CHAPTER TWENTY-FOUR

Wrath of a Mother Scorned

Take me home, Simon ... I wasn't sure that was a good idea, really, but seeing there was nowhere else to go, home is where we went. Ma held her silence most of the way. She couldn't hold her fury, however. Rage trembled off of her. The air in the cab space quivered of it. Ma continued to shake. She'd been shaking all day, it seemed— first out of fear, now out of anger. This had been a long day, and it wasn't over yet. Driving to the Midland County Bank this morning seemed like eons ago. From the bank, to the Applebee's for lunch. And on to Tall Oaks Jewelers, where a tall fellow of Lebanese descent had reached into Ma's chest and pulled the beating heart right out of her. And maybe out of me, too. The highs and lows of this day had worn me thin, and I was tired. The only thing worse than getting turned around in the storm, perhaps, was allowing yourself to falsely believe you'd found your way out. That light at the end of the tunnel had been an oncoming train, and now the train was running us over. I had failed. I'd stood with all I had, I'd fought the good fight. But in the end I'd lost. Now, there was nothing left to stand with. There was nothing left to stand *on*.

Catherine. How could she do this? Didn't she know how much that diamond was worth? Didn't she realize what kind of a situation we were in?

Maybe she still has it. If we're lucky, she'll have it stashed away somewhere.

But I knew this wasn't to be so. I'd been spoon-fed enough false hope for one day. Now I was tired. I was worn thin. A pall of defeatism and finality draped itself over me.

I turned the Roadgrader onto Williams Way. Minutes later, I was turning into our driveway. We both saw Cath's dilapidated Chevy wagon parked on a skew—half in the driveway, half on the front lawn.

"Good, she's home," Ma breathed. "Don't block her in, Simon. She'll be pulling out very shortly. You're about to witness an eviction."

"Ma, you need to get a hold of yourself," I said. "Try to control your—"

She opened her door before the Roadgrader had come to a complete stop. Then she was out her door and bouncing across the stones toward the side porch. I had to run to catch up to her. I laid a hand on her shoulder, trying to slow her down. She grabbed my hand and threw it off of her.

"Ma—"

She rounded on me. "This is between her and me, Simon. You stay out of it."

"I know, but—"

"She betrayed me, Simon. She *betrayed* me. It's bad enough that she disrespects and disregards everything I say and do, but this is outright betrayal. And I guarantee you it's the end of the line."

The truth was, I was angry, too. Catherine deserved to be scolded, reprimanded, maybe even booted out of the house. But the hawkish, predatory lust in Ma's eyes was beginning to scare me. I had never seen that look in her eyes before.

She turned and started to climb the porch stairs. We both looked up and saw the piece of paper that had been taped to the storm door during our absence. Notice of Foreclosure and Sheriff's Sale, it said in big black letters. Ma tore it free and crumpled it into a paper ball before I could read any of the fine print underneath. She pulled open the door and entered the house. I went in behind her.

*   *   *

Ma tossed her pocketbook onto the kitchen table with enough force that it slid across the wood surface and fell off the other side, taking with it two placemats and the saltshaker. The purse struck the edge of a chair seat and plopped onto the floor. I heard lipstick cylinders, some coins, and other various items rolling toward the corners.

Ma didn't seem to notice this, or care. She stormed through the dining room and into the living room, heading for the stairs. I was hot on her heels.

"Ma, wait—"

"Stay downstairs, Simon. I told you, this is between your sister and me."

I did no such thing, of course. I followed Ma step for step. A cruel part of me wanted to watch this. A part of me relished the notion of seeing Catherine get what was coming to her. After all I had done, it would be one inexplicably selfish act on her part that would bring all of us down.

But there was a second part of me, one that felt differently. As we reached the top of the stairs, turned right into the bottom part of the L hallway, then a quick left into the straightaway, I recalled the journal entry I had read—Cath's letter to Dad. *Ma drinks through it, Simon stays away. And I am the glue holding the sinking ship together.* I suppose in some respects she *had* been the glue. But you wouldn't know it from the outside, looking in. You wouldn't know Catherine had been using her body as a means of paying off Dad's debts. You wouldn't know she'd been performing dirty little deeds to protect Ma from Blackstone's hounds. Dirty deeds done dirt-cheap. There was more to Catherine's actions than perhaps met the eye.

There is not much of me left. You can't squeeze blood from a stone, but I guess you can squeeze the life out of a whore.

It had been Cath's journal entry, her desperation letter to Dad, that had served as an impetus for me to take action. That had been the turning point for me. I may not have known it then, but I realized it now. The journal entry had been the spark that had lit the fire in my belly, encouraging me to run to the neighbor's house for help that very same day. I'd known in the back of my mind that Mr. Van Ness's wife, Molly, belonged to some anonymous substance-abuse self-help group. Mr. Van Ness had gone into his kitchen and returned with the gold coin. "This coin saved our marriage, Simon." He'd given me a list of local churches and meeting times.

Catherine's bedroom door was locked. This didn't deter Ma in the slightest. She rattled the knob for a few seconds, then began kicking the door in. Wood splintered and cracked. Two strong kicks were enough to sufficiently weaken the jamb. Ma threw her shoulder into the door with more strength than I thought she possessed. The door burst inward with a sharp *crack!* Ma went stumbling into the room with so much momentum that I was sure she'd fall flat on her face.

She recovered, though, and immediately lunged to the back left corner of the room. I entered the busted doorway in time to see that Cath's bed, though unmade and unkempt, was empty. The room was mostly dark and in terrible disarray. The stale, noxious miasma of cigarette smoke and body odor washed over me, making me grimace.

Cath had been sleeping in her pile of dirty laundry. She was wearing pink sweats and an old wifebeater. Ma's noisy entrance had roused her, and I looked in time to see Cath's head upraised, eyes barely open and squinting, dry lips parted in dismay. "What the fuck—"

She never had time to finish. Ma was on top of her. "You stinking, rotten, filthy bitch, get up! *Get up!*" Ma grabbed Catherine by the hair. She dragged Catherine to her feet and out of the laundry heap. Cath's bare heels bumped across the floor as her hands flew up to her head to grab Ma's fingers, trying to wrench them free. But the combination of being half-asleep, strung out, and morbidly underweight had turned the tables in Ma's favor. It hadn't been long ago, I remembered, that these two had sparred in the kitchen late one night, and Cath had dealt Ma a blow and knocked her down. No more. Catherine was the weakling now, and Ma's temper was lit up like a jukebox.

"Let go of me!" Catherine wailed. "Let go of—"

Still holding her by the hair, Ma whipped Catherine to the left. For a moment, Catherine appeared to be flying; the toe of one foot grazed over the floor as she flew shoulder-first into the hanging closet doors. Both doors blew inward off their tracks. An overhead shelf collapsed, raining shoes and clothing onto Catherine's head and body.

Ma went for her. I stood back, horrified, as Ma bent down and seized Catherine's hair again. "How could you do this to me? Do you have any idea what you've done, young lady? Do you have any idea *what you've done?*"

Ma swung Catherine the other way this time. Hard. Catherine flew across the room in a clumsy pinwheel of legs and arms. She went headfirst into the wall, in mid-fall and mid-flight. Her head broke through the drywall, exhuming a cloud of white dust. She collapsed to the floor. A trickle of blood formed on her temple.

I started forward. "Ma—"

My mother spun around and planted her hand in the middle of my chest, shoving me backward. I fell flat on my ass and elbows.

She advanced on Catherine again. She stood towering over her, hands rolled into fists. Catherine lay feebly at Ma's feet. Cath was five-foot-nine, and maybe down to ninety-five pounds. Knobs of bone bulged against her skin. Her face had a sunken, hollow look. You could almost see her skull behind her caved-in cheeks. It occurred to me then and there that my sister was going to die. Today. Possibly here. Right now.

"Don't … hurt me anymore," Catherine mewled. "Please don't hurt me."

"That brooch was meant for your wedding day. That diamond … I trusted you, Catherine. I trusted you, and you betrayed me."

"I didn't … have a choice."

"You didn't have a *choice?*" Ma's voice was rising. "You say you didn't *have a ch*—"

"That's enough!" I said. I was on my feet and between the two of them now. "Ma, back up."

"I told you, Simon—"

"I said, *back up!*" Ma backed up. "You've done enough damage here." I turned and looked down at Catherine. "What did you do with the diamond, Cath? Wherever it is, we need to get it back. The bank is repossessing our house."

She muttered through stumbling lips, "It wasn't … my job to pay the bills."

Ma took a step forward. *"Don't you dare bring—"*

"No, Ma!" I yelled, turning toward her and thrusting both hands out. "Stay right there. Back up to the doorway." I paused, waiting for tempers to come down a little. "We're all guilty in this, okay? Let's stop pointing fingers, so we can instead focus on fixing the problem. Catherine, we need to get that diamond back."

"You can't get it back. I pawned it."

"You did *wh*—" Ma started.

"Not now, Ma," I told her. "Just hold your horses." I turned back to Catherine. "Which pawn shop did you use?"

"I didn't go to a shop. I pawned it on the street. In Newark."

"Oh, my God," Ma blathered. "I absolutely cannot believe this."

I said to Catherine, "How much did you get for it?"

"Two thousand."

Ma went ballistic. *"Two thousand?"* Her hands flew up in the air. *"You pawned a fifty-thousand-dollar jewel for a lousy two thousand bucks?"* She came in a flying rage, but I was ready for it. I caught her and held her back. *"That was a hundred and fifty years old! Seven generations! Passed down by … our … ancestors! And you had … the gall—"*

"All right, Ma—"

"—*the audacity*—"

"—that's enough—"

"—*to go behind my back*—"

"Ma, stop it! That's enough! For Christ's sake, will you get a hold of yourself?"

Ma wasn't merely shaking anymore. She was *palpitating*. Her round, bulbous eyes appeared ready to pop out of her head. Her quivering cheeks and trembling jaw were a spectacle to behold. I had never witnessed fury of such magnitude in *anyone*, much less my own mother. A scary fact here: what I was seeing lent a sober credence as to why family members sometimes kill one another. Those awful stories we see on the news and read in the papers … most of them are likely prefaced by moments like this. What if I hadn't been here? What might Ma have done?

"I couldn't take it no more," Catherine muttered. "Couldn't … there's nothing left of me. I had to end it … He said if I … paid him—"

"You have thirty minutes to gather whatever things you need," Ma stammered. "And then you will leave this house, young lady."

"But I … have nothing."

"Neither do we, thanks to you."

I interceded, "Now, Ma, wait, that's not entirely—"

"Not now, Simon, I won't hear it. Good-bye, Catherine. Good luck out in the real world." Ma checked her watch. "It's now 3:35. You will be out the door and off these premises no later than 4:05."

Ma left the room. Her heavy footfalls descending the staircase punctuated the stillness of the house.

I turned to my sister's pathetic form writhing in the corner of the room. "Look, I'll take care of Ma. She just needs some time to calm down. Pack a suitcase and go to a friend's house for the night. You want me to drive you?"

She shook her head weakly. Her eyelids were half closed. She didn't appear to have the strength to stand.

I took a half step toward her, then dropped to one knee. In a lower voice, I said, "Catherine, do you have any idea how thin you are? You need to eat something."

"Just go away, Simon." She laid her head down among the cobwebs and dust balls that had gathered on the floor along the baseboard. "I wanna be alone for a while."

"I'm gonna go talk to Ma. Start throwing some things together. I'll be back up in a bit to help."

I stood up and went to the door. Then I paused, turning around to ask, "Why only two thousand dollars, Cath?"

"Just let me alone, will you?"

Downstairs, I found Ma sitting at the dining room table. She sat hunched over with her forehead resting in one hand. Her overturned purse lay where it had fallen—her right foot was almost touching it, in fact.

I pulled a chair and sat down catty-corner to her left. Closer inspection of her face revealed she was crying.

"What are we going to do now, Simon? Where are we gonna go?"

"You should have thought of that, Ma, during the five months you weren't making payments on the house."

Her head shot up. "I believe I've already admitted to being a drunk, Simon. I don't see how rehashing that busi—"

"And you've come a long way, Ma." I reached out and took her hand. She tried to pull it free, but I held onto it. "But there's more admitting to be done, I think. Pawning the diamond was a horrible decision on Catherine's part. It was lousy, it was backstabbing—it was betrayal, like you said. But pawning the diamond played no part in getting us into the financial hole that we're in now. You share as much blame as she does, Ma … maybe a bit more, 'cause you're the adult."

"Oh, so now it's all my fault."

I was exasperated. "Can we please stop pointing fingers? It's not fixing anything. We need to put our heads together so we can focus on *fixing*."

Ma shook her head, resting her forehead in her palm again. "There's nothing left, Simon. Our ace card is gone. All hope went with it."

"No, Ma. Even when money runs out, hope doesn't. Hope never runs out." We were quiet for a while. I was still holding her hand. "Now, Ma, about Catherine—"

"She is no longer welcome in this house. I meant every word that I said up there, Simon."

"I think your anger got the best of you up there, Ma. You just threw your daughter through *a wall*. Her head broke through *the wall*, Ma."

"Well, something had to give, didn't it? Look, Simon, I've been putting up with her bullshit attitude for more than a year now. Maybe you haven't noticed, but that girl has not shown me a single ounce of respect for longer than I can remember."

"I would agree with you on that point—"

"Thank you."

"—but you need to think about how far you want to go with this. Are you aware of what you said up there? You pretty much told her to leave and never come back."

I was disquieted by Ma's laugh. "A couple weeks from now, Simon, it won't make a rat's ass worth of difference. There'll be nothing left to come back to."

"Ma, I don't think you truly *meant* what you—"

"Oh, you'd better believe I meant every goddamned syllable. Denial is not a river in Egypt, Simon; someone said that in last night's meeting. We are on the brink of being homeless."

I sighed. "I'm gonna drive Catherine to one of her friend's houses. Maybe even Don and Betty's place, I don't know. It's obvious the two of you need some time apart."

"You can let her off at a dumpster, for all I care."

"Ma, you don't mean that."

"After we get evicted, maybe she'll let us move in with her. We'll take turns raiding the McDonald's garbage bins."

"You don't mean—"

That's when the gun went off.

CHAPTER TWENTY-FIVE

DOLLARS AND SENSE

COREY'S SIXTH BIRTHDAY WAS a smash. On a cold, breezy Saturday in late February, we had a party at the house for him. He invited some friends from school, half of his karate class, and two girls from his Kindermusik class. There were the traditional games followed by the opening of gifts (a new set of bouncy balls from Samantha), and then my long-time favorite, the cake-eating—a to-die-for Boston cream cake Alisha had made from scratch. The kids went home with smiles and goody-bags.

Later in the week, we had a smaller celebration among the three of us. Alisha gave Corey some new shirts for school, along with dress pants, socks, and even a tie. He scowled a bit, opening them. "Why are you giving me clothes, Mom?"

"Because you *need* clothes," Alisha answered. "You're starting to grow out of your other things."

"I need toys," he said. I laughed.

"You've got enough toys for ten children," Alisha told him. She turned to me. "And don't you encourage him."

I gave Corey a stack of books. He opened these with mounting delight. Among the titles were some favorites from my own childhood: *Charlie and the Chocolate Factory* by Roald Dahl; *Charlotte's Web* by E. B. White; *Cunningham's Rooster* by Barbara Brenner; and a personal favorite, *My Father's Dragon* by Ruth Stiles

Gannet. The latter was published in 1948, and I'd had to visit several used bookstores to find it.

"Wow!" Corey exclaimed. "Can we start one tonight, Simon? Can we?"

February ended. March blew in on the shoulders of gusty northwest winds. The lake was covered with whitecaps most days. Bare tree limbs appeared to saw away at the blue sky. It was still cool, but you could feel the sun getting closer to the earth.

I paid Millie for the truck. I drove to her house one day with a cashier's check for eleven thousand dollars—Blue Book value for the Tacoma's year and model. She handed me a spare set of keys and the title. It was as close as I'd ever come to owning a brand-new vehicle.

By the middle of March, Alisha had all but abandoned her daytime writing efforts. It wasn't going well, she admitted, and she no longer made any pretense about it. Instead, we spent our mornings together, walking along State Street and up some of the numbered roads, chatting away and basically enjoying each other's company. Gradually, Alisha began schooling me on the laws of money—namely, on how to invest.

"The single most important rule of obtaining wealth, Simon, is to acquire assets as opposed to liabilities."

"What's the difference?"

"It's simple. Assets make money for you, liabilities take money from you. Assets make, liabilities take."

"Hey, that rhymes."

She continued, "Most people are too busy making a living to become wealthy. The majority of Americans spend their entire working lives slaving away for the next paycheck, which they then use to pay bills. Work to pay bills, work to pay bills—it becomes a repeating cycle. The money you make from your primary job is called 'earned income.' Earned income is taxed at a very high rate. Most people work January through April just to pay their yearly taxes. Can you imagine, Simon? The first four months of every year, you're working for free. You're working to pay the government."

"I've never thought of it that way," I said.

"If the withholding process were ever abolished, we'd have the biggest tax revolution in this country's history."

"You think withholding will ever be done away with?"

"God, no. The IRS would never allow it."

We were on Road 37. We came to a one-lane bridge spanning Pine Creek. Alisha went to the handrail to peer down at the water below. I went and stood next to her. Looking down into the small pool of water, I spotted a pair of brook trout riding the current, their fins gently moving.

"Getting back to what I was saying about assets …"

"Yes?"

"Any assets you acquire become a part of your portfolio. Portfolio income is taxed at a lower rate than earned income."

"Meaning?"

"Meaning that if you're studious and consistent in your acquisition of assets, there will come a day when your portfolio income surpasses your earned income. That's the definition of money making money, Simon. When your portfolio income provides enough of a monthly cash flow for you to live on, it frees you up from your regular job and allows you to do what you want. That's my definition of true wealth. It's also my definition of freedom."

"You make it sound so easy."

We started walking again.

"It is and it isn't," she divulged. "It requires discipline. Assets first have to be purchased, and they don't provide instant gratification. In many instances, they require years to grow.

"Here's another way to look at it, Simon. I'll throw some numbers at you. It's estimated that 50 percent of the U.S. population lives at or below poverty level. A recent survey found that roughly 51 percent of Americans have less than a thousand dollars in savings. Yet the average household credit card debt is around eight thousand dollars. What does that tell you?"

"People spend more than they save, I guess." Actually, what it told me was that my family had been off the charts six years ago. We were worse than the average. Ma had had fifty-grand worth of credit debt in addition to five months of missed mortgage payments, unpaid property taxes, and other assorted debts … with *nothing* in savings. It had taken a miracle of miracles to get us out of it.

"In a nutshell, yes—people spend more than they save. Lack of opportunity isn't the driving force behind poverty in this country,

Simon. Rather, it's lack of knowledge, lack of discipline, and lack of initiative."

"But you'll concur that some are born with less resources at their disposal than others, yes?"

"I wholeheartedly concur because I was one of them. I've seen it work the other way, too, Simon. I've seen people of inherited wealth blow through everything they have by age forty. They haven't worked for their money, and thus don't know how to maintain and manage it."

Our continued discussions through the latter half of March slowly forced me to recast some of my earlier-conceived notions of the type of person Alisha was. Or at least, the type of person I thought her to be. Here was a woman who started with nothing, an only child living with a single mother on a meager income. A woman who'd finished college on her own, her mother having died during her junior year. A woman who'd later put herself through graduate school, and ultimately made her own way in the world. Making one's way in this world of ever-increasing complexity is a hard enough task by itself. But Alisha had done it without any siblings, parents, or benefactors.

I asked her one day, "Tell me how you got started."

"I owned a catering business," she said. "I launched it alone and worked it alone. As the business grew over several years, I hired employees. By the end of the fourth year, I had nineteen people working for me full time. I sold the business for forty thousand dollars and used some of that money to purchase assets. I used what was left to start a title company. I later sold the title company for a hundred and fifty thousand, some of which I used to purchase more assets."

"What sort of assets?" I asked.

"Stocks, bonds, CDs, and mutual funds, primarily. I made a lot of money early on with start-up stocks of small companies going public for the first time. But those ventures are risky. I've lost money that way, too.

"Obviously, the bulk of my wealth has been made by selling books. I used some of my early book profits to buy rental properties. Rental homes can be a powerful addition to your asset column."

This came to me as a surprise. "You're saying you own other homes? Other than this one, I mean?"

"Of course. After I buy a house, I'll move in and typically live there for two to three years. I'll use that time to fix the place up exactly the way I want it before I rent it out and move on."

"How many houses do you own?"

"The Swan Lake house is my fourth," she said.

"And you plan on renting that one out, too?"

"That's the plan, yes." She was quiet for a while. We walked side by side, almost in lock-step. This was my first glimpse of Alisha Caldwell's life as a mosaic. I was also seeing for the first time her residency in Swan Lake, New Hampshire, in its proper context. She hadn't moved here to settle down, or to begin a new job, or because she enjoyed the scenery. Her stay in Swan Lake was temporary, a business decision at best. Had she known what she was getting when purchasing the Turner estate? Probably not.

Alisha said, "It's been my pattern to buy during a down market. But that factor won't come into play this time."

"Why not?"

"Well, Corey starts first grade in September. Which means our next move will happen sometime this summer. Preferably as soon as kindergarten lets out. I'd like for him to have as much time as possible to assimilate to a new community."

"Is that to be the pattern, then?" I asked. "You'll be pulling him out of a school system and plunking him into a new one every two or three years?"

She seemed to mull on this for a while. We were crossing a one-lane bridge on Road 49. Her tennis shoes scuffed across the wood planking. "No. Our next move will be a more permanent one."

"Continuity through the early grades is important."

"Yes, it is," she agreed. "And I want Corey to have that stability."

"Have you considered just staying put? Here in Swan Lake, I mean?"

"Well … Actually, Simon, I'm having a house built."

My mouth fell open. "Where?"

"South Carolina. About an hour west of Hilton Head."

"South Carolina?" I paused. Suddenly, the pieces fell into place.

"So, that's why you made the trip down there last fall. When you disappeared for a week."

"Yes."

"But why so far away?"

"Oh, Simon, it's not *that* far. It's just down the East Coast a bit." She nudged me with her elbow. "You'll have to come visit us, you know."

"Of course I will." In truth, though, I was having some trouble absorbing this new information. It was my first glimpse of life beyond Swan Lake. I still had a life to get on with, and there were still decisions to be made.

"Does Corey know about this new house?" I asked.

"Not yet. But when he sees pictures of his bedroom, he'll be excited. It's twenty by twenty-five, with nine-foot ceilings and a private bathroom."

"Pictures? The house is finished?"

"Almost. The target date for completion is May 1st."

"What about your business partnership with Mr. Bryson? The securities and investments firm?"

"I'm only a 10 percent shareholder, and I bought in for a two-year option. When my option ends, I'll sell my shares back for 20 percent more than what I paid for them."

I stared at her. "You're a walking dollar sign, you know that?"

She sidled up against me. "I'm also a nice piece of ass, and don't you forget it." She took my hand and pressed it against her right buttock, where her jeans clung firmly to her skin.

The lessons continued through March and into April, as the days lengthened and the crocuses opened and the brown grass started to green.

"Never buy luxury items on credit, Simon."

"Don't try to time the market, Simon. Invest regularly and consistently over time."

"Never play the lottery, Simon. It's the worst investment in America. Your odds of winning are something like one in a hundred and eighty million. I've seen lots of poor people spend money on lottery tickets who've told me they'll never invest in the stock market because they're afraid of losing money. Yet there's never been a fifty-year period in the market's history in which it hasn't gained in value."

"What's the most important rule?" I asked her one evening. We were sitting on the front deck overlooking the lake, sharing a bottle of after-dinner wine.

She thought it over for nearly a full minute. Her lips poised over her glass, eyes directed over the lake, she said, "I would say the most important rule is to work with character and integrity. A person's character and integrity are his two most vital virtues. When the product you produce is the best it can be—whatever business you happen to be in—you'll usually get the best in return. Always work hard, Simon, at whatever it is you do."

CHAPTER TWENTY-SIX

CATHERINE'S END

THAT'S WHEN THE GUN went off ... It was so loud, the house shook. Windowpanes rattled in their muntins. Milk glasses clinked in the cupboards over the sink and counter.

Ma's head shot up. Her eyes were large. One hand had gone to her chest. "Jesus, Mary, and Joseph, what was *that?*"

I was already backing away from the table. My heart was beating fast, and the bitter taste of bile was creeping into my throat. I ran for the stairs, knowing it was too late already, the deed was done—a dirty deed done dirt-cheap.

"Simon, what was—"

"Stay down here, Ma!" I yelled.

She was hot on my heels, though—a role reversal from fifteen minutes ago, when she had ordered *me* to remain downstairs. I hadn't listened then, and of course she didn't listen now.

"Oh, God, Simon, tell me that wasn't a gun! Tell me it wasn't—"

"I want you to stay down here, Ma!" I was halfway up the stairs, pausing to look back at her. "Stay downstairs! You don't need to see this!"

Her hands flew up to cover her mouth. But it didn't matter. The requisite horror escaped through her eyes. Ma stumbled back down to the landing. Her back slid down the wall as she fell—landing in a sitting position with her knees almost touching her chin. What came out of her mouth, partially filtered by her splayed fingers, was something like a scream and something like a cry, and yet it was neither.

"*Noooooooooo! Noo-aaaa! Aaaaaaaaaa!*"

I went up the steps alone. I made the right turn, followed by the immediate left, going up the L's shaft. My heart thundered drunkenly in my chest. My vision swam. I felt my gorge rising in anticipation of what I was going to find in Catherine's bedroom.

But her room was empty.

She'd done it in my room.

"Oh, no … Oh, Jesus, Catherine …"

My feet carried me to the room at the far end of the hall. My bedroom door was ajar. A crescent of late-afternoon light shone through the opening, but that was all I could see.

I stopped in front of the door. I put one hand up against it. Ma had stopped screaming. Probably she had crept up the stairs behind me, but I didn't turn back to look.

I went forward. Forward only. I pushed open the door. I entered my room.

The first thing I saw was my nightstand to the right of the bed. The drawer was open. I moved my eyes farther to the right, and there I found my sister. She was slumped in the far right corner of the room. Her eyes, milky and glazed, appeared to stare straight at me. Her legs were splayed across the floor in front of her. Between them lay the Colt .45. Catherine's hand was still curled around the stock, one finger caught inside the trigger-guard. I saw no blood, amazingly. I saw something else instead. Catherine appeared to be coated in white dust. Taking slow, careful steps toward her, I noticed that her eyes were active—they were tracking my movement. I looked up and saw a dime-sized hole in the ceiling. Sheetrock dust continued to stream out of the hole like snow. Most of it fell into Catherine's lap. Some landed in her hair.

I knelt down beside her. For a while, she didn't move. She stared vacantly into the middle of the room.

"I had to kill it," she murmured, barely audible.

"What?"

"I had to starve it to death. There was no other way."

"How long have you been pregnant, Catherine?"

"I starved it, Simon. It's not … moving anymore."

I heard movement behind me, and a gasp. Ma had come up.

I said slowly, "Catherine? I'm going to take the gun from you now. Please take your finger out of the trigger-guard."

She did nothing of the sort, so I did it for her. She offered no resistance. Her body was limp and gelid. Her white-waxy skin was pulled tight over bones and ligaments. I moved her hand away from the Colt .45 and brought the gun into my possession. I re-engaged the safety and put the gun back in the drawer. I turned it over to the state police the following day. I told them I never wanted to see it again. They assured me I wouldn't.

"I should go now," Catherine muttered. She started to push herself up. "I'm gonna … I'm gonna go."

"Catherine, wait …" She got to her feet and shuffled feebly across the room. "Cath, I think I ought to take you to a hospital."

She drifted across the room like an apparition. "No … I'm … Simon … fine … going … ride …"

Ma stood aside as Catherine passed through the doorway into the hall. Ma's eyes were still wide and frightened, and she still kept one hand pressed to her heart. She seemed hypnotized by Catherine's trancelike state. I think both of us were.

She shuffled down the hall, Catherine did, not stopping to duck into her room for the aforementioned essentials or even her wallet or purse. She appeared to float down the stairs wearing only her pink sweats and old wifebeater shirt.

Ma and I trailed along behind her. I said, "Catherine, where are you going? Wherever it is, let me take you. You aren't well." I didn't think she was physically strong enough to drive, in fact.

She drifted through the living room, and into the dining room. We drifted along behind her. I kept waiting for Ma to say something—something apologetic, perhaps—but Ma never did. Ma never uttered a word. Ma had endured enough shock and awe for one day, and I don't think she had anything left.

Catherine raised one arm to remove her keys from the key hook just to the left of the coat hooks. She pulled open the door.

"Catherine, wait … Where are you going? What are you gonna do?" This didn't feel like any of the other times, when Catherine hopped into her car on a whim and took off. This felt altogether different.

Out the side door and down the porch steps she went. Moving in that same mummy-like trance. The only aspect missing were the arms held out in mock B-movie fashion.

I started out the door after her, but Ma's hand fell on my shoulder, holding me back. "It's okay, Simon. Let her go for now. She'll be all right."

Somehow, I didn't think so. Catherine didn't appear capable of driving. On the road, she would represent a danger to herself as well as others. She had nothing with her, no money, no ID. She was malnourished, had recently miscarried, and had just moments earlier come close to blowing her own brains out. So why were we letting her go? Why were we just standing there letting her leave?

As my sister fired up her old Chevy wagon, backed it out of the driveway, and disappeared down Williams Way, it was her voice I heard in my head, speaking to our father. *You'll never know me, Dad,* she said. *You'll never know me.*

CHAPTER TWENTY-SEVEN

DAVID

I WAS SITTING ON an old tree stump outside the small wood schoolhouse, waiting for Corey's Kindermusik class to let out. Through the thin walls behind me came the off-tune clatter and bang of tambourines trying to keep pace with a lead guitar. It sounded like a New Orleans funeral party gone horribly awry. I decided to get up and walk.

In addition to the schoolhouse, the Barrow Hill State Park featured a five-acre pond, towering oaks and maples, a network of marked trails, with several pavilions and ample, green-grassed open space. There was also an education center and nature house, and public restrooms. The park was the site of many picnics and town functions. In the fall, local high schools held cross-country meets here.

I moved lazily down the hill with my hands in the front pockets of my khaki shorts, in the direction of the pond. It was April 30th, and the air was filled with everything blooming. Leaves were sprouting, flowers were blossoming, and the sky rained sunshine. At the water's edge, I halted, peering across the pond's rippled surface. It was often said that water had the power to heal a bruised soul.

Catherine had not come back. Not the next day or the next week, or the following month. Police found her car parked in a side street in Newark's Ironbound section two weeks after we last saw her, but there was no sign of Catherine inside it. They checked out the local homeless shelters and women's crisis centers and even the hospitals. No Catherine. No signs. No trails. Where had she gone? What had happened to her? She had left home in a miserable state, hardly able to walk in a straight line. She couldn't have gone far. She couldn't possibly manage on her own. Ma winced at the thought of having to answer the door to a state trooper at two in the morning, to learn that they'd found Catherine's body floating face-down in the harbor. When it wasn't her lost daughter she was thinking about, it was the house we were in the process of losing. "All is lost, Simon." She said it over and over again.

"No, Ma," I countered, though I knew she was right. "Not all. We still have each other, don't we?"

I turned right, walking along the east side of the pond. More than six years had passed since I'd last seen my sister. What nagged me the most, I suppose, was the destitute condition in which Ma and I had allowed her to leave. Catherine had been borderline suicidal, she'd blown a hole in the ceiling instead of her skull, and what had Ma and I done in return? We'd stood at the door like a pair of dummies. We'd watched her morbidly scrawny body limp away from us. We'd let her go. She had failed us in pawning the diamond … but in the end it was Ma and I who had failed Catherine by not holding onto her.

I walked over the plank bridge that spanned the pond's outflow creek. I stopped halfway across and propped my elbows on the wood side rail. My eyes wandered across the water's surface. Three old pilings jutted out of the water thirty feet in front of me. Ducks and geese paddled in and among the pilings as though it were some sort of intersection. A domestic goose joined the fray, honking nasally.

I caressed the bandage wrapped around the middle finger of my right hand. Corey and I had spent a lot of time fishing of late. We'd walk down to the lake a little before dinner, or sometimes after dinner, and we'd fish. We'd stand maybe ten feet apart, and we'd cast our lures. We used Blue Fox Vibrax spinners most of the time. We also threw Little Cleo spoons, Pheobes, and floating Rapalas. Around dinnertime, Alisha would come out on the deck and poke her head over the rail. "Come on, guys. Dinner's ready."

I would give Corey a ten-second head start and then race him to the top. I always won because he laughed too hard. After dessert, we'd head back down to start fishing again.

After three days of catching nothing, Corey got the idea of changing spots. I told him to go up the bank to his left thirty or so yards, but to be careful. He did. I heard him moving through the woods. There came the sounds of branches snapping underfoot and rocks rolling down the slope into the water. Minutes later he began yelling. "Simon! I got one, Simon, I got one!"

I dropped my pole and ran into the forest toward the sound of his voice. He'd probably gotten his lure snagged up in some seaweed or an old log. After ditching and ducking and dodging trees for a minute or two, I emerged onto a sandy strip of beach. Corey had walked out onto a narrow stone peninsula twenty feet down the beach. He was holding his pole out over the water, the butt tucked into his tummy. The rod's tip bounced and bucked with the weight of a fighting fish.

I ran out to assist, amazed he'd actually hooked something.

"I got him, Simon! I got him! He's a big one!"

"Okay, keep your line tight. But don't horse him in too fast, or he'll break off."

The fish boiled on the surface ten feet away from us. A large tail slapped the water. Another strong thrust propelled the fish toward open water again. The drag mechanism on Corey's reel screamed as the fish took line.

"Don't reel against your drag," I warned him. "Let him take line if he's gonna go. Keep your rod high, and keep your line tight against him. That's it, nice and easy."

"What is it, Simon?"

"It's a fish, silly."

"Yeah, but what kind?"

"I don't know, a big green one. Okay, here she comes."

Corey had landed a two-foot pickerel. This is a bony fish, not good for eating. A member of the pike family, their mouths are filled with rows of very sharp teeth. Minutes later, the fish was flopping up and down on the beach. Corey could barely contain his excitement. He jumped up and down, hollering like a banshee. "Whoa! That fish is big, Simon! It's a big one!"

"Yeah, and it's got your lure in its mouth." I held the pickerel's head with my left hand and reached into its mouth with my right. I know now why most experienced anglers carry pliers in their tackle boxes. The fish bit down on my middle finger, slashing my skin open in four or five places. "Ow, you *bastard!*" When I ripped my finger out, the lure came with it—one of the treble hooks was sunk into the side of my fingernail. You can bet your boots that felt good.

I kicked the fish back into the lake and then yanked the hook out of my fingernail. While Alisha bandaged me up later on, Corey danced around the dining room table recanting the capture of what was now the Great Fish. He was too jazzed up to fall asleep. Around 10:30 PM, his eyelids finally grew heavy. "Can we go fishing again tomorrow, Simon? And then the next day, and the next one?"

"If you get a good night's sleep," I said. "We'll see what tomorrow brings." He turned over and fell into slumber.

Ten minutes later, the phone rang. I answered it in the kitchen. "Hello?"

Alisha's voice was dusky. "It's me. I could use a break."

I spun around in place. "Are you calling me from your writing room?"

"How's your finger?"

"Swell."

"If you aren't feeling too handicapped, I've got something for you."

I walked out of the kitchen with the cordless phone, into the den. "What might that be?"

"Why don't you come and find out?"

At her office door, I hesitated. Normally, this place was off limits.

"You don't have to knock this time, silly," she said into the phone.

I turned the knob and pushed the door open. In front of me and slightly to the left was her computer. The humming machinery told me it was on and running, but the screen was blank. Her roll-chair was empty. On the floor next to the chair was her clothing.

I looked to the right—and my breath caught in my throat. She was sitting on the room-length desk with her legs crossed, her feet propped on the seat of a different chair. She was wearing a pink bra and pink, string panties. She was watching me with a smile, the phone pressed to her ear. "It's about time. I thought I was going to have to draw you a map."

I clicked off the cordless phone and advanced on her. She dropped the phone back onto its hook. She uncrossed her legs and used one foot to slide the chair a foot or so away from the desk. I moved into its place. She propped her feet on the chair once again, with her legs around me this time. I cupped my hands over the tops of her knees. I slid my hands slowly down her thighs, to where they intersected with her waist, and then I moved my hands up her sides and around her breasts, resting my hands on her shoulders. She looked up at me in the lamplight, her eyes filled with lust. Finally I kissed her. We kissed long and hard, and when her breathing began to deepen, I pulled her toward me so that I could lift her off the desk and carry her into the den.

But she stiffened. "No, Simon. In here. On the desk."

"The desk? It's awfully hard—"

"I *like* it that way." Her eyes glistened.

So we did it on the desk.

*   *   *

We'll see what tomorrow brings. Around here, it always brought the same. It always brought another day. And every day ended with some sort of a miracle. Standing on the plank bridge watching the geese and ducks maneuver among the pilings, I got to wondering about things. I got to wondering how much time I had left here. I was aware that real life didn't feel like this. Everyday life didn't feel this good. At least mine never had. Would it again, after all this was over? Maybe, but not before much soul-searching and hard work. The hard aspects of life were coming toward me, darkening my horizon. My stay in Swan Lake was a one-year moratorium on life, and that one-year term was coming to a close. What does a person do who discovers the moratorium more rewarding than the life that surrounds it? Law school seemed a long way off. It seemed to exist in a separate world. But it was a world I would have to go back to.

I left the plank bridge behind and began moving up the hill away from the pond. Kindermusik was just letting out as I reached the schoolhouse. Children streamed out the front door with music books in hand. Corey ran into my arms when he saw me.

"Whoa, there, kiddo!" I said, hoisting him into the air and setting him on his feet again. "How was music class today?"

"Good," he said. "Did you hear us playing?"

"For better or worse."

"Can we go fishing? Let's hurry up and get home so we can go fishing." It was all he could think of these days. "You wanna race to the truck? Let's go!"

He was off and running before the words were wholly out of his mouth. I let him win this time.

He talked incessantly on the ride home: what we were going to catch, where we were going to fish, and what the score would ultimately be. Since catching the first pickerel last week—the one that had bitten my finger—we had expanded our fishing area westward along the lake. The farther west we'd explored with our lures, the more fish we'd caught (I'd since purchased a pair of pliers, thankfully). Fishing is a lot of fun when you're actually catching stuff. It had become an overnight passion for both of us. We'd taped a tally sheet to the kitchen fridge, with a score column beneath our names. Starting with Corey's big pickerel last week, we'd caught a combined twenty-nine pickerel. But last night Corey had landed a surprise seventeen-inch rainbow trout. We decided that if a pickerel was worth one point, a rainbow trout had to fetch two points. The trout gave Corey a one-point lead in the score column.

He chattered all the way home. Maneuvering down the switchback driveway to the house, I slowed down to admire Josef's tulips. He had managed to get one row of bulbs into the ground before he'd died doing it. Those flowers were up now, and they were as red as red could be. "Look at that," I said.

Corey undid his belt and climbed partially over me to look. "Yeah. Look at that."

We reached the bottom of the driveway. An emerald blue BMW was parked at an angle in front of the railroad-tie stairs. Both of Alisha's Saabs were parked in their customary places, as was her Land Rover. The BMW was in my place.

"Daddy!" Corey yelled. "It's Daddy's car! Daddy's here!" He grappled for the door handle.

"Hold on, sport. We're still moving."

I parked in front of the left garage bay. Corey waited for me to shift into park and then threw his door open and jumped out. He ran for the stairs without pushing the door shut. He yelled, "Daddy! Daddy! Daddy!" all the way to the house.

I gathered his books in my arms, then slowly climbed the hill to the house. Corey had left the front door standing open. I entered the den, nudging the door shut behind me.

In one of the dining room chairs sat a man in his mid- to upper forties, dressed in business attire. He had sandy-brown hair and a thick face with chiseled cheekbones. Corey had already jumped into his lap; his small arms were wrapped around his father's thick neck. The man returned the hug, patting Corey gently on the back. I'd walked into the house in time to hear, "Hey, there, big guy! That's it, give Daddy a hug!"

Alisha, wearing a flower-print dress, sat in an adjacent chair with her legs crossed. Her eyes met mine as I came forward, and I was able to read her initial thought quite perfectly: *I didn't know he was coming. He just showed up.*

The two suitcases and brown duffel bag set on the floor near the hearth attested to this.

She got up from her chair and tapped Corey twice on the shoulder. "Okay, Corey, let the man breathe. David, I'd like you to meet Corey's chaperone. His name is Simon Kozlowski. Simon has been very helpful to us this year. Simon, this is David Kaplan—Corey's dad."

David rose from his chair, setting Corey onto his feet. He was about my height, only much broader. His eyes were a sparkling aqua-blue. He smiled and stuck his hand out. "Hey, Simon. A pleasure." He squeezed my hand hard enough to pop most of my knuckles.

"The pleasure's mine," I said. Actually, I recognized his voice from our brief phone conversations. "Thanks for stopping by."

"Oh, you bet. Been takin' care of my boy, have ya?"

"Well, yes. I obey all traffic signals, and we've had no flat tires to this point."

"Hey, Dad," Corey cried, tugging at his father's sleeve, "Simon taught me how to fish! You wanna go fishing?"

"Well, I don't know, big guy, I don't have a pole or—"

"You can use Simon's! Come on, Dad, let's go! Let's go fishing! C'mon!"

"It's all right," I assuaged. "I could use a day off. Corey'll show you where we keep the poles." I directed my eyes onto Corey. "Just be careful walking over those rocks. And remember to use the pliers if you catch a fish. Don't try to get the hooks out using your fingers."

"I know, I know. C'mon, Dad, let's go. C'mon."

"Okay, son, but let me change out of these clothes first."

"Bathroom at the end of the hall," Alisha said, pointing.

He changed into jeans, sneakers, and a white T-shirt. Pectoral muscles bulged from behind the shirt; his thick arms sprouted from his shoulders like small, hanging trees. He ruffled Corey's hair as he came up the hall past Corey's bedroom. "I can't believe how much you've grown, big guy. What are you now? Five?"

"Six!" Corey yelled.

"Six? Wow! You get an extra birthday present, then, don't you?"

Corey jumped around like an Indian. "Yeah, yeah, yeah!"

Alisha asked, "You didn't spoil him, Dave, did you?"

"Of course. We'll open presents later. Now let's go fishing."

As they paraded out the door with Corey in the lead, Alisha called behind them, "Dinner at six, guys."

After they were gone, I tossed Corey's music books onto the dining room table. "The chaperone thing is getting a bit tired."

She held out her hands, palms up. "How was I supposed to introduce you? As Corey's surrogate father, and my boy toy?"

"Is that what I am? A toy?"

"That was a poor choice of words. I'm sorry."

I went up the single stair and into the hall toward my bedroom. Alisha followed.

"Don't walk away from me, Simon. Look, I had no idea he was coming. He just showed up."

"You could've pretended you weren't home." I tossed my keys into the fish dish on the bureau and then deposited my wallet into the top left drawer where I normally kept it.

Alisha came around the bed and sat down on the edge of it, watching me. "I can't just send him away, Simon. He's Corey's natural father. I thought we had this discussion one night. You said you wouldn't be opposed to him visiting."

"Maybe I changed my mind." Two things occurred to me then. First, Monsieur Kaplan had appeared on Alisha's doorstep as though he'd just attended a board meeting, which I found a trifle odd. A traveling businessman, perhaps? And second, this was also a man currently on medication for bipolar disorder. "And that's the man who struck you the one time?"

"Yes."

"He's well-built. Strong."

"Yes. He is."

"Judging by the luggage out there, it appears as though he intends to stay for a while."

"For a couple of days, yes."

I leaned back against the bureau, crossing my arms over my chest. "Where is he going to sleep?"

"I don't know."

"Not upstairs," I said, alluding to the two spare bedrooms.

"Where would you like him to sleep?"

"I'll clear some room in the garage."

"Simon, try to be serious for one—"

"He can have this room. I'll move my stuff out temporarily."

"And where are you going to sleep?"

"I'll bunk with Corey. He always said he wanted to have a sleepover."

We spent the next thirty minutes transporting most of my things from my room over to Corey's room. This included most of my clothing as well as visible items like books, magazines, shoes, the fish dish, and generally anything that might have my name on it. Lastly, I grabbed my favorite pillow. I said to Alisha, "He can have a hard one."

When we had finished, my bedroom had once again been transformed into a spare guest room.

"Let's go for a walk," Alisha said.

"I don't feel like walking. How 'bout we go for a drive instead? Hey, we'll take the BMW."

"Will you knock it off? This is bringing out the worst in you."

She was right, of course. I really should straighten up and act my age. Why did I feel so inadequate around older men dressed in suits? It's some sort of a complex of mine.

Anyway, we went up the driveway in silence and turned left onto State Street. We walked for several miles without either of us saying very much at all. Finally, I asked, "Did you want to tell me something?"

"No. I thought you needed some fresh air."

"Oh." We turned right onto Road 23. We'd gone another half mile or so in silence before I said, "I don't want to see him touch you."

"What?"

"I said I don't want to see him touch you. You know, lovey-dovey."

She smiled. "Oh, Simon, you're jealous. That is so cute—"

"Cut it out, will you?"

"It is. It's *adorable*." She reached over with one arm to tickle me in the ribs. I brushed it away.

"Look, all I'm saying is that if he lays a hand on you, there's going to be a fight. He'll throw me through the wall, probably, but there *will* be a fight."

She sidled up beside me, taking hold of my right arm and draping it around her slim set of shoulders. "I promise to behave, darling. It's just that I'm not used to having so much testosterone under my own roof."

I made no reply to this. She removed herself from my right arm, content to hold my hand instead. After a while, she added, "David came here to visit Corey, Simon. I assure you that's the extent of it."

We stopped to rest at one of the lovelier one-lane bridges, a brick-and-mortar job arching over Hemlock Creek.

"I assume David has … other attachments."

Alisha went and sat down on the mortar-topped sidewall. I sat down on the opposite sidewall. We stared across the bridge at one another. The late-day breeze blew dust and cinders past our feet. It occurred to me that we could sit here for the better part of the day and maybe have two cars pass between us. Why did our more serious discussions have to take place on these goshforsaken bridges?

> *Light comes to darkness,*
> *Darkness comes to light.*
> *Daytime runs a'falsehood high,*
> *Tho' truth distills the night.*

> *Of lies distilled and lives fulfilled*

This bridge is but a token;
As morning breaks, the lion waits
A spirit hath awoken.

The funny thing was, I felt that spirit now. David Kaplan had brought it with him, perhaps. Either way, I was aware of its presence on my right shoulder. Was it shaking its head in reprobation? Could it be laughing? Or was it merely a silent witness, neither judge nor jury? It occurred to me in a heartfelt sense that buried beneath all those Crawford Daze canvases presently stored in Millie's vacant rental homes was a portrayal of this very moment. It would depict a young man perched on a bridge railing at day's end. The fellow's head would be bowed in thought. And if you looked closely enough, you'd see a small creature sitting on one of the man's shoulders. The creature might have a reddish-brown skin with triangular ears and a gremlin-like head. In its hands would be a Rubik's Cube or some other irrelevant object.

Finally, Alisha answered, "David is married, yes."

"Children?"

"He has three daughters."

Making Corey his only son. There's irony buried there somewhere.

"How old?" I asked.

"I don't know off hand. I think the oldest just started high school. The youngest is probably in fifth or sixth grade by now."

"You had an affair with him, then."

She nodded.

You didn't need a math degree to conclude that their tryst had taken place a little more than six years ago, being that Corey had recently celebrated his sixth birthday. Which meant that all three of David's daughters had already been born.

I asked, "Did you knowingly have sex with a married father of three? Or did he lie to you about his status?"

"I didn't say I was proud of it, Simon."

"I didn't ask if you were proud of it. I asked if you knew."

She watched me for a while. Silence is usually a proclamation of guilt. She asked, "Does it cause you to think less of me?"

That was a tricky question. Truth be told, I thought more of her now than I had last fall. But she had changed a lot since then.

I evaded the question by saying, "It just perplexes me, I guess— some of the things people do. Maybe I'm naive."

"I was living in my Pennsylvania house back then," she said. "But I was traveling a lot, always on the move. David lives in Bergen County, New Jersey, but we met in the city. He's a bond trader on Wall Street. We did some investment stuff together. He earns a Wall Street income and moves in high social circles. He's charismatic and handsome, with an Ivy League education. I'd be lying if I told you I wasn't infatuated with him back then, even if he was married." She paused before adding, "In any event, it's water under the bridge now, Simon. We all make our own beds, and we have to live with the consequences."

It occurred to me to that while Alisha was tramping around New York City, northern New Jersey, and eastern Pennsylvania at that particular junction in her life, Ma and I were groping blindly through typhoon-force winds, lost and confused and spun around three times over. It would have been around the same time. I thought that was sort of funny in a fatalistic kind of way. The timelines of different people's lives can assume some pretty odd shapes.

I asked, "What is David's wife's name?"

"How is that important?"

"Is it Diane? Or Kate, perhaps?"

"Carmen, I think."

"I'm guessing that Carmen doesn't know Corey exists."

"You're a good guesser."

"How was David able to free up his schedule to come up here without his wife's knowing? Carmen must think he went on a business trip, or something."

"Actually, Carmen took the three girls to London for the week. Carmen has family there; it's where she grew up."

"I see." I was looking down at the cinders beneath the toes of my sneakers. "It would appear that David has no qualms concerning the double-life he's leading."

"You'd have to ask him. But I wouldn't if I were you."

We started back. We walked mostly in silence. As we turned onto State Street, I said, "I used to hear you crying at night."

"You mean you were eavesdropping?"

"Not on purpose."

"You were eavesdropping accidentally?"

"Yes. The ceilings are thin."

"If you'd had any manners, you would've put the pillow over your head."

"And if I had cared, I would've gone upstairs to make sure you were okay."

"So, why didn't you?"

"You haven't answered the question."

"Maybe I don't have an answer," she said. "Unhappiness plays a role in all of our lives. Perhaps more so in mine than others."

"I find that hard to believe," I said.

"I didn't have what you had growing up. I never had a father. My mother was extremely poor, and she passed away while I was an undergraduate. I've pretty much done everything alone, Simon."

"You may have done it alone, but you've accomplished more, commercially and financially, than most couples will across their entire lives."

"It doesn't fill the hole," she said.

"You know what I think? I think Corey fills the hole, but you never knew it."

"Corey definitely fills the hole," she agreed with a smile. "You've helped fill it, too, Simon. I'd be lying if I didn't say that." It was as close as she ever came to telling me she loved me. It was as close as either of us came to admitting we loved each other.

"You shouldn't worry, though," she said, putting her arm around my waist. "I don't cry anymore."

*   *   *

Alisha got started on dinner while I got to setting the table. Corey and David returned at ten minutes before six, dirty and exhausted. They'd caught two fish apiece, but the price had been high. David had broken off three of my lures and later stepped on my rod tip, snapping it off. "Sorry, Simon," he said, handing me the broken pole. "You can bill me for the repair."

"You might want to grab a shower," Alisha told him. "Dinner will be ready in fifteen minutes."

"Sounds great. Where's my stuff?"

"Guestroom, second room on the right, before you hit the bathroom," Alisha said.

I looked down at Corey. His sneakers were caked with mud. Streaks of mud ran up both arms and one of his cheeks. Brown prickly burrs clung to the left side of his shorts.

"Were you fishing or making mud pies?" I asked.

"We took a shortcut on the way back."

"You mean you went through the swamp."

Alisha, having heard the word "swamp," came out of the kitchen to investigate. She took one look at her son and threw her hands into the air. "What in God's name have you been into?"

"We went through the swamp, Mom!"

"Well, those shoes are ruined," Alisha said. She traced her eyes along the floor, noting the muddy prints he'd walked in from the front door. "You're going to have to take a bath before we eat. Go up and use my bathroom. Simon, will you help him?"

"Sure. Okay, kid, take your clothes off here. You're not tracking any of that stuff upstairs."

He stripped out of his shirt, shorts, socks, and undies, and then ran around the room naked. He'd managed two laps around the sofa before I got after him. "You want me to swat your bare bottom with a fly-swatter?"

"Aahh! Eee! Naa!" He ran up the spiral stairs, banging the wood railing with both hands.

Dinner was moderately quiet, save for the clinking of utensils and the chewing of food. David chattered idly about life on Wall Street and the ebb and flow of capitalism. Alisha asked him where he thought mortgage interest rates were headed over the next several years. He launched into an impassioned spiel of the going-ons down at the Federal Reserve. Alisha asked if he thought that might impact T-notes and the price of gold. I mean, this stuff was boring enough to kill houseplants.

Corey eventually asked, "What are you guys talking about?"

David turned and replied, "Money, big guy. We're talking about money—quite possibly the most important thing in life."

"Where does money come from, Corey?" I asked.

He answered, "Mom's pocketbook."

"I taught him that," I said.

"Hey, you know what?" David said. "Later this week, I want to take you all out to dinner. My treat. We'll go into town, by the river."

"Really?" I asked. "You're staying that long?" Alisha, seated to my left, stepped on my foot.

"I hope it's not a problem," David said.

"Can I get french fries, Dad?"

"Of course you can, big guy. You can get anything you want."

"It sounds wonderful, Dave," Alisha said. "I'll make a reservation."

"I'll check my calendar," I added. Alisha stepped on my foot again.

After dinner, it was coffee and dessert, and then it was time for birthday gifts. I helped Alisha with the dishes while David lugged in a literal mountain of presents from his BMW. During one of his trips out, Alisha said, "You need to get yourself together, Simon. You're acting like an imbecile."

"Thanks."

"I mean it. I've never seen this side of you."

"I didn't know he was staying for the whole week."

We spent close to an hour watching Corey open his gifts. Here's a good rule of thumb: if you're wealthy and you aren't sure what to get a kid for his birthday, get him everything. David had covered all the bases. A new PlayStation video game set, along with ten new games. A baseball glove, aluminum bat, and half a dozen balls. A pair of in-line skates for playing street hockey. "You're not using those until you're twelve," Alisha said. Next was a hockey stick, which was almost twice as long as Corey's actual height. "You'll grow into it," I told him. Next came the toys. Action figures from the Spiderman series, and then the Batman series, and toys from the latest Star Wars trilogy. Tonka trucks, Matchbox cars, and a complete set of Hess trucks, including a Hess helicopter, Hess ambulance, and Hess boat. "What happened to the Hess hearse?" I asked. "Word has it Leon rides in the back."

"Who's Leon?" Corey asked.

"Never mind, Corey," Alisha told him, without looking at me. She was really getting angry now.

After the toys came the candies. An avalanche of chocolate bars, Hershey kisses, chewing gum, and taffy spilled onto the dining room table. Holy smokes and bicycle spokes—did a year's worth of dental visits come with this? I stuffed a popcorn ball into my mouth before I could add any more commentary.

As you might expect, Corey elected to have his father read him his story that night. I whiled away story time in the den, leafing through an old issue of *Time*. Alisha sat on the adjacent sofa, watching me. She sat with her legs crossed, one calf swinging slowly up and down.

The silence was unbearable, so finally I asked her, "Why are you looking at me like that?"

She said nothing. Just stared at me, her face devoid of emotion.

I folded up the magazine. "All right, I can't stand it anymore. You're driving me nuts."

"I'm driving *you* nuts?" she said.

I sighed with exasperation. I really didn't know what to say.

"You're the one acting like a child," she added. "You've lived here for eight months now. And during that time, you've shown the maturity and responsibility of a man in his mid- to late thirties. Then all of a sudden, throw an alpha male into the mix and you regress to a teenager. It's like night and day."

"Maybe I'm not cut out for a beta role," I said. "You know, in the animal kingdom—"

"This is not the animal kingdom, Simon. We walk upright, with two feet and a brain."

"Hey, I'm walking on two feet."

She didn't see the humor in that. Instead, she told me, "Look, Simon, there's no reason for you to feel insecure just because David's here. He's not competing with you for anything. He's just here to visit Corey."

"And lavish him with gifts."

"He spoils him, yes, I agree with you on that point. But in the meantime, I would appreciate if you started acting your age."

I couldn't help but smile. "I'm not used to you lecturing me about my character."

"I know you're not. Not long ago, it was the other way around. Humbling, isn't it?"

I dropped my gaze into my lap. I nodded. "Okay, I'll try to behave."

"Cutting back on the sarcasm would be a good place to start."

"That's asking a lot," I said.

"I know it is, trust me."

So, I slept on the top bunk that night, and Corey and I finally had our sleepover. It was weird being that high up, having the ceiling just three feet above my head. "Did you have a good story time?" I asked.

"Mm-mmm," came Corey's murmured reply.

"Did you have a good day today?"

"Mm-mmm."

"Did you like all your presents?"

"Mmm …"

He was sound asleep minutes later.

I, on the other hand, lay awake for more than an hour. I felt restless and uncomfortable. I wanted my regular bed back, the one David was now sleeping in. I wanted Alisha to slide into bed next to me; wanted to feel her silverish hair draped over my shoulder. I wanted things to go back to normal.

I wanted that gremlin-thing off of my shoulder. That, most of all.

Sleep dragged me down around 11:30 and held onto me, graciously, until 2:15. When I awoke to find Corey standing in the center of the room—a spectral form in his yellow Peter Cottontail pajamas—I knew the problems were starting again. His arms hung limp at his sides. His head was tilted slightly upward. He was staring into the corner. I propped myself on one elbow, squinting into the blackness between the bedroom door on the left and the far wall, in which the closets were located. Standing in that corner, swaddled in shadows and tangled in darkness, was the man in black. So help me, God, I could see him myself—though not straight on. But if I moved my eyes slightly to the right, away from the corner, my peripheral vision registered the silent movement of black fabric rippling in an unseen and unfelt breeze. The figure was tall—the top of its hood almost touched the ceiling. Was I really seeing this? I wondered. Or was I merely projecting an image of my own making? Either way, I was clearly awake, whereas Corey clearly wasn't. I climbed down the ladder and went around Corey, stepping in front of him. I waved my hands through the darkness, feeling for the robes. Nothing was there, of course. I flicked on the light switch. The corner was empty.

I decided I hadn't seen anything.

I doused the lights. I picked Corey up and put him back in his bed. He turned onto his side and nestled into his sheets, having never awoken.

*   *   *

David had decided that he wanted to assume my role as chaperone for the remainder of the week. That is, he wanted to drive Corey to and from school, and transport him to and from his afternoon activities. That way, they could maximize their time together, and it would give David a chance to see his son in action. The only problem with this was that David didn't know where any of these places were, or the times at which Corey was meant to be in those places, which meant I had to tag along as a guide. It did occur to me during breakfast that this could have been Alisha's way of punishing me for my poor behavior. In fact, when David suggested we take his car, I caught a glimpse of Alisha smiling inside her coffee mug.

"We've sort of gotten used to taking my truck," I said.

"Give your truck a day off," David said. "Save some gas. You point the way, I'll drive."

He had a heavy foot, too. We went rip-assing along some of the back roads at close to sixty. I kept stealing glances into the backseat to make sure Corey had his seatbelt on. They chattered endlessly, the two of them. My contributions to their back and forth banter consisted of, "turn left," "turn right," and "you might want to slow down." When we pulled into the Ace of Spades parking lot ten minutes earlier than normal, I checked my watch and said, "Well, that's a record that won't be broken."

Corey took my hand as we crossed the parking lot. I said to David, "In the event that Mrs. Hayes gives you the evil eye, you're to scrunch your toes and think happy thoughts." He laughed.

I introduced David to both Mrs. Thomas and Mrs. Hayes. He

offered a wide, friendly smile as he shook both their hands. I said, "David is Corey's real father. He's in town for this week, so you may see him instead of me during drop-off and pick-up."

Mrs. Thomas beamed. "So nice to finally meet you. Corey is one of our favorites; he's so soft-spoken and well behaved. Simon here has done an admirable job looking after him."

"That's what I've heard," David said. "Very nice to meet both of you."

We left the building and went back to David's BMW. All of a sudden, there I was, alone in the front seat with Alisha's ex-lover and Corey's real father. I guess this is the part where he pulls a gun and whacks me, then dumps my body in the river. Or where he decides to have a man-to-man discussion on whose penis is larger. I couldn't even tell him to get out of my truck, that was the worst thing. How had I allowed myself to get painted into this corner? What did Alisha think was going to come of this?

Anyway, we got back onto Route 513, and the silence was worse than a fork on a chalkboard. David said, "Why don't we go into town. You can show me around. We'll stop somewhere for coffee and donuts. My treat."

"We just had coffee and donuts. You're gonna make the U-turn up here."

We made the turn, and David stomped on the gas. We went shooting down the county road like a bullet traveling the barrel of a rifle.

"Where'd you learn to drive?" I asked.

"Jersey." He reached for the radio and flipped on some tunes. "I understand you're a Jersey boy yourself."

"I guess so. My mother lives in Lake Hiawatha."

He nodded. "Sure, Morris County. I'm in Bergen. Thirty, forty minutes northeast of you, I'd say."

"Have you lived your whole life in Jersey?"

"Most of it," he said. "I certainly can't retire there, though. The day I retire, I'm gone."

"Why's that?"

"Too damn expensive. There's a joke about natural disasters in this country: in California you've got earthquakes; in the Midwest it's tornadoes; in the southeast it's hurricanes; in New Jersey it's property taxes."

"I've heard that," I said.

"And you know something? It's never gonna get better. We've got blue-state syndrome. We're blue in the face, and we're just gettin' bluer."

I turned toward my side window and rolled my eyes. Well, Alisha and David definitely had one thing in common. I was beginning to see how and why they'd first hit it off.

I said, "Alisha's been determined from day one to see to it that I turn Republican. Now you."

He laughed. "Nah. Conservatism is like wisdom—it comes with age."

"I disagree. I've known lots of older, upstanding citizens who happened to be Dems."

"My parents were life-long libs. Christ, my father was a socialist. He wanted 70 percent taxation." We got off 513 to make the dog-leg into town. David continued, "Look at it this way, Simon. New Jersey has been electing Democratic senators for over thirty years now. It's no coincidence that we have the highest property taxes, auto insurance rates, and health care costs in the country."

"Where would you go, then? Alaska?" The farther, the better.

"Florida or the Carolinas. That's kind of the big thing right now."

We spent most of the morning occupying the corner booth at the front of Molly's, where I slowly, if not painfully, came to the conclusion that David wasn't all that bad of a guy. He made a concerted effort to get to know me and seemed genuinely interested in Corey's affairs and overall well-being. He listened to what I had to say with an attentive ear and an honest face. At some point, we started talking about baseball. A customer entered the café wearing a Yankees cap, about which David commented, "There's a fellow fan. You know, the good thing about Yankee fans is that they're all over the place. You'll find them anywhere in the country."

So, we finally had something in common. I told him I thought Jim Leyritz's three-run homer in the eighth inning of Game 4 of the ninety-six World Series was among the top three hits in franchise history.

He practically slammed his coffee cup onto its saucer, then pointed at me. "I was there!"

"*What?* Oh, come on—"

"I *was*, no foolin'—I was in Fulton County Stadium in Atlanta for that game. I was sitting high up in left field when Leyritz hit the hanging slider over the wall. You can't imagine the pall of silence that fell over that stadium. I mean, the place was dead quiet after that hit."

"That one swing pretty much ruined Mark Wohlers' career," I said. "He never recovered."

"The sequence of pitches in that at-bat will forever remain among the most second-guessed by fans and critics alike," David said. "Why was Mark Wohlers, who could approach a hundred miles an hour with his fastball, throwing hanging sliders to Jim Leyritz?"

"But if you remember," I reminded him, "Leyritz had fouled off several fastballs straight back, meaning he was right on the pitch. And Jimmy was always a good fastball hitter."

"Yes, yes, yes," David trumpeted, waving his hands in front of him like an orchestra's conductor, "but the old adage remains: you can't hang a fastball! If you're gonna get beaten, get beaten on your best pitch. You're right, though—that hit turned that series around for the Yanks, and Wohlers never did recover."

The following morning—Wednesday—I got up to find Alisha working busily at the kitchen table. Papers lay everywhere, and she had the cordless phone pressed between her ear and shoulder. She was chatting away and jotting things down on random slips of paper. I went to the coffee pot and poured myself a cup. David had driven Corey to school himself, now that he knew how to get there and back.

Alisha got off the phone, finally. "Good morning, Simon."

"Morning," I said. "What's all this?"

"Oh, I'm trying to coordinate the move. It's all one giant pain in the ass. The house is ready, and I'd planned to be there the first of June. But I just discovered that Corey's graduation takes place June 3rd. I can't let him miss that."

"Since when does kindergarten have a graduation?"

"Oh, the Ace of Spades has a ceremony every year. They do it at the Barrow Hill State Park. The kids get these little diplomas, and afterwards there's a big barbecue. Everyone eats hotdogs and hamburgers."

I watched her closely. "You're right. He'd be upset if the two of you couldn't attend that."

She looked up at me. "And you, Simon. He'll want you there just as much."

"Of course," I said, shifting my eyes to the floor. "I wouldn't miss it."

"It means I've got to push everything back a couple of days. Most importantly, the movers. You know how moving companies are."

"Actually, I don't," I told her. "I've never moved, and I've never owned a house."

"Hey, was that you I heard moving around last night? Between, oh, three and four?"

"It was me going after your son."

She set her pen down and sat up straighter. "Oh, no, Simon, is he sleepwalking again?"

"The last two nights."

She sat back in her chair and sighed. "But it's been so long since he's last done it. I was beginning to think that maybe he was getting over it."

I poured myself a bowl of cereal, then opened the fridge to grab the milk. "It won't last Alisha, trust me. As soon as David leaves, it'll stop."

"Why do you say that?"

"'Cause he's excited. Corey, I mean." There were other reasons, too, but I didn't voice them. "Why do you suppose it gets worse during the holidays?"

"Maybe you're right," she mused. She picked up her pen and began tapping its butt end against the glass tabletop. "But how does that jibe with your man in black theory? The man Corey is supposedly chasing?"

"I haven't quite worked that out yet," I told her. It was practically a full-fledged lie. By now, I had a pretty strong idea who the man in black was. And I knew why Corey was after him.

*   *   *

David got my fishing rod fixed. He took it to a rod repair shop, where the proprietor, known locally as Old Stan, affixed a new rod tip with Krazy Glue. The pole was now an inch and a half shorter but perfectly serviceable. Moreover, David had purchased a brand-new outfit—rod, reel, line, the works. "You use the new one, Simon," he said. "I'll use the repaired version. When I leave, all three poles stay with you guys."

"Wow, David," I said, duly impressed. "That's really nice of you. Thanks."

"You bet." He clapped me on one shoulder. "Now, what do you say the three of us go fishing?"

"Yeah!" Corey exclaimed. "Let's go!"

Alisha said, "No shortcuts through the swamp this time, okay?"

"We won't, Mom!" Corey yelled. He was already headed for the door.

We spent the rest of Wednesday fishing, and it was truly a blast. The fish were biting that day, and we caught lots of them. The three-way competition culminated, amazingly, in a three-way tie come dinnertime. We had each registered eleven points utilizing the one and two point system. No one said a word during dinner. We ate fast and furiously. We were all famished, for sure, but more so, we were eager to get back down to the lake to settle the score.

"I've never seen three people scarf down so much food in so little time," Alisha remarked. She stood and began gathering the empty plates. "All right, we'll do dessert later on. I can see the three of you are itching to go back out."

Without a word, all three chairs backed away from the table as we got up and ran for the door. I caught a glimpse of David wiping his mouth with a napkin, then throwing the napkin onto his plate as he pushed away and got up. He looked like a little kid.

The fish were really hammering when we got back down to lakeside. I won the tournament with twenty-two overall points. Corey took second with eighteen, barely edging out David, who finished third with seventeen. David gave us both high-fives when it was over. "Good job, guys. Both of you. That was the most fun I've had in a while. Now, who's up for going home through the swamp? Just kidding!"

So, we enjoyed a late dessert that night, the four of us. We gorged ourselves on apple pie and vanilla ice cream. Afterward, we rehashed fish tales of that afternoon and evening, laughing in many areas, objecting in others, and generally exaggerating wherever we thought we could get away with it. Alisha sat in a chaise lounge with her legs curled beneath her, holding a cup of tea and watching our exchange with an unfaltering smile. She listened intently as Corey expounded upon "the fish that struck his lure close to shore and broke the line you should have seen it Mom it was huge it was like three feet long," and later laughed as David gave his own version—"I was standing right there; I'm telling you that fish was no bigger than sixteen inches." My version went something like, "I was fifty yards up the shoreline, and from my vantage point the fish looked no larger than a pencil." The room was filled with laughter.

Thursday normally would have been Corey's day to see Dr. Andrews. Under my persistent urgings, Alisha had finally discontinued the therapy. Last Thursday had been Corey's final afternoon with the good doctor. Good riddance, I thought.

So, this week, David taught both Corey and me how to throw a curve ball. It was hard to do, and it took me quite awhile to get the hang of it. Corey was lucky simply to throw the ball within six feet of the target.

"Did you see it curve, Simon?" he yelled happily after one of his many pitches. "Did you see it?"

The ball had hit the garage door instead of my glove, and as I ran to retrieve it, I replied, "You're darn right I saw it. That one curved four feet out of the strike zone." David bent over laughing.

Friday night, David took us all out to dinner, as promised. The Hampton Riverside was bustling with Swan Lake's social elite. Corey looked cute as a button in his miniature jacket and tie. We stood on the veranda for cocktails, looking out over the river, surrounded by people talking about stocks and wine. Alisha commented, "When last we were here, Simon, it was a beautiful autumn evening. Tonight, it's a beautiful spring evening."

"She's right," David said. "On that note, I propose a toast. To friends, family, and good times."

We toasted. Corey and I were drinking 7-Up. Alisha was drinking white, David drank red. It didn't matter. We toasted.

Eventually we were seated, and we opened our menus. "Prices haven't changed," I said. Alisha snickered.

David said, "Hey, Simon, you can't have 7-Up all night. You're gonna have a hard drink before we're through here."

"Good luck with that," Alisha told him. "Getting liquor into him is like force-feeding a cobra."

David motioned for the waitress. She came promptly. "Bring us two Northport Nailers. One for him and one for me."

"Two *what?*" Alisha said.

"Wait a minute," I said, "I'm not sure I want one of those."

"I've never heard of it," the waitress said. "What's in it?"

"It's two parts …" David started to say, but then stopped and pushed himself up from the table. "I'll go talk to the bartender."

Alisha tried to protest. She lifted one arm and said, "Dave—" but he was gone by then.

Corey asked, "Where's he going, Mom?"

"Nuts," she said. "Your father is going nuts."

David returned minutes later, clapping his hands and rubbing them together. "Okay, two Northport Nailers coming right up."

"David, what is in one of those?" Alisha asked.

"Don't worry, it's good stuff."

Five minutes later, the waitress came back with two tumblers balanced on a tray. She set one of the drinks in front of me. It was amber colored with a red stirrer and lots of ice.

David lifted his Northport Nailer and said, "Okay, drink up. These go down easy, trust me."

I sipped mine cautiously. I was surprised to discover that it wasn't all that bad. What I mean is, it didn't have that awful battery-acid bite that I'd come to associate with hard liquor. I risked a second taste, and then a third.

"Yeah. You see? It hides the taste well, doesn't it?"

"It's actually kind of sweet," I noted.

"Sure it is."

Our dinners arrived, and we dug in. Corey had ordered a cheeseburger, which included a mountain of french fries. The kid was thrilled. America's such a great country. I got the sautéed tilapia with steamed broccoli and baked potato. The potato came with sour cream. David had asked for the prime rib—"an end cut, if you have it"—with garlic shrimp and fresh asparagus. Alisha had gotten some linguine dish.

The food was great all around. The banter among us was even better. I mean, once the dinner really got rolling, we found ourselves having a wonderful time. We laughed uproariously several times, attracting attention—not entirely unwanted, either—from nearby tables. I had sort of become the life of the party. I spoke with what was truly a silver tongue. I found myself able to recall old jokes I'd thought were forever lost.

At some point, the waitress came by, and I decided she was good-looking. "How's everything going here?" she asked.

I shook my empty tumbler. "Hey, sweetums, how 'bout another one of these?"

Alisha said, "I think you've had enough, Simon."

David said, "You know what? Bring me another, as well."

Alisha rolled her eyes. "Well, it looks likes I'm driving." To the waitress, she said, "A glass of water for me, please." When the waitress had gone, Alisha looked across the table at David. "Okay, give me the keys."

He stared back at her. "I'm fine, trust me." He burped. Corey and I laughed.

Alisha appeared mildly amused but serious at the same time. She held out her hand. "Keys, David. *Now.*"

"Be careful," I told him. "She's tenacious."

He turned to me. "And bossy."

"Oh, yes. Always gets her way."

"Incorrigible," David said.

She waggled her fingers. "Keys, please."

He handed them over.

"Thank you."

"Irreconcilable," I said.

"Irascible."

"Reprehensible."

Corey asked, "Why are they acting so strange, Mom?"

"Because they have penises, dear."

By dinner's end, I'd had three of those Northport things, David had had four or five, and we were about as drunk as two skunks in a dump. I mean, I was laughing at everything. David was telling some of the dumbest jokes in the book, and I thought they were the most hilarious things I'd ever heard. Alisha paid the bill because David had forgotten which pocket he'd put his wallet into. "Wait a minute," he said, mimicking a melodramatic game show host, "it's not in *that* pocket, so it must be in *this* one." I laughed so hard I thought I might retch. Corey was laughing because he saw me laughing. Alisha decided she'd had enough. She gave the waitress her credit card, scribbled in the tip, and out we went.

I had to lean against David in order to get to the car. The parking lot seemed like a vast sea of turbulent waves. We tottered and weaved, and it occurred to me we were straying in the wrong direction.

I yelled, "Steer! Steer, you dumb pirate!"

Alisha got us both into the back of the BMW, then slammed the doors. She got into the driver's seat and started the engine. As we pulled out of the parking lot, she said, "I have to say, Simon, I was wrong about David bringing out the worst in you. It appears the two of you bring out the worst in each other."

David thought that was funny, and he laughed. I was aware that both of our heads were lolling around on the backrest. He muttered something about not throwing up in his car, and as soon as he said it, I threw up. In his car.

"I thought I told you … not to do that."

I said, "Aw shit. What a waste of a fine, expensive meal."

I phased in and out after that. I kept reminding myself that as soon as I got my strength back I would ask David what exactly had been in those drinks. It might have to wait until morning, but so help me, I would ask him. Of course, I spent the remainder of the night and most of the next day passed out in Corey's lower bunk. By the time I woke up Saturday afternoon, David was long gone.

CHAPTER TWENTY-EIGHT

TAILLIGHTS IN THE DARK

YOU'LL NEVER KNOW ME, Dad. You'll never know me.

You'll never know me, either, Simon. You'll never meet the woman I was someday to become ... a woman I think of as Caroline. *Caroline can never be born because Catherine is dying. You can't squeeze blood from a stone, you know, but surely you can squeeze the life out of a whore ...*

Her voice haunted my dreams. I wandered aimlessly down meandering corridors, listening to that voice. I was lost in some sort of hallway maze, an amalgam of left and right turns and four-way intersections. The earthen walls writhed with vermicular life. Fingers and arms pointed at me. Admonishing whispers told me it was my fault—I hadn't stood high enough, hadn't acted early enough, hadn't utilized all that I owned.

Eventually I approached a room whose door was ajar. I started to run toward it, but in each case the gun went off before I could reach it. The gunshot was loud enough to stifle the whispers in the walls and send temblors through the foundations. Some nights, if I was lucky, it was enough to wake me.

But mostly, it didn't. I remained chained in sleep, trapped in the nightmare with nowhere to go except down the hall and through the door, where my dead sister waited. In tonight's version, I palmed the door open, and there was Catherine sitting in the corner with her legs splayed open. A stream of blood rained down from the dime-sized hole in the ceiling. The blood landed on the crown of her head and ran down all sides of her face. Her eyes were open, and they watched me. Then she tried to speak. "*I killed it, Th-imon,*" she said, mangling the S in my name due to the blood that invaded her mouth. "*I th-tarved it.*"

Suddenly, my eyes snapped open. I sat up in bed, my eyes darting around the room. Had the dream awakened me? Or had it been something else?

I rubbed my eyes and waited for my bearings to return. A glance at the clock on my nightstand told me it was 4:43 in the morning. It was still dark outside. I was about to lay down again when I realized that I heard something. I cocked my head to one side and listened. It sounded like an idling car engine.

I got out of bed and went to the windowsill behind the nightstand. It was mid-December, but I'd gone to bed with the window open about three inches due to the unseasonably warm, wet weather we'd been having. The night was damp and foggy, and a light mist may have been falling. Peering through the glass, I saw a pair of red taillights hovering in space near the end of our driveway. Someone had backed into our driveway to turn around, perhaps. But then I thought better of it, realizing that Catherine had in fact returned from her short-lived exodus. She'd been gone four days to this point, and four days is a long time when everything you own is running on empty.

I turned away from the window. I swung one leg into bed—and paused. *That's not her car, Simon. One of her taillights is busted out, if I recall.*

My heart sank in my chest as I realized it was one of Smoot's messengers taping yet another note to our door in the dark of night. *You're Out of Time*, this one probably read. Or *Game Over*, or *Thou Hath Entered Final Judgment*. I decided that bankers and loan officers, as a rule, were born heartless.

I pulled the rest of my tired body into bed and lay down with one ear against the pillow. I heard the car door open and then clunk shut again, muffled by the mist and fog. The car pulled out of the driveway and sped off down Williams Way.

I might have cried myself back to sleep had I any tears left to cry with.

*   *   *

A dry, deep slumber took me instead. Gladly I succumbed to it. I got up around 9:30 and went downstairs. It was Wednesday, a school day, and I did plan on going, but I wasn't in any hurry. I would be marked "late" again by the ladies in the front office, quite the norm these days.

Anyway, I found Ma sitting at the dining room table having a cup of coffee and an English muffin. "Hey, Ma."

She looked at me and smiled. "Good morning, Simon. Sit down, I want to talk to you."

"Can I get some orange juice first?"

"There's none left."

"I'll have some milk, then."

"I just poured the rest of it into my coffee."

"Then I guess I'll sit down."

Actually, I went to the sink first and filled a glass with cold water. I opened the fridge for good measure and saw a lot of white space. There was a half jar of relish, some mustard, some salad dressing. Condiments but no staples. I pictured myself squirting ketchup into my mouth and calling it breakfast.

I went back to the table and pulled out a chair across from where Ma was sitting. I sat down and poured cold water down my throat.

Ma said, "We need to start thinking about what we're going to do after the eviction."

Hearing the E-word coming from Ma's mouth had a stinging effect. "It's gonna happen, then, isn't it?"

"Yes, Simon, it is." She reached across the table and took my hand. "And I want to tell you that I'm sorry. There's a laundry list of behaviors and poor decisions on your father's and my part that led to this. It's no one else's fault but ours. It's not Catherine's fault, it's not your fault … it's *our* fault. I apologize for not doing more to help curb your father's gambling in the days of yesteryear. And I apologize for my own behaviors and inactions over the course of this year. I tried to pull the wool over my own eyes by getting drunk every day, which took a small problem and made it into a huge problem. I became an alcoholic, and I will always be an alcoholic in recovery."

"I …" But I didn't know what to say, so I merely nodded.

"Look, I talked to Don and Betty the other day. They know what's going on. They've agreed to open their hearts and their home to us. They said we can stay with them for as long as it takes me to get my feet on the ground again. That is, when I can afford to find an apartment for us."

"How are you gonna do that?"

"I'm going to start working again, Simon. I was offered a job at the Roundhouse, over in Netcong. It's literally three minutes from Don and Betty's house. I could walk to work until I get my license back."

"You were offered a job? Ma, that's great. What's the Roundhouse?"

"It's an antique store. Bethany Philips owns it. She's in the Program, you know. Anyway, she approached me at the Budd Lake meeting the other night and asked if I was looking for work. She says she needs a reliable person with a working knowledge of antiques. And you know how much I love that sort of stuff."

"Ma, that's wonderful!" I wanted to get up and hug her. She sensed my enthusiasm and stilled me with one hand, though.

"It's not going to be easy, Simon. There are a lot of hard days in our future. As for *your* future, you need to start thinking about college."

"How are we possibly going to afford college, Ma?"

"Where there's a will, there's a way, Simon. You'll get through on scholarships and student loans. In the meantime, I want you in school today, and in fact I want you there every day, and I want you there on time. Is that understood?"

"Yes."

"Good." She got up from the table and went out the side door to fetch the *Daily Record*—which was still being delivered, despite our probable delinquency—as I went to the sink to rinse out my glass. I was in the process of turning off the water and setting my glass upside-down in the drying rack when I heard the side door opening again.

"Simon, there's something out there."

I turned to look at her. Her face wore a nervous look. She held one hand over her heart. "What?"

"There's something on our porch." She pointed, as though whatever it was had the potential to deliver a nasty bite.

"Oh … shit." I had forgotten having woken up during the night to find the pair of red taillights hovering in space near the end of our driveway. I remembered thinking that bankers and loan officers were born heartless. Now I decided they were born gutless as well. I headed for the door and said, "One of Smoot's cronies was here last night. I heard his car pulling out of the driveway."

"Oh … but …"

I opened the side door before Ma could finish. Looking down, I saw a medium-sized brown paper bag sitting dead center on the top step. The top of the bag was rolled down to enclose its contents. I bent over to pick it up. Immediately I was surprised by how heavy it was. I cradled one hand underneath it so the bottom wouldn't break open. It was still misting outside, and the bag was pretty wet. I unfurled the bag's opening and peered inside. I saw wax paper wrapped and rubber-banded around a square-shaped object. "What the hell …"

I brought the bag into the house and set it down on the dining room table. My heart was beating loudly.

Ma came to look over my shoulder. "Simon, what is—"

I ripped the bag open, then tore off the wax paper. One of the rubber bands snapped and flew across the room. When it did, the rest of the wax paper fell apart, revealing five bricks of bound twenty-dollar bills. My mouth fell open. Ma screamed and jumped back. Her hands flew up to her mouth.

For a moment, time stood still.

*   *   *

I can't tell you how long we stood there in naked disbelief, but it seemed like an awfully long time. I heard Ma's wheezing breath behind me; heard the pounding of my own pulse in my ears and temples; heard the second hand on the clock above the kitchen range tick-ticking; and I heard, in some far-off language I could neither decipher nor entirely understand, a new definition of human kindness.

"Simon …" Ma started to say. "What is …"

I pawed through the stack of bills and found a small piece of paper folded in half. "Ma, there's a note here."

I unfolded the paper and read the note, which had been written in a flowing, cursive script, in ink. When I got halfway through it and realized what I was reading, I began muttering small expletives, like, "Oh, my God, Ma … Oh, Jesus …" I began stuttering the words after that, and when my legs grew weak, I pulled out a chair and fell into it.

Ma took the note from me. "Oh, God, Simon … it can't be … it can't be … no, it can't—"

"It is, Ma, it *is*."

She exploded into joyous, rapturous tears. She fell down against the edge of the table, and then collapsed to her knees. She laid one side of her face flat on the table's surface and cried openly for several minutes. "We're saved, Simon! God and heaven help us, we're saved!"

I opened one stack of bills and counted them, then made some quick calculations in my head. "Ma, there's eight thousand five hundred dollars here."

She looked up at me, blinking through tears. "Who, Simon? Who could have possibly left—"

"I don't know, Ma. The note isn't signed."

She reached to her left and pulled a chair toward her. She got up off her knees and sat in the chair. "Simon, think about this. It was someone who knew. It was someone who knew our plight, who knew how much money we owed. Who would know such a thing? Think now. Who have we told?"

"Don and Betty? You said you talked to them the other day—"

"But I never told them how much I owed. I only mentioned that we were deeply in debt and that we were foreclosing on the house."

"Well, I don't … I don't know who else could … You don't suppose Catherine could have come up with—"

"Get real, Simon, Catherine can't even feed herself."

"Well, look, it doesn't matter right now who left it. What matters is that we have enough to—" But I stopped myself. "Unless …"

"What, Simon? Unless what?"

"Unless it was … Ma, could it have been somebody in the

Program? Someone you told the story to, someone who was listening when—" I stopped abruptly, because now it was coming to me. I was able to hear the solution coming around the blind corner.

Ma heard it, too. "I haven't been broadcasting exact debt figures at meetings, Simon. Except …"

"The first night! The Budd Lake meeting! When you thought I was taking you to a surprise party—"

"And you waved the foreclosure stickers in front of my face, and you said how much we owed, yes, I know, but—"

"Ma, someone followed us home that night. Do you remember?"

She thought for a moment, then said, "The person with the high beams."

"Yes, he was driving with his brights on. And then he would turn his lights off altogether, and then he'd flick on his brights again."

She fell quiet for a long while. "You made me throw the scotch out the window."

"Yes, that came later."

"Do you think whoever was following us was trying to get us to pull over?"

"I don't know. But he must have followed us far enough home to have figured out where we live."

"But that was more than three weeks ago. Why wait all this time?"

"It doesn't matter," I said. "We have to call Smoot. We have to tell him we've got the money. If only I can remember where I put his damned card—"

"Hold on a second, Simon, hold on." She grabbed my arm to keep me seated for a moment. "We need to think about this first. Let's put our heads together here. We need to come up with a plan."

"What plan?" I asked.

"Simon, listen to me. You can't simply call that Smoot fellow out here and present him with a box of twenty-dollar bills."

"Why not?"

"Because it won't look legitimate, that's why. What's that man going to think if he walks in here and sees all this cash sitting on the table?"

I was beginning to get the gist of what Ma was saying, and I sort of half nodded.

"That's right," she continued, "he'll think we stole it. Or he'll think you sold drugs to get it. Anyway you cut it, it will smell fishy."

"Ma, I don't think Smoot will accept a personal check from you, given your recent history."

"No, he won't. But he'll take a bank check. It's as good as cash." Ma stood up. She headed for the door. "Get your coat and your keys, Simon. We're going for a drive."

*   *   *

An hour and forty minutes later, I was standing at the side door waiting for Smoot to arrive. I'd found the business card he'd given me and dialed his cell phone. He'd answered on the second ring. I'd informed him that he needed to drag himself out here pronto, but I hadn't said why.

Ma was sitting at the table. A serene look had come over her face, but she was fidgeting noticeably. On the table next to her hands was a cashier's check for seven thousand dollars. Following our trip to the bank had been a visit to the Municipal Tax Office on High Street. The leftover fifteen hundred in cash had been more than sufficient to pay our overdue property taxes along with interest and late fees. We had about a hundred and fifty remaining, which Ma said she would use for food shopping later today.

When Smoot did in fact show up, he didn't show up alone. Trailing his Infiniti was a white, unmarked sedan with county government plates. The two vehicles pulled into our driveway. "Here he is," I said. "He's got another guy with him."

"Who?" Ma asked.

"Don't know. I'm guessing we'll find out."

The door to the Infiniti opened, and I saw that Smoot had downgraded his level of attire. That is, he had ditched the white suit with the gold chain. He was still going Western, however, wearing cowboy boots and jeans, along with a clean shirt and tie, and a wide-brimmed rancher's hat. The man getting out of the white sedan wore brown shoes and loose-fitting navy slacks beneath a yellow rain slicker. The two men converged in the driveway for several moments to exchange some words. Smoot's hands were gesticulating. The other man listened and nodded.

"What's going on?" Ma asked.

"I don't know, they're standing there talking. Here they come now."

Smoot came onto the porch first. I opened the door for him. "Good day, young fellow," he said.

"The name is Simon."

"Right. Simon, this here is Joe Donovan, Morris County Sheriff. He'll be in charge of the sheriff's sale. I thought it appropriate that he accompany me on this visit. Do you have any objections to his being here?"

Smoot had sort of sandbagged us by dragging the county sheriff along with him unannounced, but given the circumstances, I really had no problem with it. "It's okay. Come in, both of you."

They both entered. I shook hands with Joe Donovan. He was a pleasant-enough looking fellow with a soft grip and a mustache. His face carried the slightly embarrassed look of one who is partially grateful at being invited into a home that he and others would be repossessing in short order.

They rubbed their shoes on the mat. I said, "This is my mother, Carol Ann Kozlowski." Ma smiled, but didn't stand up.

Smoot removed his hat. He nodded toward Ma. "Good day, ma'am."

"Hello," Donovan said.

The introductions were followed by an uneasy silence. We all sort of stood there looking at one another.

Finally, Donovan said, "I understand that this is a very difficult process for everyone involved. But I can assure you that with your cooperation, things will move smoothly—"

"We're not leaving," I said.

"What?"

"We're not leaving," I repeated. "We came up with the money."

Smoot gave me a tired look. He put his hand up and said, "Look, son—"

"No, you look, Mr. Smoot," Ma said. "We're paying off the balance of what we owe. I have a bank check here for seven thousand dollars." She slid the check across the table's scarred surface.

Smoot afforded himself a moment or two. "Look, uh … Do you mind if we sit?"

"Please do," Ma said.

The two men pulled out chairs. I sat down, too.

Donovan, who had chosen a chair at the end of the table, seemed suddenly perplexed. He was absently stroking his mustache and looking at the check at the same time. Smoot had taken the chair to my left … and he didn't appear to care that the check existed. His eyes remained fixed on Ma.

He went on, "Look … Ms. Kozlowski … Simon … We've given you a lot of time. In fact, you've had a lot more time than you might have had with a different lender. You went five solid months without payment—six, now. Most lenders would have begun lis pendens after three months of default. That being said—"

"I told you we'd come up with the money," I said. "Now we have it, and I expect you to keep your word."

Smoot regarded me a moment. "What word is that, son?"

"For the last time, my name is Simon. And you said we had roughly three weeks to come up with the money, that you would stall for time—"

"Yes, Simon, I remember *you* saying that, but I don't really recall my agreeing to it. And in any event, you're ascribing to me powers that I don't have. You see, this is—"

"You said that once the case entered final judgment, it was out of your hands and into the court system."

"That's correct, and—"

"Well, then?" I said. "Have we entered final judgment yet? You're required by law to notify us when such a status is reached. We've been checking the mail every day, and we haven't seen any official documents."

Smoot paused. He may have been getting a little frustrated. He went on, "I inquired early in the week as to the current status of this case. It's considered an uncontested foreclosure, and I was told that it would be entering final judgment by the end of the week. Today is Wednesday, midday, so if it hasn't happened already, then it *will* happen tomorrow or Friday. The ink is hitting the paper as we speak. Look, what I'm saying is … it's over. I'm sorry, but it's too late. You're simply out of time."

"And what I am saying," I replied, leveling Smoot with a steady gaze, "is that you're wrong."

He sat back in his chair. "What?"

I took out the note that had been folded up and stashed inside the bundles of bound twenty-dollar bills. I held the note in front of me and began to read, verbatim: "The New Jersey Fair Foreclosure Act, effective December 1995. The Act permits reinstatement of any residential mortgage loan by payment of the amount which would have been due in the absence of the default together with court costs and attorneys' fees in an amount not to exceed those permitted by the New Jersey Court Rules. The right to cure by payment exists at any time up to the entry of Final Judgment."

I lowered the note and met Smoot's eyes. He watched me carefully. Donovan said, in a lower voice, "Actually, Norm, the kid's right. We don't see this too often in the uncontested cases, but ... well, the law does allow for the right to cure by payment at any time before final judgment is reached."

Ma slid the bank check closer to Smoot. "It's for seven thousand dollars. That covers any late fees we've incurred and also meets this month's requirement. Whatever's leftover, you can put toward the principle."

Smoot slid the check toward him, and gave it a glance-over to make sure it was legit. On his face was the smug half smile of a man who knows he's been beaten at his own game. He picked up the check in his fingers and clicked its lower edge against the table's surface several times, producing a smart *click-clack*.

He sighed and said, "Well, I can make the necessary calls, and we'll begin processing this immediately. You're still left with one very big problem, however."

"Yes?" Ma asked.

"There's no way First Equity will keep you on. This money will get you caught up, but you can rest assured you're going to have to find a new lender. Given your recent delinquency, you're going to be classified as high-risk, which may translate into higher-than-normal interest rates. Provided that you're able to procure a new lender, you may find yourselves unable to meet the new payment on a month-by-month basis."

"Actually, Norm, you're wrong about that, too." I held the note up once more, and read, aloud, the rest of it: "The borrower may reinstate the loan by paying only the past due periodic payments, court costs, and permitted counsel fees. If this reinstatement right is exercised, the default is nullified as of the date of the cure, and any acceleration of the underlying obligation is rescinded."

"That was well put, son," Donovan told me. "I mean, Simon." He turned to Smoot. "The kid's right, Norm. He read it right out of the nomenclature."

"You had some help with this," Smoot observed, looking from me, then to Ma, then back to me.

"Maybe," I said.

"So, how'd you come up with the money, then? If you don't mind my asking."

"We got lucky." *We stood with all we had.* I added, "You know, Mr. Smoot, sometimes when you love someone that much, and when you try hard enough ... well, you end up getting lucky, that's all."

"Indeed." Smoot folded up the bank check and stuck it in his breast pocket. Then he stood. Joe Donovan stood as well. "Well, congratulations, Simon. And congratulations to you, ma'am. It looks as though you've got yourself a house."

*   *   *

When they were gone, Ma and I went out and sat on the side porch. Ma brought a pair of scissors with her, along with her wallet, and a trash can. One by one, she cut up all fourteen of her credit cards. I held out the trash can as she sliced and diced. She laughed during the process. "You know, Simon, I'm feeling freer by the moment. With every card I cut up, in fact."

"Me too, Mom."

"There's still all that credit debt to pay off, and I'm not sure how I'm going to do it, but ... well, first things first, right?"

"That's right," I said. "One day at a time."

"To thine own self be true," she added. I laughed.

When she was finished cutting, I set the trash can aside and put my arm around her. I may have never loved my mother more than I did at that moment.

She put her arm around me, too. "You know what, Simon?"

"What?"

"I don't believe a mother has ever had a more loving son. How lucky am I to have you as my son?"

"Pretty damned lucky."

Ma laughed. "And modest, too. Well, I know your father would be awfully proud of you if he were here."

"You know something, Ma? We may never learn who left the money on our porch."

"We may not," she ceded. "But that doesn't mean you or I can't repay this act of kindness to someone else down the road. You know what I mean?"

"Yeah," I said. "Yeah, I do."

Some of the clouds were drifting apart in the west. We both looked up and saw this perfectly round hole of blue sky forming above us. And for the first time in what seemed like an eternity, the sun poked out.

CHAPTER TWENTY-NINE

BOOK OF REVELATIONS

ALISHA MOVED HER TOES up and down on my bare chest. This felt good, but it tickled, so a while later I took hold of her foot and began giving her a foot massage. I positioned both thumbs beneath her arch, and began moving them in slow, undulating circles. "Oh, Simon ... oh, that feels so good."

I asked her, "Is it possible for a woman to have an orgasm as a result of a foot massage?"

She smiled but didn't open her eyes. "Depends how good the massage is, I guess. Why don't you give it a go?"

"All right."

The square floating dock made lazy revolutions beneath an aqua-blue sky. The aluminum decking was warm against my skin, a welcome relief after a cold swim. It was mid-May, and the weather had been hot of late, and the lake was warming quickly. The water temperature was still in the mid- to upper sixties, however, which made for a fast swim. There was no small talk while treading water.

Anyway, I went to work on her foot, kneading her sole with my thumbs while spreading the rest of my fingers around her bridge in a spider web pattern.

"That's ... a little higher, Simon, a little ... oh ... right there ... oh, God, yes, yes, *yeeesss* ..." She pointed her chin toward the sky and arched her back. She moaned and thrust her hips forward. When it occurred to me that she was obviously faking it, I gave up on the massage and resorted to tickling. She laughed and jerked her foot away.

"You're a terrible faker," I told her.

"I thought I was pretty good."

"Maybe *you* thought it was good. I, on the other hand, know the real thing when I hear it."

She turned her body parallel to mine and rolled toward me. It occurred to me that she looked like a twenty-four-year-old in her white bikini rather than the forty-two-year-old woman she actually was. Anyway, I cradled my arm underneath her neck, and she sort of propped her chin on my shoulder and said, "Hey, guess what?"

"What?"

"I finished it. Last night."

"Finished what?" But I knew before the words were entirely out of my mouth. "Oh … well, when do I get to read it?"

She pattered her fingers up and down on my chest the way she'd done with her toes earlier. "Oh, it'll be a while. It's only the rough draft. I'll send you a galley before it's published."

Then again, if it was similar to her previous books, maybe I was best off to wait for the movie. "What's it called?"

"I don't know yet. That'll come later. I'm just glad I finished it. I knew I had to finish it while I was still here."

"Why's that?"

She shrugged. "It's just the way things are sometimes. Have you noticed the house looks different from out here?" She lifted her head off my shoulder so she could view the house right-side up instead of sideways. I watched her lift a tress of silverish hair away from her eyes to better her vision. Then I turned to look at the house.

She added, "The way the windows show through the leaves and trees … it almost gives the impression that the house is watching us."

"A home always looks after its occupants," I said. "Especially if it's a happy home. Hey, you should write a book about that."

"Someday, maybe." She pushed herself up. "I'm ready to go in if you are. I have to say, I'm not looking forward to this swim."

I stood up next to her, stretching my limbs and girding myself for the agony of the cold dive. "If we wait long enough, maybe a boat will come." She laughed. "Hey, did you know I used to swim out here every morning?"

"When?" she asked.

"End of last summer, when I first arrived."

"Really? And what did you think about while you were out here?"

"I wondered what the hell I was doing swimming in a lake when I was supposed to be doing road construction. I was supposed to be working with my hands, some sort of manual labor. It was my father's advice. So that one day, when I was ensconced in my chosen profession, I would have a better awareness of what I had."

"Your father gave you excellent advice," Alisha said.

"I guess so. But it didn't turn out the way he said. Nothing turned out the way he said."

"I'm glad it didn't. Road construction is miserable work, Simon. It doesn't pay as well as I do, and the sex isn't half as good."

She dove into the lake.

*   *   *

"Some of the larger items will stay," Alisha said. "For example, the kitchen set and spare bedroom sets. The dining room table in the den will go, but everything else there stays."

The man from the moving company followed Alisha through the downstairs portion of the house, holding a pencil and clipboard. Glen was his name. He was a tall, thin fellow with a balding pate and a large nose.

"Basically, it's the master bedroom, my son's bedroom, and most of the stuff in my office that goes with us."

"What I'll do," Glen said, "is give you a set of color-coded stickers. Green goes, red stays. Very simple."

"What about yellow?" I asked.

"Not now, Simon." Alisha turned back to Glen, who had given me a perplexed look. She said, "As for the smaller items, such as books, glasses, and knick-knacks, we'll have it all packed into boxes and ready for transit. Do you need a green sticker on every box?"

"Absolutely. I'll leave you plenty, don't worry."

"What kind of deposit do you need? Fifty percent?"

"That's fine," Glen answered.

"I'd also like to see copies of your valid insurance papers if you've got them."

"No problem."

Later in the afternoon, Alisha and I were in the kitchen boxing up some of her finer, seldom-used crystal and expensive dinnerware. It was a tedious process. Each item had to be individually wrapped in tissue paper and then placed carefully into a box.

At one point, Corey came into the kitchen holding a book. "Mom, can I take this book with me?"

"Of course you can, honey."

Ten minutes later, he reappeared, holding another book. "Mom, can I take this one, too?"

"Corey, you can take all of your books."

"Do they need stickers?"

"No, honey, the sticker goes on the outside of the box. Simon will help you pack up your books and toys over the next couple days. They don't have to be packed just yet."

"Mom?"

"Yes, dear."

"Can, um, can we take Playworld with us, too?"

"I put a red sticker on it," I said.

A smile went flitting across Alisha's face, but she told Corey, "Yes, Playworld can come with us. The new house has a great big playroom in it, perfect for Playworld. You can help Simon take it apart later this week."

"Maybe the movers can get it in their truck in one piece," I suggested.

"They'll never get it out of the basement in one piece."

"I don't understand why you're leaving a lot of the furniture behind," I told her.

"When the house goes on the rental market, I can advertise it as being partially furnished. It'll push the rent up a little bit. And besides, I'll be picking out mostly new furniture for the new house."

"How do you plan on finding tenants and collecting rent and all the other work that goes with being a landlord if you're living a day-and-a-half-drive away?"

"There are companies that do that for you, Simon. You don't see me running back and forth to my other rentals now, do you?"

I brought up another subject. "Alisha, you've still got a garage full of junk leftover from the Turners."

"I'm aware of it, yes. I'll be making several trips back once Corey and I are settled down south. I'll probably hire an outfit to come in and clean everything out. Feel free to grab anything you deem useful or valuable," she said.

"Do you plan on bringing Corey back up with you?"

"Not if I can help it, no."

"Who will look after him?"

This caught her by surprise. She stopped what she was doing and looked up toward the ceiling. She stood that way for several moments before turning toward me. When she did, I was a little surprised to see that her eyes had taken on a wet, shiny complexion.

Leaning back against the counter, she folded her arms over her chest and crossed one leg in front of the other. "I guess I'll have to find a good babysitter. You know any?"

I shook my head.

She dropped her eyes to the floor for a while, then looked around the kitchen before meeting my eyes once again. "I guess you and I need to talk, don't we?"

I nodded. Had I seen this coming?

"Give me a day or two to think first, okay?"

Again, I nodded.

"It's not like you to be speechless, Simon." She offered a pained smile. "You normally have a comment for everything."

"Maybe I need a couple days to think also," I said. I turned and walked out of the kitchen.

*   *   *

And so David Kaplan had come and gone, taking with him his charm and good looks and his Wall Street income and his spontaneous sense of fun. What had he left behind? Why, his gifts to Corey, of course, and the new fishing pole … and the small gremlin that continued to shoulder-hop over my head. I found it odd and even a bit crazy, in a way, to realize that David's visit had not only altered the chemistry among Alisha, Corey, and me, but that I sort of missed his presence on top of it. Somehow, he had grown on me, and toward the end of his stay, we had gone from a trio to a quartet. But we hadn't necessarily gone from the quartet back down to the trio. Because something was different. Something had changed. That little thing sitting on my shoulder and swinging its legs back and forth as it turned the Rubik's Cube wasn't going away. My time at Swan Lake was ending, and when the Rubik's Cube showed solid colors on all six sides, my stay would be over. That gremlin-thing was my future, the gremlin was reality—morning was breaking, the lion was waiting, the spirit was waking. What was this false reality we were living? I was young enough to be Corey's big brother, and young enough to be Alisha's oldest son, and yet I was neither. I had entrenched myself as Corey's father and Alisha's husband, and yet I was neither. What did that mean, exactly? Where did that leave me?

It leaves you at the end of the road, my friend. It brings you back to where you started. Sometimes you can see the end before you see the beginning. Now the end is near.

*   *   *

I spent the next several days helping Corey break down his bedroom. It took us an entire afternoon to box up the books alone. Corey's favorite part of the operation was putting the stickers on the boxes once they were packed and taped shut. "How 'bout this, Simon," he suggested. "You load the boxes, and I'll put the stickers on."

"Or, better yet," I said, "how 'bout I load you into a box and then cover it with stickers?"

Laughing, he shouted, "No!"

I spent some time in the garage sifting through the columns of junk left behind by the Turners. I salvaged what I thought might prove useful down the road, but I really didn't want anything. Removing some of the trinkets and trappings from the pegboard along the back wall seemed to make the emptiness more real. I was aware of a hollowness spreading like a cancer through my innards and into my extremities. It had begun the day David had arrived, but only now was I able to ascribe a name to it. I spent my last week at Swan Lake wishing I were ten years older and Alisha ten years younger. But if wishes were dollar signs, we'd all be wealthy, wouldn't we? We had missed each other by twenty years, and there was no amount of magic that could make up for lost time.

Eventually, we walked. At the top of the driveway, we made a right onto State Street. She didn't take my hand this time, and I wondered if she'd already broken up with me. We walked in silence for a long time. The morning was warm, in the low eighties. State Street was mostly shaded by the many towering pine boughs, but you could feel summer trying to usher its way in three weeks ahead of schedule. We both wore shorts. Alisha wore a white, spaghetti-strap tank top and sandals.

I was unaware we'd gone halfway around the lake until I looked to the right and saw the first of Millie's three houses. The driveway to the middle house was empty, and I surmised Millie was at her store. Passing the last of the three houses rekindled the memory of the painting in which the blue tarp had been ready to burst. *The weight of water*, I thought. *The entire world swooshing through that gash in the tarp.* I remembered the stiletto claws rending me open, and the life draining out of me.

"The boy and the apple tree," Alisha said.

"What?"

"When I think of you and Corey together, that's what I'll think of. The boy and the apple tree."

"You think of me as a tree?"

She chuckled. "Native American tribes had a ritual, Simon, of assigning an apple tree to every newborn child. Each boy and girl had his or her own tree while growing up. The tree remained his or hers until marriage. The tree's symbolism was threefold: it served as a play toy—the child could climb among its many branches; its many limbs provided shelter from the elements; and it bore fruit for sustenance."

"Did you make that up?" I asked.

"No."

We made a left onto Road 17, which I'd never been on. It was a winding, dirt and gravel lane with steep slopes dropping off both sides. The terrain below was dark and swampy. The air was ripe with skunk cabbage.

"It's funny," I said, "when I first got here, the notion of looking after a child was completely foreign to me. I felt like an idiot the first time Corey held my hand crossing the school parking lot. Now I can hardly bear the thought of losing him."

"You won't be losing him, Simon. And he won't be losing you. Both of your lives have been enriched by having the other in it. You understand that, don't you?"

"I suppose my brain understands it, yes."

"You love him, don't you?"

"I … well, yes, I guess I do, but … Alisha, why are you crying?"

She wasn't sobbing outright, but her upper lip was trembling and a tear slivered around the corner of her mouth. I put a hand on her bare shoulder. "Come on. Don't cry now."

"Should I cry later, instead? It's just that … I've never seen another person love my son the way you have. You came into my life by accident, and I hired you as a chaperone, and yet you loved Corey like a father. As his mother, I can't tell you what that means to me."

"Well, Corey is special," I said.

"You're the one who's special, Simon. That's why I can't take you with me."

A dagger to my chest couldn't have lanced my heart with more precision. I looked up and discovered we'd happened upon another one-lane bridge, this one arching over Fire Creek. The Fire was the smallest of the eight outflows exiting Swan Lake, but it was said to run the fastest. I limped over to the wood handrail along the left side to sit down. Alisha, quite appropriately, went to the right side. There we sat again, facing one another. It occurred to me that wherever my life took me, when I closed my eyes in an attempt to envision Alisha Caldwell's face, it would be these one-lane bridges I would remember her by. She would always be the woman sitting on the other side of the bridge, her face framed by the forest beyond. In my memory, she would never speak. She wouldn't need to. We wouldn't need to speak to each other. We would *always* be sitting on opposite sides of the bridge.

> *And from this bridge I'll see your face*
> *And words are never spoken …*

Alisha continued, "I've been thinking of the girl lately."

"What girl?"

"Sometimes I can see her face, but usually I can't. Sometimes I think I can smell her shampoo. Other times, she's in my dreams. She doesn't know I'm watching. She doesn't know I can see her."

"Alisha, what are you talking about?"

"She's special, Simon, this girl is extremely special. She doesn't know where exactly her life is taking her. But it will intersect with yours, somehow and some way. And I can't … I can't take you away from her. She's meant to have all of you. The best I can ever do is to have some of you. And that's not a fair bargain. Not to you, and not to her."

"I don't believe in fate, Alisha. I believe in chance."

"Oh, Simon, there's no difference. If you don't find her in one place, you'll find her in another. She won't choose you, Simon. You'll choose her."

"What if I don't want to choose?"

"You will, Simon, it's the way of the world."

I swept a forearm against my brow to wipe the tears off my face. I felt everything slipping away from me. "You're a writer, goddammit. I'd expect you to come up with a better ending."

She laughed in spite of her broken countenance. "Happy endings can make for good books. But real life doesn't have an epilogue after it. There's always another page in real life. In eight years, I'll be fifty. I'll have wrinkles as you're entering your thirties. By the time you hit forty, I'll be white and shriveled and two inches shorter. Before you know it, you'll be pushing me around in a wheelchair. How would you like to walk into the bathroom in the morning and see my false teeth marinating in a cup of water?"

Tears sputtered out of my eyes as I bent over laughing. "Christ, Alisha, don't be so hard on yourself."

"I'm not being hard, I'm being real. You're meant to meet the woman of your dreams, and to have your own children, and to have your own career, and to be a pillar in your own community. Those were your goals when you came here, and they must continue to be your goals when you leave."

I lowered my head and thought about these things for a while. I looked up and said, "Maybe you should forsake romance for science fiction. That way—"

"I know where you're going with this," she cut in. "You put me into deep freeze for twenty years, until your age catches up to mine."

"How'd you know I was gonna say that?"

"Because it's been done a thousand times," she said. "And what happens when you meet a girl your age who, as it turns out, you end up liking better? Meanwhile, there I am hanging on the wall, stuck in a block of ice. What then?"

"*That's* the book you should write."

"Someone's written that one, too, trust me."

We both stood up. We walked toward each other and met in the middle of the bridge. She took both of my hands in hers and held them for a while, looking down at me and then looking up. Finally, she asked, "Are you okay, Simon?"

"Yeah, I'm okay. But … Alisha?"

"Yes?"

"What if I never feel this again?"

"You will, Simon. Trust me, you will."

*   *   *

Corey's last day of school was Friday, June 1st. He came running across the school parking lot as I was climbing out of my truck. "Simon! Hey, Simon!" I noticed a stream of loose papers flying out of his open backpack behind him, swirling and twirling, and ultimately coming to rest on the asphalt and the hoods of parked cars. Well, there you have it—a six-year-old boy can indeed leave a paper trail.

"Whoa, there! Slow down, camper, you're littering."

"Guess what, Simon? We get trophies at our graduation!"

"Do you now?" I asked, walking past him to pick up some of the papers. "You're one up on me, then. I've never gotten a trophy for anything."

"They're real ones, Simon! They're real trophies!"

"Okay, well, let's get these papers picked up first, and then we'll celebrate."

We got the papers picked up, then walked back to the truck, sans celebration. I noticed Corey was holding some sort of arts and crafts creation made of Popsicle sticks.

"What's that?" I asked.

He looked down at the thing he was holding. "It's a dog."

"Oh. Well, that's cute. He's even got ears. Looks like the tail is coming off, though."

"It needs more glue."

I drove out of the parking lot and onto 513. "So, you guys are gonna get trophies, huh?"

"Yeah! Big ones!"

"What are they gonna look like? A big K for kindergarten?"

"I don't know."

"Hey, do I get a trophy, too?"

"No!"

"I might have to steal yours, then."

"Nooo!"

I made the U-turn onto 513 South. We drove along for a while. I asked him, "So, how's it feel to be finished with kindergarten?"

He shrugged. "I don't know."

"It feels the same?"

He nodded.

"Are you excited to be in first grade?"

He nodded vigorously, his eyes a brilliant blue. "Yeah, yeah!"

"When you go to your new school in South Carolina, you get to ride the school bus."

"Mom says my new bedroom is gonna be really, really big."

"That's what I hear. Maybe you can fit Playworld in there."

"Is your room gonna be close to mine, Simon?"

"Actually, our bedrooms are going to be farther apart than they've ever been," I said.

"Why?"

"Because I'll be sleeping in New Jersey. You'll be sleeping in South Carolina."

He paused. "What do you mean?"

"What I mean is that I'm not going to the new house with you. You and your mom are moving there by yourselves. I'm going back home to my mom."

"But … why?"

"Because …" *Because your mother will always be the woman on the other side of the bridge.* "… because that's the way things are, kid. It's time for me to go home now."

Frown lines were appearing in his forehead and chin. His lower lip was starting to pucker out. "I don't want you to go home. I want you to come with us."

"I know you do, kid. But I can't. I have to go back to school too, just like you."

"But I thought you were done with school."

"I have to go back for a few more years, so I'm not done yet."

"After you're done, then are you coming with us?"

He was actually making this much harder than I'd anticipated. I shook my head and said, "After your graduation on Sunday, you and I will be saying good-bye."

"No, I don't want to say good-bye!" He started to cry. "I want you to come with us, Simon! I thought you were coming with us!"

"Hey, come on—"

He erupted into a full-fledged tantrum. He started beating his fists against the dashboard. He threw the Popsicle-stick dog into the floor well in front of him, and proceeded to stamp his feet through it, breaking it apart. He continued to stomp on it until no two sticks remained joined.

I switched my blinker on and pulled onto the shoulder.

"Okay, that's enough now." I reached a hand toward him, but he batted it away. I undid my seatbelt and slid across the seat toward him, but he began punching me in the chest.

"No, I hate you! I hate you, Simon!"

"You do not hate me—"

"Yes, I do! I hate you!"

"If you hate me so much, then why do you want me to come with you?" I asked. He bit his lip and pouted. It's so easy to trip up little kids under cross-examination. I'm halfway to my law degree already.

"Huh?" I persisted. "Why do you want me to come with you if you hate me so much?"

"Because you're supposed to take care of me," he said in a tiny voice.

"Your mom is going to take care of you. She's perfectly capable."

He looked up at me through wet, shiny eyes. A thin sliver of snot was leaking out of one nostril. "She can't do it all herself."

He hadn't meant it to be funny, but I laughed all the same. "Are you that much of a handful? That it requires two people to look after you?"

"But she's too busy."

"No, she isn't. I promise you, she's gonna be the best mom in the whole world." I forced a smile. "And besides, you're getting bigger. You're gonna learn how to read in first grade, and lots of other things. Pretty soon, you won't be a kid anymore."

"But who's gonna take me fishing?"

"Your mom can take you fishing," I said. "Look, there's nothing your mother can't do."

"Can she get the hook out?"

"Okay, that's one thing she can't do. You'll have to do that yourself. Look, Corey, it's not as if we'll never see each other again. I'll come down to your new house to visit. We can have a sleepover and go fishing."

He sat still and resolute, his lip puckered out—the defendant trying to decide whether or not to accept the terms of a plea bargain.

"Come on," I said. "Give me a hug. Let's go."

He undid his seatbelt and gave me a hug.

"All right. Feel better now?"

He nodded glumly, but his lip was still sticking out.

"Good. Seatbelts on, then. Let's roll."

"Where are we going?" he asked.

"We're going home to get your horseback riding gear. Today's your last lesson."

*   *   *

We stayed up until eleven o'clock that night, packing. Saturday morning, we were up at seven to continue the process. The devil's in the details, let me tell you. I worked until two in the afternoon disassembling Playworld. Have you ever noticed you can never get products back into their boxes exactly the way they'd come out? I'm going to call it Simon's Law of Irreversibility—SLI for short.

Following a short nap, I took an hour or so to get my own things organized and ready for departure. I didn't have much, really. Some clothing, including the new suits Alisha had bought me, along with some books and several tools I was salvaging from the garage. My largest acquisition was Josef's Tacoma, which meant I didn't have to rely on public transportation to get home. But I'd be leaving Swan Lake directly from the graduation tomorrow, so it was imperative for me to have my stuff loaded into my truck when we left for the Barrow Hill State Park in the morning. I phoned Ma around suppertime, letting her know I'd be home late in the day tomorrow. She said she couldn't wait to see me. I told her I couldn't wait to see her either. I found it difficult to believe that we hadn't seen one another since last August.

I spent the remaining time Saturday helping Corey with his bedroom toys. It was almost as bad as Playworld. By 9:30 that evening, we'd loaded twenty-three boxes, taped them shut, and affixed the requisite green sticker to each. We carried them out to the den, where Alisha was working. By this time, the den resembled a department store warehouse. Rows of boxes stood at odd, intersecting angles. Any higher, and the den would be transformed into a maze.

Back in Corey's bedroom, we stood with our hands on our hips, surveying the naked walls and the empty shelves. The bookcases were bare. The bureau drawers were likewise empty—all of Corey's clothing had been packed away save for tonight's pajamas and tomorrow's outfit, both of which Alisha had neatly laid out for him.

"I guess that's it, kid. Are you gonna miss this room?"

"Yeah, a little." He looked down and picked up the roll of green stickers we'd left on the floor. "We still have a lot of stickers left, Simon."

"Hey, I've got an idea," I said. I took the stickers from him. "Now hold still."

In ten minutes' time, I'd covered his face, neck, and arms in green stickers. "Now we can call you the Green Lantern. Now go out and tell your mom you're ready to be shipped out."

He went running out into the den in his bare feet. I waited a few seconds, then moseyed along behind him. Moments later, I heard Alisha laughing.

"I'm ready to go, Mom! I'm ready to be shipped out!"

"Well, I guess you are. We'll have to load you onto the truck, won't we? Let me get a picture of you before you start peeling them off."

I had never seen Alisha take any photos of her son before, but she quickly produced a camera, telling me to kneel down beside him. "Get close to him, so I can get both of you in. That's it." She snapped two or three quick ones. "Oh, that is so cute."

It took us fifteen minutes to peel off all the stickers. Corey got into his pajamas, and as we sat down on the edge of his bed, it occurred to both of us that we'd packed away all of his books. "Well," I said, "that just means your mother will have to read you two stories tomorrow night."

Alisha was leaning against the doorframe. "Are you kidding? We'll be lucky to arrive at the new house by midnight."

I turned to Corey. "That's *three* stories the following night. You see how quickly women get into debt, kid?"

All Corey wanted to discuss was the trophy he'd be receiving tomorrow. He could barely contain his excitement. "Mom, it's gonna be a big trophy. A really big one!"

"Wow," Alisha said. "What are you going to do with a trophy that big?"

"I don't know. Can I put it in my new room, Mom?"

"Of course you can. But right now, you need to get into bed. It's late. Tomorrow is going to be a long day. Your graduation starts at ten, which means we need to have the Land Rover all packed and ready to go by nine."

When he was tucked in and the lights were out, Alisha and I went out to the kitchen for a cup of decaf. "Are you seriously intent on driving straight through tomorrow?"

"That's the plan, yes."

"The ceremony will be more than an hour. You won't get out of there before noon. It's at least a twelve-hour drive from New Hampshire to South Carolina. Probably more. Drive halfway, and get a room somewhere. Make it easier on yourself."

"We'll see how it goes," she answered. "I can be quite driven once I've got my mind set on something."

"Trust me, I know."

We said our goodnights, and I wandered into my bedroom to

lie down. I could scarcely believe that this would be my last night sleeping in this bed, in this room, in this house. I switched off the light and lay down with my arms crossed beneath my head. Staring up at the ceiling, I ran the muntins for a while. Left, right, up, down, all around. This room had become my room, over time. These walls had become second nature to me. I knew their corners and where the shadows lived. I remembered the very first night I'd lain down on this bed, how strange and foreign and displaced I had felt.

I'd fallen asleep that first night to the sweet memory of Molly's rhubarb pie sliding across my tongue and down my throat … and how long ago that now seemed. It seemed like forever. It seemed like a lifetime.

*   *   *

My eyes fluttered open around five in the morning. A light rain pitter-pattered the screens and windows. A pre-dawn grayness pervaded the forest beyond. I turned from one side over to the other, and later onto my back, but sleep would not return. So I lay on my back and stared at the ceiling. There were no muntins to run at this hour, but there was a lot to think about.

I thought about the Turners. Nels and his wife and their son, Crawford. Crawford, who had been blind at birth, who had been possessed of an extraordinary talent. A boy who could paint what his eyes couldn't see. A boy whose eyes had swum into focus moments before his death, enabling him to look upon his mother's face for the very first time. I recalled the painting I'd seen in front of Millie's store the first afternoon, the portrait of the house as viewed from the lake, with the suffused greenish light in the corner window. I now understood the happiness the Turners had known as a family. The happiness Alisha, Corey, and I felt while together may well have mirrored that of the Turners. I recalled the initial insight that had illuminated my brain upon seeing the painting on the sidewalk that first day: *There is no happiness in that home. But there used to be.* Happiness had come full circle, had it not? Alisha, Corey, and I had replaced that which had been lost from this once-happy home.

I had never shared these insights with Alisha. I had never told her what Millie had told me of this home's previous occupants. I'd never told Alisha that a blind boy had once lived here, a boy with an eye in his head—with a vision so keen it sometimes saw into other people's lives. It occurred to me that she ought to know these things.

I lifted myself out of bed and went into the hall. The den was a gray mausoleum of towering boxes. I maneuvered through them and tiptoed up the spiral stairs. Going up the hall, I came to Alisha's bedroom door, which was ajar. I pushed the door open.

She was sitting on the edge of her bed. Looking almost spectral in her white nightgown. She turned and saw me standing in her doorway.

"How long have you been awake?" I asked.

She appeared to be wringing her hands together. "I don't know, twenty minutes."

"I …"

"Come lay down next to me, Simon. Just for a while."

I walked around to the other side of her bed and lay down on it. She lay down beside me, taking both of my hands into both of hers. She snuggled close to me, with her chin resting on my shoulder, her face close to mine.

"It's raining," I whispered.

"It can't rain today."

"It is."

"I'm glad you came up."

"I wanted to … tell you—"

"Shh. You don't have to, Simon. Just hold my hands for a while, okay? Hold my hands."

*   *   *

I still couldn't sleep, so I lay there and held her. I worked one of my hands free and stroked her hair softly, ever so softly, as her breaths deepened and grew farther apart. Morning's dismal light advanced slowly around the walls. Morning was breaking, the lion was waiting. I heard tree limbs bending in the breeze, the leaves brushing back and forth in the canopy. Rain tapped against the shingled roof.

I forced myself to get up. I went into Alisha's master bath and took a shower. For ten minutes, I stood with my face turned into a scalding hot spray. I got out and wrapped a towel around myself.

Back in the bedroom, I took hold of Alisha's shoulder and gently shook her. "Hey. You'd better get up. I'm going downstairs to make some coffee."

"Mmm," she murmured, rolling onto her back and stretching. "What time is it?"

"Quarter after six. What time do the movers get here?"

"Around nine, give or take. Bring me up a cup, will you?"

I went down to the kitchen to put the coffee on. On the way back to my room, I ducked into Corey's room to check on him. He slept soundly, with one thumb in his mouth. I decided to let him sleep for another hour.

I returned to my room and put on some fresh clothes—jean shorts and an aqua-blue Polo shirt. In the downstairs bath, I shaved and brushed my teeth. I heard the shower running upstairs.

In the kitchen, I poured myself a cup of coffee and sat down at the table. After ten minutes or so, I poured Alisha a cup and took it upstairs for her. She was out of the shower by then. She sat at her vanity in her master bath, wearing a white robe and running a hairbrush through her long, silvery hair. I've always been amazed at the length of time women spend brushing their hair. They can sit there for hours, it seems, brushing away.

Anyway, I set the mug on the vanity in front of her. "Oh, thanks, Simon." She raised the mug to her lips. "Mmm, that's perfect—just the way I like it." She put the mug down and resumed brushing. "You know, you're the only guy who's ever brought coffee up to me in the morning on a consistent basis."

I leaned against her bathroom sink with my hands in my pockets. She was watching me through her vanity mirror. I said, "You're the only woman I've met who knows how to tie a tie."

She laughed. "Is Corey up?"

"No. I didn't see the harm in letting him sleep a little while longer."

We were quiet for a while. The only sound in the room was Alisha's brush sliding through her hair. Morning rain danced across the bathroom skylight.

I crossed my arms over my chest. "I wanted to ask you something."

Her eyes met mine in the mirror, though only briefly. She continued to run the brush through her hair.

"Last August, I gave you a list of names and phone numbers as references. There were five names on the list, as I recall. Did you call any of them?"

Still brushing. "That's an odd question to ask at this juncture."

"Well? Did you?"

Her eyes did not meet mine in the mirror. She continued her brushing. "I called three of the five, but I can't remember which ones."

"Well, that's funny," I said, "because I called all of those people over the Christmas holiday, to wish them a Merry Christmas and all. And not one of them remembered getting a call from you."

She switched the brush to her other hand. A slight smile may have tweaked the corners of her lips, but if so, it was gone just as quickly. "You'll make a great attorney, Simon."

"I want to know why."

"It's a good thing I wasn't under oath. You wouldn't send a woman to jail, Simon, would you?"

"Alisha, I'm serious. You didn't know a thing about me when you first met me. I very easily could've been someone with a questionable background."

"I'm good at judging people. I did say that, didn't I?"

"Bullshit, Alisha. The next caregiver you give a passing grade to could be an Internet sex predator. All I'm asking is that you be a little less cavalier about the next person you hire. For Corey's sake, will you please do a background check?"

She said nothing. The brush continued to move through her hair.

"Promise me, Alisha."

Finally she set the brush on the vanity in front of her. I noticed that somehow her expression had changed—her face wore an intent, serious look. "I would never compromise Corey's safety."

"You did by hiring me, without knowing a thing about me. You got lucky."

"I knew you were a genuine person the first time I met you." Her eyes had fallen in the mirror. She appeared to be staring at the vanity top.

"I was down and out the first time you met me. I didn't have a job, I didn't have a car, I was practically homeless …"

"You were so brave …"

"The hell I was. I walked into the café 'cause I was exhausted and hungry."

"Your mother was so scared …"

"What? My mother—"

But I stopped. And froze.

"I remember … I remember her eyes, the look in her eyes. The way they darted back and forth. She didn't know where she was. She didn't know any of us. She wanted to run. And she tried to run, but you wouldn't let her. You held onto her. You held onto her, and you were every bit as frightened as she was."

I tried to say something. Nothing came out. My lower jaw hung open.

Alisha's eyes rose up to meet mine in the mirror. "I've never seen bravery of such magnitude, Simon. I've never seen someone on the cusp of losing everything stand so tall and unwavering in the face of total uncertainty. The way you held on to her arm that night … you had nothing but love to stand on."

I felt myself sliding down against the edge of the bathroom sink. I had to prop both arms against it to steady myself. My heart banged so loudly against the inside of my chest I thought it would break through.

She turned on her stool to look me straight in the eye. "That event changed me in some small measure. I don't know how, it … it altered the way I viewed the world. It made me want to help in some way."

"You … It was *you* who left the bag …"

"I wasn't attending those meetings for me. I was … with someone. A friend. I went with him for support. We followed you home that first night. It was my idea, I told him to follow you. His car … it was an older model … a Jetta, I think. It had a broken fuse, so the low beams wouldn't work. We followed you all the way home with our high beams on."

I remembered waking up in the middle of the night several

weeks later, seeing the red taillights hovering in space near the end of our driveway. It would have been Alisha in her own car then, acting on her own. I remembered Ma stepping out onto the side porch the next morning, then staggering back in with her hand over her heart. *There's something on our porch, Simon.*

I was aware of a burning sensation in my eyes. My eyes were hot, and they burned, and then my vision swam out of focus. I felt tears tracking down my cheeks.

"I … it … you were … it was you who …"

I stood with all I had … and by itself it wasn't enough.

"I had to help, Simon, I had to do something." A single tear slid free from one eye and curled easily around the side of her nose and over her lip. "And then … when you walked into Molly's last August, I recognized you immediately, and that's how I knew you were a good person, and I … I'm … I'm sorry I didn't tell you who I was … I didn't want you to think—"

I went to her. I grabbed her by the arms and lifted her off the stool while she was in mid-sentence and pressed my lips against hers. She stiffened at first, but quickly relented, kissing me hard and thrusting her tongue into my mouth. *The world cannot be so small,* I thought. *And yet …* I pulled loose the white sash holding her robe together, then moved my hands to her neck to push the robe off of her shoulders. She let her arms down, allowing the robe to fall. *And yet …* And her bare body stood before me, and her eyes searched me, and her silverish hair lay damp across one shoulder. I pulled her toward me. We kissed again, and then I took her hand and led her into the bedroom.

And yet, it is. The world is indeed small enough, and the world still has miracles in it.

I pushed her softly onto the bed and stripped out of my clothes. Then I took her into my arms. Outside the house, wind battered the treetops. Rain lashed against the roof. Alisha beckoned me into her, and we made love. Our rhythm was perfect. Her curves met mine like pieces of a sensual puzzle, and at one point, I felt her heartbeat through my own chest. We stared at one another with our chins touching, her eyes moist and true. She whispered, "Promise me you'll be strong today, Simon. Promise me."

"I'll be strong," I said. "I promise."

"There's one more thing that troubles me," I said. Alisha and I were standing in the kitchen. Corey was in the bathroom brushing his teeth. My truck was loaded up. The Land Rover was loaded up. The movers would be here any minute.

Alisha tilted her head from one side to the other. She wore faded jeans and a light blue J. Crew V-neck shirt. She had applied minimal make-up on this rainy morning, and I thought she'd never looked more beautiful.

"You told me you attended those AA meetings to support a friend. Right?"

She nodded but didn't volunteer any more information.

"It wasn't David Kaplan, obviously. Not the way he was forcing those Northport Nailers down our throats the one night. And I can't picture David driving an old Jetta with broken headlights."

She shook her head miserably, scrunching her eyes shut. "I'm not sure I can take much more of your inquisition, Simon."

"It's not an inquisition. It's a search for the truth."

"I don't see how it pertains—"

"It does," I said. "Who was he? Who were you with at those meetings, Alisha?"

She was quiet for a long interlude. We both heard Corey tapping his toothbrush against the rim of the sink. Finally she answered, "His name was Jack. Jack Rappaport. He was a liquor store salesman, single, never married. Hooked on his own product. I tried to help him."

"How close did the two of you get?"

"We were friends."

"How close did you get?"

"That's personal information, Simon, and it has nothing to do with—"

"Because it occurs to me that this all took place a little more than six years ago. Shortly before Corey was born."

Her eyes burned into me, but not with anger. Her lips appeared tremulous. "Simon, please don't insinuate—"

"How close did you and Jack get?"

"It was a periodic friendship. We'd known each other for almost a year."

"So you spent time with him during the same time frame in which you were seeing David. Correct?"

"Yes, I suppose."

"Okay, then answer the question. How close did you and Jack get?"

One of her cheeks was ticcing. Her lips were trembling. "Why can't you let it go, Simon? Why do you have to put me through this?"

"How close?"

She lowered her head as though to look at the floor. "We were close on several occasions. But it wasn't as if—"

"He's the father. Jack Rappaport is Corey's biological father."

"Simon, that's preposterous."

"It's true."

"It's conjecture, that's what it is. You have no basis—"

"Did either David or Jack submit to a paternity test?"

"Of course not—"

"Then you don't know, do you?"

"I'm Corey's *mother*, Simon, I know in my heart. Can't you accept that as an answer? Besides, how would you know otherwise?"

"He's the man in black …"

"What?"

My gaze ran around the room, transfixed and captured. I said, "Jack Rappaport is the man in black. The man in Corey's dreams. The figure he's been chasing ever since the two of you got here."

"Oh, Simon … come on, now. How could Corey possibly know—"

"He doesn't know," I said. "Not in his conscious self. But the unconscious is practically another person, Alisha—a person who lives beneath us. And that person knows a great many things that we ourselves do not."

The mystery was finally solved. Alisha hadn't truly known who Corey's actual father was … so she had *chosen* the father. She had chosen the man more befitting of her aristocratic tastes, and to whom she saw better fit for her son to exemplify. I saw the collage of Alisha Caldwell's adult life spread before me. Never before had it been clearer. Here was a remarkable, overachieving woman who had accomplished everything—a true cosmopolitan who fancied herself too good for most men, but who'd waited too long for the *perfect* man. The Alan Mercers of the world had stood her up, and the David Kaplans were already taken. Inexplicably, she'd wound up on a station's platform whose train had already passed or flat-out wasn't coming. I saw her as a woman unable to reconcile the fact that her one and only child had been fathered by a liquor store salesman who drove an old Jetta—and not the bond trader with the Wall Street income who drove a BMW and traveled in elite circles. She had somehow made it a habit of falling in love with men she couldn't have, and wanting to fall in love with men who wouldn't have her.

Corey emerged from the hall and entered the kitchen. He looked up at his mother, who appeared to be holding her face in one hand.

"Hi, Mom. Are you okay?"

She ran her hand through his damp hair. A cowlick stuck up on the back of his head. "I'm fine, big guy." Her voice was unsteady. "Are you ready to go?"

He nodded. From outside came the sound of a vehicle stammering down the driveway. The movers had arrived.

"Go get in the Land Rover, then," she said.

As Corey left the kitchen, I said, "Look, Alisha ... I'm sorry if I upset you. Hey, it's just a theory, okay?"

But we both knew my theory was correct. As if to emphasize this point, she said, "Again, you'll make a great attorney, Simon. Are you ready to go?"

"Yes."

"The day has hardly begun, and yet it seems hours and hours old. I'm already exhausted."

CHAPTER THIRTY

THE WEIGHT OF WATER

THE RAIN ABATED SOMEWHAT as we drove south, but the sky remained gray and swollen. Battalions of dark, portentous clouds lined the firmaments as far as the eye could see, pushed by a stiff northeast wind. Temperatures were in the low seventies, but the wind made it feel colder.

The parking areas in the Barrow Hill State Park were as filled as I'd ever seen them. There were vehicles parked on the grass, and others double-parked along both sides of the driveway—and people everywhere. Kids along with siblings, parents, and even grandparents were streaming en masse down to the park area, toward the pavilions.

We parked side by side in one of the upper adjunct lots, and got out to join the downstream flow. Corey held his mother's hand, looking around anxiously for fellow classmates. A gust of wind whipped his hair up and about. The sky spat raindrops for ten or twelve seconds, and then stopped. Alisha stared down at the pavement as we walked.

I said, "I had no idea there'd be this many people here."

"You and me both," Alisha joined.

"We won't all fit beneath the largest of the pavilions if it begins pouring."

"Maybe they'll call it off."

We entered the lower lot, however, and my heart sank when

I saw the immense blue tarp that had been erected on the grassy knoll overlooking the pond. A large group of people had gathered beneath it, and the rest of the crowd appeared to be heading in that direction.

"We'll at least be sheltered if the skies open up," Alisha pointed out.

No. That thing isn't safe. The tarp is going to rip.

We passed through the lower lot and stepped onto the wet grass, heading for the blue tent. The tarp itself was gigantic—sixty feet long and probably thirty feet wide. It was all suspended by aluminum poles. Three long poles held up the center of the tent from beneath, giving it its height. These three center poles were probably sixteen-footers. The rest of the poles were eight-footers, studded around the perimeter, including the four corners.

Alisha and Corey passed beneath the tarp's edge without a moment's thought. But I hesitated, remaining outside the tarp's boundaries.

"You two go on," I said. "I'll be with you in a minute."

"Simon, it looks like they're ready to start."

"I just want to check something. Go on, I'll be there in a second."

They moved in to join the formation now assembling beneath the tent's midsection. I took several minutes to walk around the outside of the tent's perimeter, passing on the outside of the anchor stakes to ensure that I didn't trip over any of the anchoring ropes. I circumnavigated the entire setup, searching for flaws or abscesses where rainwater could potentially collect, but I didn't find any. The tarp was taut and perfectly stretched. Everything appeared copacetic. I focused my eyes on the tips of the center poles where they protruded through the tarp's centerline, remembering the odd bird emblem I'd seen in Crawford's painting. *It reminded you of a lightning rod, remember?*

I saw no emblems at the tops of the three poles. I detected no low spots in the tarp's diagonal slope. Heck, it wasn't even raining, save for a slight drizzle. For once, Crawford had been wrong.

"Psst! Simon! Come on, will you?"

Alisha was holding her arm out from within the throng of adults.

I went in and joined her. We stood hip to hip. "Are you auditioning for OSHA?" she whispered.

"Something like that."

Around us, the crowd jostled anxiously. All the kids—the *graduates*—were sitting near the front of the tent in small, metal folding chairs. The venerable Mrs. Hayes was quieting them, and perhaps coaching them on what was about to happen and what they were meant to do. A small pulpit stood at the very front of the tent, and behind the pulpit stood Mrs. Thomas, who appeared to be readying herself for an inspiring speech. She smiled from ear to ear as she began, "Welcome parents, welcome graduates, welcome all. I am so pleased that all of you could make it. Weather notwithstanding, this is a bright and momentous day indeed for our young graduates as they sprout their first wings in preparation of advancing to the first grade. For an entire year, they have labored. They have learned, they have played, they have laughed, and they've all endured ..."

Blah-blah-blah. And their parents have paid a steep tuition, lady—that's really why we're here. The hotdogs better be Ball Park. My eyes wandered to the left of the pulpit, and there was the table with all the trophies on it. My heart dipped a second time when I saw what the trophies really were: birds. Each trophy was a bronze replica of a bird standing upright with its wings spread. I guess they were supposed to symbolize kindergartners flying up to first grade or something, where they would later get beaten up by third-graders. The bird trophies weren't exactly what I had seen in Crawford's painting, but they were pretty damned close. Thirty-one such trophies stood on the corner table, waiting to be distributed.

Mrs. Thomas was introducing today's guest speaker. I hadn't caught the speaker's name, but she was apparently a local figure—some sort of feminist-artist type. She prattled on for twenty minutes. I glanced around and noticed some of the older socialites holding their chins high and nodding with faux appreciation. The wind kicked, the tarp rattled and snapped. A heavy rain fell for ten minutes before slackening. I turned, searching the crowd behind me and to my left. Vivian smiled at me. Standing next to her was Karl Spencer. They were holding hands. Karl saw me looking and winked. I faced forward again.

Finally, the crowd was applauding, and the guest speaker was leaving the pulpit. Mrs. Thomas began reading the names of the graduates. They came up, one by one, to accept their trophies from Mrs. Hayes. Cameras clicked, flashbulbs flickered. When Corey's name was called, he jumped out of his chair and practically ran up to the trophy table, his smile carving his face in half. He held his trophy up in both hands, trying to locate his mother's face in the crowd. He found Alisha's face, and mine as well. "Way to go, kid!" I yelled. Alisha snapped a quick succession of photos as Corey returned to his seat.

Alisha turned and gave me an endearing look. *Gosh, look at him, will you? Our boy is getting older.*

I smiled, squeezing her hand.

More names were read, more trophies were handed out. Tommy Spencer was the last to have his name called. "Atta boy, Tommy! Atta boy!" came Karl's cries from several feet behind me.

"I would like to thank all of you for coming," Mrs. Thomas said. "As for the Kindergarten Class of 2006, congratulations! You are now first-graders!"

The crowd erupted into applause. Mothers and fathers cheered. Siblings whistled.

"Good luck, first-graders! Go boldly, go bravely!"

"And if you can't do either of those, then just go," I said. Alisha elbowed me in the ribs.

"… hotdogs and hamburgers in the west pavilion … sodas … refreshments … please help yourselves!"

The crowd disbanded. There was a great deal of confusion as children sought to reunite with parents. Some of the children remained near the front of the tent, talking to each other. Many parents were already lining up to voice their thanks and good-byes to Mrs. Thomas and Mrs. Hayes. I followed Alisha through the bustling crowd. We emerged into the open air again, and into a breezy drizzle. Corey came around the outside of the tent and ran up to us.

"Mom! Mom! Can we stay for hotdogs?"

"Yes, but not for too long. We have a long drive ahead of us. You're gonna need to say good-bye to your friends."

As we struck out for the west pavilion, I turned back several times, searching for imperfections in the blue tarp. Still, I could find none. It wouldn't matter if the tarp ripped now anyway—most of the crowd had filed out.

"Simon, what are you looking for? Why do you keep looking at the tent?"

"Nothing," I said. "Just a funny feeling." *A feeling that something has gone wrong, that we missed something.*

I faced forward again, looking down at the wet grass. I felt Alisha's eyes on the side of my face, but I didn't return her stare.

We made our way to the west pavilion, where enough food had been laid out to sustain an army. There were burgers and dogs, chips and pickles, potato salad, macaroni salad, soda, juice, coffee and tea. I helped myself to a hotdog and a pickle, though truthfully I had never felt less hungry in my life. I watched Alisha as she dabbed a spoonful of potato salad and several Doritos onto her paper plate. We mingled with some of the other parents as Corey went around saying good-bye to his classmates. Alisha and I eventually got separated, and I found myself conversing with some of the parents I'd met at the father-son breakfast. I answered their questions with simple nods or shakes of the head, in some cases not fully knowing what I was responding to. A paralyzing numbness seemed to be enervating my body from limb to limb. I dropped the paper plate with the half-eaten hotdog on it into the trash and set out to find Corey.

I found him on the far side of the pavilion, talking with two of his friends. I went up to him and put my arm around him. "Come with me a minute. I want to show you something."

We moved away from the crowd, toward a copse of pine trees forty yards away. He came willingly, holding onto his trophy. "What do you want to show me, Simon?"

"Do you remember the time I showed you the spit bug? The little green bug on the blade of grass?"

He nodded.

We entered the copse of pine trees. I knelt down and picked up a pinecone. "Did I ever tell you what's inside one of these?"

"More spit bugs?"

"No, silly. The pinecone is actually a husk, which holds the seeds for a new tree. But the husk is extremely tough. It's so tough that it only opens under one condition—fire. The intense heat from a forest fire causes the husk to open, and then the seeds fall out so new trees can grow. So you see, when the temperature around it is at its greatest, the pinecone is at its best. Can you remember that?"

Nodding. "I wish you could come with us, Simon."

"Me too. More than you know, kid. Okay, give me a hug."

He threw his arms around me and embraced me. I squeezed him tightly, patting him on the back with one hand. "You take care of your mom, okay?"

I looked up to see Alisha walking toward us from the pavilion. The wind caught her silverish hair and blew it sideways in a fantail. A wave of fat raindrops fell over us, followed by no rain, followed by more drizzle.

The three of us started up the hill. I said to Corey, "Run ahead so I can talk to your mom." He went sprinting along with his trophy.

"What were you telling him back there?"

"I told him to take care of his old lady."

She laughed. "I'm glad I got to know you, Simon. You're a very special person."

"You think you'll miss this place?"

"I think I'm going to miss a lot of things. How about you? What will you miss?"

"Our walks. Corey's innocence. The smell of your shampoo."

She took my hand in hers, squeezing my fingers. She didn't seem to care if anyone noticed or not. We were halfway up the hill now, getting closer to the upper lot. It seemed there was so much to say but no way to say it. I felt a heaviness in my chest spreading outward, slowly working its way around my torso. Our vehicles came within sight, and as we drew nearer, I found myself reaching inward and downward for those final words that would summarize and paraphrase all things as we knew them—and I realized I didn't have them.

Corey was waiting for us on the passenger side of the Land Rover. "Get in the car, Corey, and put your seatbelt on," Alisha told him. "I'll be right there."

He did as told. Alisha and I walked around the back of the Land Rover to the driver's side, adjacent to which my truck was parked. We stood facing each other for several moments.

"Look, Alisha ... I want to pay you back. For what you did for us six years ago."

She shook her head.

"With interest, preferably—"

"You already have, Simon." Her voice cracked as she said it. "You changed me. You *changed* me, Simon, don't you see? You fixed me. I don't know what was wrong, exactly, but you fixed it." She reached up with one hand and caressed the side of my face. "And for that, I will always remain in your debt."

I reached up and took hold of her hand, keeping it pressed to my cheek. I felt the weight of water growing inside me. When I blinked, tears brimmed over the lower rims of my eyes.

"I'm afraid …" I started to say.

"I have your address, and we'll write to you once we're settled. I promise."

"I'm afraid that I …"

"Don't be afraid, Simon." *Be strong. Promise me you'll be strong.*

"I'm afraid that I might not see you again."

"You will," she whispered. She looked down at the pavement, then up at me again. "And who knows? Our lives have crossed paths twice. Who's to say they won't cross again?"

She pulled me closer and kissed me quickly on the lips, and then pulled me into a tight hug. I felt her lips move against my ear as she whispered, "I felt your heartbeat against me this morning, and I know that it's strong."

We pulled apart. "I'll be in touch," she said. She opened her driver's door and climbed in. She pulled the door shut and started the engine. I stood back as the Land Rover backed out of its space, then nosed slowly out of the lower end of the adjunct lot. The two of them waved as they passed by on the main drive, Corey bent over his mother's lap and waving both arms. The last I saw of him was his smiling face and his bright blue eyes as the Land Rover sped past with a double honk of the horn and the back tires kicking out sprays of water. It climbed the hill and disappeared over its crest.

I stood in the newly vacated parking space, looking down at the wet pavement with my hands on my hips, allowing several minutes to pass by. Allowing the Land Rover to get far enough ahead of me before I set off. The wind gusted, bringing a squall of rain with it as people ran for their vehicles. It felt strange to be standing here by myself, alone in this alien place.

I went around the front of my Tacoma and climbed in. As I backed out of my space and exited the adjunct lot, I glanced down the hill to my right, where the blue tarp bucked and swayed in the breeze. I faced forward again, pointing the truck toward home.

I crested the hill and drove the remaining quarter mile to where the Park Access Road bisected with Garrison's Hill Road. Left onto Garrison's, and then I was coasting downhill through a tunnel of dripping pines. At the bottom of the hill was County 513. Cars were jetting left and right, raising rooster tails of water behind them. As I swung onto the right-hand dogleg that would put me onto the northbound lane, I caught a glimpse of the Land Rover on the other side of the road, pulled onto the southbound shoulder. Evidently it was Alisha's intent to drive directly and immediately south, whereas my intent was to backtrack through town and then cut east, and later south, returning home the way I had come.

She had come to the end of Garrison's Hill, crossed over 513, and immediately pulled over. As I streaked down the dogleg, I craned my head to the left, squinting through the rain and gloom. It was enough for me to catch a quick glimpse through the Land Rover's side window. I saw a woman's form slumped over the wheel, her hair spilled back over her shoulders. I was on the road then, moving north and putting distance between us. I heard the wipers thumping and the tires rolling … and I took my foot off the gas. My foot hovered over the pedals as the truck began to slow. And I knew that it wasn't too late. It wasn't too late to change things. I knew there was still time …

Promise me you'll be strong today, Simon. Promise me.

I buried the gas pedal. The Tacoma sprang to life. I leaned forward, hunkering over the wheel with my foot pressing the pedal to the floor, going as fast as I could. I felt my insides bubbling over, my eyes growing hot and wet as the tears ran down my face and dripped off my chin. I began to cry in earnest—hard, racking sobs as the abscesses filled in and the weak spots gave way behind the weight of all that water. I was still gaining speed as my sides split open and the life fell out of me. Suddenly I was more alone than I'd ever been before, and there was no one to hold my hand. There was no guiding force to hold me steady as I passed from the brightest light I'd ever known into a darkness more absolute than that which any of my life's previous trials had inflicted upon me.

> *Light comes to darkness,*
> *Darkness comes to light.*
> *Falsehoods fly, the days go by,*
> *But truth will end my plight.*
>
> *Of lies distilled and lives fulfilled,*
> *This bridge is but a token;*
> *As morning breaks, the lion waits*
> *A spirit hath awoken.*
>
> *So from this bridge I'll see your face,*
> *And tho' words are never spoken,*
> *Of this life I leave behind*
>
> *… I know my heart is broken.*

PART III

After the Fall

CHAPTER THIRTY-ONE

SUMMER OF DISCONTENT

ICELANDERS HAVE A SAYING: *Home is where the hearth is warmest.* Our versions aren't much different: *Home is where the heart is; home is a place to hang your hat on.*

To me, home felt like none of those things. It felt like an old place I was groveling back to. In the space of six hours, I'd left the place where I'd been a man and returned to the place where I'd been a boy. Where, in a manner of speaking, I would always remain a boy. In one corner of my old bedroom stood the hockey sticks and Wiffle bats of my youth. Pictures hung from the walls in places they'd occupied for ten years or more. The wallpaper brought to mind past struggles and old desires. Even the floorboards squeaked in the places I remembered them.

I was tired, empty, and depressed. Ma prepared some hearty meals for the two of us, so thrilled was she to have her son back in her house. Truthfully though, I had no appetite. All I wanted to do was sleep. Sleep is what I did. I slept the nights away, then slept straight through the mornings. There was no reason to get up. I had no one to take care of. Around noon, I'd drag myself out of bed and into the shower. I'd spend the rest of the afternoon driving around town or taking walks or staring out the windows at nothing in particular. At four o'clock, I would take a nap. I'd sleep until Ma came up and woke me for dinner.

After three days of this, Ma came into my bedroom one morning around 11:30. I was sitting on the edge of my bed with my hands on my knees. Ma sat down next to me. She glanced up at the ceiling, close to where the old bullet hole had been spackled and painted over, and then she looked at my face. She put her arm around my shoulders. "Simon, I want you to talk to me."

I shook my head. This wasn't exactly something you could talk to your mother about. "There's nothing—"

"Yes," she said, "there is. Don't pass me up for stupid, Simon. I know what you're going through. So let me ask you: do you understand why it is you can feel such pain? Hmm?" She rubbed my shoulder with the hand of her encircling arm. "The answer may surprise you. It's because you can feel love. You cannot feel one without the capacity to feel the other. It's part of what makes you human, Simon. It makes all of us human. The pain will go away in time."

"What if I don't want it to go away?"

"It must, and it will."

I inhaled some sniffles and blinked away some tears. "What am I gonna do, Ma? What am I gonna do?" The tears came anyway. I was crying openly when I turned and met her eyes.

"You're gonna do what I did. You're gonna take it one day at a time. If that doesn't work, you'll take it one hour at a time. A minute at a time, if you have to."

I had little use for clichés at this point. It suddenly seemed my whole life had been a book of clichés. But maybe Ma was right. When you were as deep in the dark as I was, maybe the worst clichés were the best rules to live by.

*   *   *

"You'll need to find a job," Ma said. We were sitting at the dining room table. I'd gotten into the habit of getting up early each morning to have breakfast with Ma before she left for the antique store.

"I don't need a job. I've got more money now than I've ever had."

"I'm not talking about money, dear. I'm talking about *service*. I'm talking about *time*. We all need a reason for getting up in the morning. We all need a sense of purpose to occupy the hours in our days."

"But my purpose ..." *My purpose was taken away from me. My purpose is gone.*

Ma may as well have read my mind. For she shook her head as she reached over the table to put her hand over mine. "You glimpsed your adult life too early, Simon. You reaped the rewards and benefits of years and years of hard work without having done the work. It's time now for you to do the work. And *through* the work will your purpose emerge."

This seemed contradictory to everything I thought I'd believed about my life before I'd gone to Swan Lake. Before Swan Lake, my outlook had been simple. Now my life was a mess. Swan Lake had turned me upside-down and shaken all the loose change and old priorities from my pockets. So, how could Ma lecture me on "purpose emerging through work" when I didn't even know what I wanted the work to be?

"But ..."

"Trust me, Simon. You have to trust me on this."

She got up and came around the table to kiss me on the cheek. "I'll see you for dinner. Love you. The world over."

"The world over," I said.

I went online and enrolled to take the LSATs. Then I began looking for work. Because it was already June of 2006 and I had yet to take the exam, much less begin the law school application process, I was staring at another full year of moratorium before potentially attending classes in the fall of 2007. Never before had I felt so estranged in life, so hopelessly awash in that tidal inlet that separates the undergraduate years from the adult years. I felt like a boat without a rudder, without a mast, without a pilot—truly a ship lost at sea.

I took a job with a roofing contractor. Starting pay was fifteen dollars an hour with nominal benefits. Ernie was the contractor's name. He was a squarish, muscular fellow with a black mustache and a crew cut. He kept a pencil tucked behind his left ear at all times. His cell phone rang no less than eight times an hour. He employed a staff of seven men. Three were legalized Mexicans who spoke practically no English. Two were African-Americans from Newark who stuck together and did their best to avoid contact with the Mexicans. The sixth was a white guy who'd been paroled in April. His name was Jared, though according to him, his friends addressed him as Jaycee. Both biceps were riddled with tattoos, and his nose and lower lip were studded with jewelry. The one aspect all six of these guys had in common was physical strength. Each was well built, showing off thickly muscled shoulders and washboard abs in the sweltering summer heat.

And then there was me. I was the smallest of the lot by a long shot, a literal goat among oxen. My physical stature was the butt of many jokes early on. I made a lot of mistakes in the first three weeks because the work was new to me. The other guys would usually raz me, but tempers would sometimes flare if I committed too many miscues in a short space of time. The Mexican guys had short fuses. They would rant and holler in Spanish when I screwed up badly enough, sharing their hostilities with each other but directing them toward me. I would stare at the three of them with my hands on my sweaty hips, with the summer sun burning into my bare back and threatening to set my skin ablaze. Eventually, Ernie would walk over and calmly explain what I'd done wrong. He'd mutter something in Spanish to the angry trio and then clap his hands once or twice, signaling that we were moving forward with the job.

I grew to like Ernie over time. He was a businessman who knew what had to be done, how to do it well, and how to get the most from his workers. Secretly and silently, I think he grew to like me as well. I showed up on time every day, worked to the best of my abilities, and, despite my early stumbling, I never made the same mistake twice.

As for the work itself, I loathed every minute of it. And I reveled in the loathing. I reveled in the physical abuse my body endured in scraping off old shingles and sheathing in the blistering sun; I learned to drown my sorrows in the rivers of salty sweat that rolled off my arms and shoulders on a daily basis; I channeled my misdirection and occasionally my anger into every roofing nail; I absorbed every verbal barb to come at me before answering with a return serve; as the summer months waxed and waned, I felt myself slowly sweating out my past. I banked the cash, every cent. I attained a new focus, became stronger both physically and mentally. School began to look palatable again. I began to recognize this year as that in which I worked with my hands. The previous year, I had worked with my heart.

*　　*　　*

I started going to church with Ma. She attended a Baptist church in Parsippany. After the service, we'd go out to lunch. After lunch, we'd cruise through the countryside for an hour or so. We talked about Dad a lot. Occasionally, we talked about Catherine, about where she might be, but Ma was too easily upset by this subject. To Ma, the mention of Catherine's name on a Sunday was one step below blasphemy. Mostly we made small talk.

To her credit, Ma never asked about Swan Lake.

I utilized the remainder of Sunday afternoons studying for my LSATs. I studied hard, bent low over the desk in the back sewing room from two o'clock until six. I ran practice tests and later calculated my scores. My renewed vigor began to pay off. As July melted into August and August phased into September, my simulated scores gradually rose.

Mondays, it was back to work. Back to the rooftops. We spent much of the morning listening to Lon and Chester, the two black guys, blither back and forth to one another about the women they'd boned over the weekend. It had become a Monday ritual, you might say.

At one point, Chester turned to me and asked, "Yo, whitebread. How many mud pies did you poke this week?"

"None. And you?"

"Three. Isn't that just *fat?*"

"What were their names?" I asked.

Chester gave me a hollow look. "Names? Uhh … shit, I can't remember!" He burst into laughter. He and Lon high-fived, low-fived, and then knocked elbows. It was sort of their secret handshake.

Later in the week, I found myself having lunch next to Jaycee. We were sitting on a flat portion of the roof with our legs dangling off. On a whim, I asked, "Hey, Jaycee, what did you get busted for?"

"I stole."

"Stole what?"

"Money."

"Who'd you steal from?"

"A gas station."

"What made you choose a gas station?"

"I knew where the money was kept. Cuz I worked there. You know how a lot of gas stations and deli's have these signs that say, 'No safe on premises'?"

"Yeah."

"Well, it ain't always true. The station where I worked, we kept a cash box under the floor mat in the booth. There was a secret compartment in the floor."

I thought for a while, then asked, "Jaycee, why did you do it?"

"Do what?"

"Why did you commit the crime?"

"I needed the cash."

"And you stole from a gas station at which you were an employee?"

"Yeah."

"And it never occurred to you that you'd be among the first suspects police would think to question?"

"Naw."

*   *   *

I took the LSATs on the first Saturday in October, at a local community college. I thought they went well. That is, I felt in command throughout most of the exam process. I had practiced the different portions of the test so many times that nothing seemed new to me. However, it was an exhausting day all around. I drove home in a kind of mental fog. When I walked into the house, I thought I'd never been readier for—or more deserving of—a long afternoon nap.

Ma was sitting in the living room, reading a book. "How'd it go?"

"Okay, I think. But, holy cow, it took everything out of me."

"A letter came for you today. I left it on the table."

"A letter from wh—"

But I stopped when I saw the red envelope resting on the corner of the dining room table. I immediately recognized Alisha's thin, slanted writing. My heart sped up in my chest. I picked up the envelope and passed the pads of my fingers over its rough, almost sandpapery surface.

The return address in the upper left corner read simply: Caldwell – P.O. Box 397 – 7 Springs, SC 93597. I saw my name, Mr. Simon Kozlowski, written above my address.

Mister. Alisha had addressed me as *mister.*

I took the envelope up to my room. I sat on my bed, where I opened it and unfolded the enclosed note.

> *Dearest Simon,*
>
> *It's been four months since we parted company on that rainy, windy day in New Hampshire. It may interest you to know that Corey and I did not, in fact, drive straight through to South Carolina that day. What a fool I was to think I could pull that off. I was barely able to get down the first hill to the county road because I was crying so hard. We must have sat there for ten minutes, honest to God. I actually entertained thoughts of turning the car around and going after you—I knew you'd be heading north initially. I'm glad you were strong that day, Simon. Thank you for being so strong.*
>
> *I trust you've had time to heal. Those wounds may never close completely, but they do grow smaller over time.*
>
> *So, how are you doing otherwise? Are you working? Have you taken your LSATs yet? How is your mom doing? How's Josef's truck holding up? Everything is pretty much on hold for me. I've put off editing the new manuscript, as well as finding new work. Right now I'm focusing all of my efforts into being a mother. You've helped me in this regard, Simon. You've helped me become the best mother I possibly could be. Some mornings I wake up, and I think to myself that I love Corey so much it actually hurts. Thank you for saving his life, and*

*thank you for saving mine. You've saved mine in
more ways than one. Corey is doing okay, but he's
had a lot of transitional difficulties. He misses his
friends, he misses the old ways, and of course he
misses you. He talks about you all the time. He's
always asking when you're coming down to take
him fishing. Anyway, the school system we're in
is not what it should be. There are no reputable
private schools within driving distance, so Corey
is in the public school system for now. He doesn't
like the first grade half as much as he did the
kindergarten in the Ace of Spades. I keep telling him
to keep his head up.*

*Well, I've got to get started on dinner. Corey
gets off the bus at 3:45. Simon … are you okay? I
hope that you are. I know that you are. You're a
strong person with a solid core, and you're special in
so many ways. I hope you are continuing along your
career path, as we discussed over Fire Creek the one
day. I cannot stress the importance of this enough.
You know what you have to do, so go out and do it.*

*Be strong, and be well, and always keep your
courage. I have several photos for you, which I'll
send along at a later date. In the meantime, may
your heart continue to beat strongly. You are a
unique person, Simon, and I meant what I said
when I told you that I'll always be in your debt.
I'll be in your debt until the day I die. And until
that day comes, you will always have a place in my
heart.*

Yours,

Alisha

I finished reading the note, and when I'd wiped the wet glaze from my eyes, I read it a second time. I noticed several places where the ink had blotted, creating these dark, asterisk-like marks. It occurred to me that Alisha had wept as she'd written the letter, and—perhaps unbeknownst to her—several of her tears had hit the stationery.

*   *   *

I took several days to digest Alisha's letter before writing a reply. At the end of the reply, I scribbled my phone number, along with this: *It would be nice to hear your voice. Call me.* I stuffed the letter into an envelope and mailed it off.

On Friday of that week, I announced to Ernie that I would be getting out of the roofing business in two weeks' time. He smiled slyly, saying, "Well, I have to say, you lasted longer than I thought."

I signed on part-time with an independent plumber, a guy named Steve. For the first two weeks, I did nothing but carry tools and copper tubing to and from the truck. Steve did the actual work, and I watched. By the third week, I was applying plumber's putty to the places that needed it, as well as turning a wrench here and there. After four weeks, I was sweating pipes and replacing elbow fittings on my own. Six weeks, and I was replacing hot water heaters. Steve stood back with his arms crossed, critiquing my movements. "Okay, good," he would say. Or, "Excellent." Or, "Not so much torque this time. You want the fitting to be snug, nothing more."

I signed up for real estate school. I can't say why, exactly, other than the fact that it seemed like the right thing to do. Classes were held in the evenings, three nights a week for five weeks. I was easily the youngest in attendance. When asked by the instructor why I'd signed up, my reply went something like, "Well … I'm here to learn the language, I guess."

I also began investing. Alisha had taught me how to pay quarterly taxes on self-employed income, i.e. the money I'd made working for her. After taxes and the purchase of Josef's truck, I had about forty grand lying fallow in a bank savings account. I helped Ma with the mortgage and utilities each month—four or five hundred dollars, say—but that came out of my current income. It occurred to me that my forty-thousand-dollar nest egg wasn't doing much for me.

I tried to remember some of the lessons Alisha had taught me. *Avoid penny stocks, Simon. They're dangerous.* Or: *Calculated risk is okay, but never, never put too many eggs into one basket.* Or:

Remember to offset your risk with conservative funds. Or: *Diversify, Simon.*

These maxims didn't help me a whole lot when it came to starting out. I didn't really know what to invest in. So I invested in everything. I opened a money market fund, where the interest rate was higher, and parked the forty large there. Then I slowly began allocating small bits of capital into different areas. I bought some mutual funds, some stocks, and some bonds. I read books on investing, on capital appreciation, and I attended seminars on weekends. I absorbed knowledge like a sponge sucks up water.

The gargantuan task of applying to law schools stood before me. I made phone calls requesting literature on various programs in the tri-state area. After several weeks' time, I'd narrowed my top choices down to the following four schools: Rutgers, Seton Hall, Fordham, and my alma mater, William & Mary. I notified administrators of my intent to apply. "We'll need your undergraduate transcript as well as your exam scores," the lady from Rutgers informed me. "The sooner, the better."

My LSAT scores came in the mail on December 2nd. I'd scored a 159. This was slightly higher than most of my simulated scores, so I figured I was off to a good start. I spent the better part of December filling out the actual applications and getting them out in the mail. Then the waiting game began.

I didn't hear from Alisha again until the 23rd of December. I opened the cream-colored envelope and withdrew her Christmas card. Inside the card were four color photos. My breath caught in my throat when I saw the one on top. It was a picture of Corey and me. Corey's face and arms were covered with green stickers. He was grinning from ear to ear. I was kneeling down beside him, my chin level with his shoulders. I was flabbergasted seeing the smile on my own face. It was like looking at a different Simon, a Simon from a different life.

The second photo showed Corey hoisting his trophy on graduation day. His smile and bright beaming eyes all but illuminated the dark underbelly of the blue tent.

The third photo was at first a mystery to me. I was in it, as was Corey, but neither of us was looking toward the lens. I was squatting down with my back to the camera, while Corey stood next to me.

It appeared I was handing him something. Then I noticed several surrounding evergreen boughs, and realized it must have been the moment I'd told him about the pinecone. *When the heat around it is at its greatest, the pinecone is at its best.* Alisha had seen us from a distance, evidently, and taken a picture.

The fourth and final photo was a recent Christmas picture. Here were Corey and Alisha together, smiling for the camera. Their heads were touching cheek to cheek, temple to temple, with Alisha's arm wrapped around Corey's neck. I must have stared at that photo for a full ten minutes, studying every minute detail—Corey's brilliant row of white teeth and large round eyes, a blonde whip of hair tracing across his forehead; Alisha's quicksilver eyes, her head tilted slightly to touch her son's. Her cheeks bore a vague tinge of pink, and her lips were full and glossy. I traced my finger down the perfect crest of her nose, to the shallow impression just above her upper lip. This was my first glimpse of the two of them since graduation day, and oh, how I missed them. How tremendously I missed them.

But there was something else at work here, something that nagged me. At first I couldn't decide what it was. And then I knew what it was.

They looked *happy* in this picture. It occurred to me I'd never seen Alisha and Corey in a picture together in which happiness transcribed and transcended every facial nuance, every brow and dimple. Could it be they really *were* happy? Happy without me? Had they moved on, outgrown my absence? *A picture may be worth a thousand words, Simon, but a picture is but a moment in time.*

Then again, didn't I *want* them to be happy? Isn't that what I *wanted*? Surely, it was pure selfishness to wish ill will on someone simply because they'd moved on in life without you. Wasn't it?

I set the photos aside and opened the card. It contained a short note along with some Christmas euphemisms. Corey had written, in large capital letters: Hi Simon! We Miss You! Seeing his writing made me think of him wearing his Peter Cottontail pajamas, with the rabbit hood and long floppy ears. I could practically smell his shampoo and the soft aroma of his skin.

At the bottom of the card, in Alisha's thin slanting script, was a phone number.

*   *   *

Ma and I celebrated a quiet Christmas. We exchanged several small gifts before attending the morning church service. Midway through the sermon, Ma leaned over and whispered, "I believe in the power of prayer now, Simon. I'm going to pray for Catherine."

I smiled and rubbed her shoulder. "I will, too."

We went to Don and Betty Reinhardt's place for dinner that night. We drank hot cocoa in front of a warm, crackling fire and talked of small things while listening to carols on the Bose radio. Ma and I got home around nine. Ma kissed me goodnight and headed up to bed. I pulled out Alisha's Christmas card and sequestered myself in the back sewing room with the cordless phone. My hands were shaking as I dialed the number. As the line began to ring in my ear, a string of thoughts flew through my head in rapid-fire: *The machine will pick up, it always does in such cases; she's already gone to bed, she'll be upset you called so late; she'll have company over, and won't be able to—*

But she answered on the third ring. "Hello?"

"Hello, Alisha."

A hesitation. And then, "Simon."

"How are you?"

"I'm well. And you?"

"I'm okay. I'm not calling too late, I hope."

"No, I'm up. I'm reading a novel and drinking tea. And … well …"

"What?" I asked.

"Well, I had a feeling you might call tonight."

"You did?"

"Yes. You got my card, obviously."

"A couple days ago. Thanks for the photos. I'd forgotten about the green stickers."

"Did you have a nice Christmas, Simon?"

"Ma and I had a quiet and uneventful Christmas, which I interpret as a positive thing these days."

"How's your mom doing?"

"She's never been better. She's working, she's active in the

Program, goes to church every week. She's got her credit card debt shaved in half, almost."

"You're paying her some rent, I hope."

"I help her out as much as I can each month. But the fact remains, we wouldn't still have this house if it weren't for you, Alisha."

"And Corey and I wouldn't be alive if it weren't for you, Simon. The world's a funny place, isn't it?"

"You give me too much credit."

"You don't take enough credit. How're you coming along with your studies, Simon?"

"I don't think I've ever worked harder." I brought her up to date on my exam scores and where I was in the law school application process. I told her about real estate school and some of the investment seminars I'd attended. "Last summer, I worked full-time with a roofer. Now I'm working part-time with a plumber. I've actually got calluses on my hands, Alisha."

She laughed. "Most Americans have calluses on their hands, Simon, and some have blisters. That's how the world is." She paused before adding, "Your father was right, wasn't he? The advice he gave you?"

"Yes, I suppose he was right—but for more than one reason. If not for his advice, I wouldn't have met you and Corey. How is Corey, anyway?"

"He's doing fine. He's made some new friends in school. And he's learning how to read."

"You're still reading him his bedtime stories, I hope."

"Of course. Every now and then, I let him take a line. Before long, Simon, he'll be reading to me."

"Are you writing again, Alisha?"

"I've given that up for a while."

"What about your manuscript from last year? When's it coming out?"

"When I get around to editing it, I suppose. Right now I'm focusing on being a mother. You might say I've got a little catching up to do."

"I think you're a fine mother, Alisha. I can't express how much Corey loves you. You mean the world to him."

"Thank you," she replied, with a barely suppressed sniffle. She took a moment to gather herself, then asked, "Would you like to speak to him? I can wake him, if you'd like."

"No, let him sleep. I'll talk to him another time." Quite suddenly, I asked, "Are you seeing someone, Alisha?"

"No, not right now. Though I've been asked several times. You?"

"No. And I haven't been asked by anyone."

She laughed. "They don't know what they're missing, Simon. Women can be fickle, you know. Especially when they're young."

"So, maybe I need someone older."

"Not twenty years older."

"I would drop everything in a minute if it meant being close to you and Corey. You know I would."

"Yes, I know you would … and I know you *can't*. Remember what we discussed on the bridge over Fire Creek the one day. You do remember, don't you?"

Yes, I did remember. But I didn't necessarily want to remember. Because sometimes doing what was right also meant doing what was hard. And the hard things in life could wear you down.

We made small talk for a while. I had some investment questions for her, to which she provided coherent answers, some of which I jotted down on a piece of scratch paper.

Finally she said to me, "Has it occurred to you what tomorrow is, Simon?"

"Tomorrow? December 26th—" I slapped my hand over my open mouth to stifle a gasp of incoming breath. "Oh, Jesus. It happened the day after Christmas, didn't it?"

I closed my eyes and glimpsed the darkness of complete and utter whiteness. Whiteness around, whiteness above. A ceiling of snow up there. It was like standing in the middle of a centrifuge, with snow whipping past horizontally on all sides. Looking down and seeing my boots, but nothing else. Completely lost and turned around in the storm, all while walking on thin ice—ice that had already been breached where Alisha had plunged through. Trying to locate Corey in that mess and knowing it was impossible. Eventually coming to grips with the possibility of dying myself. However, death was preferable to slouching back to the house empty-handed, and I'd fallen to my knees several times, overcome with shame and grief, knowing full well that Corey was long dead and I wasn't far behind, and—

And then something had happened. Something amazing. Something miraculous. Something I would never be able to explain.

"Simon? Are you okay?"

"I'm fine," I lied. I was beginning to shiver just thinking about it.

"You never told me what happened out there. You never told me how you found him."

"I ..." Closing my eyes and remembering the compass. Some of the crazy things the compass had done. "I ..."

"What, Simon? Tell me."

"I stood with all I had."

"What does that mean, exactly?"

"It means I got lucky."

*   *   *

I was rejected by Fordham. But the next three responses were acceptances. By late March, I had made my decision. I would be attending the Seton Hall School of Law in Newark, New Jersey, as a member of the fall class of 2007. I would be one of sixty-five full-time students chosen from a pool of over three thousand applicants. Tuition was thirty-eight thousand dollars a year (Fordham was closer to sixty) for three years. I decided I would borrow the money rather than tap into my savings. Like most law students, I would finance my education with a combination of subsidized and unsubsidized Federal Stafford Loans.

Ma and I celebrated by going out to dinner. We each had a steak. I paid the bill.

I quit the plumbing job in mid-March, deciding I'd learned all I was going to learn from it. Steve was disappointed but not angry. We shook hands. In early April, I took the H & R Block Tax Preparation Course. I learned how to file a return, instead of paying someone else to do it.

In late April, I began working for a surveyor. It was interesting work, and best of all it was outdoors. Like the other jobs, however, the novelty wore off quickly. And because I was into novelty and all about learning new things, I didn't stick around. I learned the language and moved on.

In the summer of '07, I painted. The man I worked for was named George Walin, Jr. He carried a two-man crew. Actually, it was one man and one woman. The man was a mildly retarded fellow named Benny. The woman was a deaf-mute named Betty. Benny and Betty. Both were in their twenties. George himself was in his fifties, and I learned later that he had a PhD in history and a master's in sociology. I asked him why he was painting houses. He told me he found solace in painting, and that the brush always did what he wanted it to do. Neither Benny nor Betty drove, so George picked them up in his van every morning. Betty—aside from some basic lip-reading skills—was largely incapable of receiving verbal instructions, but George was fluent in signing, and Benny knew some basics from watching George.

When I finally got the nerve to ask George why he'd hired a pair like Benny and Betty in the first place, he told me, "They've withstood time. I've had others come and go, some only lasting a week or even a day. Benny and Betty are like rocks in a river—they're content to simply stay put. And you know something? They never complain, they never talk back, and they both have great eyes with the brush."

I worked for George Walin for the rest of that summer. We were an eclectic quartet—the PhD painter, a law student-to-be, a mildly retarded man, and a deaf-mute woman. We would break for lunch at 12:30 every day. Benny would say grace out loud while the rest of us bowed our heads in reverence. It occurred to me at some point that our mealtime conversations were small miracles unto themselves: George talking while he ate, holding his butter and cheese sandwich in one hand while signing with the other, translating his own speech so that Betty could follow the conversation. When it was Benny's turn to speak, George would sign Benny's words for Betty. If Betty had something to say, she would flash the signs to George, and George would parlay them to Benny and me via the spoken word. If Betty didn't quite understand something, she would tilt her head and squint one eye at George as if to say, *Say that again, I didn't quite catch that.*

We painted everything, from houses to barns to fencerows. We painted interior and exterior. We handled big jobs and small jobs and all jobs between. The one rule to which George adhered was that we always worked together. He would never split the group among jobs. The lone exception to this was that during the long days of June and July, I would sometimes stay a half hour or an hour later if a piece of trim needed doing, or a lone wall, or some edging-in with the brush. I was often the last to leave the jobsite in the evening and the first to arrive the following morning.

Such were the circumstances that found me working at Stella Carver's house one night in late July. Mrs. Carver was an eighty-one-year-old widow who still lived on her own in her home in rural Mendham. I was outside on the ladder at sunset, trying to tie up some loose ends with the window shutters. It wasn't quite dark yet, but the mosquitoes were flying, and I was getting bitten. Mrs. Carver must've heard me slapping bugs, for she appeared on her front porch and said, "That's enough work for one day, Mr. Simon. I can see there's no quit in you. Now get yourself cleaned up, and come inside for a cup of tea."

I had no interest in staying for tea, but neither did I want to sound impolite, so I washed out my brush and went inside. Mrs. Carver had put the kettle on, and she poured tea for both of us.

"Go on, sit yourself down, Mr. Simon. Right there, in that chair."

I sat down at her kitchen table, which was cluttered with mail, newspapers, and clipped coupons. "That's very kind of you, thank you. And you can just call me Simon."

"Well, you are a workaholic, Simon. I trust you have family at home, yes?"

"Just my Ma. And you know what they say: the bird works best when the sun's in the west."

Mrs. Carver laughed. She talked while we drank tea, and before I knew it, I was hearing her life story. She told me about her husband, Danny, who'd passed away nine years ago, and all about her three grown children, who were spread around different parts of the country. "Oh, they call me all the time to ask how I'm doing. They're all wonderful children, but they're so *busy*, what with their work and their own families, and kids, but we see each other on holidays. I'll be heading out to Seattle this Christmas to stay with my oldest,

Dave, and his wife, Wendy, and they have two of the most adorable little girls you've ever seen, oh, they are just the *cutest* things …"

At one point, I tried to make a little room on the kitchen table for my empty mug, and succeeded in knocking over a stack of financial statements. It occurred to me as I was bending over to scoop them up that none had been opened.

" …wouldn't worry too much about that," Mrs. Carver was saying. "They send so much paper through the mail these days, and who has the time to go through it all? Those things have been piling up since Danny passed on, he was always in charge of that kind of stuff, and I never much understood it anyway."

I did my best to arrange the stack of unopened envelopes into a close approximation of how I'd found it. "These are financial statements, Mrs. Carver. You might want to go through some of these."

She waved a dismissive arm. "Whatever's there, my children can have. I certainly don't need it. What with Danny's Social Security check, plus my pension, why, it's more money than I know what to do with. I end up giving half of it away anyway, after my taxes and utilities are paid."

"You're saying you haven't opened one of these statements in—what—almost ten years?"

She smiled merrily. "Sounds about right. Would you like more tea, dear?"

I ignored the request. "Mrs. Carver, I hope your children are listed as beneficiaries of this account. Do you know if they are?"

She went to the sink, where she moved some dishes around. "Danny was in charge of that stuff, like I said. I assume he took care of it."

And Danny may have died sooner than he'd expected, leaving unfinished business behind. A lot of people do.

I fumbled around the table, looking for a knife. "If you don't mind my seeing your statement, Mrs. Carver, I can tell you in about five seconds. I don't mean to be intrusive, but …"

She hesitated a fraction of a moment, turning to look at me, and I feared I'd gone too far. But she flashed her carefree grandmother's smile, and said, "Golly, dear, go ahead. You seem like a smart boy."

As she walked back to her chair and sat down, I opened the

envelope with a bread knife and withdrew the statement. The first thing I noticed was that Mrs. Carver had a lot of money. The second thing I noticed is that no beneficiaries were listed in the account status.

"Mrs. Carver, are you aware you've got three-point-one million dollars of liquid capital in this account?"

She crossed both arms over her chest and laughed. "Golly, that much? Go figure—I'm too old to use it."

"Well, I don't see your kids' names listed as beneficiaries anywhere on this statement. So, let me ask you this: do you have a will?"

A shadow darkened Mrs. Carver's face for the first time that evening. "Truth be told, I don't know. That would have been in Danny's department. And besides, I put my faith in the Lord. It'll all be in God's hands when I'm gone."

I put down the statement. "Actually, Mrs. Carver—no disrespect—but if you don't have a will at the time of your passing, it won't be in God's hands. It'll be in the court's hands."

"But you need a lawyer to get a will, don't you?"

"Typically, yes."

"Well, lawyers are *expensive*, dear."

"Actually, it doesn't cost much to have a will drawn up. In the state of New Jersey, a two-page will costs a hundred dollars—and then five dollars for each additional page. In your case, you may have a four-page will, which will cost a hundred and ten dollars."

"Oh … Well, that's not much at all, is it?"

"You also have to consider your house and property. You have a copious amount of land out back. What is it—ten acres?"

"Give or take."

"You may want to have it surveyed," I told her. "Look, Mrs. Carver, with your home, and your land, and your financial assets contained in this account … you may be looking at a five-million-dollar portfolio."

"You mean I'm rich?"

"And then some. But look, if you truly love your children and grandchildren, then you have to take care of them after you're gone. And that means having a will."

"What happens if I don't have a will?"

"One of your children will have to be named as administrator of your estate. That child will need to go to the Surrogate's Office in the county courthouse. And he will need," (I began counting things off on my fingers), "a copy of your death certificate, a list of all your assets with fair market values ascribed to them, the names and addresses of the other two children, renunciations from those children signed before a notary, and a check for a hundred twenty-five dollars for administration fees. The administrator will sign the application, and then a bond form.

"Next, the administrator will have to take that bond to an insurance company. The insurance company will sign on as a third party. And the administrator will pay a bond premium for a full year, up front ... and this is *without having any access to the estate*. If your estate is worth five million dollars, then the administrator will be bonded for that amount. And he cannot be released from the bond until the court says so. This entire process may take one to two years. And considering none of your children live locally ..."

Mrs. Carver was staring at me with one hand covering her mouth.

"Generally speaking," I continued, "people with estates exceeding two million dollars should really consult a reputable estate attorney for tax planning purposes. The attorney can help you set up trusts to avoid federal and state taxes. This isn't difficult to do, Mrs. Carver, and it can be done in one day. More importantly, it can save your children thousands of dollars in tax consequences, not to mention lots of headache."

Mrs. Carver continued to stare at me. Finally she said, "Honey, what are you doing painting houses?"

"Oh, this is just temporary," I told her. "I'm starting law school in the fall."

"Well, that's nice." She smiled. "Do you like biscotti?"

CHAPTER THIRTY-TWO

SHARON

I HIT LAW SCHOOL feet-first and running. Head down, eyes low to the ground. I was running a fast race these days, faster than most. I rode the train into Newark in the morning, then home again in the afternoon. My four courses for the fall semester were all required: Legal Research & Writing 1, Contracts, Torts 1, and Civil Procedure. I didn't spend a lot of time looking sideways in the classroom, but when I did, I saw others who looked like me. Many were fresh out of college. Some were coming off one- or two-year moratoriums like I was. There were middle-aged adults, as well—professional types in their thirties and forties embarking on career changes. They all had one thing in common: they were sharpies. These weren't day laborers punching time clocks. No longer was I the big intellectual fish in a small pond of muscle and repetition. These were lifers, brainers, people with get-up-and-go. People with *plans*.

No matter. We each run our own race, and none of these people were running in mine. I maintained a forward vision and kept my eyes focused on the finish line. At home, I studied four to five hours a night, breaking only for dinner. Lights went out at nine o'clock. The sooner I got to sleep, the sooner the morning broke. The sooner the morning broke, the sooner I could launch myself into sleep the next night, and so on. This was the race I was running. I ran it alone. I kept my head down, studied hard, and tried not to notice the time. The less I noticed it, the faster it moved.

*   *   *

The girl with the long, black hair sat behind me in every course. In every *class* of every course. In most cases, I was the first student to enter the classroom, so I sat where I wanted. The girl with the black hair would saunter in later, sometimes last … and invariably she'd sit directly behind me. If the seat behind me was taken, she'd sit one or two seats over in the row behind mine. In the several instances in which I glanced over my shoulder, she never once made eye contact with me. She was really into the color black. She wore black lipstick most days with black mascara, and a black leather jacket.

I didn't speak to her until the first week of spring semester. The spring curriculum for first years looks like this: Legal Research & Writing 2, Criminal Law, Constitutional Law, and Property. She sat behind me in every class. She'd come walking in wearing her black jeans and black boots, the heels of her boots *klip-klopping* over the tiled floor. As she passed behind me, I'd hear the *klip-klop* of her footfalls until she fell into the desk behind mine.

One day, I finally turned around and asked her, "Why do you always sit behind me?"

Her blue eyes flitted toward mine. They may have been the coldest eyes I'd ever seen. "Why do you always sit in front of me?"

"I don't. You're not in the room when I sit down."

"Are you sure of that?"

I rolled my eyes and faced front again.

Anyway, her name was Sharon, and she caught up to me on the sidewalk outside the campus later that day. I heard her boots *klip-klipping* at a rapid pace behind me, so I wasn't completely surprised when she called out, "Hey!" I turned and saw her walking toward me. She was taller than I'd thought, almost my height. The boots may have given her another inch, however. She drew even with me and said, "I hope I didn't spook you earlier. I'm not a psycho or anything."

"You didn't spook me at all. I was just wondering—"

"Look, the only reason I sit behind you in class is because I'm superstitious. I like to do the same thing over and over, especially when it brings good results."

"Good results?"

"Well, yes. I aced all my exams."

"You got straight A's last fall?" I asked her.

"Of course. You didn't?"

"I got three A's and a B."

"Ouch. What'd you get the B in?"

I couldn't believe what I was hearing. "Torts."

"Well, look, three A's and a B is pretty good. What's that work out to—a three-eight?"

"Three-seven-five."

She pushed up her jacket sleeve so she could check her watch. "I have to run. I promised my father I'd meet him for dinner. I have an hour commute. Look, I'll see you tomorrow, okay?" With a laugh, she added, "Save my seat." Then she ran off toward the parking garage.

*   *   *

I did my best to stay in touch with Alisha and Corey. There were seasonal letters and holiday phone calls. But the normal course of things was beginning to exact a toll. The phone calls were growing farther apart and the letters were getting shorter. And Alisha was thinking about moving again.

"Back to New England?" I asked.

"No, farther south. Georgia, maybe."

"When would this happen?"

"Over the summer, if I can find a place."

I told her I was thinking about visiting her and Corey this summer.

"Let's wait and see, Simon, okay?"

"Okay."

I ran through spring semester at full tilt. I got three A's and a B again. Summer came, and I went back to work for George Whalin. Benny and Betty were still with him. I found painting a frustrating business for someone trying to accelerate time. The days were long, and the weeks were longer.

Alisha sold her house in South Carolina for a neat profit and moved into a smaller home in the Atlanta suburbs. By the time she and Corey were settled, however, I was back in school. And running faster than ever. I was sprinting to the tune of Alisha's words in my head: *Our lives have crossed paths twice, Simon. Who's to say they won't cross again?*

On the first day of fall semester, I walked into my Appellate Advocacy class and took a seat in the middle of the room. Sharon entered moments later, dressed in black as usual. As she climbed the stairs along the left side of the desk rows, it occurred to me she looked ten pounds lighter. Also, her hair was shorter, and she wore shoes instead of boots.

Instead of opting for her customary seat behind mine, she turned into the row in which I was sitting. She came toward me, closer and closer … and took the seat directly next to mine. There were only three students in the room at that point, and here we were sitting elbow to elbow.

I stared at her. "What, you're breaking tradition?"

She got comfortable, then smiled at me. "It's a new year; you're allowed to start new trends. I've an idea you're pretty good luck, so I've decided to stick close to you."

"But we have all the same classes."

"Yes. Looks like you're stuck with me for a while."

*   *   *

That was the year Sharon and I became friends. Her full name was Sharon Louise Welsh. She was a Jersey girl, but she commuted from farther away than I did. She lived with her father in Somerset County. We began walking to classes together out of habit. We teamed up in the library, helping one another with our research. She became a fixture during our study times, always seated across from me, occasionally tapping me on the foot with the tip of her shoe if she had a question. We went to lunch together a couple days a week, but soon it was every day. Not because we were dating, but because it was the way of things, the path of least resistance, a comfort zone.

She was as superstitious as they come. She never parked her car on the odd side of the street. When we traveled the sidewalks around campus, she never stepped on the cracks between cement slabs. I did my best to counteract this by stepping on every crack I possibly could. When paying for lunch in one of the many diners we frequented, loose change could not be left touching the table's surface. Coins could only be left resting on top of paper money, and all the coins had to face heads-up.

"Christ, where did you come from?" I asked her one day. It was mid-December, and we were having lunch in a Chinese place called The Stellar Dragon. A light snow was falling outside. Sharon was poking at her food with a metal fork—she refused to use chopsticks because she thought they were bad karma.

Instead of answering the question, she asked me, "What area of law do you want to go into?"

"Estate. You've asked me that before."

"I know. For some reason, I keep envisioning you as a defense attorney."

"I've little interest in criminal law. But I can certainly picture you as a prosecutor."

"Oh, yeah?"

"Sure. With all your superstitions and idiosyncrasies, you'd never lose."

"Are you ever going to ask me out, Simon?"

I almost choked on my eggroll. "Excuse me?"

"You heard me. Are you ever going to ask me out?"

I fumbled for words. "W—Well, we go out every day. We're out now."

"You call this a date?" She slid a piece of broccoli into her mouth.

"Well, uh …" I lowered my eyes to the tabletop. "I'm … kind of seeing someone."

She paused before saying, "Look me in the eye and say it."

"What?"

"Look me in the eye and tell me you're seeing someone."

I looked her in the eye and told her I was seeing someone. She was quiet as she chewed her food. Finally she said, "I've never seen her."

"Of course you haven't. She doesn't go to school here."

"You've never mentioned her. You never talk about her."

I dropped my gaze again, not knowing what to say. Only knowing that I had to run faster. *Because she's getting farther away from me. Farther every day.*

"I'm … sorry," I muttered.

Sharon laughed. "Don't be *sorry*, Simon, geez. If you're seeing someone, then you're seeing someone. I'm happy for you." She took a swig of her Diet Coke. "It's just that ... well, I get asked out a lot, and ... lately I've been saying no. I wasn't ... wasn't sure, you know, where you and I stood, but—"

"Shit, I'm sorry—"

"No, it's okay, really—"

"Sharon—"

"I'm just happy that you're honest with me, that's all."

We were quiet for some time. I stifled the awkwardness by stuffing noodles into my mouth. I watched Sharon steadily, but she refused to make further eye contact.

Finally, I said, "Sharon, you're mad."

Laughing, almost. "I am *not* mad, Simon. Get it out of your head."

"You're pissed off, I can tell."

"Well, I'll get over it. I'm a big girl." She began digging in her purse for money.

"Look, I'll pay for today—"

"No, it's my turn. It's bad luck to deviate from the pattern; you should know that." She withdrew exact change, plus five for the tip, and tossed it onto the table. Then she was standing and shuffling into her coat at the same time.

I sighed. "Sharon—"

"We need to get moving, Simon, or we'll be late. Federal Income Taxation starts in ten minutes, and you know how Professor Crosby feels about tardiness."

As she moved away toward the front of the restaurant, I slid out of the booth and stood up. I was reaching for my coat when I saw that the three coins she had put down—two dimes and a quarter—had not landed on the pile of bills like they were supposed to. They lay scattered on the Formica in a sort of evil triangle.

*   *   *

"You're quiet tonight, Simon. Everything all right?"

"Everything's fine, Ma. It's Friday, end of the week. I'm kinda bushed."

"You're pushing your food around your plate more than you're eating it," she noted. "It's not like you not to have an appetite. Is the meatloaf okay?"

I smiled. "The meatloaf is fine, Ma. It's the best."

"When do exams start?"

"Very shortly. I'm gonna hit all four this time, instead of hitting three and leaving one in the sand trap. You watch."

"Don't look now, but I think my son's becoming a perfectionist."

"I prefer to think of myself as a realist."

"Yeah, a real perfectionist." We both laughed.

At that moment, there came a knocking at the side door. Ma and I looked at one another in surprise.

"Who could that be at this hour?" Ma asked.

I got up to see who it was. "Are all the bills paid up?" Ma didn't reply. Bad joke.

I flicked on the outside light and pulled open the solid oak door at the same time. Standing on the porch stoop in the yellowish cone of light was a young woman and a little girl. I studied them through the glass storm door for a moment, deciding they were door-to-door carolers or Salvation Army go-getters, or both. I took a closer look at the woman. I saw lush blonde hair fanning out from beneath a red, wool Christmas cap. I saw full, cream-colored cheeks framing a perfectly formed nose. She was tall and well proportioned, wearing jeans and brown leather boots. As I pushed the storm door slightly open, I started to say, "Can I help—"

But her eyes stopped me, the knowing look in her eyes. I covered my mouth with my hand and muttered, "Oh, my God."

"Hello, Simon," Catherine said. "Merry Christmas."

"Is that …?" Ma had heard the familiar voice, had gotten out of her chair, and was now coming around the table. "Tell me that's not … tell me it isn't …"

Then Ma was standing behind me with both hands shielding her gaping mouth, her eyes wider than teacups. And for the first time in … what, nine years? … mother looked at daughter. And daughter looked back.

"Hi, Mom," Catherine stuttered. Her jaw was shaking badly, and tears started rolling out of her eyes. "I missed you."

"Oh, *Catherine!*" Ma charged past me, shoving the storm door aside and reaching for her daughter. Catherine came forward and threw herself into Ma's embrace. Ma hugged her, squeezing her tightly with both arms and rocking her gently side-to-side, weeping joyously at the same time. "Oh, my Catherine's come back to me! My little girl has come back!" They pulled apart to look at one another more closely. "I knew it," Ma breathed, cupping Catherine's wet cheeks in her hands, "I knew you'd come home someday, and I prayed for it. I've been praying for it ever since you left."

"I've wronged you, Mama. I've come to beg for your forgiveness."

"It is *I* who have wronged *you*, darling, believe me. I'm just so happy to see you. Oh, come inside, please come inside, won't you?"

Ma stepped back, allowing Catherine and the younger girl to enter. Ma turned to me and said, "It's a miracle, Simon, don't you agree?"

I was in full agreement—so much so, I was speechless. I couldn't take my eyes off Catherine, couldn't reconcile the fact that the starved and destitute girl who had staggered off of these premises close to a decade ago had blossomed into this full-throated, beautiful woman.

I looked at the little girl standing at my sister's side. She had hair of spun gold, wavy and alpine and falling past her shoulders. Her eyes were a sharp, piercing green. Her face was lightly spattered with freckles. She held her chin high, exuding the confidence of a child well cared for.

Ma asked, "And who is this precocious young lady I see standing before me?"

"This is Natalie," Catherine said. "Natalie, can you say Merry Christmas to your grandmother? And to your Uncle Simon?"

"Merry Christmas," Natalie said. "It's a pleasure to finally meet you both."

"And Merry Christmas to *you*, sweetheart," Ma crooned, bending over slightly. "And … oh, dear—I get my daughter back, and a granddaughter, to boot! Well, if this isn't cause for celebration, then I don't know what is!"

Catherine and Natalie had come to the door by themselves, so I didn't imagine there was a father anywhere nearby. Not out in the car, and probably not at home, either. And suddenly I was struck by an idea so powerful and heavy, so overwhelming … so terrific and horrific at the same time, that for a moment I couldn't breathe. It felt like I'd been hit in the chest with a medicine ball.

I looked at Natalie again, but much more closely than before. Judging by her height and level of speech, she was at least eight years old. Eight, at the very least. But no older than nine. Catherine had left home nine years ago, and she'd been a very sick girl at the time. *I starved it, Simon. It's not moving anymore.* I gasped, putting my hand over my mouth. It was Natalie she'd been starving. Natalie was the miscarriage.

*   *   *

"Much of what happened after I left home, I can't remember. Only that I wanted to die and that I didn't have the courage to do it myself."

We were seated around the dining room table, the four of us drinking hot chocolate. Natalie sat erect in her chair with both hands clasping her mug, watching and listening. It occurred to me to wonder if she'd heard this story before. She didn't show it, one way or the other.

"I drove around listlessly for a while, without a plan or destination. Somehow I wound up at my friend's apartment in Trenton, although I don't remember driving there. Bella took one look at me and drove me across the river to her mother's house in Newtown."

"Who's Bella?" Ma asked. "I don't remember a Bella."

"Just a friend, Ma. Anyway, when we got to her mother's place in Pennsylvania, they loaded me into her mom's Volvo after some heated discussion, and then we were off again."

"Off to where?" I asked.

"I have little recollection of that car ride. I remember lying on the backseat in a fetal ball with my head on Bella's lap, wanting to die. Praying to die, *willing* myself to die. And Bella's mom driving, just driving, driving into the night, on and on to God knows where. It was raining, and I remember hearing the thump of the wipers, and songs by Johnny Cash on the car stereo …

"Some time later I awoke, and I was no longer in the Volvo. I was lying on a bed, in a strange room. The room was Spartan, old-fashioned, with wood walls and wood floor. The walls smelled of cedar. Other than the bed, there was no furniture save for a night table and one chair. A dimly lit lamp on the night table gave the room its only light. I would have begun screaming at that point had a woman not entered the room. She came with a tray. On the tray was a steaming bowl of soup and some bread. She set the tray on the night table and said, 'Try to eat some of this. It'll make you feel better.'

"I'd never seen her before. She wore a red sweater. She had dark hair and kind, loving eyes. I asked her, 'Where's Bella? And her mom, where are they?'

"The woman answered, 'Your friends have gone home. They left several hours ago.' She laid one of her hands on mine and added, 'You needn't worry. You're safe here.'

"'Where am I?' I asked her.

"'You're in a safe place.'

"'Who are you?'

"'Try to save your strength. Eat some soup. I'll be back.'

"The woman in the red sweater left, closing the door behind her. Outside, in the hall, were other voices. Whispers conferring with other whispers, or so I thought. I tried some of the soup. It was the best I'd ever tasted. I don't even know what kind it was—minestrone, perhaps. I ate all of it, and some of the bread, and then lay down again. I may have dozed, I'm not sure. It seemed I was having all sorts of mangled dreams. Every ten or fifteen minutes, I would open my eyes, and sometimes there'd be a person in my room, a woman. Not the same woman as the first, but always wearing a red sweater. It seemed they were all wearing red sweaters.

"At some point, I was awakened by a girl wearing jeans and a sweatshirt. When her face swam into focus, I realized she looked no older than me. She said, 'Catherine, if you need to use the ladies' room, it's right there.' She pointed to an alcove at the back of the small room. It had a wooden door, which stood ajar. 'All the rooms have their own baths,' she added.

"I looked at her and asked, 'How do you know my name?'

"Instead of answering, she said, 'My name is Jennifer. I want you to know that you aren't being held against your will. You can get up and leave at any point.' She smiled and added, 'But I hope you'll stay.'

"'Where am I?' I asked her.

"'Do you believe in God, Catherine?' she asked me. I thought it an odd question in light of the circumstances and the time of night. I shook my head as if to signify that I didn't know. She said, 'Because where you are now is the closest place to heaven.'

"'Who are the ladies in the red sweaters?' I asked.

"'Those are the Sisters. They're the closest things to angels.' My eyelids fluttered, and I felt myself slipping away again, felt the world dimming around my eyes and ears. Jennifer said, 'Rest a little more. Auntie Murrell will be up a little later. She wants to talk to you.'

"'Who's ... Auntie Murrell?'

"Jennifer smiled and said, 'A very special person.' And then I was out again, adrift on an up-and-down sea. It was the most surreal night of my life, awake for ten minutes, then asleep for twenty, awake for five, asleep for thirty. Often unable to distinguish dream from reality. Different women coming and going, quiet voices cooing, soft hands touching. And then ..."

"What?" Ma asked. "And then what? Tell us, Catherine."

"And then I awoke at some point, and I looked up, and I saw a woman sitting next to me. She was sitting on the edge of the bed, carefully massaging my forehead with the back of her hand, and smoothing out my hair with her fingers. She was African-American, in her fifties or sixties. She was wearing a white fleece pullover. She said, in this rich, rolling voice, 'Sit up, girl, if y'can. Sit up so I can get a good look at ya.'

"I sat up. We were inches away from each other. She took one of my arms in her hand and made a loose fist around it, so that her thumb and fingers touched. Then she ran a hand over my neck and beneath my chin. She looked down at my midsection and ran the backs of her knuckles along my exposed ribs. She said, 'Oh, girl, you done hit bottom. Ain't nuthin' left of you.' She looked me in the eye and said, 'My name is Mrs. Murrell. Most'a the girls 'round here jus' call me Auntie. You can call me anythin' you want, sugah, I won't cry.'

"'Where am I? What is this place?'

"''Tis a place of miracles,' the black woman told me. ''Tis a place women come to start over.'

"'I don't want to start over,' I told her.

"'Oh, honey, don't say that.'

"'It's true,' I said, 'I don't deserve to live.'

"'Ah, hell, sweetheart, neither do I. But lookit, I'm still here, ain't I? And there's somethin' I want to show you. Later today, after the sun's up. It might change your mind.'

"'I killed my baby,' I told her.

"She watched me with eyes that were caring and nonjudgmental. Then she opened her arms, and I went to her, and she hugged me. I started to cry, softly at first, and then fiercely. Auntie Murrell held onto me while I sobbed, my body shaking and trembling out of fear and shame. I cried and cried and cried—at times, my cries escalating into screams—uncontrollably, without respite, for three minutes or more. It felt longer, though. It felt a lot longer. But the old woman never let go of me. She never let go."

*   *   *

Ma went around and refilled all of our mugs with fresh hot chocolate. She slid a dish of mixed nuts onto the table for good measure. Then she took her chair again. "Continue, Catherine. What happened when you woke up? What was it this Murrell lady wanted you to see?"

"I slept until ten o'clock," Catherine resumed. "One of the Sisters came in with breakfast on a tray. I was given a clean set of clothes and asked to shower in the little bathroom. Auntie Murrell came up and hooked her elbow around mine. I'll never forget her smile. Her smile was like the sun. Always shining, always full of hope. I asked where we were going. 'The grand tour,' she said. 'Come, sweetheart, you see fo' yourself.'

"We went down three flights of stairs. We were in some kind of Plantation-style boarding house. The first floor was divided into large, wide-open common rooms. I saw some of the Sisters walking around. They smiled at me as they went about their work. I saw other girls, too, girls like me. Girls my age, some even younger.

"'Where are we going?' I asked.

"'This way, sugah.'

"Auntie led me through a series of rooms and into a back hall. We were heading toward a set of gray, wooden doors in the back of this back hall. She pushed one of the doors open … and we stepped into another place, into a world of sunlight, and flowers, and open space. My mouth literally dropped open. It was some sort of greenhouse. Some sort of … *magical* greenhouse. Simply a mammoth, gigantic, *gargantuan* greenhouse. Bigger than anything I'd ever seen. My eyes couldn't take it all in. It was over two hundred feet wide. The high, arching walls formed a ceiling sixty feet up. The walls and ceiling were made of some frosted material—glass or Plexiglas, or something similar. I could barely see to the end of the greenhouse—it seemed to just go forever.

"'It's almost a quarter mile long,' Auntie Murrell told me. 'The ceilings are retractable. We open them in the spring and summah.' I saw red leaves everywhere, as far and wide as I could see. And I saw honeybees. Bees inside the building, in the month of December. 'The bees live in here year-round,' Auntie explained. 'The bee-houses are out in the middle. As you can see, this is the Poinsettia House. We grow nothin' but poinsettias in this house.'

"'You mean there are other houses?'

"'There are *seven* other houses, sweetie. All like this one. The eight houses radiate out from the central mansion like the spokes on a bicycle wheel. Poinsettia House sits between Orchid House, to the left, and Rose House, to the right. You follow?'

"'Where are we? Geographically.'

"'Central Pennsylvania. Twenty miles outside of Lancaster. I employ over four hundred people, local people. They work in the houses, and in all facets of the business, including shipping, receiving, and billing. There are twenty-five Sisters employed full-time, with another two dozen or so who work part-time.'

"'You mean … that this … this is …?'

"'A capitalist enterprise. Last year, we did seven million dollars in gross sales.'

"'You're saying I have to work here?'

"Auntie pitched her head back and laughed. 'Oh, sweetie, I don't get to make that choice.'

"'Who does?'

"'You do,' she said. 'You and no one else.'

*   *   *

"'*As we work, we grow. As we grow, we build discipline. As we build discipline, we learn to love and respect ourselves.*' That was Auntie's credo, her mantra. In the six years I lived there, she broke me down completely and rebuilt me from the ground up. My values, my belief system, my work ethic, my sense of responsibility. I began by working two hours a day. As my strength improved, I went up to four hours a day, and so on. I was paid for whatever hours I worked. I got raises as I moved up. By the end of my stay, I knew all the ins and outs of the business, from seeding and pruning to billing and processing.

"There were other girls like me. Sometimes as many as fifty or sixty at a time. Some stayed one day, then ran off. Others stayed a year, others five years. For those who stayed, Auntie instilled in us, over time, a moral code and a sense of personal responsibility. We had our own bank accounts at a local branch. We learned to manage money. We learned how to invest money. The Sisters led spiritual meetings every night. We went to church on Sundays." Catherine paused, turning to smile at Natalie, sitting to her left. "And some of us learned how to raise children and how to be responsible parents."

"But I thought … when you left here …" The words died in my mouth.

"Once I'd been there a few days, the baby started moving again," Catherine proffered. "I can't explain it either. I guess I was wrong."

Ma asked, "So, Natalie was born at this … plantation?"

"In a nearby hospital, yes. The business gave us complete medical coverage. Everything, including check-ups and vaccinations. Natalie lived with me in the mansion. She went to kindergarten and first grade in the local school system."

We were quiet for a while, all four of us looking at each other. This had been one hell of a long day. I remembered Sharon shuffling into her coat and walking out of The Stellar Dragon in a tiff. Had I lied to her? It seemed like such a long time ago.

"I would say," Catherine went on, "that whenever I think of Auntie Murrell, the image that comes to mind is that of the bees flying around her. She would sit there clipping roses and smiling and talking—and the bees would buzz right under her arms and around her head as if she was part of the scenery. At times, they made little rings around her head. They never landed on her, and she never swatted at them or shooed them. One summer day shortly after

Natalie had begun walking, Auntie and I were working side by side in the Tulip House, and the bees were flying all around her, but at the same time ignoring her. Without looking up, she said, 'Someday, honey, you'll have wings like one of these bees. And you'll fly away from here.'

"It frightened me a little, her mentioning my leaving. 'How will I know when I have wings?' I asked.

"'You'll know, honey. Trust me, you'll know.'"

*   *   *

"You have your wings," I said.

Catherine smiled. "I do."

"Where are you living now, Catherine?" Ma asked.

"Pennsylvania. Natalie and I own a townhouse an hour north of Philly. I'm a department manager for a shoe distributor."

"A manager," Ma breathed.

"The Sisters keep after me. I'm constantly in touch with them, and Auntie, via phone and e-mail."

"Oh, Catherine, I'm so proud of you," Ma said. "I'm glad you came back."

"Mommy, why do they keep calling you Catherine?" asked Natalie.

"Well, that used to be my name, honey, before I changed it." Catherine looked at Ma, then at me. "I'm Caroline now. Caroline Ann Gates. I had it legally changed when I turned twenty-one." She paused, waiting, perhaps, for a reaction. "Mama, you're not mad, are you?"

Ma paused herself, then shook her head. "No, sweetheart. I'm not mad. I … Well, it'll take some getting used to, that's all. Caroline and Natalie Gates." She said it again, then a third time. She smiled. "Yes, I think I can get used to that."

"I still owe you an apology, Mama. It was a terrible thing I did … the diamond …"

Ma reached across the table and took her daughter's hand. "I know what you were doing, Cather—Caroline, I mean. Simon told me what … what you were doing … how you were trying to protect us. I know the truth now, and the truth speaks volumes. And besides, what they say about diamonds is false: diamonds are *not* forever. A diamond is a lump of coal that made well under pressure. Family is what's forever. You hear me, hon?" Ma shook her daughter's hand, tightening her grip on it. "*Family* is forever."

I saw a glisten in Caroline's eyes. "Thank you, Mama." She recovered reasonably well and added, "I wasn't sure if … if you'd still be here. In the house, I mean. I know there were problems, financially, when I left." She looked at us plaintively. "How'd you get out of it?"

"That's a long story," I said. "It's another story for another night."

*   *   *

After church on Sunday, I drove out to Sharon's house. Her father owned an old split-level in Basking Ridge, just off the I-287 corridor. She was waiting for me on the front steps when I turned my Tacoma into the paved driveway. She was wearing her black leather jacket, with black gloves and a black hat. I parked behind her black Pontiac and got out.

"You found it okay, looks like," she said, standing.

"I drove right to it. Your directions were perfect."

She smiled. A gust of wind blew her raven hair across her face. "Come inside and meet my dad. He's watching the Giants game."

Mr. Welsh was short and balding, with a gentle voice and soft brown eyes. I took him for around sixty or sixty-two. He shook my hand firmly and proudly, saying, "Hey, there, fella, nice to meetcha. Studying hard, are ya?"

"Yes, sir. Every day."

"Good. The world needs more hard workers."

We talked football for a few minutes, though I didn't know jack-squat about the game. "You know it takes three thousand cows to supply all the NFL footballs for a single season?" I said.

"Christ A'mighty, that's a lotta steak," Mr. Welsh replied. We both laughed. I managed to steer the conversation over to baseball, which was a wise move because Mr. Welsh happened to be a Yankee fan. He seemed a down-to-earth guy, with no trace of his daughter's superstitions or fantastic beliefs.

I voiced this outside. Sharon and I went for a walk along the road. She turned off the road, onto a narrow footpath that wound its way through the woods. I ducked in behind her, saying, "He seems all wit and wisdom, your dad. Are you sure you came from him?"

"I'm told that I did. Why, you don't think I have wisdom?"

"At least there are no cracks in the sidewalk out here," I said.

"You're dodging the question."

"How old were you when your mom died?"

"Fourteen."

Eventually the path grew wide enough for us to walk side by side. "You still think about her?" I asked.

"Every day. You still think about your father?"

"Yeah," I answered. "But not every day. You think that's a bad thing?"

She stopped walking, turning to face me. We'd come to a place where the trail split into three others. Three earthen paths appeared to diverge in completely different directions. I took a moment to examine those paths before looking back at Sharon again.

"What did you want to talk to me about, Simon?" She sauntered over to a sawed-off tree stump and sat down on it. It wasn't the first time I'd been left standing.

I fidgeted for a while, looking down at the ground with two hands buried in my pockets. "My sister … came back the other night."

Sharon didn't know the full story, but she knew enough of it for her eyes to widen. "Oh, my God. Simon … that's wonderful."

"Yes, it is. But it got me thinking about what I told you on Friday. At the restaurant. And …"

Sharon watched me, saying nothing.

… And she's getting farther away, with each passing day … and I cannot run faster, though try as I may …

"And I … I may need to revise my answer."

"What are you talking about, Simon?"

I opened my mouth. Shuffled my feet. Steam on my breath.

"What answer?"

"I'm …" I closed my eyes, and in the dark theater of my memory saw Alisha Caldwell sitting on the opposite rail of a one-lane bridge. When I opened them, I saw Sharon Welsh sitting on a tree stump.

"I …" I couldn't get the words out. The words wouldn't come. "I …"

"You're *not* seeing another person? Is that what you're trying to tell me?"

"I'm not … I mean, yes, I think … I think you're right."

"Jesus Christ, Simon, speak English. What are you saying?"

I was losing my grip on them, I was feeling them slip away from me. What did that say about all my pretensions? All of my dreams? All of my running? Where did it leave me?

"Look, Simon, I like you a lot, okay? And I think you're a great guy. But you've got to tell me what's going on in your head. You've got to tell me what you're chasing."

I spun toward her. "Chasing?"

"Yes, *chasing.* You're chasing something … some dark-clad figure on horseback over a sea of desert. You're always preoccupied. It's move, move, move with you. It's finish one thing so you can get on to the next. You're not enjoying the ride, Simon—you're trying to *outrun* the ride. You have been from the moment I met you."

I'm chasing the man in black. The hard weight of the truth made me stagger. I felt my legs turning to Jell-O. I reached out with one arm, but there was nothing to grab onto. I was in an open space looking down upon three diverging paths, three different ways, and I was on my way to the ground, falling. *All this time, I've been chasing the man in black. I've been chasing the wind, trying to catch the wind's shadow.* Falling, falling, falling. And I knew that my fruitless chase was over. I was standing in a vast wasteland of salt and sand, where one could look in all directions and see only shadows getting farther away. Where one could taste the alkali grit of truth and darkness, and know, as he fell, that he was alone.

But I never hit the ground. Sharon's arms were suddenly around me, and somehow they supported me as, together, we swayed and tottered and sank slowly to our knees. I held onto her with what little strength I had, my face buried in the depths of her black jacket. In the dimming theater of my mind, I caught a final glimpse of the man in black as he melted away into a shimmering haze. I would never catch him, and he could never be caught.

Instead, it was Sharon who caught me.

CHAPTER THIRTY-THREE

THE END OF WHAT I KNOW, THE BEGINNING OF WHAT I LOVE

WE MARRIED STRAIGHT OUT of law school. It was a small wedding, with family and some immediate friends. Caroline and Natalie were flower girls, dressed in matching blue gowns. Ma sat in the front row with a box of Kleenex.

I mailed wedding announcements—with photos galore—to Alisha and Corey, who had moved again and were then living in Florida. They sent replies of congratulations and best wishes. I've tried my best to keep up with them over the years—letters, calls, and Christmas cards. But time is a trickster, making liars out of most of us. And as the years went by, time slowly took them away from me.

Time, and the wind.

*   *   *

I never saw Alisha Caldwell's name in print again, though I can't profess to have spent a lot of time looking. I was a busy man through my twenties and thirties, working for a small law firm in Ramsey, New Jersey. The firm needed a good estate attorney, and I was the guy. Sharon went into business for herself as a real estate closings attorney, and was able to work from home. This was convenient to us both because she was also a mother. Three years out of law school, she gave birth to our first daughter, Kendra. A year later, our second daughter, Marissa, entered the world.

In the delivery room the second time, moments after the birth, Sharon took my hand and told me, "That's it, I'm done. I can't do it again, Simon."

"You mean you're tapped out?" I said.

She wiped sweat off her brow and forehead. "I'm tapped out, all right. I think men should give birth in the next life." The nurses in the room laughed.

So, we took to raising our two daughters, and we loved them as much as any two children have ever been loved. Deep in her heart, though, Sharon knew that I wanted a son—that I'd *always* wanted a son. I began pleading my case anew as we rode into our mid-thirties. For three years, I quietly pecked away and delivered my subtle exhortations. Sharon wouldn't hear it. She'd pretend not to listen. Eventually, however, it reached the point where she'd argue back verbally, and I knew I was making progress.

"We have two, Simon. Two is a great number, a safe number. Three is an odd number, and cosmically unsafe. Universally, 'three' brings with it much uncertainty."

How the hell does one answer that? The one thing I've learned with Sharon over the years is not to respond with words or implied logic. She'll shoot them down like a marksman taking clay birds out of the air. Instead, you take her hands in yours and look her in the eye. No words, no logic. Eye contact only.

"Simon, don't start that with me …"

A year later: "Simon, no …"

Another year: "I'm not playing that game with you …"

Six months later: "Simon, goddammit …"

And so one night she came to me in a black negligee. The doctor had given us a three-day window, during which, he said, our fertility chances were optimal. The way I saw it, we should be doing it all three nights, but Sharon said no, I'd pushed my luck far enough as it was, and luck was not something to mess around with.

"It's the father who determines the sex of the child, you know," she said, climbing onto the mattress on her knees. "You're sure you don't want to go back for more oysters?"

"Christ, woman, do I look like I need more oysters?"

Smiling, she straddled me and slowly moved her hands up her thighs. "This is your last chance, cowboy. Don't screw it up."

*　　*　　*

Four and a half months later, the doctor told us we'd be having another girl. Sharon laughed. I shook my head and said, "We'll keep trying, that's all."

"No, we won't."

"We'll have a dozen kids if we have to."

"The hell we will."

"You know what, make it a baker's dozen. Lucky thirteen, and all that."

"Face it, Simon—you're destined to be surrounded by women. You can only fight destiny for so long."

I hung my head and laughed. Even the doctor laughed. We all laughed together.

The next day, Ma had a stroke.

*　　*　　*

They kept her in the hospital for ten days. From there she went to a rehab facility in Chester, where she would remain for close to a month. The stroke had been a bad one, they told us, but it hadn't been devastating. The damage was to the right half of Ma's body. That side of her face drooped a bit, and she spoke in a slur. Her right arm didn't want to cooperate, and her right leg she dragged along like a tree stump. She underwent occupational and speech therapy every day, and made considerable progress during her stay. But we all knew a decision would have to be made about where she went next.

And then Caroline did a wonderful thing. She said to me over the phone one night, "Look, Simon, I think we should move Ma back into her home."

"She can't go home, Caroline. She can't be on her own."

"I'll move in with her. I've been thinking it over lately, and I think I'm ready to do it."

Caroline had sold her townhouse in Pennsylvania and moved back to New Jersey five years ago. She owned a two-bedroom condo in Convent Station, and worked as a hospital administrator in Morristown. I said to her, "Caroline, you don't have to do that."

"I want to do it, Simon."

"Do you realize the commitment you're making? Ma's only sixty-three, Cath. She may live another twenty years. You've got to think about your own life."

"It doesn't have to be permanent. Look, I can put my condo on the rental market and see what happens. And with Natalie leaving for college this fall ... I'll be by myself anyway."

I sighed into the phone. "I don't know. Are you sure you want to do this, Cath?"

"Simon, you're doing it again."

"Doing what?"

"Calling me by my old name."

I tended to do that when my nerves were up. "Sorry. Look, I just think—"

"Simon, you took care of her the first time. I ran away."

"Come on, Caroline, reciprocity doesn't make the world go round. You were sick when you ran away, and we both know it."

"And were it not for Auntie Murrell, I may have never been made whole again." I heard defiance in my sister's voice this time, and I loved her for it. "Ma wants to go home again, Simon, and I want her to be happy. I'm going to move in with her. I'm going to take care of her."

*   *   *

Time never speaks, it only whispers. And it mostly does so at volumes too low for us to hear. Can you hear time whispering? Can you feel the wind brushing the backs of your ears?

Caroline moved in with Ma. Three years later, Caroline moved out again. Ma wanted her independence. Ma wanted Caroline to find a good man. A year later, Caroline did.

More time. More wind. Brown leaves hissing across open sidewalks.

Snowdrifts building, then receding. Crocuses springing open. Lush grass and baseball diamonds, the buzz of lawnmowers up the street. Acorns a'falling, sunsets a blaze of orange.

My little girls grew up. Kendra, Marissa, Arianna. Swing sets and seesaws, pink dresses and Barbies. My dream home with my dream woman. A house of wholeness, a house of mirth.

Time, wind. The ice hardens in Winnipeg. The snow melts in Kansas. Rivers rise and fall through flood and drought. High tide, low tide. Full moon, new moon, half moon.

Time never speaks, it only whispers. Can you hear time whispering?

*   *   *

I'm forty-three years old now. It's safe to say I've lived half of my life—one hopes, anyway—and it's been a good half, all told. I wouldn't describe myself as an introspective man by any stretch of the imagination, nor do I spend large reams of time reflecting on the past—what was, what could have been, and what really is. But I've never forgotten where I came from, and those I've met along the way, and the ways in which those people have affected me. I've never forgotten Millie Frustoff's lesson on the circles our lives make.

I've learned a lot about the circumstantial nature of happiness. I know that happiness is not a plateau one reaches. You don't just pitch camp and stay there. More so, it's a byproduct of what you're doing with your life as well as the people with whom you surround yourself. The happiness I knew during my year in Swan Lake was lost. In the years since, I've slowly managed to reconstruct that happiness, in my own ways and through much hard work and devotion. I left the law firm in Ramsey years ago and went into business for myself. Today, I work out of a small office in Harding Township, New Jersey. I have one secretary and one paralegal. I do a fair amount of municipal work because it's steady and keeps the bills paid. But estate planning is my bread and butter. I come highly recommended because I'm good at what I do and I'm well versed in the relevant tax codes. Sharon works out of our home in Mendham. She deals exclusively with house closings.

Caroline married an architect named George Vasher. They live in Mountain Lakes today, ten or fifteen minutes from Ma. Ma is pushing seventy and doing well. She still works three days a week—not because she has to, but because she wants to. The only thing Ma can't do is drive, but given the number of friends she has, she's rarely in want of a ride. Natalie is out of college and currently working her way through dental school. Can you hear the wind blowing? Can you hear time whispering?

On a warm spring day around lunchtime, there came a soft knocking on my office door. Sandy Knight, my secretary, stuck her head in and said, "Sir, there's a young man here to see you."

"Does he have an appointment?" I asked without looking up.

"No, sir. He says his name is Corey Caldwell."

The pen in my hand stopped moving. I sat stock-still at my desk for a moment, then slowly raised my eyes up to meet Sandy's. "Who?"

"Corey Caldwell. A friend of yours, or something, from a long time ago? He said you would recognize the na—"

"He's here? Now?"

"Yes, sir, he's waiting for you in the lobby."

As I pushed away from my desk and stood up, I quickly ran the numbers through my head. The last time I'd seen Corey, he'd been leaning across his mother's lap in their Land Rover, waving frenetically as they pulled away from me on their way out of the Barrow Hill State Park. He was six years old then, I was twenty-three. *Dear Bellamy, that was twenty years ago. Twenty years in the blink of an eye.*

I moved across my office and through the door, practically pushing Sandy out of the way. I went into the hall, made a left turn, then a quick right, and stepped into the lobby.

Only one of the six chairs was occupied. The young man stood up when he saw me. I froze for a good, hard moment, staring back at him. Old wheels clicked and chugged as my brain strived to achieve pattern recognition. Only in the arresting blue eyes, however, could any vestige of the boy be seen. Past that, his features had changed. His face had become thinner, more angular, as his boyhood cheeks had melted off. The dimples were gone. And his blond hair had darkened to a faded, almost dusty brown. He stood about five-ten and weighed probably around one-sixty. In other words, he appeared fit and trim, and in relatively good standards.

He wore clean, pressed pants and a white Polo shirt. When he spoke, the lowered range of his voice threw me for quite a turn. "Hello, Simon."

"Corey?" I was breathing pretty hard. "It's ... My God, it's really you, isn't it?"

He laughed a little. "Yeah, it's really me." He stepped forward and held out his hand. "How you been, man?"

I took his hand and shook it, then decided *what the hell*, and pulled him into a hug. He laughed again and hugged me in return.

I stood back from him a little, my hands on his shoulders, surveying him at arm's length. "Jesus, look at you. All grown up, after all these years. What brings you to these parts? Are you living nearby?"

"Well, no, I live in Texas, actually."

"Wh—*Texas?*" I gasped. "Holy cow, what do you do out there?"

"I'm a teacher," he said. "I teach eighth-grade science. I'm about ten miles west of Austin."

"Wow, gosh, a teacher ... that's wonderful, it's great. So, what brings you all the way up here? You have friends in the area?"

"No, I uh ... I came to find you, actually." He looked down at his feet for a moment, then met my eyes once more. "My mother passed away three weeks ago."

"Oh, no." I covered my mouth with my hand, then spoke through my splayed fingers. "Gees, Corey, I'm sorry. She was in Texas also?"

"No, she lived in Florida. She had a small house with ten acres."

I crunched more numbers in my head. "Your mother couldn't have been that old ..."

"She was sixty-two. She had leukemia."

"Oh, shit." I rubbed the side of my face with one hand. "How long did she have it?"

"It was diagnosed a year and a half ago."

"And you traveled all this way to tell me?"

"Sort of," he said. "My mother's attorney, a Mr. Martin Matlick, sent me to find you. He's the executor of my mother's estate. Apparently, she ... well, it appears she left you something."

I was dumbstruck into silence for a moment. "She *left* me something? What?"

Corey shook his head. "I don't know. It's in a sealed envelope. You're the only one allowed to open it."

I stood there looking at him with my mouth hanging open. We stood there looking at one another.

"Do you have it with you?"

He nodded. "It's out in the car."

"Sandy?" I'd almost forgotten she was standing in the doorway behind me.

"Yes?" she asked.

"Clear my schedule for the remainder of the afternoon."

"Um, sir, you have two appoint—"

"Clear it, Sandy."

*   *   *

Corey and I went outside, into warm air and bright sun. His rented Camry was parked in one of the slanted spaces in the front of the small parking lot. He opened the passenger door, then reached into the floor well, where a briefcase lay. He set the briefcase onto the passenger seat and opened it. He withdrew a six-by-ten-inch padded envelope, taped and sealed. He handed it to me.

"That's it?" I asked.

"That's it. It's yours, whatever it is."

Written in black permanent marker on both sides of the envelope were the words, To Be Opened by Simon Kozlowski Only.

I held the small parcel in both hands, turning it over, then over again. It weighed practically nothing. I asked Corey, "Were you aware she was leaving me something?"

"Not until last week, when the attorney went over everything with me. Look, you don't have to open it now if you don't want to."

"Don't be silly." I stuck my finger under the sealed flap and tore it open. Then I turned the envelope upside-down and attempted to shake out the enclosed item. Onto the palm of my left hand landed a brass key attached to a white fob.

I slowly curled my fingers around the key and closed my eyes at the same time. In my mind, I tried to call up an image of Alisha

Caldwell as I'd known her all those years ago. What I saw, not surprisingly, was her long, silver hair and her quicksilver eyes as she watched me from the opposite rail of a one-lane bridge. It was on this other side of the bridge she had promised to stay, and it was a promise she had kept.

My eyes were poignant and moist when I opened them. I noticed Corey was still staring at the key. "What does it go to? That house? The house by the lake?"

I nodded. I knew my voice would crack if I attempted to speak.

Corey placed one hand on my shoulder. "Hey, Simon … you all right?"

"Let's walk for a while," I told him.

We set off on the sidewalk, which paralleled a crumbling stone wall for a while, before we made a left into the crosswalk, crossing Bleeker Street. We went past Amy's Pastry Shop and walked onto the bridge looking down over the river. Halfway across, we stopped, resting with our elbows propped on the concrete wall, looking down over the water.

I said finally, "She should have left it to you. The house, I mean. It's an appreciable asset."

"She left me three other houses, with properties. Not to mention a seven-figure trust fund that I can collect when I'm thirty. And whatever's left from her own estate. Christ, Simon, I can retire if I want to."

"You gonna?"

"Probably not. A man's gotta have something to do, doesn't he? And I really enjoy teaching. I feel like I'm making a difference."

"You married, Corey?"

"Not yet."

"Involved?"

"Yeah, I've been going with a girl for, oh, maybe a year now. We'll see."

"Did your mother ever get married? Or at least settle down with someone?"

"She never got married, no. She saw different men over the years. Became pretty serious with one of them, a surgeon out of Orlando. I know they lived together for five or six months before going their separate ways."

"Was she alone when she died?"

"Romantically, yes—if that's what you mean. But she wasn't alone-alone. I was with her."

It saddened me to know that she hadn't found someone. I felt none of the spite or satisfaction a jilted lover often knows upon learning he or she has gone on to have the more fruitful life. I felt, instead, an emptiness, a sense of unfulfillment—both *for* her and *through* her. If hindsight was indeed twenty-twenty, then what I know now is this: I had wanted her to be happy. I had *always* wanted her to be happy.

"Corey?"

"Yes?"

"In your opinion, was your mother content in her later years? Your answer is important, so take your time."

He took his time. He crossed his arms and looked upriver for a while. Gazing upstream and waiting for the thoughts to flow down to him.

"I don't know, Simon, it's … it's hard to say. My mother wasn't an easy person to read. She certainly never seemed *un*happy—not to me, at least."

"She taught me a lot of things, your mother."

Corey smiled. "She said you taught her a lot of things. And … well, she said you saved both of our lives once. I guess there was a snowstorm?"

"Was there ever. I haven't seen a blizzard like that to this day. Do you remember it, Corey? The storm?"

He shook his head. I thought, *You died, son. You were dead when I found you. And somehow, you came back.*

"Let's walk some more," I said. Remembering the storm was giving me the chills. We went the rest of the way across the bridge and later found an empty park bench along the river's edge. As we sat, I asked, "What do you remember? About the house, or the whole year in general. Do you remember me?"

"Yes, I remember you. Beyond that, it's mostly bits and pieces. I remember tossing paper airplanes in the woods. I remember sledding in the winter, going down a big hill …"

"The driveway, yep." I smiled as I allowed the memory to

complete its circuit. Remembering the scent of Alisha's shampoo as her hair blew past my face.

"I remember fishing a bunch of times," he said. "I remember you showing me the spit bugs."

"You remember the spit bugs, huh?"

He nodded.

"It's funny what you remember, isn't it? What sticks with you and what doesn't."

"Yeah," he said. "Yeah."

"Did your mother ever say why she quit writing?"

"Not really, no. Actually, it's funny you bring that up, because I never knew her as a writer. Her writing days were mostly when I was real little, or before I was even born. When I got older, she used to say she was on permanent sabbatical. Tongue-in-cheek, of course. She did want to go back to it someday, and she always said she would. But … for some reason, she never did. It was always my belief that she'd simply lost interest."

"Was she a good mother to you, Corey? Through your boyhood and teen years?"

"The best," he answered. "She was the best, most loving mother a kid could ever have hoped for. I wouldn't have had it any other way."

*   *   *

"Okay, people, keep your fingers crossed," I said as I slid the key into the keyhole. The lock clicked. I opened the front door and pushed it gently inward.

Immediately, my three girls went bustling past me, whooping and hollering. Kendra, Marissa, Arianna … ages twelve, eleven, and seven, in that order. They were a whirlwind of glee and discovery.

"Daddy, this is great!" Kendra cried. Her head tilted back, looking up at the high ceiling and the loft railing.

I stepped into the house, followed by Corey, and then Sharon. I heard Sharon's voice behind me: "Wow, this is something."

"Hey, look, guys, look!" Arianna was standing halfway up the spiral staircase, grinning wildly.

"Go all the way up," I told her, "and check out the upstairs."

To her older sisters, Arianna said, "Come on, guys! Come on!" She went stomping up the casement with Kendra and Marissa hot-to-trot behind her.

"So, what do you think?" I asked Corey. "Does it all look familiar?"

He stood with his hands propped on his hips, head tilted back, looking up and around. "Yes, it does, but I can't get over how small it seems now. It seemed palatial in my memory."

Sharon offered, "That's because you were a little boy back then. I had the same experience when I went back to visit my elementary school soon after I'd finished high school. I could've sworn the halls and classrooms had shrunk to one-third of their original size."

"Gosh, look at that," I muttered quietly. "The same sofas and love seats are still here."

We wandered into the kitchen together. Sharon walked around the island counter, admiring the stainless steel appliances and the cherry wood cabinetry. "It's nice," she commented. "Looks like it was built yesterday."

"It's exactly as it was," I said. "And here's the kitchen table, where we had all of our meals." I pulled one of the chairs out, remembering the soft noise of the padded feet sliding over the floor.

We moved slowly out of the kitchen, whereupon we made the left turn that would lead us to Corey's old bedroom and, immediately after, the room I had occupied. I insisted that Corey lead the way. He did, his hands thrust in his pockets and his head rotating up and around, his eyes taking in all the angles and corners. I found it truly amazing to watch this adult man relive and rediscover a place of his youth. He'd been a boy here, an innocent, amorous little boy, and you could see the memories flooding back into him just by watching his face. As my daughters tromped up and down the hallway above us, Corey turned the corner, entering his old bedroom. I went in behind him.

Sharon remained in the doorway, watching us.

The dark blue wall-to-wall carpet was all that remained here. But memories filled in the gaps with startling clarity.

Corey uttered a, "Whoa," followed by a, "Wow." I knelt down on one knee in an effort to slow my racing heart.

"I recall exactly what this room looked like," he said. "The bureau for all my clothes was here, along the wall, below the windows."

"That's right," I said.

"And there," he added, pointing with his arm fully extended, "was my bed. The big bunk bed—"

"Exactly."

"—and I slept on the bottom bunk—"

"That's right."

"—and that's where you used to read me stories, Simon!"

"Yes, yes," I said, nodding.

"My God, it's all coming back to me," he added. "It's all coming back to me. It was special, living here. Wasn't it?"

"It was very special," I answered.

We moved over to my room. All the old furniture remained. I took a long, wistful look at the queen-sized bed I'd slept in for close to a year. It hadn't been moved. None of the furniture had been moved. I moved toward the windows. I laid a hand on the bureau surface, remembering the ceramic fish dish and the key with the white fob. On one corner of the bureau was a red sticker roughly the size of a nickel. I had put it there myself. *I'll be damned.* I turned and quickly surveyed the room, checking all the furniture. Every piece had a red sticker on it.

"This house has been empty," I said slowly, "ever since we moved out. Your mother never rented the place out, Corey, did she?"

"I don't … I have no idea. Maybe not."

I found it hard to imagine that someone with Alisha's business savvy would continue to pay taxes over the years on an asset producing zero income other than its own appreciation. It ran against every grain of logic I could think of. But the more I looked around, and the more I examined the juxtaposition of the furniture—with all the red stickers exactly where we'd stuck them—the more convinced I became that Alisha, Corey, and I had in fact been the last tenants here, exactly twenty years ago.

"If what you're saying is true, then someone has been taking care of the place," Sharon pointed out. "I mean, the house is pretty clean, there's not much dust. Even if the water and electricity are off, the heating system has to be maintained."

"She would have paid someone to do that. Probably one of her management companies." I looked out the window at the lake. The floating dock was gone. Other than that, all else appeared the same. I saw Millie's three houses on the far shore. I wondered if Millie was still around, much less living. Had her properties been sold? Was there a new owner over there?

No new lakeside houses had been built. There'd been no new construction here. Nels Turner's old ordinance had kept the developers and bulldozer treads away. State Street was still a dirt road.

We filed into the den as the girls came spiraling down from the loft en masse.

"We're picking out our rooms!" Marissa declared.

"I want the big one upstairs!" Kendra claimed.

"Don't get ahead of yourselves, girls," I told them. "Your mother and I haven't decided if we're even keeping this place."

"Technically, we don't own it," Sharon said. "All we have is a key."

"Matlick has the title and deed, I'm sure," Corey said. "I'll give you all his information."

"Are you sure you want to give this up, Corey?" Sharon asked. "You must have mixed feelings."

"It's not mine to give up," he replied. "If Mom wanted you to have it, then that's what I want. I live all the way out in Texas, don't forget."

I said to the girls, "Why don't you go down and check out the basement and garage. Corey will show you where it is."

As Corey led them down the cellar stairs, Sharon started her way up the spiral casement. She paused halfway. "Are you coming, Simon?" I shook my head. I wasn't ready to brave that old territory yet. Sharon, who knows the story from beginning to end (save for one tiny part), smiled understandingly. "I'll be back in a minute."

With Sharon going up, and Corey and the girls going down, I found myself alone for a while. On a whim, I went into Alisha's old office. Most everything was gone: computers, chairs, books, and knickknacks. What was left were bare shelves where books had once lived. And in front of me, paralleling the front wall and running the length of the office, the long desk space on which books had once been written. I recalled the many sunlit hours Alisha had spent sitting here, sipping coffee and staring through the windows at the water beyond. A blank screen in front of her, nothing on it save for a blinking cursor. She had attempted liftoff on one of her new novels, one of her "smut" novels. For whatever reason, though, the plane couldn't get off the ground. She couldn't get going with it, and the book's recalcitrant progress, or lack thereof, had reflected in her mood. Then Christmas had come along, and her spirits had lifted a little. And then the storm had struck … and everything changed. After the storm, she'd begun writing at night. Not *just* writing, either, but *humming*. Really making the keys sing. This hadn't been the smut novel she'd hoped to start, this had been something altogether different. A new idea, a new story—one that had galvanized her from top to bottom. And perhaps one that had changed her. This manuscript she had finished. But for some reason, it had never appeared in print. She'd never published it.

Can you hear time whispering? Can you hear the wind sifting over the salt flats? If you listen closely, you may hear a voice in the wind. It may tell you a secret.

I bent over and began opening some of the wood drawers in the bare desk space. They were empty. But the fourth drawer I pulled out seemed heavier than the others. Inside it was a manuscript wrapped in Saran Wrap. I lifted it out with trembling hands and set it flat on the desktop. Slowly I peeled away the multiple layers of plastic wrap. The top page was blank—a protector page. My pulse pounded like a kettledrum as I removed the top page. It revealed a title page:

> *The Boy and the Apple Tree*
> A Novel by Alisha Caldwell

I flipped over the title page. Beneath it was a dedication page:

> Dedicated to the End of What I Know,
> and the Beginning of What I Love.

On the next page, the text began. And went on for another 492 pages of double-spaced typeset. Close to five hundred pages of untold secrets lying fallow for twenty years.

… The end of what I know … The beginning of what I love …

When Sharon found me, I was out on the front deck, looking over the lake with my forearms resting on the side rail. She rubbed the back of my left shoulder, saying, "It would make a nice vacation home, that's for sure. I think I could get used to it." She was quiet for a moment, watching me. "Simon, how are you doing with all this? It must be … difficult, in some ways. Share your thoughts with me."

"Do you remember the storm, Sharon? You remember what I told you about the storm?"

"Yes, of course. Alisha broke through the ice. You pulled her out and … and carried her back to the house. You couldn't see the shore because the snow was blowing so heavily, but you … There was a light, you said you saw a light—"

"It was the house," I said. "The light came from the house. What next?"

"What?"

"What did I tell you happened next?"

"You went back out and found Corey."

"Where? How?"

"You said you found him under a dock, some sort of a floating dock."

"That part isn't true," I said.

"What do you mean?"

"I made that part up, is what I mean. It's not what happened. I never told Alisha what *really* happened."

"What did happen, Simon?"

"I gave up. I looked for more than two hours in a complete whiteout. And I couldn't find him. He was gone. He was gone, Sharon. And I … began to fear for my own life. I was cold and tired and beaten. And so I gave up. I called off the search. I gave up. I left him for dead. I left him. I *left* him."

"Simon, what you're saying doesn't make sense. If you left him, then how did you find him?"

"I had a compass with me. It was Corey's, actually. I'd given it to him for Christmas the day before. I knew that the house sat on the south shore of the lake. When I decided that Corey was dead and that I'd be joining him if I didn't get indoors, I used the compass to take me in a southerly direction. It worked fine for a while, but then the compass began to malfunction."

"How do you know it was malfunctioning?"

"Because it was spinning in circles. Counterclockwise, and nonstop. I tried shaking it, then hitting it with my gloved palm. I tried breathing on it. Nothing worked. It just went right on spinning. It spun so fast I couldn't make out the letters."

"So, what did you do?"

"I prayed," I told her. "I got down on my knees and prayed to a God I wasn't sure I believed in. I was so scared, Sharon. I thought I was gonna die. I was scared for *me*, Sharon, for *me*. Not for him anymore."

"Christ, Simon, I'd be scared, too. There's no reason for you to feel guilty. Go on, finish. What happened next?"

"What happened was that my prayer was answered. I looked at the compass and saw it had steadied. It was no longer spinning. I climbed to my feet and pushed on, heading south. I walked for what felt like another twenty minutes, maybe more. I held the compass in front of me, watching it the whole time. And finally I looked up, and … I saw something."

"Saw what?"

"A large, dark shape. An outline of something that shouldn't have been there, considering which way I was moving. I stood there contemplating this … this thing for a minute or more, and began moving toward it. And then suddenly I knew what it was. I recognized it. It was the clubhouse on the bathing beach. I was looking at one corner of the clubhouse roof. I'd been walking in the wrong direction. I hadn't been walking south at all. I'd been moving dead east. Maybe slightly *north*east. All that time, I'd been going the wrong way. I started to take another step, and I felt something against the toe of my boot. I looked down and saw a piece of red cloth sticking out of the snow—the Superman cape. I was standing over Corey's body. It was practically between my legs."

"Oh, my God, Simon." Speaking through the hand now shielding her mouth. "And he was …"

"Yes, he was. The rest of the story you know."

The girls came running out of the house and onto the deck. All three of them talking at once; yelling, giggling, and pointing.

Corey walked onto the deck behind them, a huge smile pasted

to his face. "Simon, you're not gonna believe this. Our old fishing poles are down in the basement."

"You're kidding."

"No, he's not," Kendra said. "We saw them, too, Dad."

Corey said, "I had no idea we'd left them here. I don't think I've cast a line since."

I threw a sidelong glance toward Sharon. "You think you and the girls could find something to do for an hour?"

Smiling, she answered, "We drove up in two vehicles. Knock yourselves out. Meet us back at the bed-and-breakfast." She pecked me on the cheek.

So Corey and I grabbed our poles and walked down to the lake. The monofilament line was old and dreadfully coiled, but still useable. We made slow, careful casts, turning the reel handles and getting the feel of it again. "How could I possibly have forgotten how much fun this is?" I mused. "You remember how to do it, Corey?"

"It's comin' back to me, yeah." He nodded, smiling ear to ear.

We talked quietly as we fished, filling in the years and remembering old times. We worked our way carefully down the bank the way we used to—Corey straying ahead while I followed loosely behind. We lapsed into silence here and there, just casting and reeling, then casting again. I thought about Alisha, how she used to call us in when it was time for dinner, then listen to our tales and send us out again. I'm roughly the same age today as she was back then, and what I've learned is this: there comes a time in our lives when what we know becomes less important than what we love. And that what we love, when all is said and done, might be the most important of all things.

My thoughts were interrupted by a shrill cry, followed by loud hoots and hollers. I spun to my left and spotted Corey fifty yards down the shoreline, standing on the tip of a rocky peninsula. I saw the bend in his rod, and the rod itself thumping and bucking with the weight of a fighting fish. I dropped my pole and started running, my feet splashing in the shallow water, my elbows pumping at my sides. I felt the smile stretching across my face as I ran … and for a bleary, fleeting moment, I was twenty-three again, racing toward a boy of six.

"*I got 'im, Simon! I got 'im!*"

ACKNOWLEDGMENTS

I would like to thank Brooke and Richard Schumann for their research assistance. And thanks to Susan Osberg. Your contributions have not been forgotten.

Lastly, I owe a special thanks to Ron and Beth Delaney, the best neighbors a guy could hope for. I owe a debt of gratitude to Ron for the technical support necessary in getting this manuscript to press. I am equally indebted to Beth, for allowing me to monopolize her husband's time, and who, as it turns out, makes the best vegetable soup on the planet.

Lightning Source UK Ltd.
Milton Keynes UK
UKOW041137240712

196486UK00005B/35/P